Take My
Breath Away

Glancing up from that flawless descent, Cole tried to see details of her, but was out of luck—or maybe in luck. Who knew? The next few minutes were pure torture as the blades of that copter slowly *whap-whap-whapped* to a stop. During this, Ariel leaned down until she was completely out of sight as she fiddled with something inside the cabin.

"Patience," Thaddeus said.

Cole pretended not to hear.

"She'll join us in good time," Thaddeus added.

That's what Cole was afraid of as the door to that copter finally popped open and Ariel stepped outside.

She was immediately surrounded by Thaddeus's house-keeping staff that had run across the lawn to the helipad. As Ariel came around the copter door and bent at the waist to lower something to the ground, she was again obstructed from view.

Cole wondered if that was a good omen . . . or maybe a bad omen of things to—

His thoughts suddenly paused as the staff moved aside just as Ariel straightened.

Thaddeus called out, "Please be certain you get those books she's brought to me!"

The staff chorused a "Yes, sir!"

Thaddeus leaned toward Cole. "Ariel's found a simply delightful bookstore that deals in rare volumes."

Cole nodded absently to that.

Thaddeus shouted more directives to his staff, the gist of which escaped Cole. Lowering the bottle of beer from his lips, he pushed up in his chair as his gaze simply prowled over Ariel Leigh.

Patience, Thaddeus had said.

Not a chance, Cole thought. He couldn't explore every part of her quickly enough. She was a tall woman, probably five-ten, with a sleek and well-toned body that was a delicious caramel color from days spent outdoors. As she moved fully into the sun now it intensified the color of her hair. That reddish gold mane was worn in a thick braid, while delicate tendrils danced over her tawny cheeks with the constant breeze.

Warmth continued to flood through Cole, settling in his groin. *That's Ariel?* Not only was she nothing like what he had feared, but she was exquisitely female—the real deal, not the Hollywood version of what femininity should be. From this distance it appeared she wore little, if any, makeup.

She didn't need it. Her charm was natural, her beauty unique and more stunning than anything Cole had seen in Los Angeles where plastic surgery and excess were the norm. Even Ariel's clothing was simple, yet elegant—a white, sleeve-less cotton top, white shorts that revealed an amazing expanse of her sleek legs, and white moccasins on her feet.

Cole's body continued to respond as he imagined licking her long, slender toes before he worked his way up those taut calves and creamy thighs to those delicate curls between her legs. Were they auburn, too?

A man could hope. A man should really know.

Of course, to do that, he would definitely have to stay longer than just tonight, possibly several days, which wasn't out of the question if he played dumb about this survival stuff, pretending he knew absolutely nothing about it. That would get her to show him everything she knew for as long as was needed. That would give them time to get to know each other, like each other, make love with—

"Young man," Thaddeus suddenly said, breaking into Cole's thoughts.

Cole nodded as his gaze continued to hunger over Ariel.

"I am over here," Thaddeus said.

Uh-huh. Getting his bearings, Cole finally looked at the old guy. "Yes, sir."

Thaddeus quietly regarded Cole before continuing. "As I so clearly stated just a few minutes ago—before this is over, you will dearly love Ariel."

"Okay."

Thaddeus frowned. "I believe you misunderstand." Gripping his cane, he leaned forward in his rattan chair and spoke in a voice only Cole could hear. "Men can so easily fall in love with my niece because of her obvious charms. But I warn you, young man, you are not to romance her, nor seduce her, nor lead her on, nor touch her in any way while she is with you. Any and all desire that you feel you will keep to yourself. If you do otherwise, you will never make another film or work in this business or any other again—not even the Marines—is that understood?"

Cole said, "Yes, sir," to that and only that.

Thaddeus knew. Narrowing his pale blue eyes, he added the coup de grace. "Believe me, I had to use all my powers of persuasion to get Ariel to do this, given that she abhors Hollywood types."

Okay. So maybe it was time to reconsider his first thought that she wanted a film career, which given her effortless sensuality Cole knew he could easily deliver. *God*. Not only did she not want that, but she abhorred Hollywood types, which Thaddeus presumably thought he was, and which she probably did, too.

"But I'm certain all will turn out well," Thaddeus said as he leaned back into his chair and smiled. "You stay on your best behavior, and there will be absolutely no reason for Ariel to deal with you in her usual fashion."

Cole wasn't about to ask what that fashion might be, sensing it didn't involve lingering kisses or wild lovemaking. And here he had thought the Hollywood powers-that-be were tough to deal with.

Suppressing a frown, Cole warned himself not to look in her direction. A moment later, his full attention was back on her, because he couldn't fucking help himself. He was a man, for God's sake, and damn, but she was some woman.

She was at the rear of the copter now and bending at the waist as she checked something out. Cole hadn't a clue what that something might be as his gaze remained on the edge of her shorts that fluttered in the wind, while the waning sun kissed the backs of her seamless thighs and outstanding butt.

Every part of Cole's body responded to that amazing scene as he imagined her in that position within his room, willingly presenting herself to him, remaining open and vulnerable as he slowly lowered those shorts from her achingly soft flesh, exposing it for his use and their pleasure.

Cole's cock stiffened even more, his tightened balls simply ached for relief, but he didn't dare adjust himself in his chair with Thaddeus still eyeing him.

A trickle of perspiration ran from Cole's temple to his jaw as he finally wondered why she abhorred Hollywood types.

Had she been in love with one, then deeply hurt? Had she been engaged to one? Divorced from one?

Damn. Was she still married now? Was she engaged? Was she free?

She was finally straightening and turning as she exchanged pleasantries with the young man who had secured the copter, then those staff that were taking her bags. At last, she saw an older woman approach and held out her arms in welcome. As the two women embraced, Ariel smiled.

Cole's fingers paused on his temple. That smile was simply radiant and aroused him beyond reason. It was the kind of smile that brought a man to his knees, making him return home again and again no matter how dangerous or difficult the journey might be. It was a smile that made anything possible.

Inhaling deeply, he watched as the two women finally parted and Ariel headed in his direction.

Her step was light, her movements fluid, her gaze on the small bag slung over her shoulder before she abruptly looked up.

In that moment, her gaze touched Cole's. In that moment, her step actually paused.

Well, well, well, Cole thought.

She seemed as suddenly taken with him as he was with her.

And no matter Thaddeus's admonitions, Cole just couldn't help but stare.

Several of those auburn tendrils continued to wiggle in the persistent breeze that pushed against her clothing, revealing the gentle swell of her breasts and the flare of her hips. Cole looked from that back to her eyes. They were light enough to be blue or green. They remained on him as if she could not— or would not—look away.

Ariel, his mind whispered, while his heart raced and his body continued to respond.

At last, he smiled.

Ariel's gaze touched that smile. She was quickly warmed by it and completely confused.

This couldn't be the man she was supposed to teach survival skills. This couldn't be the man whose safety would be hers to keep, whose presence would be a constant throughout that instruction.

Ariel moistened her lips at that possibility, then pulled in her tongue when she saw his gaze lower to her mouth. There his attention lingered before he again glanced up.

Her belly fluttered as he unexpectedly pushed back in his chair and stood. Was he coming to greet her? Would he actually touch her?

Have you lost all good sense?

This man—or rather *no* man—would dare touch her under the watchful gaze of her uncle.

Nor would she touch such a man, since she wasn't into Hollywood types or shallow guys. Long before today Ariel had vowed never to get involved in a one-night stand or a casual relationship or, worse, a fraud of a marriage stuffed with extra-marital affairs like the one her parents continued to have, with that being something she really didn't want to think about now.

Of course, it was either that or think about the time—all the time—she would be spending with this man.

Despite her convictions and all the precautions in the world, Ariel wasn't so certain she would survive that.

Oh, he was something. Well over six feet with a build that

was lean, muscled, wonderfully hard, and definitely ready for anything. Oddly enough, it wasn't the kind of physique one got from gym equipment, but rather outdoor activity.

Her gaze drifted over his white linen shirt, the sleeves of which had been folded back to mid-forearm, and then to his beige linen slacks. Wind continued to push the fabric of both against his broad chest and what looked to be his erection.

Ariel's mouth went dry. She ordered herself to lift her gaze from that lovely bulge.

When she finally did, he was still regarding her, and there wasn't a thing Ariel could do except meet his gaze. His eyes were as richly brown as his hair. Those dark, silky waves danced across his forehead with the breeze and curled around his ears. Though clean-shaven, his face was shadowed with beard as night approached.

He was quite beautiful; nothing on earth could convince Ariel otherwise. His features were enticingly masculine, his skin deeply tanned, his presence certainly not what she needed. Oh, no, not this, *please;* not a shallow Hollywood type. Not someone who would have the same problem with honesty and fidelity as her parents had, and who would worry more about image than substance. Nope. No damn way. The sooner this was over, the better it would be for all involved.

At last, she got moving again.

Cole saw the change in her expression. Whatever had gone on in her mind just now, she was suddenly a woman on a mission, because her gaze was no longer open and vulnerable.

Now it was all business.

Oddly enough that didn't change one damned thing for Cole. Desire so quickly flooded through him, he was forced to lock his knees and endure an arousal that was overwhelming and would not be easily satisfied.

She knew it, too. Cole had seen her expression when her gaze had dipped to his erection. In that slice of time she had looked aroused, not disturbed—and that's what mattered most, not her cool demeanor now.

"My dear," Thaddeus said first.

She nodded at her uncle's greeting even as her gaze remained on Cole. When she, at last, looked away, she took Thaddeus's outstretched hand and brought it to her cheek. With her other hand, she lifted the old guy's Panama hat to reveal a bald, freckled crown circled by wisps of hair in varying shades of auburn and white.

Leaning down, Ariel delicately kissed that shiny pate.

He quickly complained. "Stop that. You're messing up my hair."

Ariel gently replaced his hat, then spoke in a very sweet voice. "What hair?"

Thaddeus arched one grizzled brow and looked at Cole. "See what I have to put up with?"

You lucky bastard, Cole thought as his gaze remained on Ariel. She was now so close he could see that her eyes were a grayish green and appeared far cooler than her manner allowed.

There was heat in her cheeks and throat. There was still wonder and interest in those amazing eyes.

"Well now," Thaddeus said after a charged silence, "I suppose it's time for you two to meet." He sounded vaguely annoyed.

Cole was damn near giddy. "Yes sir, it is."

Ariel looked at him. Cole smiled, and just like that her gaze softened.

Before she got too giddy, Thaddeus smacked his cane against the table's wrought-iron leg. Ariel flinched with the *clang.*

Thaddeus continued speaking as she glared at him. "Ariel, dear, this is Cole Ryder. Now, as I explained when I begged you to join us—yes," he said, speaking above her, "I *begged* as you were hardly enthusiastic. At times, you were downright rude, but I forgive you. Anyway," he said, as her cheeks flushed, "as I explained at the time, Mr. Ryder is a writer and a director who comes to us from Hollywood. However, unlike many writers and directors who were once unemployed actors or waiters or who-knows-what else, Mr. Ryder did have a real job at one time when he was a Marine."

Ariel's slender brows rose with that news. She looked at Cole in amazement or maybe disbelief.

Cole wondered why. Was it that surprising that he had had a real job before getting into this unreal one? Or did she doubt he could have survived the rigors of the military if he was now a Hollywood type?

"Of course," Thaddeus continued, "Mr. Ryder simply stumbled into this new career by serving as a military subject matter expert on the movies of other writers and directors who were once unemployed actors, or waiters, or who-knows-what-else. Because of Mr. Ryder's expertise in the military field, in particular the Marines elite Force Recon unit, where I've been told he distinguished himself again and again in quite dangerous military operations, he's been given a chance to make his own movies. Political and military action thrillers I believe they're called. Life is strange, wouldn't you say?"

"At times," Ariel said.

Despite her continuing surprise Cole forgave her, because she had an outstanding voice. Sweet, silky, and so damned enticing he might have smiled again, if not for Thaddeus. The old guy was watching them like a drill sergeant, because he damn well knew what Ariel's direct gaze and amazing voice did to a guy.

"Young man," Thaddeus suddenly said.

Cole resisted the urge to roll his eyes and finally looked at him. "Yes, sir."

Thaddeus regarded Cole, his gaze a warning not to *seduce her, romance her, lead her on,* or *touch her in any way.* "This is my niece, Ariel Leigh."

Yes, sir. "Ariel," he said, then stepped around his chair so that he could offer his hand.

Before he got that far, Thaddeus put out his cane, stopping Cole. "Not so fast," he said.

Suppressing a sigh, Cole lifted his gaze from that rose-wood cane to those suspicious blue eyes.

"There is nothing Ariel doesn't know about survival in the wild," Thaddeus explained. *"Nothing."*

Cole slowly nodded, figuring what the old guy really meant was survival from the wild.

"Though Ariel is quite young," Thaddeus added, "only twenty-seven, by the way, she is still quite amazing at what she does."

"I have absolutely no doubt of that." Cole met her gaze. "You did a fine job landing that bird."

Her cheeks quickly flushed to that compliment, after which she arched one brow.

Cole arched his right back.

She seemed surprised at his teasing, then unexpectedly smiled.

It was luminous, dimpled, and so damned honest it melted Cole's heart.

"Mr. Ryder," Thaddeus said, then continued when Cole frowned at him. "How old are you?"

How old am I? "Thirty-three . . . why?"

"Old enough to know better, then," Thaddeus said in answer to the question. "Old enough to be cautious of dangerous situations and to heed *all* warnings."

Cole was not about to comment on that.

Thaddeus's eyes suddenly twinkled. That mischievous note was back in his voice as he said, "With Ariel's youthful enthusiasm and your caution, you two make a good match."

Cole looked at her.

She was staring at her uncle as if the old guy had lost his mind.

Thaddeus pretended not to notice. "Go on," he said, as if he were a headmaster at a school dance, "say hello."

Ariel cautiously turned to Cole. After a brief pause she said, "Mr. Ryder."

There was such regard and obvious welcome in her voice, he was momentarily stunned.

"Cole—please," he finally said, then went to her and offered his hand.

Ariel slipped her own inside.

Her fingers felt incredibly delicate, moist, and hot, while her grip was really firm.

For some crazy reason that made Cole want to show her how strong he was. If need be, he'd carry her from here to the other end of the island and back, then pleasure her until dawn, if she allowed it.

"So, Cole," she said, as her thumb stroked his, "you and I will be spending the next few days and nights together."

He opened his mouth, then closed it without saying a word. For a moment, he wasn't certain he had heard her correctly, given that blood was whizzing in his ears as she continued to stroke his thumb.

You and I will be spending the next few days and nights together?

Cole's head swam to the thought of not one, but a few nights with her stripped bare, her dewy nipples puckered in the candlelight, her hair freed from that braid, that cinnamon flesh scented with arousal, her gaze welcoming, her lips—

"On research and only research," Thaddeus said, cutting into that carnal fantasy, "isn't that correct?"

Cole certainly hoped not. "Two nights?" he asked, guessing that was what she meant by a few.

Her expression suddenly changed. She pulled her hand from his.

Cole looked from that to her.

"Did you want to change it to only two nights?" she asked.

Only? Good God, how much time had she planned to give him? "Not at all . . . how much time do you have?"

She seemed surprised by the question. "Three days and nights, not including tonight." She looked at Thaddeus. "Just what *you* said was needed—no, I believe you used the word *required*—when you *begged* me to do this, remember?"

Thaddeus smiled blandly, then looked from her to Cole. "So, I suppose the two of you are really hungry now."

Cole spoke without thinking. "I am."

Ariel looked at him.

He looked right back.

Again, Ariel was caught off guard, not to mention quickly aroused, because this time his expression was stripped of pretense. He knew what he wanted, and for the moment he appeared to be hungry for her.

Ariel was completely captivated, not to mention vaguely annoyed, and not only at him.

What was the matter with her? She didn't want just a moment, she had never been willing to settle for that. She demanded far, far more than he, or any other man, was willing to give. Did he really believe that three days and nights would do it for her or any other woman? Did he really think that passion could be turned on and off?

As far as Ariel was concerned she needed a man's love for a lifetime to satisfy the ache in her heart and the longing in her soul. Didn't he know that?

"Are you all right?" he asked.

The question surprised her. Was she that transparent? "Sure."

He smiled.

Her gaze lowered to his rich mouth, that oddly tender smile. With that her resolve again weakened, while her mind begged her to be careful, because she certainly wasn't being smart.

Oh, no. Cole Ryder was a dangerous man, even more so than a Hollywood type. He was an ex-Marine, the ultimate bad boy with a polite manner, disarming smile, and an undeniable masculinity that would be hard to resist when he got her alone.

And he would, for three whole days and nights.

"Are you absolutely certain of that?" Thaddeus asked.

Ariel's skin continued to tingle as she pulled her gaze from Cole and looked at her uncle. "I'm sorry . . . what?"

"Really, Ariel, you must pay attention."

She leveled her gaze on him.

Thaddeus's cheeks crinkled with his wide smile. "Are you absolutely certain that you're feeling all—"

"Yes."

"I see," he said to her expression. "Then is it safe to say that you're ready for supper?"

She wasn't ready for anything, except spending some time alone with Cole Ryder—an ex-Marine—to teach him survival skills and nothing more. So it was best that they just got on with it. "Actually, I am."

Leaning heavily on his cane, Thaddeus pushed to his feet. "Time to freshen up, then." He looked at Cole. "You may also retire to your room, Mr. Ryder. Supper will be served in precisely forty-five minutes on the piazza. I warn you, don't be late." He offered Ariel his arm. "I'll escort you to your room. By the way," he said to Cole, "I took the liberty of faxing Ariel the copy of your script that was forwarded to me. She will discuss it with you while we eat . . . won't you, dear?"

It was either that, Ariel thought, or discuss the three days and nights she would be spending alone with him that her uncle had apparently failed to mention to Cole.

Ariel had seen Cole's surprise and felt his gaze on her now as she walked toward the compound. Despite the steps that separated them, that gaze continued to arouse and disturb her.

Thaddeus finally noticed. "Why, dear, you're breathless," he said as they reached the entry of the main house. "Am I walking too fast for you?"

Ariel slid her gaze to him. "Walking too fast for me? With that cane? Are you kidding?"

"Now, now, if you want a cane, too, I will gladly purchase one for—"

"I don't want it, and you don't need it."

Thaddeus smiled slyly, then followed her into the lush foyer where countless ferns, banana trees, and tropical flowers thrived beneath the skylight. Beyond this, rich Mexican-pavered floors led to countless white-washed rooms where priceless wall hangings and furniture from around the globe offered both comfort and an undeniable feeling of home.

Lifting his cane as if it were a shotgun, Thaddeus took aim at an African mask on the wall. "I believe Mr. Ryder thought I was infirm."

Ariel crossed her arms under her breasts and leaned against the rough-textured wall. "More like crazy," she said, when her uncle used that cane as a prop as he did a vaudeville soft-shoe down the low-ceilinged hall.

After a few more steps, he stopped. Despite his age and *infirmity*, he wasn't breathing all that hard. "You don't like my cane?"

The question was whether Isa liked it. Isa was her uncle's cook, whom Ariel had hugged outside. "Why do you keep trying to get Isa's attention with dumb stuff like that?"

"My cane is not dumb. It's elegant and commands attention."

"It makes you look infirm."

He grinned. "That's one way to get attention."

Good God. "Uncle Thaddeus, why don't you just ask that poor woman on a date? Take her to one of the casinos on the other islands. Live a little. Spend. The. Night."

"I am working up to it," he mumbled, "not that it's any of your business."

Uh-huh. Uncrossing her arms, Ariel pushed away from the wall. "I guess you didn't fill me in on the details of this job, because that wasn't any of my business either, right?"

Thaddeus studied his cane's brass handle. "I have no idea what you're—"

"Sure you do." Ariel glanced over her shoulder to make certain they were alone. Although they were she still kept her voice low. "You said he was a Hollywood type."

Thaddeus nodded distractedly, then finally looked at her. "He who, dear?"

Ariel briefly closed her eyes. "You know damn well who. The ex-Marine out there. The Force Recon dude. You said he was a Hollywood type."

Her uncle looked surprised by the accusation. "He is. He's a writer *and* a director, and I believe he's also a produ—"

"Who used to be a Marine. Who used to be in Force Recon."

"If memory serves me correctly, he also graduated from the Naval Academy."

Oh, please, she thought. This was getting better—or maybe worse—by the minute. "*Now* you tell me?"

"Are you saying I misled you?"

"I'm saying you didn't tell me he was ex-military, and so beautiful, polite, and intelligent." *Not to mention dangerous to my heart and good sense,* she thought, but didn't add.

"You noted all of that in the short time you've known him?"

Ariel arched one slender brow.

"If I had told you about his military education and service, his beauty, his chivalrous manner, and his intelligence," Thaddeus asked, "would it have made any difference?" His expression again grew mischievous. "Does it make a difference?"

Ariel frowned. "Of course not." She continued to lie. "This is simply another job. Which, I might add, you obviously didn't tell him would last three whole days."

"And nights."

She ignored that.

"Very well," he said, "I confess that I forgot to mention the matter of scheduling to him. But what does it matter, dear, if this is simply another job? That is what you're implying, correct?"

Okay, so he knew she was lying. He always knew when she lied, starting with that first moment she had come into his life as a lonely little kid who told him she didn't need anyone, especially him.

At the time Thaddeus had nodded gravely and told Ariel that despite her independent spirit, which he greatly admired, he still needed her. "So, indulge my needy heart," he had said.

Given that Ariel was only ten at the time, she hadn't been absolutely certain what he meant by *indulge my needy heart,* but the softness of his voice and the hurt she had put in his eyes had bonded her to this man for the rest of her days. He had willingly been her family when no one else wanted the job. Ariel knew she would protect him with her very life and would love him until the end of time.

Of course, that didn't mean she was going to tell him how she already felt about Cole Ryder. "Yes," she continued to lie, "that's what I'm implying."

"And that's what I thought," he said in a voice that betrayed his lie. Taking her arm, he walked her down the hall that led to his room. "So, you'll be pleased to know that I took care of the matter."

"How?"

"I told Mr. Ryder that his time with you is strictly business, and he is not to seduce you, romance you, lead you on, or touch you in any way while you two are alone."

Ariel's step paused. Thaddeus looked at her. "Is something wrong, dear?"

Of course something was wrong. "You actually said that?"

"He actually agreed to my terms."

She frowned.

Thaddeus smiled now as he had years ago when she was a wayward little girl. Gently patting her hand, he said, "Don't you worry, dear. Men always want what they cannot have . . . or have been warned they cannot have."

"Excuse me?"

"Have I ever not taken care of you?"

"You've always been more than wonderful," she quickly admitted, "but—"

"Of course," he interrupted, "I'm not going to be around forever, and we do have your future to think about. So that settles it."

"Whoa, whoa, *whoa*. Settles what?"

"Really, dear, if you keep pausing like this, we're never going to get to our respective rooms to freshen—"

"Don't play dumb with me," she said. "All this stuff about him not touching me and not romancing me is simply a smokescreen. You're trying to fix me up with this man."

Thaddeus looked at her with an expression that was all innocence. "Now, why would I do that? He is a Hollywood type."

He's an ex-Marine, Ariel thought. A delicious, sensuous ex-Marine with a sharp mind, a tender smile, and a mischievous nature just like her uncle. "You've played this game in the past. Remember that pilot you thought I'd like and that—"

"Mistakes, all of them mistakes," Thaddeus said, then gently urged her down the hall until they reached his room.

"And Cole Ryder," Ariel asked, "what is he?"

Thaddeus looked from the doorknob to her. "A job. Nothing more. So don't you worry, dear, the young man has been warned not to make any move on you at all. Tomorrow I'll warn him not to even think of you. I'd do that tonight, but I'd rather not ruin supper. See you in a bit." With that, he left her in the hall.

Ariel's shoulders sagged. What had she gotten herself into? No, she quickly amended, what had Thaddeus gotten her into?

Shaking her head, Ariel went to her room that had never been changed, even though she had had her own place for years. There were the same beautiful wall hangings and carpets from Spain, the same canopy bed from England, and the same snowy linens from Ireland that she continued to enjoy alone.

With that being a matter her uncle seemed determined to remedy.

Already he had tricked several men into coming here as he

hoped against hope that she might like one of them and, even more importantly, that one of them would love her as deeply and steadfastly as he did so that she wouldn't be alone when he was gone.

It hadn't worked. The first of the lot, a corporate pilot, had used the only thing they had in common, which was flying, as a way to one-up her. In the end, her piloting skills proved better than his, and the guy couldn't whiz out of here fast enough.

A semi-famous animal trainer was next. That guy was game for some serious action, until his fake Aussie accent and oozing charm gave Ariel a bad case of hives, her first ever.

And then there was the CEO of a luxury hotel chain, who turned out to be the worst. Not that that was entirely her fault, given that he preferred all of the male staff to her.

Sighing deeply, Ariel dropped her bag on the floor, crossed the room to the bank of windows, then leaned against the last jamb as she faced an awful truth. When it came to her luck with guys, there simply wasn't any. Her choice of a career turned off most men and scared the hell out of the rest. Those that did stick around long enough to want sex only did so because they just had to prove they could outdo her in some activity. Her direct manner and poor flirting skills made her a pariah on the dating scene, while her height and aversion to makeup wasn't what any guy was looking for.

Except, it seemed, for Cole.

He was still outside.

Why? Ariel wondered as she watched him from the window. Was it to give her and Thaddeus some time alone or to plan his escape?

She turned into the window as he gazed at the sky. What was he thinking? What was he hoping? Would he be leaving?

No, she told herself, at least not tonight. He had already lowered his gaze and was now moving toward the compound with the ease and confidence of a man used to infiltrating hostile territories, the least of which was a woman's wary heart.

Despite her own caution, Ariel liked him already. If she allowed herself to consider it, he was a man she could all too easily love.

His smile was a wonder, mischievous yet tender; his gaze hungry, his body—*oh, his body*—it had been coiled for pleasure that could be primitive and wild, but gentle, too. It was that tempered strength that made a woman feel feminine; it was a gift that had been too absent from her life.

As he disappeared from view, Ariel finally turned away from the window and looked at her bed. In that moment, she allowed herself to imagine how it might feel to be in that bed held by his strong arms . . . using his broad chest as a cushion, feeling his thickened shaft plunging into her, filling her, anchoring her for all time to his world, his life, this bed that would become theirs.

Then, and only then, would she feel completely protected, safe, cherished—all the wonders that women craved and so few received.

You and I will be spending the next few days and nights together, she had said.

It didn't even amount to a week. It certainly didn't come close to a lifetime.

And she had to remember that; she had to be strong. No matter how vulnerable she was feeling right now, no way would she allow it to go further. This was a job. She would give him the benefit of her knowledge and would make his movie the best it could be. As a professional, she would give nothing less.

As a woman, she would offer nothing more. No way was she going to fall for a Hollywood type, not even if he was an ex-Marine with a tender, engaging smile and a seeming hunger for her that took Ariel's breath away.

Not even if he was a man she couldn't wait to be alone with during the next three days and nights.

She would make all of that very clear, too, beginning at supper.

Chapter Two

Given his military training, his desire to see Ariel again, and good old common sense that told him not to piss off Thaddeus—at least not knowingly—Cole had every intention of being on time for his supper.

After a quick shave, shower, and change of clothing he left his room and, with a staff member's help, found the piazza.

It faced the churning sea and was flanked by torches that lent an amber glow to the Mexican pavers, black wrought-iron chairs, and glass-topped tables that reflected the setting sun. To the left was an expansive buffet with silver containers perched above flickering flames so that the fragrant fare inside remained hot. Bowls of island fruit—mangoes, pineapples, bananas, and papayas—rested nearby, lending their scent to the balmy, perfumed air.

On the table directly in front of him, white linen napkins, expensive china, ornate silverware, and the finest crystal the world had to offer marked each place setting.

Cole wondered which was his since no one else was here.

You may also retire to your room, Thaddeus had said. *Supper will be served in precisely forty-five minutes . . . I warn you, don't be late.*

Okay, so he was ten minutes early.

Twenty minutes later, however, Cole was still cooling his heels as one staff member after the other returned to the buffet to check on the piping-hot food or to deliver more trays that held ornate desserts. Cole's stomach growled to this feast, while every other part of him hungered for Ariel. Once more, he checked the time on his watch.

"Don't you worry," a voice from behind said in heavily accented English.

Cole looked over his shoulder to see that same older woman Ariel had hugged outside. In this muted light, the woman's skin was a rich coppery shade, which was complemented by her beautiful black hair that was faintly streaked with gray. That color was only a shade darker than her flawless white uniform and shoes.

Cole faced her. "Excuse me?"

The woman lifted her chin even more as if that regal bearing would make up for her scant height. "I said, don't you worry."

He nodded good-naturedly. "Okay." He teased. "About what?"

The older woman crossed her arms under her ample breasts. "Little Ariel. Mr. Thaddeus." She frowned. "Who else?" She quickly smiled. "They are coming. Little Ariel first, then Mr. Thaddeus." She uncrossed her arms and went to Cole. "Little Ariel is not usually this late. Why she's behaving like this, I do not know. Mr. Thaddeus, well, he cannot be rushed." Her frown returned. "Always later, I am promised. *Always* later." She glared at Cole. "The man will *not* make a move!"

Cole wasn't certain whether to acknowledge that or not, or to ask why Ariel was late, especially as the woman started swearing in Spanish, which she obviously didn't know he knew.

At last, Cole cleared his throat.

She abruptly stopped, then stepped back as she smoothed her uniform. "Forgive my rude manners. I am Isabella."

Cole offered his name and hand and wasn't a bit surprised her grip was as firm as Ariel's. "Nice to meet you, Isabella."

"I am called Isa," she corrected, then frowned. "By little

Ariel and Mr. Thaddeus, not by you. To you, I am *Miss* Isa. To me, you are Mr. Cole."

"Yes, ma'am."

She smiled broadly this time, showing her beautiful white teeth. She leaned closer and murmured, "Get ready, you hear?"

Cole glanced down as the woman pulled her hand from his. Before he could ask, *Get ready for what?* she had already moved past him.

Cole looked over his shoulder to see where she was going and saw Ariel instead.

My God. Her hair was loose and being stirred by the breeze as it tumbled over her narrow shoulders in thick, glossy waves. Its color matched her top and wide-legged pants made of some silky fabric that draped her curves. Cole stared at the plunging neckline that left little to the imagination. There, the fabric skimmed over Ariel's luscious breasts, while those tiny capped sleeves fluttered around her slender arms.

Nice. But definitely not all. His gaze dipped to the edge of that top. It was cropped very short so that it bared her midriff, just as those pants hung low on the flare of her hips to reveal her taut belly and navel.

That small depression was pierced and sported a ring from which tiny diamond stars dangled and glittered, catching all available light.

It was the only jewelry she wore. It was all she needed.

My God, Cole thought again as he imagined sweeping aside those stars to get to the woman beneath.

Inhaling deeply, his gaze continued to roam over her.

In that moment, Ariel understood what it meant to be desired and knew she hadn't been foolish to have dressed like this. The truth of that was in Cole's expression.

He liked the way she looked. The man was damn near stunned by the way she looked.

He had no idea how hard it had been for her to do this.

For too long Ariel had troubled over what to wear. When

nothing she had packed seemed right, she had gone through her closet finding this outfit, which she had purchased after the disaster with that pilot. He hadn't been the man of her dreams, of course, but he was a man; so after his rejection Ariel had bought these racy clothes, and others, and had gotten her navel pierced so that she could wear those tiny diamond stars. It seemed a foolish reaction, of course, but at the time she had wanted to feel like a woman—sexy and desired.

She hadn't worn the stars since then. She hadn't even recalled the outfit until tonight.

Against all good reason, and with Isa's less-than-gentle prodding, Ariel had decided to wear it no matter what was to come.

"Don't be like me," Isa had warned. "You go for it."

Ariel had, and how glad she was.

The unmistakable surprise and continuing delight in Cole's eyes was a gift she would keep in her heart forever. He thought she was beautiful.

She had brought this bad boy—this ex-Marine—to his knees, and she was going to revel in that as she admired him.

His previous outfit had been replaced by a black shirt and slacks. The well-tailored fabric fluttered around his strong, solid body with the persistent breeze. It also revealed his desire. This time, Ariel wasn't surprised at his lovely erection. This time, she was more than pleased, because she had caused it. She *owned* it.

"Hi," she said.

Cole's nostrils briefly flared. When he spoke, his voice was downright husky. "Hi."

She smiled.

"So," Thaddeus suddenly said from behind, "I see we're all here."

Ariel's smile paused.

Cole frowned, at least until he noticed her uncle was walking as spryly as a man half his age and without the aid of his cane.

Arching one brow to that and the toupee Thaddeus sported, Cole stepped aside as two young men starting serving the meal, filling plate after plate with shrimp and lobster known as camarones and langosto; gallo pinto, a dish of delicately spiced rice and black beans; deep-fried plantain called patacones; smoked marlin that the islanders knew as pescado ahumado, and fragrant turnovers bursting with beans, cheese, and meat that everyone referred to as empanadas.

As the staff set the filled plates on the table, Cole pulled out a chair. "Ariel?"

Mmmm. She liked how he said her name. She was also very pleased with his manners. Most of the men she had known seated themselves first, fully expecting that she get her own chair—perhaps even build her own chair given that she was so very capable at everything else.

Not Cole. In his heart he was still an officer and a gentleman. Of course, his ego had yet to be tested out in the wild. But that would come later. Giving him a smile, Ariel next leveled her gaze on Thaddeus with an expression that said *behave.*

"Are you all right?" her uncle quickly asked.

Ariel briefly closed her eyes. "Fine." After Cole seated her, she looked up at him. "Thanks."

"My pleasure." He gently touched her shoulder.

"Well, now," Thaddeus said, "perhaps you'd care to help me with my chair."

Ariel spoke before Cole could. "We could ask Isa to do that."

Thaddeus shot her a look, then muttered something beneath his breath as he easily pulled out his chair and seated himself.

"Legs not hurting you anymore?" Cole asked.

"He's had a remarkable recovery," Ariel answered, then smiled sweetly at her uncle. "Haven't you?"

He muttered something else.

Cole wasn't about to get into that fray. "Glad to hear it." Seating himself, he straightened his legs and touched Ariel's.

Her delicate nostrils flared slightly, but she said nothing, nor did she move.

Neither did he. Cole kept his gaze on her as his heart beat hard and Thaddeus said, "Well, what are you two waiting for?"

Ariel's eyes widened slightly before she looked at Thaddeus.

The old guy arched one grizzled brow. "Dig in," he ordered.

You have no idea what you're asking, Cole thought, but nodded good-naturedly. Reaching for the serving spoon at the same moment Ariel did, their fingers touched.

Cole's gaze jumped to hers as heat flooded his chest, belly, and groin. He knew he should bring back his hand, but could not.

Nor did she. Her cheeks flushed, and her eyes sparkled.

She was as aroused as he was, and Cole didn't want it to end. He wanted her beneath him, open and willing. He wanted her on top of him, working his cock until both of them cried out. He wanted her bent over the dresser, back arched, legs spread wide, presenting herself for his pleasure. He wanted her mouth on him, licking his length, before taking him inside.

He wanted to know each part of her; to touch her, to fill himself with her scent; to taste her tight, hard nipples; those long, slender toes, those adorable stars, her plump nether lips, and those delicate curls between her legs.

Were they auburn, too? he wondered again.

A man could hope. But a man could hardly know if he had been warned not to romance her, or seduce her, or lead her on, or touch her in any way while they were together.

I can't do this, he thought.

Ariel's eyes widened slightly. She brought back her hand.

Thaddeus leaned forward in his chair. "Can't do what?"

Cole's heart started to race. Dear God, had he spoken his thoughts aloud?

He looked from Thaddeus to Ariel. She seemed disappointed, wounded.

"Eat," Cole lied. He turned to Thaddeus. "It's too hot."

The man narrowed his eyes at Cole, then grabbed a fork and speared a bit of the patacones. Chewing quickly, then swallowing, he continued to frown. "Hot? It's tepid at most and barely spicy. I must have a talk with Isa about this."

Ariel pressed her fingertips to her right temple. "I believe Cole's referring to the outside temperature, not the food."

"Is that right?" Thaddeus asked, then looked at Cole as if the younger man had lost his mind. "Why, it's no more than seventy-five degrees out here, and the breeze is quite pleasant. But you're still hot?" He looked at Ariel. "Are you hot, too?"

Cole actually felt himself blush.

Ariel, on the other hand, was now helping herself to the gallo pinto and the pescado ahumado as if her uncle's behavior wasn't the least bit embarrassing.

"I'm fine," she finally said in a tone that betrayed none of her emotions.

"That's good to hear. Now, Mr. Ryder," Thaddeus said.

Cole reached for his water and finished half the glass before coming up for air. "Yes, sir?"

"You best be careful."

Cole looked at the man, then at the water he had just drunk, then Ariel. *You best be careful?* Of what? With that, he'd had it. If the water wasn't purified, that might cause a bit of a problem—but he would survive. However, if he was going to be spending three fucking days and nights with a woman he wasn't allowed to love, in any fucking way, that was definitely going to be a problem, especially if she wanted him.

And she did. Cole saw it in her eyes and in the way her body responded each time he looked at her. Heat rose in her cheeks and throat, her breathing picked up, her nipples tightened, and those precious lips parted as if to welcome him inside. Damn right, she wanted him.

And by God, he wanted her. So if touching her, kissing her, and making love with her got him thrown out of the film business—so fucking what? Could be a blessing in disguise— at the very least, it might be a relief.

"And why is that?" Cole finally asked, ready to have it out with the man.

Thaddeus wasn't in such a rush. Spearing a bit of the langosto, he carefully dipped it in melted butter before bringing it to his lips. Slowly chewing that delightful bit of food, he moaned briefly after he swallowed, then asked, "Why else?" He paused to tap his mouth with a napkin before continuing. "There is no end of danger out there." He glanced to the right, that part of the rain forest that crowded the beach, but was now hidden by darkness.

Cole wasn't certain what to make of this. The old guy was suddenly talking about the rain forest, not the danger he faced if he pursued Ariel? "It seems benign enough."

Thaddeus smiled. "Except for the poisonous plants, snakes, and all those nasty insects. But," he added, "Ariel is an expert at wilderness survival, in addition to being a black belt in karate and an expert markswoman. So rest assured, young man, she knows how to deal with those pests, and any other kind there is."

Uh-huh, Cole thought, then decided it wasn't worth it to fight the old guy, since playing along might be more fun. Looking at Ariel, he asked, "And how do you deal with pests—of the insect variety, that is?"

She finished swallowing a patacones as her gaze moved from Cole to her uncle. As much as she loved the man, she really wanted to smack him.

Thaddeus knew. He mumbled something beneath his breath and finally concentrated on his meal.

Looking back to Cole, Ariel waited until his gaze lifted from her breasts to her eyes. Once it did, she quietly regarded him.

His gaze grew quickly heated.

It touched Ariel's soul and thrilled her to the core. Whatever had made him say *I can't do this* had passed. Ariel knew she shouldn't be glad, but she was. She knew she shouldn't be reading too much into this, and she wouldn't. She'd simply enjoy this bit of pleasure while it lasted. It wasn't smart, but it was what she craved. "Are you certain you want to hear this?"

Cole nodded distractedly, then stopped. "Hear what?"

Ariel suppressed a smile. She leaned forward in her chair and couldn't help but tease. "How I get rid of pests—of the insect variety, that is."

Cole's gaze dipped to her cleavage, lingering there, before returning to her eyes. "Shoot."

"Careful what you ask for," Thaddeus mumbled.

Cole ignored him. So did Ariel. "One of the easiest ways," she said, "is to eat large quantities of onions."

Cole stared for a moment, then smiled broadly. "With a burger?"

Ariel's brows arched. She had been trying to impress, not amuse him. "No," she finally said. "Of course not. Onions give you a scent that helps to repel insects."

"Not to mention people."

She did not return his smile. "You're missing the point. You're not seeing the beauty of nature. It has all you need. Take for example if you get hurt out there, the juice from onions—and especially garlic—is a natural antiseptic. All you have to do is rub it all over yourself."

He looked skeptical. "Not just on the wound?"

"Well, if you want to do it the easy way."

"Don't make any of this easy," Thaddeus suddenly warned. "The more perils in this story, the more exciting it will—what?" he asked, interrupting himself as both Cole and Ariel looked at him.

Cole spoke first. "Are we talking about my film here?"

We are now, Ariel thought. After giving her uncle a hard stare, she looked at Cole. "You can clearly use what I just said. In fact, you should use it."

He looked uneasy.

"If you don't believe me," Ariel said, "I can show—"

"I believe you," he said. "It's just that I wanted something better."

"Than onions?"

He laughed.

Ariel did not.

Cole quickly sobered. "Better than that remedy," he said. "Filmmaking needs something different, something exciting, something unique. Surely there's another way to repel insects and treat wounds. Something the audience would enjoy."

Like what? Ariel thought. Female medics and pest control workers dressed in bikinis parachuting into the jungle to give shots of penicillin to a bunch of horny guys, while also spraying for bugs?

"There is another way, isn't there?" Cole asked.

"Of course there's another way," she said, "but using it would depend upon your familiarity with the terrain. From what I've read of your story, I don't believe your guy knows much about the tropics or anything else for that matter."

Cole started to nod, then stopped when he realized what she had said. It wasn't that he expected her to love his story or that her approval of it would even be necessary to have her plug in a few facts. Even so, it didn't thrill him to have her suggest that his lead character was deadly dumb or that he knew absolutely nothing either. Maybe it was time to let her know that he *had* studied some of this stuff while in Force Recon, even if the subject of gorging on onions had never come up.

"Screenplay," he corrected, "and it's called a lead."

She looked confused. "What is?"

"My *guy* is called a lead, and my *story* is called a screenplay or a script."

She didn't comment on that. As her gaze remained on his, she speared a slice of mango and brought it to her lips.

Cole's gaze dropped to her mouth. He watched as she slipped that succulent fruit inside, chewed slowly, then swallowed.

"You know what the problem is, don't you?" she asked.

With her way over there and him way over here and Thaddeus chaperoning the whole sorry mess, he had a pretty good idea, not that he figured she was speaking about that. "Problem?"

Ariel nodded. "You do know what it is, correct?"

Cole hadn't a clue. He wasn't even following this new conversational direction. "'Fraid not."

Ariel nodded as if she already knew that. Lowering her fork, she crossed her arms over the edge of the table and leaned closer. In the light from the torches her eyes sparkled, while that amber glow flickered over the satiny sheen of her flesh. "You need a woman," she said.

Cole's fork stopped halfway between his plate and his mouth. He was about to look at Thaddeus to see if the old guy had nodded off, and maybe that's why Ariel had said what she did, but at the last moment Cole thought better of it. "Excuse me?"

"You heard me."

That he had. God, but she was direct. "I need a woman?" he asked.

"For your screenplay."

Uh-huh. "Of course. For my screenplay." He smiled. "And that's why I have you."

Thaddeus loudly cleared his throat.

Ariel ignored him. "*In* your screenplay," she amended. "You should put a woman into it, to make it more interesting."

"Not Ariel," Thaddeus quickly said. "I will not have her exploited in that—"

"Mister Thaddeus!" Isa suddenly shouted. "You are needed in the kitchen!"

"Thank God," Cole mumbled.

Ariel looked at him, then her uncle. "Go," she ordered. "Isa needs you." She turned to the woman and spoke the words the two of them had rehearsed earlier. "Whatever the problem is, Isa, don't you worry about keeping him too long. Keep him all night if you need to."

Thaddeus shot Ariel a look. Isa winked.

Once they were out of earshot, Cole said, "None of my business, I know, but is she sweet on him?"

Ariel nodded. "For ten years."

"Ten years?"

"She's very patient."

"She's a damned saint."

"You mean you wouldn't wait that long to show someone you wanted them?"

Cole's expression changed. Leaning forward against the table, he murmured, "No, I would not."

Ariel already knew that, but it was nice to hear it from him. Even so, she wasn't about to rush anything. It felt too good to have him want her. Once he got her, everything could go downhill fast. Given that she would never be ready for that, she said, "About your story."

Cole seemed surprised by the change in subject, but then, as if sensing her caution, he leaned back in his chair. "You think my screenplay needs a female character."

"Your story's desperate for one."

Desperate? he thought. "It's a political-military thriller. There's no room for females in it. There's no need. From the opening sequence senior government officials—politicos, military, and operatives—are at this secret island location planning intelligence to avert a global disaster. The public can't know; they'd panic. But others know that these few men know about the conspiracy, and the decision is made to neutralize them. In the very first scene the assassins arrive, and the targets are taken out except for my lead, who's forced to escape undetected into the rain forest. Since these subversives have taken over this compound to relay counterintelligence, my lead has to work his way to the other side of the island where he can signal for help. And just in time, too, I might add, to stop what could be the end of this world as we know it."

Ariel didn't comment.

Cole frowned. "It's an action film. It doesn't need—"

She finally interrupted, "You say your guy is—"

"My lead," he corrected.

Ariel nodded. "This guy," she said, then continued over Cole's sigh, "is a pampered politician, so how is he supposed to—"

"Hold it right there. I never said he was pampered."

Ariel smiled as if he were a naïve little boy. "Do you know any politicians that aren't pampered?"

Cole crossed his arms over his chest.

She didn't miss a beat. "Given that pampering, how is he supposed to know how to survive out there?" She glanced to where Thaddeus had earlier, the rain forest.

When she looked back at him, Cole offered a sexy smile. "Well, that's why I have you, isn't it?"

Ariel crossed her arms over her chest. She wanted him to want her for more than just that. She also needed for him to respect her work. He would disappoint her greatly if he did not. Keeping her voice cool, she said, "You have me to fix your story. And that's why your guy needs someone like me in your story. A girl hero."

Fix his story? "Female lead," he said.

"Right."

"Wrong. This is a political—"

"It'd be more interesting with a male and female lead," she said. "He could remain a useless and obviously clueless politician, but what would it matter when she's the one who could get them through this?"

Get them through this? "And how is that?"

"She'd be a kick-ass Marine like you."

Cole's frown paused to the awe he heard in her voice. "You think I'm kick-ass?"

"Well, I don't know. I haven't seen you in action, so I'm working at a disadvantage. So just stop me if I'm wrong."

He arched one dark brow.

Ariel smiled. "This lady would know how to survive in the rain forest, even though they don't teach it at the Marine school, and that's because she—"

"The Marine school?"

She nodded, then uncrossed her arms and started talking fast. "She learned it from her uncle, who was this great expert. If that doesn't work, she could be a native from this island who turned into a Marine, and—"

"*Turned* into a Marine?"

She nodded, more slowly this time, but continued to talk fast. "By being a Marine and using her native smarts she can help him survive both the initial assault and the rain forest. When he gets injured in the initial assault—and he should be injured," she quickly added, "she, the native-turned-Marine, could help him into the jungle. There, she'd just have to remove his clothes to see the extent of his wounds. His injuries would be bad, but not fatal. At first he'd be delirious, but she wouldn't panic. Oh, no. She'd be too skilled for that. After she got him through the worst days of his fever, he'd finally come out of it, weakened but on the mend. When he finally awakened after maybe a week, she'd be asleep, exhausted from caring for him. He'd look at her as she rested against him, her body protecting his. He'd be surprised at first, but then his memory would come back. He'd recall how she gently cleansed his wounds and used the available plant life as an antiseptic. He'd think back to how she tore strips from her own clothing to bind his wounds. He'd know that's why her shirt and pants were so tattered, barely covering her. He'd recall how she kept watch over him, wiping the perspiration from his brow, running her fingers over his bristly cheeks, resting her hands on his strong shoulders, pressing her face against his broad chest, listening to the steady drumming of his heart, liking it, wanting it, kissing him when he didn't know it, caressing him when he needed it, loving him when he asked for it, and well, you know the rest."

Still breathing hard, Ariel grabbed her glass and finished the water in one long drink. Lowering the empty container to the table, she mumbled, "She could do all that."

Cole slowly nodded. "Yeah . . . they could definitely do all that."

"All that what?" Thaddeus suddenly asked as he rejoined them at the table. "And who is they?"

Cole looked at Ariel.

She pressed her fingers to her right temple. "You done with Isa already?"

Thaddeus blushed. Readjusting his toupee, he said, "The problem was minor. We fixed it, all right?"

Ariel looked at Cole.

"So," Thaddeus said after a lengthy silence. "What were you two talking about when I returned?"

"The leads in Cole's screenplay," Ariel answered first, then told Thaddeus how she plotted it.

Cole noted how she left out all the R- and X-rated parts.

"Sounds good," Thaddeus said, then looked at Cole. "Use it."

Huh? Before Cole could respond to that, his cell phone rang. After checking the number, he looked at Ariel and Thaddeus. "It's my business partner and co-producer. Sorry, but I really have to take this."

"Do it here," Thaddeus said as Cole was ready to leave the table. "Don't want you keeping any secrets from us, isn't that right, dear?"

Cole looked at Ariel. Her cheeks were still flushed, her voice very soft as she asked, "Would you do that?"

Not to her. *Never* to her. For Ariel, he'd be scrupulously

honest, because that's what she obviously wanted. Of course, he might lie a little when it came to critiquing her plot points for his story.

Thinking of that, he finally answered the call. "Gwen—hi."

"What's wrong?" she asked.

"Nothing. Why?"

"You sound weird."

"As compared to what?" After all, Gwen was a former stunt woman turned dental hygienist turned co-producer. It just didn't get weirder than that.

"Something bite you?" she asked.

Cole looked at Ariel. Her gaze was lowered to her food as she pushed it from one side of the plate to the other with her fork. "Not yet, but I'm hoping."

Ariel looked up.

Gwen chuckled. "Ah, you met a native girl."

"Actually, Ariel Leigh," Cole corrected, "the young woman I'm pleased to say will be serving as my subject-matter expert."

Ariel smiled.

So did Cole.

"Do I actually detect a note of affection here, and already, too?" Gwen asked.

"You called because?" he asked.

"If you're going to be that way," she said, "I'll be brief. Pitt, Cruise, and all the other biggies said no way to your script. They think it sucks."

Well, that hurt. Even so, Cole shrugged it off. "So what if we don't get a big name to play the lead? Besides, the script's not finished yet. I still have—"

"Nobody wants to be in your story?" Ariel asked.

"What was that?" Gwen asked.

"Just a minute," he said to her. "We'll sign somebody," he said to Ariel.

She frowned. "Is that what you want—somebody? Is that what you're willing to settle for—somebody?"

Now he frowned. "Well, I'd like Tom Cruise or Brad Pitt, but I'm also a realist so—"

"Give me the phone."

"What?"

"I didn't say a thing," Gwen said. "You told me to shut up."

"I told you just a minute," he corrected, then looked at Ariel. She was wiggling her fingers, wanting his phone.

"Why?" he asked.

"Why what?" Gwen asked.

"Will you just be quiet?" he said.

"Well, hell, quit asking me questions and I will!"

"Give Ariel your phone," Thaddeus said.

Cole frowned at the old guy. "Why?"

"I need to talk to Gwen about your story," Ariel said.

"Screenplay," he corrected again.

Ariel arched one brow. "Shouldn't you be more worried about who's going to play your guy than whether it's called a story or not?"

Cole gave up. "Gwen," he said into the phone, "meet Ariel." He handed the damn thing to her.

Ariel gave him a smile, then brought the phone to her ear. "Hi, Gwen, Ariel Leigh here. I'm Thaddeus Leigh's niece."

"Now, you mustn't mention me at all," Thaddeus interjected. "You're an expert all on your own. Give me the phone, I'll tell that woman that."

Dear God, Cole thought.

"Thanks," Ariel said to her uncle, "but there's no need—no, Gwen, I was speaking to my Uncle Thad—what?" Ariel listened for a moment, then said, "Well, you know, that's what I wanted to talk to you about, the flaws in Cole's story."

Right. He glanced around the area to see if there was any hard liquor.

"I see," Ariel said to Gwen, then paused and listened some more. At last she smiled. "Yes, he did say that."

Cole looked from the buffet to her. *Said what?*

Ariel's gaze moved to him, then roamed all over him—his face, his chest, his arms—as she listened to whatever Gwen was saying. After a few moments, Ariel said, "Yes, he is."

Is what? he thought.

Pushing back in her chair, Ariel stood. "You're right," she said to Gwen. To Cole and her uncle she said, "Excuse me."

Cole turned in his chair and watched as she left the area.

"Remind me to speak to your woman about Ariel's abilities," Thaddeus said. "I want to make certain she knows that Ariel is the very best at what she does."

Cole looked at the old guy, then again glanced over his shoulder as Ariel laughed.

It was youthful and carefree, the kind of laugh that tore a man's heart in two. It was also the kind of laugh that got a man to wondering just what in the hell she and Gwen were talking about.

"Perhaps I should have Ariel's biography printed up and faxed to your woman," Thaddeus said. "That way she and all of your staff would know—"

Ariel laughed again. A hearty, throaty laugh that stirred Cole in a way he never believed possible.

He imagined her gifting him with that laugh after they shared a private joke. He thought she might also laugh like that while he straddled, then tickled her.

He couldn't imagine a world without that laugh.

"Well, what do you think?" Thaddeus asked.

Cole looked at him and took the easy way out. "Whatever you want."

"Then that settles it. We'll have posters and other advertising printed up concerning Ariel's part in making your story a success. It will be good publicity for all."

Cole started to look for that hard liquor again. Before he spotted any, Ariel returned.

Those diamonds dangling from her navel glittered so wildly, Cole found it hard to breathe.

"No, no, please sit down," Ariel said as both men got to their feet.

"Was your conversation good?" Thaddeus asked as he sank to his chair.

"Amazing," Ariel said, then handed Cole his phone. "I didn't know Gwen started out in the business as a grip."

Neither had Cole. He had thought she got started as a stuntwoman.

"What's a grip?" Thaddeus asked.

Ariel lifted her shoulders.

Cole suppressed a smile.

"Anyway," Ariel said, turning to him, "Gwen agrees with me completely. There should be a female hero in this. She should have the largest part."

Cole frowned. "Role," he corrected. "And," he quickly added, "that's not how these stories go, at least not the ones I've worked on, and they've all been big hits."

"This can be bigger."

My God, she actually meant it. Worse, she believed it. He held back a sigh. "You don't understand. What you're proposing isn't my type of story."

"It could be."

Before Cole could protest, Thaddeus said, "Let's compromise."

Compromise? Cole thought. On his screenplay?

Given the way Thaddeus and Ariel were now looking at him, it had already become their story.

God help me, Cole thought. "How do you propose that?" he asked Thaddeus.

"I have all of the movies you worked on. Once we finish eating we'll retire to the screening room so that Ariel can see what you usually offer the public, after which she'll tell you how she can improve it."

Chapter Three

This time her uncle had gone too far. Ariel saw that in the way Cole stared at the man, then looked out to sea as if Cole wished he—or maybe Thaddeus *and* she—were there.

Ariel hoped it would pass. If she was going to help him in this, if he wanted to make this story really authentic—and she sensed he would, given he was an ex-Marine and not just some shallow Hollywood type—he'd just have to come around to her way of thinking.

Gwen already had.

Talking to that woman felt like talking to the brother Ariel had always wanted, but never got. Gwen swore like a sailor and didn't take any crap, but most importantly, she was fiercely loyal to Cole and was actually receptive to the idea of talking about the flaws in his story so that it could be really great.

"He takes his role in this way too seriously," she had said. "It's like he's planning a fucking military campaign. I'll bet when he ran down his plot for you, he used words like operatives, insurgents, subversives, counterintelligence, neutralize, and oh, yeah—his favorite—the end of this world as we know it."

"Yes, he did say that," Ariel admitted, which had gotten Cole's full attention as he looked from the buffet to her.

Gwen chuckled. "You'll have to forgive Cole; he's like that

sometimes—very gung-ho about everything. Guess it's because of his military past. But he is a nice guy, the very nicest I've ever known."

Of course, Ariel had thought as her gaze drifted over his beautiful face, deliciously broad shoulders, strong chest, and luscious arms. In his heart, he was still an officer and a gentleman—a kick-ass ex-Marine. "Yes, he is," she had said.

"Ah-ha!" Gwen said. "You like him, don't you?"

Ariel couldn't lie. "You're right," she answered, then excused herself. When she figured neither her uncle nor Cole could overhear, she asked, "Am I that transparent?"

"Of course you are, but at least you're not drooling like he was."

Ariel couldn't help but laugh.

"I can tell by his voice that he likes you," Gwen said. "And that he respects you, too."

Always a good combination, Ariel thought, but was still hesitant. "Then you're saying he's not currently involved?"

"He's not married or engaged, if that's what you mean. But, my guess is not too many days have passed since he's been in the sack with—"

"I get your point," Ariel said, then bit her lower lip before she asked, "Is he serious about any of the women he's dating?"

"Let me put it this way—I don't know. Cole doesn't share his romantic escapades with me. Thank God. That said, I do know he has never used the same tone of voice when speaking about anyone else as he did when he mentioned you."

Ariel smiled, then sighed. "I think I've pissed him off with my suggestions."

"He'll get over it. What are they?"

She told Gwen about the native girl turned into a Marine who nursed the useless politician back to health and brought him to safety, while also averting that global disaster.

"Ah, a love interest, the promise of sex and the struggle to survive against the bad guys. Sort of like Adam and Eve in the Garden of Cretins."

Ariel laughed.

"Not bad," Gwen had said.

Maybe. But the jury was still out as far as Cole was concerned. As Ariel walked arm-in-arm with her uncle to the screening room, Cole brought up the rear.

"Now we must concentrate on your biography," Thaddeus said as he gently patted her arm. "It's important that the audience know what *you* did to make this movie a success."

Ariel thought it was far more important that Cole knew she was doing this only because she wanted him to succeed.

As her uncle continued going over his plans to make her a household name, Ariel wondered if Cole was even behind them anymore. She listened for his footfalls and didn't hear any.

My God. He couldn't have left. There was no way to leave.

Glancing over her shoulder, Ariel saw that not only was Cole still following, his gaze was riveted to her butt.

"Now I have another idea," Thaddeus said, "and I want you to tell me what you think of it."

"Uh-huh," Ariel said, her voice distracted as she continued to look at Cole. At last, his gaze slowly lifted to meet hers.

She arched one slender brow.

He wiggled his.

"Ariel," Thaddeus suddenly said, then came to a halt, "are you all right?"

Not entirely. Cole's teasing had made her knees go briefly weak. "Fine," she said.

"Good to hear," Thaddeus said, then swung his gaze to Cole. "Here we are."

As Thaddeus led Ariel into a room furnished with ornate Spanish tables, forged-iron lamps, and richly tooled burgundy leather chairs that faced a huge plasma TV, Cole remained in the low-ceilinged hall.

It was one thing to have the world view the movies he had worked on. It was another to have Ariel do so.

Already he wanted her to respect his work, even if she didn't particularly like it. Already he needed her to believe in him just the way his mother still believed in his dad.

You're one lucky man, Cole thought, and decided he was going to tell his dad that, too, the next time they talked.

Of course, to do that he'd have to get through tonight first.

As Ariel turned to him, Cole's gaze lowered to those sparkling stars dangling over her taut belly. Despite his misgivings, those stars drew him inside.

Ariel smiled. She gestured him to the chair nearest hers.

"Thank you," Thaddeus said, taking it.

Ariel's smile faded. Cole frowned.

"Go on," Thaddeus said, casual as could be, "sit down, my dear. We have numerous movies to get through tonight—hours and hours, in fact—so you best be comfortable." He looked at Cole as if he expected an argument.

Cole would have given him one, too, if it would have stopped this damned screening, which it would not. Thaddeus was going to make certain Ariel saw these films so she knew how truly awful his work was. And why not? He was an ex-Marine, not tech support, and certainly not a writer or a director. How could he have been so crazy to have left his real career to get involved in this unreal one?

"You know," he said, giving it one last shot, "we really don't have to do this."

"Nonsense," Thaddeus said, then gestured Cole toward the TV. "That DVD on top—*Force Recon Response,* I believe it's called—play that first. Ariel needs to know how bad these movies are so she can make your new one better."

Cole quietly regarded the old guy, then looked at Ariel.

Her expression was apologetic, her smile gentle. "I'm certain they're wonderful," she said in a very soft voice. "Please, I want to see the response one."

Suppressing a sigh, Cole did as he was told and slid the DVD into the player.

When he turned, Ariel's gaze was leveled on her uncle as she spoke to him in a voice that could not be overheard.

During that lecture, Thaddeus continued tapping the remote control against his knee. At last, he muttered, "Yes, ma'am." He looked at Cole. "Mark my words," he said, "she's going to be keeping you in line, too."

Cole looked at her. "I don't mind."

Ariel's face and throat flushed. She sank into her chair as if her legs would no longer hold her.

Cole's felt the same, so down he went.

Thaddeus pointed the remote to start the film. "You will mind, believe you me," he said, then leaned toward Cole's chair and spoke in a normal tone. "Especially if you don't heed my advice to keep your hands off, understand?"

Blood rose to Cole's face, stinging his cheeks. Even so, he held Ariel's gaze as he answered her uncle. "I understand fully what you're saying, sir."

Thaddeus nodded as if that settled it.

Ariel knew it did not. Cole hadn't actually promised to keep his hands off of her, given that's what her uncle meant. He had simply stated he understood her uncle's demand.

Her heart caught to the implication, then raced as her gaze lowered to Cole's large hands resting on his thighs. Ariel imagined those long fingers curled around her breasts while the blunt tips stroked her pebbled nipples. She saw those muscular thighs pressed to hers, his broad chest crushing her breasts, his shaft thickened and hard, his mouth demanding all she had to give and then wanting still more. His tongue would be hot and wet, his touch insatiable, his lovemaking that of a man like none she had known before, a kick-ass ex-Marine.

"Better be good," Thaddeus suddenly said.

"Oh, he will be," Ariel said.

Cole's eyes widened slightly, while Thaddeus swung his head to her.

As both men stared, Ariel looked at the TV which displayed the FBI warning that preceded every movie. "I wonder if anyone's ever been arrested and jailed for that?" she asked.

Beat the hell out of Cole. As she continued to stare at that screen, he stared at her. Whatever had just gone through her mind, it still had her breathing pretty damned hard. Up and down her chest went, which caused her breasts to quiver and those delicate stars to twinkle wildly.

It was a potent combination and completely enchanting. Oddly enough, though, Cole's mind kept returning to how she had defended his work to her uncle.

I'm certain they're wonderful, she had said.

In that moment, a wave of gratitude had so quickly washed over Cole it left him totally defenseless.

He quietly regarded her in this room's faint light. His gaze traced the curve of her cheek, the delicate line of her nose, that lush mouth, those slender brows, that amazing hair.

She wound a strand of it around her right forefinger as her gaze remained on the screen, the thunderous action that had opened this movie and was still continuing.

Whether she enjoyed that or not, her expression remained neutral. Like a juror in a murder trial she seemed to be withholding judgment, at least until she had all the facts.

Cole sighed.

Thaddeus looked at him, then pointed to the TV screen as if to say *the movie's over there.*

Unfortunately, Cole thought, then finally forced himself to watch. For the first few minutes he found it impossible to concentrate. Once he had, he was sorry he did.

No, no, NO, Cole thought as the lead dismantled a bomb with the same finesse that a kid opened a present at Christmas.

Good God, why hadn't he noticed that before? In the real world that man's thumb would have been responsible for blowing up a sizeable portion of the village he was trying to save.

When the action briefly slowed so that the lead could help a group of frightened locals, Cole sank farther into his chair.

That guy was now carrying one kid on his back, and two others in his meaty arms, as he dodged hundreds of whizzing bullets, while grenades with the punch of small A-bombs exploded in the background.

Dwellings were flattened, vegetation was scorched, the bad guys flew this way and that, while the star had the presence of mind to shout, "I won't leave you! I will not leave you!"

Like any man could? Like a damned Marine would even consider it? Like there was time to shout that stuff when you were running for your freaking life?

Cole nearly groaned, then cringed as the action again picked up and got really bad. More firepower was being used in this flick than in all of World War II; there was absolutely no character development and absolutely no women. Not even mothers for those kids. Why hadn't he noticed any of that before? Why hadn't he thought of it?

He was about to look at Ariel to see if she was cringing, too, but thought better of it. Glancing at Thaddeus, Cole was surprised to see the old guy's head and toupee were lolling to the side. He was fast asleep, bored into it by this stupid film.

Least it was good for something, Cole thought, then looked past Thaddeus to Ariel.

Her gaze was already on him, her expression thoughtful, honest, open.

Faster than Cole would have believed possible his heart knelt.

A second later, something new exploded in the film.

Without looking at it, with her gaze still on him, Ariel said, "That was really something."

Cole's mouth went dry to the aching tenderness in her expression and voice. "You think?"

Her gaze slowly traveled his face, then moved up and

down his length, before returning to his eyes. "I don't believe I've ever seen anything more amazing."

Okay, so they weren't talking about the film anymore, and that got Cole's heart pounding. "Really." He paused, then decided to ask something he had never asked another woman in his life. "You're not just trying to be nice, are you?"

She glanced at her uncle, who was still asleep. Looking back at Cole, she said, "Not about this."

He believed her. "So tell me," he said, "what exactly do you find so amazing?"

Her gaze became unexpectedly playful, dipping to his chest, then to his groin. Given the sudden heat in her cheeks, she knew he was hard. "It's so powerful." She looked up. "Don't you think?"

Damn straight, he did. "It goes on and on, too."

She wound a strand of hair around her finger as she slowly moistened her lips. Bringing that tongue back inside, she murmured, "Well, I would hope so." Leaning on the arm of her chair that was closest to him, she asked, "How long do these types of activities usually last?"

"Some go on for hours."

"Really?" She seemed genuinely surprised and completely intrigued. "How exhausting."

"Not for a Marine."

Those delicate nostrils flared ever so slightly as her gaze trickled back to his groin. "You're saying that Marines don't tire easily? They're always ready for action?"

Cole worked his mouth so he wouldn't smile. Damn, she was something. "That's right."

"How nice," she said, meeting his gaze.

The invitation was there, and Cole decided to take it.

He had just gotten to his feet when Thaddeus opened his left eye.

That blue orb settled on Cole. "Is it time for the next movie already?" he asked. Without waiting for an answer, he yawned lustily, then adjusted his fake hair before looking at Ariel. "Why, dear, you must be warm. You're very flushed." Without waiting for her comment, he looked back to Cole. "What are you waiting for? Change the movie. We've got several more to get through tonight."

"I don't think that's necessary," Ariel suddenly said.

Thaddeus looked at her. His gaze noted the way she was rubbing her temple. "Do you have a headache?"

If she had to watch another of these films, she might. God, but this one had been awful, not that she'd ever tell Cole that. Actually, he seemed to know that, given how he'd been squirming in his chair.

Poor baby, she thought, wanting to assure him that his contribution to the movie was good, even if the rest of the story sucked. Of course, now he had her to help out. Not only would she make the tropical survival skills realistic as all get out, but the story and people in it would be better than good; they'd be great. "I'm just tired," she said.

Thaddeus narrowed his gaze on Cole. "Are you tired, too?"

"You seem to be," Ariel said.

Cole looked at her with a really hopeful expression, as if he expected that they would now retire to one of their rooms to make love *Marine*-style all through the night.

How Ariel wanted that. A few minutes before she had been so caught up in the moment it hadn't even registered that this was her uncle's house.

She remembered that now. No way did Ariel want to show him any disrespect; he had done far too much for her. At last, her gaze darted to Thaddeus, before returning to Cole.

Given the way his broad shoulders sagged, he understood immediately that there would be no lovemaking tonight. "Yeah," he mumbled, "I'm bushed, too."

"Then that settles it," Thaddeus said. Pushing to his feet, he offered Ariel his arm.

"Just a sec." She turned to Cole and offered her hand. The moment he took it, she regretted leaving him. "I'll see you in the morning with some ideas I have."

He slowly nodded as his thumb gently stroked hers.

Although Ariel craved that stroking and far, far more, she finally pulled her hand from his and escorted her uncle into the hall.

Once they were out of earshot, Thaddeus said, "You think I'm too hard on him."

"If you weren't," Ariel said, "I would be."

Thaddeus stopped and turned to her. He looked truly surprised. "You can really take care of yourself?"

She smiled and hugged him hard. "Of course not. I still need you. I'll *always* need you."

"Yes, yes," he said, gently patting her back, before easing away. "But I won't be with you while you instruct Mr. Ryder . . . will I?"

"No, you won't," she quickly said, "but I swear I'll be careful."

Lifting his weathered hand, Thaddeus held her chin between his thumb and forefinger. "You best tell him to be careful not to break your heart."

Ariel blushed. "I wouldn't allow it. I *won't* allow it."

"You like him?"

Oh, yes. Far too much. Far too soon. And because of that, Ariel turned her face into her uncle's hand lightly kissing it, before she stepped back. "I'll see you in the morning."

Before he could say another word or ask any more questions Ariel was not prepared to answer, she turned and ran down the hall to her own room.

After closing the door, Ariel kicked off her sandals and padded to the wall that separated her room from Cole's.

Several minutes later hinges squeaked as his door was opened, then closed.

Pressing her ear to the wall, Ariel listened as he moved across the room, presumably getting ready for bed.

She wondered if he slept in the nude. Given what Gwen had said, Ariel wondered if he ever slept alone.

Had he ever been deeply in love? Did he still long for someone from the past?

Ariel's heart quickly sank, but she pushed that hurt aside. She had just met the man, and no matter how beautiful he was, or how charming, mischievous, and wildly military he might be, she was not going to let her emotions or hope run wild.

At the most, they would probably be good friends—after they became momentary lovers.

You are such a fool, she thought, because she had already caved. But then she was lonely, too, and if Cole could fill that emptiness for even a moment, Ariel was not about to pass up that chance.

Thinking about that, she rapped gently on the wall.

There was a brief pause before she heard the unmistakable slap of Cole's shoes against the pavers as he moved toward the wall.

She rapped lightly again.

A moment later, he rapped back.

Ariel smiled and rapped once more.

At last he called out, "Is this Morse Code?"

She laughed. "No! I just wanted to see if you were asleep!"

There was another pause before he said, "Not even close."

Leaning against the wall, Ariel smiled to his husky tone.

"How about you?" he asked.

"If I were, I wouldn't be talking to you."

"I meant, are you sleepy at all?"

No, she was not, but she couldn't tell him that. Resting her fingers on the wall's rough surface, she lied, "Very. I'll yawn for you if you'd like."

He laughed.

"I just wanted to tell you that I enjoyed the movie," she said. "The stuff you contributed to it, all the Marine and military things, was very good."

He sounded amused and depressed. "Really?"

"Really," she said, meaning it, then added, "and in this new one, I'll help you make everything else just as good."

He was briefly silent. At last he said, "I know you will, Ariel."

The tenderness in his voice touched her, as did the respect.

He has never used the same tone of voice when speaking about anyone else as he did when he mentioned you, Gwen had said.

Ariel felt honored and more than a little scared. It was one thing to hope for love. It was another to believe it might be close, finally close, and have it too quickly slip away.

Not wanting to think about that, wanting only to lose herself in sleep, Ariel said, "Good night, Cole. I'll see you in the morning."

Chapter Four

Morning, to Cole's way of thinking, was easier said than done.

Just a wall away there was the promise of great pleasure, the comfort of completion with a remarkable woman whose fiery hair warmed her honeyed skin, whose cool grayish green eyes contradicted the heat in her gaze, and whose sole ornament—those incredible diamond stars—aroused him beyond all control and offered absolutely no relief.

After tossing, turning, and swearing, he finally fell into an exhausted sleep and dreamt of natives that morphed into Marines who then chased Ariel, who hid from them in the rain forest, only to be discovered by him when he saw those twinkling diamond stars dangling from her bared navel.

Cole had been licking them and her in his dream when Isa pounded on his door, then warned him—in her own delightful way—that it was time to get up.

Like he hadn't been there already, and for most of the damned night.

Once Cole had shaved, showered, and dressed, Isa ordered him out to the area where the tables with the umbrellas had been set up.

"You are being waited for," she said.

He immediately thought of Ariel and was about to smile, until he recalled Thaddeus. "By whom?"

"Get out there," she ordered. "Make it fast."

"And leave you?"

She laughed to his teasing, then frowned. "Do you want to make little Ariel wait for you?"

"See you later," he said, then went outside.

Dew still sparkled on the bright green grass, while palms and ferns shivered in the breeze that was scrubbed clean by the restless ocean.

In the distance birds cried out to each other, monkeys jumped from branch to branch, and flowers lifted their heads to the unrestricted sun, delivering a riot of color and fragrance.

It was everything paradise should be, but just across the lawn was far more—what Cole had been waiting for all night, and perhaps even longer.

Ariel.

She stood by that first table. As wind rustled the blue-and-white umbrella above her, her gaze remained on him. Beckoning. Welcoming.

Never had Cole accepted an invitation faster.

Never had a journey seemed as long or been as rewarding.

She looked amazing, fresher than Cole had felt in all of his days, as if she had had fifteen hours of uninterrupted sleep. He sensed her dreams had been far more satisfying than his, and couldn't have been happier.

As he neared her, Cole allowed his gaze to slowly ride over that glorious hair being stirred by the breeze, then to her simple cotton top and shorts that were the same color as her eyes. Trouble was, they were also covering those diamond stars.

If she had been his, Cole would have demanded she wear nothing but brief tops and low-slung pants so that he could always see those stars. She'd disagree, of course, but a man could hope.

At least, until Thaddeus showed up and ruined everything. Thinking of that, Cole glanced past her to see if the old guy was around. Oddly enough, he wasn't. Even odder was the rack of clothes among all the other tables.

What in the world was that all about?

"Morning," she said.

Cole looked from those clothes which flapped in the breeze to her. "Hi."

Ariel's smile was luminous and dimpled. "Sleep well?"

Now, there was a question that didn't need an honest answer. "As well as you."

Ariel's smile paused. She wondered what he meant by that. Had he heard her feet slapping against the pavers last night when she finally went into his room to see if he was sleeping since she could not?

At the time he seemed dead to the world. He didn't stir once in the ten or so minutes Ariel had watched him. He didn't even snore.

He did sleep in the nude, since he was facedown on the bed, bare butt to her when she went inside.

It was all Ariel could do not to touch, kiss, or lick—

"What's this?" he asked, cutting into her thoughts as he glanced at the rack of clothes.

"Costumes."

Cole's brows rose briefly as he looked at her. "You're throwing a costume party?"

She laughed. "No." She sobered quickly. "These are some ideas for costumes that I had for your story and the movie."

Cole's gaze slid to that rack of clothes, before returning to her. "You're planning the wardrobe for my screenplay that I'll be using for my film?"

Not if he used that incredulous tone of voice, Ariel thought. "Gwen thought it was a good idea."

He looked stunned. "You spoke to Gwen about—" He abruptly paused as his cell phone rang.

"That's probably her now," Ariel said.

Cole looked from the cell phone to her. Opening it, he brought it to his ear. "What?" His frown deepened as he listened to the caller. "Who? Huh?" he said, then listened some more. "Ariel?" he asked, then listened and finally handed her the phone. "For you."

"Gwen?" she asked.

Cole arched one dark brow.

Gwen, Ariel thought and took the phone. "Morning. Sleep well?"

"Better than he apparently did," Gwen said. "You keep him up late?"

"Nope."

"No wonder he's so grumpy. Probably tossed and turned all night."

"Actually, I saw no movement at all."

Gwen was briefly silent, and then she asked, "Did you spend the night with him?"

"Not exactly."

Gwen laughed. "Hon, either you did or you didn't."

"I did. He didn't."

Gwen inhaled so sharply she choked. When she finished coughing, she asked, "You actually watched him sleep?"

"It wasn't that weird, okay?"

"Who says it's weird? Does he sleep in the nude?"

Ariel's gaze slid to Cole.

He was already looking at her. "What are you talking about?"

Ariel said the only thing she could to get him to back off. "The flaws in your story."

He frowned. "You saw no movement at all in it? I thought you said there was too much action."

So much for him backing off. "There is, but not with the people."

He looked confused. "They're hardly standing still."

Good Lord. Ariel started to perspire. "That's not what I meant."

"Okay. What did you mean?"

She thought fast. "They never became better people. They

didn't go from bad to good. There was no movement at all with that."

He didn't look as if he were buying it. "You said 'I did. He didn't.' Did and didn't do what?"

"Don't answer that," Gwen said.

"Just a sec," Ariel said to her, then spoke to Cole. "I did like the changes I suggested to correct the flaws in your story, and you didn't. If you don't mind," she added, "this is a private conversation."

Cole lifted his hands in surrender and walked away.

As he did, Ariel's gaze drifted over his loose white cotton shirt, cotton pants, and those huaraches. God, he had nice feet. Large, with really long toes.

"Hey," Gwen said, "you still there?"

"Just barely."

Cole turned around to that and looked at her.

"Thanks for helping me get the costumes," Ariel said to Gwen. "Bye." Closing the phone, she slipped it into her shorts pocket and went to him. "Sorry about that. Now, where were we?"

Cole lifted his gaze from her pocket. "Well, you were talking to *my* co-producer on *my* phone."

Definitely grumpy, Ariel thought, pulling the phone out of her pocket and handing it to him. "Sorry. I'll take nothing else of yours while you're here, I promise."

He looked disappointed.

Okay, so he did still want her. For that, Ariel was glad, even though every minute with him whittled away more of her caution, making her act like a fool. First, she had worn that outrageous outfit and body jewelry; then she had stolen into his room to watch him sleep; now she wanted to cup his wonderful face in her hands, draw her thumbs over his freshly shaven cheeks, and kiss him until all the loneliness she had ever felt was completely forgotten.

She was obviously losing all control and needed to cool it.

"About the costumes," she said.

Cole glanced at them, then the small black monkey that had just jumped on the table where breakfast was being laid out. Chattering loudly, it grabbed and peeled a banana, then chomped on that fruit as it watched them.

"Let me guess," Cole said. "Is he going to be in my film, too?"

Ariel smiled. "She. Her name is BooBoo. Hey, baby," she cooed to the animal.

BooBoo ignored all that love in favor of food. Ariel looked at Cole and couldn't resist teasing. "If I did put her in the movie, would she get her name mentioned with the other actors and actresses?"

He laughed. "No." He sobered. "Actresses? Now you're suggesting more than one woman be in this?"

"It's your story."

"Screenplay."

Ariel lifted her brows, then went to the rack of clothes and gently stroked the cargo pants that the male lead in *his* story might wear. "One woman will probably be better for you." She looked over her shoulder at him. "Don't you think?"

Actually, Cole didn't know what to think. Her tone was playful, but her expression was dead fucking serious, while every part of her was causing his cock to thicken and his balls to ache. "I'd prefer it."

She smiled, and Cole was ready to fight a fucking war for her.

"Good," she said, "what would you like for me to wear?"

Cole glanced at the clothing knowing he'd prefer her nude, but that obviously wasn't an option. "Excuse me?"

"We need to decide what I'm wearing—and what you're wearing—when the bad guys show up and wipe everyone else out except for the female and male lead that are forced to escape into the rain forest. That, of course, is us."

Cole wasn't following and wasn't all that certain he wanted to. "You want us to star in the film now?"

"God, no." She laughed. "I just want to act it out so that we're certain it can be done and that it's totally accurate."

My God, he thought, she was serious. "You and I are going to act out my screenplay?" He pointed over his shoulder at the rain forest. "In *there?*"

"Sure." She narrowed her gaze as she regarded him.

"What?" he finally asked.

"That's what you do in the Marines, isn't it? You have dry runs of—"

"Maneuvers," he corrected.

"Exactly," she said. "They don't sit you down at a desk and tell you to read about blowing up buildings and taking down the bad guys and stuff; they let you do it. They let you practice at it."

Not exactly, but he got her drift.

"You're not scared of a little rain forest, are you?" she asked. "I mean, it's perfectly all right if you—"

"Hell no, I'm not scared." Cole would have laughed at the thought if he hadn't been so pissed about her wanting them to spend the next couple of days in a damned rain forest. Jesus, he hated the idea.

She, on the other hand, loved it. Cole saw that in the way her eyes sparkled and in the heightened color of her cheeks.

"You're sure?" she asked.

"I'm with you on this, okay?"

"Sure." After giving him a relieved smile, she went to the table and grabbed her copy of his unfinished screenplay. Rifling through it, she finally stopped and jabbed her finger at a part halfway down the page. "Here you say that the bad guys will be attacking during breakfast and that they burn down the politician's compound." Ariel lifted her gaze to his. "Do you think that's really wise?"

Cole looked past her to the ocean. *Mark my words,* Thaddeus had said last night, *she's going to be keeping you in line, too.* Not to mention taking over his film and dragging him through a fucking rain forest. Crossing his arms over his chest, he looked back at her. "Yeah, I think it's wise. I think it's good cinema."

"I've hurt your feelings," she said. "I'm sorry, I didn't mean to."

His frown paused. Never in his life had he known a woman who was so direct.

What in the hell was the matter with her? Why couldn't she be like any other woman and just lie to make him feel good, if only for a moment? Why did she have to keep bringing him to his knees with her guileless expression and vulnerable gaze? "You didn't hurt my feelings."

She looked *so* relieved. "Good. Then we really should start—"

"But you are rewriting my screenplay," he interrupted. "You're supposed to be showing me tropical survival skills, not rewriting my story and choosing costumes for my characters."

Ariel crossed her arms over her chest. "I'm simply trying to correct the flaws in your story."

Cole tightened his arms and stepped toward her. "Flaws?"

She tightened her arms and stepped toward him. "Yes, flaws. If you have your bad guys show up while it's light, everyone on this island will be able to see them, especially since this is the highest point on the island and gives quite a good view. *And,*" she continued, speaking above him, "if you have them burn down the compound, people on the surrounding islands will see the smoke and will alert someone, don't you think?"

Of course he had thought of that. But he was also trying to wed reality to good cinema, and good cinema usually won out when everyone demanded that the focus be purely on the action. Until now, it hadn't bothered Cole to compromise. Of course, after seeing *Force Recon Response* again, and really noticing how his expertise had been inaccurately applied, Cole was thinking maybe he should get out of the business altogether. Not that he was about to admit that to her. "The fire's good cinema. We need it." He paused, then shook his head as he moved still closer. "*I* need it."

Ariel leaned toward him. "No, you don't." She spoke above him again. "What you need is the cover of darkness to make this scary."

"Scary?"

"Thrilling," she corrected herself. "You should have these bad guys coming at night, maybe while some of your no-good politicians are boozing it up and—"

"No-good politicians?"

"Hey, it's your story."

He laughed. "Screenplay!"

Ah, she got him to laugh again. It was a wonderfully rich sound that rumbled in his broad chest, crinkled the corners of his beautiful brown eyes, and aroused Ariel far too much.

And Cole knew.

It was in his gaze as his laughter turned to a brief smile, and then to something else. Looking at her with an expression that was all male, Cole uncrossed his arms and took that last step until he was directly in front of her.

Ariel's lips parted, she lifted her face to his. In that moment, Cole's eyes grew hooded. In that moment, every part of Ariel felt his need. It made her giddy and dizzy as her gaze drifted to his mouth. She imagined those lips—so heated, so soft—covering hers. She imagined them pressed to her throat, her breasts, surrounding her nipples; his desire and strength refusing to allow her escape or release until she had fully satisfied him and he had pleasured her until she whimpered and begged for more.

God, would she beg for more.

But not now. Ariel saw the change in Cole's expression as he quickly looked past her.

"Good morning," Thaddeus suddenly said from behind. "What are you two up to?"

"Work," Cole said in a surprisingly casual voice, then

looked at her and murmured, "We'll continue this later, understand?"

Ariel's skin tingled. She nodded slowly, then gave herself a moment to calm down before turning to her uncle.

He was waving at BooBoo, who was sprawled over the table, scratching herself.

Ariel took another deep, calming breath.

"What are you working on?" Thaddeus asked.

She looked at Cole. He pretended not to notice. Ariel rubbed the back of her neck and shrugged. "Just the costumes for Mina and Henry."

That got Cole's attention. "Who?"

Ariel looked at him. "Ah, so now you want to hear this?"

"No. But I think I better. Who's what's-her-name and—"

"Mina," Ariel said. "She's the female star of this. Her name means *mine* in Spanish, which fits perfectly with her being a native girl who was raised by the government because of her brilliant mind and native expertise, which they used when they turned her into a Marine. And Henry is the name I picked for your lead guy, the useless politi—"

"Whoa, whoa, *whoa*," Cole said. "Mina? Henry? Native girl raised by the government that turned her into a Marine? I don't think so."

"I like it," Thaddeus said.

Cole looked at the man.

"Gwen likes it, too," Ariel said. "She said the money people would like it. They're the ones you're trying to please."

Cole crossed his arms over his chest and lowered his head. Thaddeus whispered loudly to Ariel. "Is he all right?"

"He is fine," Cole answered for her.

"We just need to work out the kinks in this," she said.

"Of course," Thaddeus said, "wouldn't want you unprepared when you disappear into the rain forest tonight."

Disappear? Cole thought and lifted his head. Thaddeus was already moving toward the periphery of the forest with BooBoo in his arms. That monkey clung to the old guy as if she were a little girl, while Thaddeus cooed more than Ariel had.

Cole looked at her. She was already watching him with an expression that was really hesitant, as if it just killed her to piss him off.

Hell. Even a wild-eyed, drooling hit man couldn't stay mad after looking at that.

"We're going to disappear tonight?" he asked.

She nodded cautiously. "Like I said, this should happen under cover of darkness. The other no-good politicians are eating and boozing when they're shot, strangled, banged over the head, gutted, annihila—"

"I get your point," Cole said.

She smiled.

God help him, but so did he.

Just like that she got her second wind and started talking fast. "Now, here's how I see it—while the others are being taken out by the bad guys, Henry is in—"

"Roarke," Cole corrected, wanting some part of his work to remain. "My character's name is Roarke."

"And it's a good name," Ariel said, then went to him and lightly rested her fingers on his chest. "But it doesn't fit. No politician would have a strong name like that. Remember, this guy went to all those Ivy League schools and is good at making rules for other people—but can he take care of himself?"

Cole heard the question in her voice, but hadn't been paying attention to the words. His gaze was still on her fingers as they lightly circled the buttons on his shirt, then stroked it. "I'm sorry, what?"

"Can Henry take care of himself?"

"Who?"

"Roarke, who is now called Henry." She lightly tapped her forefinger against Cole's chest for emphasis. "My thinking is he can't take care of himself until Mina shows him how. At that point, she'll start calling him Hank—to show that he's becoming more of a man, to show that his character is changing."

Cole lifted his gaze to hers. "You're really enjoying this, aren't you?"

She looked surprised, maybe even a little hurt. "Aren't you?"

"Yes, I am," he said, bringing her hand back to his chest so that she could tap and stroke it or continue fondling his buttons. Whatever she wanted. "Go on. What's next?"

"Sure you want to hear this?"

"No, but I guess I better."

She smiled. "I figure in the beginning of this story the no-good politicians will be drinking rum and smoking cigars out here at these tables. They'll be pretty drunk, but Henry won't be. He'll have already left to go to bed and—"

Cole interrupted, "With Tina?"

Ariel paused. "*Mee-nah,*" she corrected, her mouth forming the syllables as she slowly enunciated the name.

Cole's gaze lowered to her mouth, those dewy lips. "Okay."

She shook her head.

"It's not okay?" he asked.

"They won't be in bed together."

Cole arched one dark brow. "Whose idea was that?"

"At that time," she explained. "They'll make love later . . . like you just said."

His brow lowered. He wore that same expression from before—focused and completely male.

Even if Ariel had wanted to take back those words—which she did not—it was too late now. She had finally—and so quickly—lost all control and was now committed to delivering herself to this man for his pleasure and her own.

"When?" Cole asked.

Her heart quickened at the need in his voice. Need she had put there. "When they're hiding out from the bad guys."

"Uh-huh," he said, then leaned close and murmured, "Care to tell me how that will come to pass?"

"Sure you want to hear this?"

"Actually, I can't wait."

She nodded gently. "When he accepts *all* of her ideas on survival and what they should do to save themselves from these bad guys and get rescued, then she realizes he's worthy of her, and only then does she offer her heart and passion."

Cole had stopped nodding words ago.

"But we're getting ahead of ourselves," Ariel said.

"From what I can tell, the only thing that's moving on either of us are your fingers."

She stopped stroking him and brought back her hand.

He looked from that to her. "Is this our first fight?"

"If you agree with everything I say, there won't be a fight."

He murmured, "Conflict is what makes life interesting."

"You don't want me to help you with this?"

His expression changed. He straightened. "I didn't say that."

"Good. What do you want to wear to bed tonight before we go out?"

Cole wasn't certain he had heard her correctly. "What?"

"I want to make this authentic, for your audience," she added, "so if you're going to be playing Henry, and I'm going to be playing Mina while we're doing this, I need to know what you plan to wear when the bad guys strike and you're in—

"I sleep in the nude."

She nodded as if she wasn't at all surprised.

"So," he said, "how about you?"

"I don't wear pajamas or any other type of clothing to bed if that's what you mean. But given the navel ring I wear, technically I'm not totally nude. Not that it matters," she added to his expression, "because I won't be in bed when the bad guys strike, but you will."

Cole tried to picture that, but somehow just couldn't get past his memory of that navel ring.

"Your being nude is definitely going to pose a problem," Ariel said.

"For you?"

She arched one brow.

"For Mina?" he asked.

"For Henry, your hero, since he wakes up and hears the bad guys and within seconds he and Mina have to flee into the rain forest where they'll have to survive off the land using nothing but Mina's wits and skill."

Cole warned himself not to laugh. "Is she going to weave him some clothes while they're out there?"

"Hardly." Her frown softened. "Of course, she could make those eventually if she used the gauzy fibers at the base of coconut leaves. She *can*," Ariel said to his laugh.

"Oh, God, you're something," he said.

"So are you."

She said it with such wonder, Cole's laughter paused. As the world continued around them, noisy and impatient, all he heard was her soft voice saying, *so are you;* all he saw was the honesty in her gaze.

No wonder Thaddeus didn't want any man to lead her on.

"So, anyway," she said, then shrugged as if embarrassed, "back to this. By the time she gets to his room to wake him up, because she knows he's not a skilled Marine commando like she is, he'll have already put something on." Ariel gestured to the clothes hanging from the rack. "Pick out what you want, but be certain it is what you want. You'll be wearing it when we go out tonight."

Cole didn't move one inch, nor did he look at the clothes rack. *Marine commando?* he thought. He was about to shake his head when he saw the expectant look on Ariel's face. She was so into this, Cole didn't have the heart to say no.

Inhaling deeply, he went to the rack and chose the first cotton shirt and cargo pants hanging there. "These are good."

"They're olive green," she said.

Cole looked back at them, noticing the color for the first time. "Yeah . . . so?"

"Dark colors, especially ones that resemble foliage, attract mosquitoes . . . are you absolutely certain you want—"

"How about this?" He pulled out a white shirt and pants.

"With that much white, you'll be obvious against all the green in the—"

"Why don't you choose for me?"

"You're sure?"

Like every other man on Planet Earth who turned his wardrobe over to a woman. "Let's just say I'm not much into clothes shopping, which begs a question. Are these even my size?"

"Of course." Ariel rattled off the sizes he wore, right down to his shoes and socks.

Okay. "Either you're very good at guessing or you've been rummaging through my overnight bag."

Her cheeks flushed as she went to him. "Gwen got your security company to let her into your house to check out your clothes for me so I could have this stuff flown in. Of course, that was well after she argued with me about you staying here for three days. I told her that was your decision to make, not hers. Just like the survival stuff and what we wear is mine."

Cole had already closed his eyes.

Ariel rested her fingertips on his cheek. "You want this to be authentic, don't you?" she asked, her voice soft, vulnerable.

What he wanted was to haul her into his arms for some X-rated R&R, then say to hell with the film industry, this stupid picture, and spend several months here just making both of them happy. He held back a sigh. "Unfortunately."

She murmured, "Then it will be, I promise."

That's what was beginning to worry him. Covering her hand with his own, Cole lowered it from his cheek, then cradled her fingers in his palm. "Now, let's see what I think you should wear."

Given the look in his creamy brown eyes, Ariel figured he was thinking of skin. Because she liked him—really, really liked him—she had a surprise she knew he'd just love. "I was thinking I'd wear what I had on last night; you seemed pretty taken with it."

Cole grinned, then leaned toward her and said, "I was."

Ariel smiled. "Okay, I'll wear that. Once we're in the rain forest, I'll have to use the available plant life to repel insects, since I'll be wearing a color they're attracted to, and I'll have to use something for shoes, since my sandals are pretty flimsy, and then I'll have to—"

"Whoa, whoa, whoa," Cole said, sobering quickly. "I was only kidding. You can't actually be considering going out there in that outfit with flimsy sandals."

"Mina would do that. In the story she would have just left the politicians, who had gotten pretty tanked, and after fighting one of them off was on her way back to her room when the bad guys struck so—"

Cole interrupted. "You're not going out there like that. You're going to be wearing shoes. You're going to be wearing something sensible. You're not risking your health or safety, understand?"

Ariel's eyes widened to his commanding tone and the seriousness of his expression. The Marine in him was back, and God was it turning her on, while his obvious concern for her caused Ariel's heart to smile. Only one other person in her life—her Uncle Thaddeus—had ever bothered to holler or to demand like Cole was doing right now.

Everyone else—her parents and those few men that had been brief lovers—either didn't care or figured she could go it alone since she was so damned capable.

Ariel was honestly touched by Cole's expression and words, but hardly moved by such authority. As Thaddeus had said early on, she did have an independent spirit. "I want this to be authentic."

"Screw that. You're going to be safe."

Ariel arched one slender brow and pulled her hand from his. "I can choose what I want. I am an adult, after all."

"What you are is Mina. *Mine,* remember? And so long as this is my screenplay and my film and the characters in it belong to me, you're going to have to do what I say, if you intend to do this at all. And I'll not have you risking your safety, got it?"

All the way down to her tingling toes. "Yes, sir. So," she said to his arched brow, "what do you think I should wear?"

"Whatever a female-native-turned-Marine-commando should wear."

She laughed, then chose a sensible cotton top and cotton pants in a deep beige color that would blend in with the sun-dappled foliage, but still not attract insects. "How about this and moccasins?"

"Not as nice as that thing you had on last night, but it will just have to do."

"Yes, sir."

Cole smiled. "This is really beginning to sound good."

Uh-huh. "We've just started. During breakfast we'll go over all the changes I made in your story, and then we'll start acting it out for research and authenticity's sake beginning tonight."

Chapter Five

We've just started, she said.

To Cole, those words could be good or bad depending upon how he interpreted them.

If she was talking only about the research, then he was a dead man. Throughout breakfast, lunch, and now, as supper approached, Ariel continued to plan his screenplay with the same zeal a general used to organize a major operation.

Cole, on the other hand, continued to think about her promise.

They'll make love later . . . just as you said.

We've just started.

That was the honest-to-God's truth. They had shared quiet gazes, a few brief touches, and some pillow talk, but not even so much as a kiss.

Not that that had stopped her from choosing his wardrobe, penciling in ideas on his screenplay, crossing out parts she didn't like, calling Gwen to confirm strategy, and getting the woman to side with her against him.

And Cole allowed it. Oddly enough, it wasn't because he expected to sleep with Ariel—he did—but even if he had not, many of her ideas made more sense than what he had come up with, and she seemed to honestly care about his success with this project. It seemed vital to her that it not only be good, but great.

Hell, not even his own mother had been this dedicated to his future, and that woman dearly loved him.

Cole's gaze followed a strand of Ariel's hair that the breeze was lifting away from the rest. He ached to touch that strand, to smooth it down, then bury his face in that incredible silky hair, inhaling deeply of its sweet scent; to press close to each part of her so that they could begin anew and in earnest, and forget this stupid script.

The damned thing had barely been on his mind since she had flown into his life like an avenging angel.

Men can so easily fall in love with my niece because of her obvious charms, Thaddeus had said.

Can or have? Cole continued to wonder.

Did she make her other clients feel like this; did she take over their lives, too . . . or was he really that special to her?

As Cole thought about that, the torches surrounding the outside tables flickered in the wind, but that scant light didn't keep Ariel from ruthlessly editing his screenplay.

Her head was bent to a part she found particularly troubling. She wrote something, then quickly erased it. She lined through something he had written, then shook her head as if she hadn't meant to do that. So absorbed was she, BooBoo had no trouble at all playing with the ends of her hair, while Cole regarded her legs through the table's glass top.

She was sitting cross-legged on her chair, all pretense gone as she absently scratched her butt.

Cole arched one brow. Never had he seen anything more adorable or arousing. What in the hell was happening to him?

He should be pissed at what she was doing. Hell, any other woman wouldn't have dared do it. He should be demanding that she stop. He should be informing her in no uncertain terms that no damned way was he going into that rain forest tonight, because no screenplay was worth the hell she planned to put him through and all for the sake of authen—

Cole's thoughts paused as Ariel unexpectedly looked up. Just like that, she sensed something was wrong. Her expression was now as cautious as her voice. "What?"

How was he supposed to answer that when she was looking at him as if he might say something to wound? "The monkey's playing with your hair."

With those words the hesitation disappeared, and her eyes sparkled. Glancing over her shoulder, Ariel blew BooBoo a kiss, then looked back at Cole. "Did you want her to play with yours?"

He laughed. "No."

Ariel regarded him, then asked, "Do you want me to stop making changes to your story?"

Yes ... no ... hell, I don't know. "Not if what you're doing is still good."

"What you did was good."

Cole glanced at the page she was currently on. He could barely see his original work beneath all her edits.

"I'm just refining what you did," she quickly said. "You're the one who came up with the military parts, which I haven't changed at all. They're too good to change. You really put your heart and soul into this."

Not to mention several gallons of sweat. He was no writer, that was for sure, but even though he had just fallen into this career, Cole found he actually liked the challenge of putting all the pieces together in the hopes that the money people, the talent, Gwen, and now Ariel, wouldn't tear them apart. "'Fraid that's not enough sometimes."

"That's why you have me," she said.

God, you are something. "Let me see what you've done this time."

Ariel wasn't reluctant at all. After handing him the script, she leaned back in her chair, arms above her head, as she allowed herself a lusty stretch that arched her back and pulled her top up to reveal low-slung shorts and those stars twinkling wildly from her navel.

God help him, but Cole wasn't altogether certain he'd be able to control himself in those hours when they were supposed to be doing research.

Maybe that's why she had insisted on it actually taking place in a rain forest. There he'd be busy fighting off insects, animals, poisonous plants, and a fucking bad mood instead of his passion.

"Everybody," Isa suddenly said, slapping her hands together as she approached the table, "we are going to serve supper now. Be ready."

"We will," Ariel said, then continued stretching as she watched the older woman go to Thaddeus. When the two of them started talking about something that soon had Isa giggling, Ariel turned back to Cole. "Don't eat," she ordered.

Don't eat? He might have asked why, but at the moment, Cole had other things on his mind. He looked right back down to those diamonds twinkling from her navel until her top suddenly covered them as she lowered her arms and straightened.

Cole frowned.

She smiled as Thaddeus came to the table. "You look happy," she said.

"You look exhausted; you work too hard," he scolded as he bent down to kiss her cheek.

Ariel's gaze slid to Cole. "I don't mind."

Thaddeus went to his place at the head of the table. "You should." He leveled his gaze on Cole. "So what have you been doing all day?"

"Helping me," Ariel quickly said.

Thaddeus nodded as if to say *he had better.*

Cole sagged back into his chair and just let the good times roll as the staff, directed by a hand-clapping Isa, delivered water, beer, and the meal that consisted of typical island fare from the universally known arroz con pollo to the more exotic ackee, a fruit that oddly enough tasted like scrambled eggs.

Not that Cole was supposed to taste it or anything else.

Don't eat, Ariel had ordered.

During the next few minutes, Cole watched her wolfing down everything in sight, while Thaddeus was trying his best to keep up with her.

Okay. Grabbing his fork, Cole was about to dig in until BooBoo suddenly hopped on the table next to his plate. With her little butt swaying back and forth, she bent down to his chorreados y natilla, corn pancakes with sour cream.

"She dearly loves that," Thaddeus said.

No kidding, Cole thought as she sniffed and sniffed.

To his relief she finally bypassed that dish for a wedge of coconut. Chattering loudly at him, she then pushed the treat into her mouth.

"Ah," Thaddeus said, "I see you have a way with women."

Ariel laughed, until Cole looked at her. "Actually," he said, "women usually have their way with me. Right, Tina?"

She gave him a wicked smile. "It's Mee-nah." Her plush lips caressed that name as she slowly enunciated it. "And you really shouldn't be eating that." She pointed to where his fork was now headed—the ceviche, a dish of chilled sea bass flavored with lemon, chopped onion, garlic, and red peppers.

Cole looked down. "Why? Did Boobala spit in it?"

Ariel laughed again. "BooBoo," she corrected, then sobered. "No. But in the screenplay you—"

"Story," he corrected.

She arched one slender, auburn-tinted brow. "You're making fun of me."

Thaddeus muttered, "Not if he wants to do his movie on my island, he won't."

Grabbing his Dos Equis, Cole brought it to his lips.

"You really shouldn't be drinking that, either," she said.

Cole lowered the bottle a bit and frowned at her.

She leveled her gaze right back at him. "In the screenplay you weren't feeling well, which is why you went to bed early, without your supper or booze."

Thaddeus chuckled, "I told you Ariel knows how to deal with bad boys."

Uh-huh. "By starving them or by rewriting every single line of their stories?"

Ariel and Thaddeus exchanged a glance.

"I don't think he wants you to help him anymore," Thaddeus said.

"He's just tired," Ariel said. "We have been arguing all day."

Thaddeus frowned at Cole, then looked back at his niece. "He *argued* with you? He raised his voice to—"

"No, of course not," she quickly said. "And it wasn't really an argument. We disagreed until I simply used reason to bring him around to my way of—"

"Ah, people," Cole finally cut in. "If you're going to discuss me, at least wait until I go to bed without my supper."

Thaddeus chose to ignore that.

Ariel suppressed a smile. *Poor baby.* Despite his pissy mood, Cole had been the perfect gentleman throughout their brainstorming sessions.

At times, he seemed too perfect. In those moments when she had gone on and on about her ideas, Cole's gaze had remained so fixed on her, Ariel figured he was thinking of escape. But each time she asked if he was listening, he answered with amazing questions about the logistics of what she had planned.

Over and over he proved that he had heard her, and that he was taking her seriously.

For that, and freely admitting that some of her ideas were better than his, he had captured another piece of her heart. And she would reward him with everything he—and she—wanted.

When we're finally alone, she thought. *Away from this place. Oh yeah.*

"What?" Thaddeus suddenly asked.

Ariel's gaze snapped up to his incredulous tone. *Oh, crud.* Had she spoken her thoughts aloud? She glanced at Cole, then back at her uncle. Both men were already staring at her. Cole seemed intrigued, but happy; her uncle did not.

"It's getting late," she said, then pushed back in her chair and stood. Looking at Cole, she said, "We have to put on our outfits so—"

"Costumes," he corrected.

Heat rose to Ariel's cheeks with his teasing and the adventure they were about to embark upon. "We have to get dressed. The sun's been down for a good hour. The bad guys are already on their way. We need to time this correctly. It has to be accurate. It's got to be perfect. And just what we both want." Before he—or Thaddeus—could respond, Ariel grabbed two bananas and fled.

As she ran across the lawn to the compound, Cole watched. The wind pushed her hair this way and that, while her intelligence, passion, and what she had just mumbled a second before had him tied up in a knot of desire and tenderness.

You are really *something,* Cole thought, resisting the urge to tear across the lawn after her, to bring her down to the ground and simply gaze at those amazing eyes and those satiny lips, while her uncle bitched up a storm.

Cole looked at Thaddeus, who was, of course, watching him.

"You take care of her, understand?" Thaddeus said.

Cole spoke without pause, "Yes, sir. But I have to say, that's one amazing lady. She doesn't really need anyone to take care of her."

"Of course she does." Thaddeus frowned. "So you do that or you'll hear from me."

"No harm will come to her. I give you my word, sir." Cole pushed back in his chair. "See you in a few days." He left the table.

Before he got too far, Thaddeus called out, "You'll see me well before then if you take advantage of my niece's good heart or do anything to lead her on, young man!"

Lord. Cole increased his pace and hoped to God Thaddeus didn't run after him.

To his relief, the old guy remained at the table to holler at BooBoo. As the monkey shrieked in return, Cole hurried toward the villa.

Once inside his room, Cole kicked off his huaraches and padded to the wall to listen to Ariel.

She was moving around her room, opening and closing drawers, as she loudly hummed the musical theme that had played endlessly in *Force Recon Response*. When she finally paused it was to belch loudly, as if she'd too quickly eaten those bananas.

Cole lowered his head, suppressing his laughter. He heard another drawer being closed, after which water was turned on in the bath.

His gaze turned inward as he imagined her stripping down to her stars so she could bathe as she got ready for the first of their three nights together.

Nights in which he had been ordered not to touch her in any—*Wait a sec.* Cole suddenly recalled what the old guy just said.

You'll see me well before then if you take advantage of my niece's good heart or do anything to lead her on, young man.

Yeah, yeah. But where was the ever-present threat not to seduce or touch her?

Had Ariel talked to her uncle about that? Had she told him to back off, to allow her what she wanted?

Cole had no idea and decided to hope for the best. Pulling off his clothes, he padded into the bathroom and shaved, brushed his teeth, then took a prolonged shower, figuring it'd be the last civilized one he'd have for the next few days.

As he toweled off, Cole left the bathroom and stopped dead to Ariel sitting on his mattress.

She was back far enough so that her slender feet were off the floor. As she gently bounced her long legs up and down, her gaze ran over his nudity, lingering on his suddenly thickened cock. After she had had her fill of that, she casually regarded the dark thatch of hair above his still-thickened cock, the half moon of his navel, the dark hairs on his chest, and finally that ragged scar just below his left shoulder, a souvenir from one of his Force Recon operations.

Cole spoke without thinking. "What are you doing in here?"

Ariel briefly met his eyes before her gaze again caressed his erection. "You're taking too long."

He was taking too long? Was she kidding? He had just gone from zero arousal to standing-at-attention and ready to go-go-*go* in less than five seconds flat. "Excuse me?"

She tapped her fingers against the screenplay on his bed as her gaze continued to roam his nudity. When she finally spoke, her voice was very distracted. "You're supposed to be out of bed by now . . . you're getting dressed when I come in . . . I'm here to alert you to those—well, you know, the people in your story, which you've already heard outside . . . as Henry, not as you. That's why you woke up . . . it's all there on page three."

Cole nodded slowly, even though he hadn't really heard a word she'd said; he was too focused on whether he should cover himself. It wasn't that he had ever been bothered by nudity before, especially his own. It was that she didn't seem to be bothered by his nudity, or even momentarily surprised by it. If anything, she seemed really taken with the way things had turned out. Of course, she wasn't buck-naked and sporting a hard-on that had nowhere to go.

"Sorry," he said.

Her gaze trickled all the way down him, then inched right back up. "What?"

"Sorry," he said again.

She nodded slowly, then stopped and looked kind of worried. "About what?"

Hell, everything, beginning with the fact that they weren't going to be staying here tonight, but out there with a zillion insects and all of BooBoo's less-than-civilized cousins. And while out there, it was going to be fucking hard to find an appropriate location in which to stop so that he could haul her into his arms to enjoy her in all the ways he craved, which was probably why Thaddeus hadn't mentioned the no-touching stuff tonight with all the other new threats.

The old guy hadn't been ordered by Ariel to back off, nor was he forgetful; he knew Cole was screwed.

Frowning, he said, "For taking too long." Moving past her he went to get his costume for tonight. As he pulled the shirt off its hanger, he glanced over his shoulder and saw that she was studying his bare ass, then the backs of his thighs, then his feet, then his bare ass, again.

Damn, she was definitely something. Cole finally murmured, "Enjoying yourself?"

Ariel was not about to answer that, nor was she going to pretend embarrassment or look away.

No, sir. Her gaze continued to admire Cole's broad, muscular back. It was deeply and uniformly tanned, except for a few freckles on his shoulders that she really wanted to lick. Pulling in her tongue, she studied his butt again and liked the way he was tensing those muscles. The man was really turned on and, given the length and stiffness of his thickened shaft, ready to satisfy, just like the kick-ass, ex-Marine he was.

God, how she liked that.

God, how she would have worried about him if he had still been in the service.

She figured that's where he had gotten that terrible scar just below his shoulder. Had the wound threatened his life? Had it taken him long to recover? Had a lover nursed him back to health?

Ariel wanted to ask, but figured it was best that she keep on track with the story, script, screenplay—whatever in the hell it was called—and would do just that, as soon as she finished getting her fill of him. After all, they were both adults, and she had every right to look at a naked man; if he didn't mind, of course.

You don't, do you? she thought, then lifted her brows in delight as Cole unexpectedly turned to face her.

When she looked up, he was already glancing down as if suddenly recalling his nudity.

Ariel had never forgotten it. Her gaze drifted over that delicious male fur covering his firm pecs, the tautness of his flat belly, and finally his beautifully stiffened shaft against those tight, tight balls.

"Don't what?" he asked.

She shook her head, not following. "I'm sorry, what?"

"You said, 'you don't, do you?' Don't what?"

Her throat and chest got hot. Lord, she had to quit thinking out loud. "Mind getting started on our escape." She looked at him. "You don't, do you?"

"Do I have a choice?"

She smiled. "No."

Cole arched one dark brow and started getting dressed. "Then let's pretend you've just awakened me, and while you've been enjoying my nudity, you'll also pretend to be scared of the bad guys out there."

Uh-huh, Ariel thought, then used her most casual voice. "Uncle Thaddeus is not out there—at least, not yet."

Cole laughed.

"You two on schedule?" Thaddeus suddenly called out from down the hall, with that being followed by BooBoo's ear-splitting shriek.

Cole mumbled, "So much for your assurance about bad guys."

"Well, he wasn't there a moment ago, before you started taking too long." Looking over her shoulder, Ariel shouted, "We're fine, Uncle Thaddeus! We're great!"

"I wouldn't go that far," Cole said as he finished pulling on his cotton slacks. "You're still dressed."

Ariel gave him a look that said *bad, bad boy*, then shouted, "Go watch one of your movies, Uncle Thaddeus!"

"It won't be one of mine, will it?" Cole asked.

"Relax," she said, "he likes those old Gene Kelly musicals where everyone sleeps in separate beds and never has sex, but still wakes up singing and dancing . . . Are you laughing at me?"

God, he couldn't help himself. Cole's shoulders shook with his suppressed laughter as Thaddeus's loud grumbling filled the hall. Apparently BooBoo had effected her escape and was now running everywhere but where Thaddeus wanted. At last, the old guy coaxed her back with a beloved treat, after which there was the sound of a heavy door being slammed shut.

"That's our cue," Ariel said.

Grabbing the screenplay, she pushed off the mattress and went to Cole. "Time to make our escape."

Chapter Six

They only made it to the door of his room before Ariel stopped. Lifting her forefinger to her lips, as a warning for Cole to be silent, she pressed her ear against the door and listened.

All Cole heard was their respective breathing with Ariel's having slowed somewhat since he got dressed.

Leaning down to her, he whispered, "Is Isa out there? Is she going into your uncle's—"

"*No*—I don't know." Ariel's shoulders shook with her suppressed giggles. "I hope so."

Well, hell, so did he. At least that would get the old guy out of their hair to—

Ariel interrupted his thoughts. "I'm listening to what's happening out there—the bloodshed—just like in this story." She lifted the script.

Uh-huh. "You're going to act out every single bit of—"

"You don't want this to be accurate?" She turned her face to his and frowned. "You don't want this to be perfect?"

With her this close and already in his bedroom, Cole really didn't give a fuck if this story was worse than the one in *Force Recon Response.* Not that he was about to admit such a thing to her hard stare. "I don't know if this level of detail is entirely necessary."

She arched one brow. "So when you practiced with the

other Marines for all your coming conflicts, you guys just paid attention to some details, but not all, because it wasn't really real?"

"Ariel, we were preparing for engagements that could have meant life or death. This is only a film."

Only a film? she thought, knowing he couldn't have been more wrong. It was his film, and she wanted it to be perfect so that stars like Tom Cruise and Brad Pitt would never turn him down again. Hell no. They'd beg to be in all of his movies, and Cole would turn them down because they weren't good enough. "It's my first, so please indulge me."

His expression said *good God.* But, at least, his voice surrendered. "Go on. Lead the way."

Ariel had already planned to. Cracking open the door, she looked into the empty hall, then did what she figured her girl hero Mina would do—or should do—to get the useless politician Henry out of here alive.

Taking Cole's hand, Ariel pulled him into the hall and tried to hurry down it to the kitchen, but he held back.

Glancing over her shoulder at him, Ariel whispered, "Come *on.*"

Cole didn't budge as he looked past her.

Ariel turned to see what he did.

In that moment, and without warning, he used his body and superior strength to quickly back her into the wall, holding her there with his full length.

Ariel's free hand pressed against the wall's rough surface. Her breathing hitched, nuzzling her breasts farther into his chest, while his thighs hugged hers.

The man's erection was back and in full force.

Ariel's mouth went dry. When her dizziness finally passed, she looked up at him.

Cole's gaze was still to the side as he quietly regarded the empty hall. A vein in his throat throbbed with his accelerated heartbeat.

"What are you doing?" she whispered.

He didn't answer.

"Cole?"

At last he looked at her, and Ariel's heart raced. His eyes were hooded, his gaze intent. They were so very close, the scent of his freshly washed skin, its heat, became hers, and all else faded away.

In this moment, he was her world. She saw beads of water trapped in his shower-dampened hair and a small mole on his right temple. She noticed how long his lashes were and that they were even darker than his brows. She felt his stiffened shaft as he continued to press his body into hers, taking charge now in a way Ariel had never allowed anyone else.

Cole Ryder was different. He was lusciously male, more so than any man Ariel had ever known, and yet that innate power was tempered with a gentleness and respect that made her feel not only wanted, but safe.

It was an incredible moment, one Ariel wanted to last, only not here in the hall. "What are you doing?" she whispered once more, then inclined her head in the direction of her uncle's room.

Cole's gaze slowly lifted from her mouth to her eyes. There was heat in his expression and in his touch; heat he controlled just like the ex-soldier he was—an officer and a gentleman. At last, he murmured, "I'm protecting you from the insurgents by using nothing but my wits and my body."

Uh-huh. She arched one brow. "You're making fun of me."

"I'm having fun with you."

You will, she thought, then whispered, "Not now. Not here. We need to go outside."

Cole glanced over his shoulder to her uncle's room just down the hall. Suddenly, there were high-pitched giggles coming from it. "Isa?" Cole asked.

Well, it surely wasn't BooBoo. "We could stay here and find out."

Cole looked at her. "I thought you wanted to go outside."

"I want this to be perfect." And it would be, even if it killed him.

She pushed against Cole until he was really grinning, but finally stepping back. Grabbing his hand, Ariel led him down this hall, then down the one to the right that led to the kitchen and eventual escape.

As soon as they entered the area, Ariel stopped and bounced on her heels. "Evening," she said to the kitchen staff. "Don't mind us," she added, as they looked from her to Cole, then to their joined hands. "We're leaving."

When Cole again held back, Ariel frowned over her shoulder at him.

He hardly noticed as his gaze was on the chorreados y natilla, while his stomach just growled and growled.

"Don't worry," she said, "there's plenty to eat in the rain forest."

His gaze slid to her.

"I promise, it'll be nicer than you ever imagined. Night all," she said to the others as she led Cole through the enormous kitchen, then to another hall and the back door.

He stopped her before they reached it, this time pulling her into himself, her back to his front.

Ariel's breath caught. Her lids fluttered closed as his strong arms wrapped around her waist, holding her to him, not allowing escape.

Lowering his mouth to her ear, Cole whispered, "It better be."

She swallowed. His sweet, hot breath tickled her ear, his stiffened shaft pressed against the seam of her buttocks, and his right hand was now sliding up to her breasts. "Better be what?"

Cupping her left breast in his palm, Cole's long fingers trailed over the side and casually worked her flesh as he whispered, "It better be as good as you promised."

It was far better than Ariel had ever dreamed. She could feel the heat of his palm through her thin cotton top and bra, and the satiny warmth of his lips as he pressed them to her neck.

Her back slowly arched, pushing her buttocks into his stiffened cock. *My God.* A low moan escaped her. Lifting her free hand, she caressed the side of his face. "It will be," she murmured.

Cole pressed his lips to her ear. "Will be what?"

"As good as I promised." She drew her thumb across his freshly shaven cheek and turned her face into his. "The food's amazing out in the rain—"

He interrupted, "That's not what I'm talking about and you damn well know it."

"No?" she asked, innocent as all get out.

He wasn't buying it. Keeping his voice lowered, he said, "If this weren't your uncle's house, you damn well know what would happen now."

Ariel gave him a wicked smile as his thumb played with her tightened nipple. "But since it is my uncle's house?"

"I guess I'll just have to settle for this."

She gasped as he tickled her. *"Nooooo,"* she cried, then gasped again as she tried to get away.

Cole wasn't having it. Holding tight with one arm, he used his free hand to torment her, while warning her to be quiet so she wouldn't alert the insurgents.

"Or your uncle," he added in a dry tone.

Who the hell cared about any of that? Ariel wiggled, she squirmed, she kicked Cole a couple of times, too—and may have even shrieked once—but he wasn't about to let go. At last, she surrendered. Turning into him, arms and script scrunched up between his chest and hers, she trembled and softly moaned. "Stop. *Please.*"

"Aw, baby," he murmured as he gently stroked her back, "we haven't even started."

She trembled again; her body puddled against his as she rested her head near the hollow of his throat. She felt the powerful thrumming of his heart. She ached to press her lips to his flesh, to run her tongue over it, but knew that once she got started, she wouldn't be able to stop. *Damn.* "This isn't in the script," she finally complained, pulling the stupid thing from between them as she paused to swallow.

Bringing his lips to her ear, Cole murmured, "It is now. And I want no arguments from you, understand?"

Was he kidding? She could barely breathe, much less argue. "We really need to go outside, Cole."

"If you insist."

Ariel's lids fluttered open as he eased away.

"Can you stand by yourself?" he asked.

She struggled to lift her head and continued to breathe hard. This, when he was calm as could be. "I'll let you know if I have any trouble."

Smiling, Cole took her free hand. Once they were outside, he started across the lawn to the rain forest.

"Wait a minute," Ariel said, holding back.

Cole looked over his shoulder at her. His damp hair glistened in the light from the compound and the nearly full moon, while his eyes seemed even darker, filled with sweet danger and what appeared to be hope. "Have you changed your mind about our spending the night in the—"

"No, of course not . . . I just want you to wait."

Now he looked really cautious, as if she were about to suggest something worse than dining in the rain forest. "Wait for what?"

"Me," she murmured. *This,* she thought as she lifted her face to the sky.

The night was a miracle. Balmy, with a gentle breeze that was scrubbed clean by the ocean and scented with the fragrance of a thousand flowers. Stars dusted the sky, and Ariel responded in quiet awe.

She knew she needed to remember this—all of it—the scent of the breeze, the sounds of the ocean, the beating of her heart, the feel of this man beside her as they began their journey. One that would last for only a few nights, no longer; one that she knew would too quickly end.

Don't do this, she ordered herself, but was unable to stop. *Just have some fun,* her mind cried, but her heart wouldn't listen.

She simply wasn't the type of woman that could enjoy something and blithely move on when it was over. Oh, no.

For Ariel, events had always moved her too deeply, even when she read them wrong, like that first time she thought she was in love. It was a moment that had happened on a night like this.

She had been twenty at the time and had returned here for her college spring break accompanied by the boy she had just started dating. Having a man by her side had been a first for Ariel. She was far more used to blind dates that never worked out. This one had, and she had been so damned proud of her conquest.

Thaddeus noticed, and had willingly opened their house and his arms to her choice in a young man.

Ariel couldn't recall that boy's face anymore or the sound of his voice, but she did remember how they had laughed, played, and casino hopped on the bigger islands, which led her to believe that that had to be love. What else could explain the good times they shared?

Because of that, Ariel gave herself to that boy as she had never given herself to anyone else. They had made love everywhere, but the beach was her personal favorite.

How those acts and the virgin nights convinced her that that boy adored her as much as she adored him. With him by her side, Ariel knew she would never again feel lonely. Nor would she remain the sole geek in her group of friends with those girls so effortlessly attracting every male within reach.

Not that Ariel wanted every guy, just this one.

He, on the other hand, was young and wanted to play around. The defining moment in *her* life had been nothing more than a pretty good vacation to him.

Ariel survived, of course, and was eventually able to move on from him cheating on her with a college roommate.

But his infidelity, and that of the few other guys she had dated, also changed something deep inside. It made Ariel a realist; it made her understand that enduring love didn't really exist, even though her Uncle Thaddeus had tried to convince her otherwise.

He had been far too hopeful.

She was at last far too weary and had long ago accepted what she couldn't before. That the infidelity her parents had engaged in when she had lived with them, then continued even after she was gone, was the norm for male-female affairs.

Starry nights on an island paradise was not about to change that. Not even tonight.

My God, how that still hurt.

Feeling that pain at the base of her throat, Ariel wondered if Cole had ever been deeply wounded by a woman. Or if he had unwittingly hurt one because he just couldn't love that girl as much as she loved him.

Ariel knew she wouldn't ask. Despite her survival skills and all she had faced against the elements, she wasn't *that* brave.

At last, she sighed.

A moment passed before Cole cleared his throat. When Ariel didn't respond, he leaned toward her and whispered, "Everything all right?"

No. "Sure."

His silence said he accepted that, until he asked, "Then what are you doing?"

What else? She was behaving like a fool. Getting her bearings, Ariel said, "Looking at the constellations." She pointed. "See? That's Ursa Major." She moved her finger slightly. "And those are the five points of Cassiopeia." She met Cole's gaze and felt her heart ache far more than a realist was allowed.

His expression grew troubled as if he was worried about her. Or maybe he was worried about himself since she was his guide during the coming days and here she was acting like a lovesick fool.

Clearing her throat, Ariel said, "Those constellations are opposite each other, you know. Always opposite, never together."

"Okay."

She shook her head and sighed once more.

Cole misunderstood. "That's interesting, really. I'll remember to write it down once we're through. I'll try to use it in my screen—that is, my story when . . ."

As he continued to stumble through that explanation, Ariel's heart continued to ache. He was telling her what he thought she wanted to hear, when she wanted only the truth. He was saying he would try, when she needed far, far more.

Fidelity for one. Love for another.

Of course, that's hardly what Cole kept babbling about. He was here to learn tropical survival skills. She was here to teach him. That was the sum total of it. Nothing more. At last, she interrupted, "You don't have to write it down or do anything you just said. I already have it in here." She lifted the script. "Didn't you read any of the notes I made for you?"

He was briefly silent, then slightly peeved. "Actually, I did. But I'm figuring the people in my story don't really need constellations to direct them out of a lighted compound and into the relative safety of a dark forest that's right over there." He pointed.

Ariel's brows continued to draw together.

Cole noticed. "Okay, fine, don't believe me. But surely Minnie knows that, doesn't she?"

Ariel lowered her head to his damned teasing and warned herself not to laugh or cry. "Mee-nah!"

Cole cleared his throat. "I thought his name was Chuck."

Ariel covered her face with her free hand. Dammit, but he

was too freaking charming and masculine and everything she wanted and wasn't going to get, because romance was a myth, it never lasted, and she had better remember that. He would take her breath away, steal her heart, and leave her holding the goddamned bag. Oh, yeah.

Dropping her hand, she turned on her heel and talked over her shoulder as she headed for the rain forest. "Let's go."

Let's go? Cole thought. Suddenly, she wanted to go when just a moment before she looked as if she were rooted to the spot? Obviously something had just happened here, and he hadn't a clue what it might be.

First, she came out of that villa and looked up at the sky with an expression that said she was going to wish on one of those stars. But then she looked as if she was recalling something pretty damned painful. After that, she kind of pulled herself together and gave him that stuff about the constellations *always* being opposite each other, *never* together, as if she really hated that—and as if that made any sense at all, or even mattered when the characters were simply supposed to leave the danger of the villa and run headlong into their only other option—a dangerous, not to mention dark, rain forest. Which Ariel was headed toward right now.

Bolting across the expansive lawn, Cole caught up just as she reached the edge of the vegetation. Capturing her free hand, he brought her to a stop. "Whoa. What's the rush?"

She took another hitching breath, then looked at him. Her eyes sparkled in the moonlight.

My God, he thought. *Is she crying? Why?*

"What's the rush?" she asked, parroting him.

He slowly nodded. "We have tonight and two more days to do this."

Ariel's eyes narrowed; she pulled her hand from his. "And that's enough for you?"

God help him, Cole hadn't a clue why she was so suddenly pissed, unless he had played too dumb this afternoon when she was attempting to explain survival skills—some of which he already knew. Of course, he hadn't wanted her to know that, because then she might have put the kibosh on their spending these days and nights together.

"Hold on," he said, blocking her from going into that damned rain forest. It was definitely time to make peace, even if he didn't understand why. "I'll stay longer if I have to."

Her expression changed. "You'd do that?"

She seemed surprised. Hell, he was surprised. He had a boatload of work waiting for him back in LA and could hardly spare the time here. Still, he had said it. More importantly, he meant it.

Being out here with her was like nothing Cole had ever experienced. Despite her enthusiasm for this stupid project, despite her determination to get it right even if it killed them both, despite what might take place in that fucking rain forest with God knew what lurking there, he was actually enjoying himself.

"Yes, ma'am."

She smiled.

It was so luminous, Cole's heart knelt.

She murmured, "I'm glad."

He was already way beyond that. Cole felt super alive, as if his senses were on full alert, the same as when he had been engaged in one of his Force Recon operations. Suddenly, he heard sounds coming from the forest he hadn't noticed before. Animals called out in the darkness, leaves rustled, branches tapped against each other. Beyond that the ocean whispered against the beach, while the wind pushed past.

Here, Cole's heart continued to pound, and his thickened cock simply ached as Ariel met his gaze.

Her eyes were still sparkling, though not in sorrow this time, but excitement. And those delicate nostrils flared ever so slightly, while her voice sounded breathless. "Are you ready to continue with the enactment?"

Cole watched her lips hugging those words as his mind recalled the first three—*are you ready?* For too damned long, he thought, craving that mouth and every other part of her until it was nearly more than he could bear. He wanted to anchor her to him, to fill her mouth with his tongue, to give his cock the home only she could provide. To feel her beneath him, willingly trapped by his body, while her tight, wet heat imprisoned his flesh, owning that part of him because that's what she needed, too.

Was he ready?

Fucking A. No matter what hell he had to go through to get closer to the heaven she promised, he was definitely ready. "Yes, ma'am."

Ariel's breathing quickened as her gaze held his. "Me, too." She paused to swallow. "So, I guess we probably should start."

"Yes, we should."

"At the beginning."

"That's right. I don't want to miss one damn thing."

She nodded slowly, then stopped and shook her head. "Neither do I."

"I'm glad to hear it."

Her gaze lowered to his mouth, lingering there before she said, "Where were we—wait, don't tell me." She paused, then nodded. "It appears we've just escaped the bad guys, right?"

Only if Thaddeus was still in his bedroom making Isa giggle hysterically. "It would appear."

"And that's good," she said, then lifted her gaze to his, "even if it's only for the moment. I mean, now we're at the edge of this secondary jungle." She inclined her head in that direction.

Cole nodded, but didn't look.

Ariel didn't seem to mind. With her gaze still on him, she moistened her lips.

He went so dizzy with need he had to close his eyes.

She stepped toward him. "Are you all right?"

Her voice was softer than Cole had ever heard. As his

heart continued hammering against his chest, he opened his eyes and nodded.

Ariel regarded him as if to make certain, then continued speaking in that same achingly soft voice, "I'm glad."

Cole hoped to be.

"So," she said, "it seems the problem we're facing now is this jungle."

Well, it sure as hell wasn't a suite at the Ritz-Carlton. Not that Cole was about to say that. He wanted to hear it from her first. "That's right . . . why?"

Ariel's gaze lifted from his chest. She seemed distracted momentarily. "Ah, this type of jungle, the one right here, doesn't completely obscure the night sky and the moon like the actual rain forest that's just beyond." She gestured in that direction.

For the second time tonight, Cole didn't bother to look.

For the second time tonight, she didn't seem to mind. Pausing to take a deep breath, she finally continued, "The rain forest offers a solid canopy and would protect us if the bad guys started to search by air."

It was amazing, he thought, the way each word she said trembled the soft swell of her breasts. "Uh-huh."

"That's a good thing," she said.

Actually, it was amazing.

"But what if they don't do that at first?" she asked.

Cole lifted his gaze to hers.

Those delicate nostrils flared in response. Her gaze got kind of fuzzy, too. "What if they search by foot?" she asked.

Cole was about to ask "they who?" but then remembered, the assassins . . . unless she was talking about Isa and Thaddeus. "That would be bad."

"Uh-huh. So do we run headlong into the actual rain forest when visibility in daylight is only about fifty meters?"

"Probably not," he said, then stepped toward her.

Ariel's gaze noted that. Looking back up, she licked her

lips again before continuing. "So that is kind of a problem, and right now we *are* basically hidden by the darkness, so long as we stay out of the moonlight—but are we actually safe?"

Not from each other, he thought.

"Is this the wisest choice?" she asked.

Cole wasn't about to answer that.

She paused briefly, then asked, "What should we do?"

With that question, Cole's gaze lifted from her mouth to her eyes. In that moment, all caution was lost, all of Thaddeus's admonitions forgotten. In that moment, nothing else mattered, not his stupid script, not the goddamn film, not Hollywood, not anything but touching this woman, *tasting* this woman.

Moving into her until their bodies touched, Cole cradled her face in his palms.

Her flesh was silky and hot, her breath moist, her eyes widened in wonder as he tilted her face to his.

"This," he said in answer to her question about what they should do. Neither his tone nor his touch tolerated any argument before he lowered his mouth to hers.

Chapter Seven

She was his without pause, the script finally forgotten as it fell unnoticed from her hand.

Cole heard it landing on a pile of leaves. Ariel whimpered, then lifted her arms, sliding them over his shoulders even before he had pulled her into himself, allowing no escape.

Ariel's body, her response, said she wanted none. She wanted more of this and him as their mouths joined and her lips parted.

They were delicate and welcoming, guiding him to a sweet refuge that begged to be filled.

Cole wasted no time, already too much had passed. Thrusting his tongue into Ariel's mouth, he inhaled sharply to her wet heat, to the way her lips suckled him.

Dear God, but this was what life was all about. This feeling of unbearable comfort that Ariel delivered, a cleansing of all the bad, a renewal that made Cole feel like a boy, and yet—more of a man than he had ever been before.

All the kick-ass Marine maneuvers and combat in the world couldn't do that. Winning battle after battle in foreign locales and Hollywood boardrooms hadn't done that.

Being wanted by a woman who was your equal in every way was the only thing that could make that possible.

How Cole craved this feeling. How he wanted it never to

end as Ariel tilted her head, then opened her mouth still farther inviting him more deeply inside.

He quickly accepted and was fully lost.

To Ariel, his passion was a gift; his touch a balm. For a moment, she simply couldn't get enough of the man. She suckled his tongue with a reverence she hardly knew existed. She worked her fingers through his thick, silky hair, keeping his head lowered, his mouth to hers.

Cole's response was to deepen the kiss.

A low moan escaped the back of her throat; she molded her body to his, thigh to thigh, hip to hip, clit to cock.

His need fueled hers until she was breathless and weak.

Even then, the man did not let go. As his embrace tightened, his kiss grew tender, exploring. When he withdrew his tongue, Ariel groaned in protest, then whimpered as he pressed his lips to each side of her mouth, her chin, her throat. Here, Cole lingered, licking her flesh until she shivered in delight. At last, he returned to her mouth, covering it with his own, then coaxed her tongue inside.

He tasted of hot tropical nights and the cool comfort of a midnight swim. He tasted of male arousal and punishing need.

He tasted of hope and the future and love.

I'll stay longer if I have to, he had said.

The woman in Ariel believed him; the realist in her knew the score. No matter how long he gave this research, it would never be enough. Forever would barely begin to satisfy the need in her heart, a loneliness that had always been just beneath the surface.

Ariel had felt it with her parents, with her first love from college, and with those few other men she had known.

Only Thaddeus had temporarily eased that pain, but even he knew the truth.

I'm not going to be around forever, dear, and we do have your future to think about.

She loved the man for worrying, but was pissed as hell at him for putting her in this spot.

Already she craved Cole Ryder as she had never needed anything else before. Not the love of her uncle, not the attention of her parents, not the acceptance of her peers.

This was what she needed. This man who listened to and respected her, who laughed with and teased her, who kissed her now as if she were the most important thing in his universe.

At least until their time was over, and it would be.

Thinking of that, Ariel's response became wild, greedy, insatiable. Her mouth, hands, and body were consumed with giving him pleasure and taking it right back. She needed to imprint this moment in her memory and his.

At last, though, even that had to end. When it did, she forced herself to pull her mouth from his and immediately felt the loss. Pushing that aside, Ariel warned herself to be realistic as she continued to step back.

She had just brushed against a fern when Cole opened his eyes. Still breathing hard, he looked at her.

Ariel's heart caught. In the moonlight, his expression was one of lingering passion and complete confusion.

And why not? She was a wild woman one minute, and yards away from him the next.

She wanted to explain, but hardly knew how. It wasn't as if she could just tell Cole she was already falling in love. Men just didn't take that news well.

If memory served her correctly, after she had told that boy from college that she adored him, he mumbled what sounded like "fuck," then disappeared from her life only to show up in her roommate's.

Days later, when Ariel saw the two of them walking hand-in-hand down the street, that guy had looked at her blankly, as if they had never even met.

This, after spending a week on her uncle's island and sleeping with her dozens of times.

She sighed.

"Come back here," Cole ordered.

Ariel arched one brow and remained where she was.

He frowned. "What's wrong?"

"Nothing."

"*Nothing?* Are you joking? You're way over there and I'm way over here, that's the first thing." He planted his hands on his lean hips. "One minute you're kissing me like there's no tomorrow, and in the very next you're pulling away, that's the second—"

"I know, I know, I know!" She breathed hard, then lowered her voice. "But that's not what they would do."

Cole's expression said she was nuts. "Not what who would do?"

"Your characters, Minnie and Chuck."

He went to her, then bent down until their lips nearly touched. "That's Mina and Hank."

Ariel cleared her throat. "Henry," she corrected, her voice still breathless. "He's not Hank until he proves himself worthy."

Cole straightened. "I thought I just did. Hell, you surely did."

Ariel chose to ignore that. Moving around him to the edge of the forest, she said, "Now, what would they do at this—"

Cole interrupted, "You didn't enjoy the kiss?"

Was he kidding? Did he think she responded like that when she was turned off? Hell, if she had enjoyed it any more than she had, he'd be sporting bruises all over his body, not just on his lips. Looking over her shoulder at him, Ariel said the only thing she could, since men just didn't take news of a woman's love all that well. "It's not in the script."

"Actually, it is," he countered. "I penciled it in along with a scene where we're making love." He raised the pitch of his voice to parrot hers: "'They'll make love later, when they're hiding out from the bad guys.'" Cole opened his arms, then glanced at the leaf he just hit. When he spoke again, it was in his normal voice. "We're hiding out from them right now." He looked at her and wiggled his fingers, gesturing her closer. "So now is obviously later."

Ariel warned herself not to smile, then dug her toes into her moccasins so she wouldn't go one step closer to him. That wouldn't be prudent. Already she was missing his taste and scent. Already her mouth felt empty, her body bereft without his warmth pressed to it; the promise of his hot, hard rod filling it.

"You're talking about page ninety-eight of the story," she said.

"So you did read it."

Of course, she did. Again and again and again. "We're still on page five, and until we get past it, we'll never get to page ninety-eight."

Cole lowered his hands and frowned. "Just to let you know, this is *my* screenplay." He pointed. "Which you're standing on."

Ariel looked down. The top page now bore imprints from the soles of her mocs. "Sorry." She picked the thing up and threw it, hitting him in the navel. "There's *your* screenplay, which fell on *my* uncle's island."

It was down there again as it fell off of him, except for the last page which was damp and stuck to his crotch.

Peeling it off, he hunkered down and placed it with the rest. "You really didn't enjoy the kiss, did—"

"You know I did." As he pushed to a standing position, she went to him. "So quit asking such a foolish question and let's just get on with this, shall we?"

Okay, this was obviously their very first fight, and Cole hadn't a clue why. Every other woman he had known had been soft, yet eager after a kiss, not demanding he stick to a script he couldn't care less about.

So why was she acting like this? Why did she have to be so damned honest?

Of course he knew she enjoyed the kiss; only a coma

would have made him oblivious to that truth. Still, he wanted her to admit it without a fight—to be fucking honest about *that* and maybe discuss the high points until they were both so aroused, they'd be right back in each other's arms. Foolish or not, Cole needed to be told, without prompting, that she desired him as much as he craved her.

What he got was the look a mother gives a wayward son.

"Fine," he said, using the same short tone she had. "Let's get on with this." Turning, he headed for the guts of the forest.

"Hey!" Ariel shouted. "What are you doing?"

Cole stopped and looked over his shoulder at her. "Getting on with it."

"No, no, no," she said, then jabbed her finger at the ground, "come back here."

Turning to face her, Cole arched one brow. "Change your mind already?" He lifted the now damp and muddy script. "Want to jump ahead to page—"

"Cole, I want to keep you safe."

The way she said his name surprised him. The concern in her voice gave him pause.

She sounded really worried, and that quickly worried him.

Not moving one inch—hell, he was barely breathing—Cole glanced around the shadows surrounding him. "Is there a poisonous snake near—"

Ariel interrupted. "Probably not, and there won't be that or scorpions if we don't go any farther into the forest tonight and make certain to stay away from fallen logs and debris."

"I swear I will," he said, his gaze darting everywhere as he moved toward her, "as soon as I can tell which is which."

"Exactly," she said. "In this darkness everything looks the same."

Cole glanced up. "Well, not everything."

She lowered her head and sighed.

"Okay, fine," he said, "you look exactly like me, except for your chest. Say what you want, but I know it's bigger."

Her shoulders started to tremble.

He hoped to God she wasn't crying. Hell, he was just trying to lighten the moment. "Ariel?"

She let out a low, throaty laugh.

The sound drew Cole to her faster than any command.

"You're not paying attention!" She laughed.

"Hon, I'm staring at your chest right—"

"Not me," she interrupted. "This!" She swung her arm to the side. "You're not paying attention to what's surrounding us!"

Cole leaned forward and murmured, "I can't pay attention to what I can't see."

"Exactly!" As her laughter turned to momentary giggles, she pressed her thumb and forefinger to the inside corners of her eyes. "With only the moon to see by, it's hardly wise to go into a place that obscures it. Nor is it wise to leave this area at night when mosquitoes are biting." She dropped her hand and looked at him. "We have no repellent or prophylactics until I can see the plants. Could be that's *aguakalat* in those shadows; could be it's something that might kill us. Who knows in this dark?"

Uh-huh, Cole thought as he glanced over his shoulder to where she was pointing. "Aguakalat?"

"You know it as allium or wild garlic and onion."

Ah. He turned back to her. "What you said I should be eating to repel insects."

"Exactly."

"You really want me to use that in the screenplay, don't you?"

She was briefly silent. "This afternoon when I explained how we could get around that, you asked several questions that indicated you were paying attention. Now I'm not so sure."

Okay, so he was busted on the insect stuff, but he had been paying attention since the moment they met. He now knew the contour of her mouth by heart and could locate that tiny mole on the curve of her right cheek even if he were a blind man, which given the complete darkness behind him was pretty damned close. Not that Cole was about to point that out to her and risk frowns or tears instead of her wonderful laughter. "There's a lot to remember."

Again, she was silent. "Did you really serve in the Marines?"

Okay, that stung. "Yes, ma'am, I did."

Her voice sounded skeptical. "Then how come you don't know any of—"

"I didn't serve in the tropics. Let's just say I'm more attuned to the broiling desert where most of the people, especially the women, are draped from the tips of their noses to their toes in burkas, which really protects them from everything, including foolish questions."

She had gone too far. The hurt in his voice was unmistakable; hurt Ariel knew she had put there. God, what was the matter with her?

"Cole, I'm so sorry. I shouldn't have said that."

He shrugged as if it were no big deal.

"Really," she said, "I was out of line. Forgive me, please."

"Sure. Is this where we kiss and make up?"

Ariel's head fell forward. Her shoulders shook with her suppressed laughter. "That doesn't happen until page one-twenty-five!"

"Ninety-eight," he corrected.

"See," she said, lifting her head to look at him, "you do have long-term memory when you want to."

"I recall that your eyes are a grayish green."

Ariel's cheeks flushed, and then her belly fluttered as Cole took that last step to cross the space that had separated them. Before she lost all control and pulled him to the ground so that he couldn't get away from her mouth, hands, or body for the rest of this miraculous night, she stepped back. "We need to get on with the research for your—"

Her words abruptly paused as his cell phone rang.

Cole looked down at her pants, which were the source of that ringing. "You brought a cell phone?"

"I brought your cell phone." She pulled it out of her pocket. "I figured I might need it."

Cole lifted his gaze to her. "To give updates to your uncle?"

"Of course not. We need to give them to Gwen." Ariel opened the phone. "Could be I'll think of something for your story that needs to be run by her before we—"

"Uh-uh," he interrupted, then shoved the script under his left arm and took the phone. Bringing it to his ear, he said, "Gwen? Hi. Don't call again. Bye." He turned off the phone and put it into his pocket. "Okay, let's get rolling."

Ariel crossed her arms over her chest. "Yes, let's. Go on, what should we do?"

Cole figured suggesting another kiss or sex was totally out of the question, at least for now. But come page ninety-eight—watch out. "I guess we should find a safe place on the periphery of this non-rain forest, at least until dawn, at which time we can go farther into it to get to the real rain forest, which we'll hack through to get to the other side of this island like the proverbial chickens we are."

Ariel looked as though she was trying very hard not to smile. "You want to stay in the villa and fight a bunch of drooling, wild-eyed bad guys who are armed to the teeth when all you have are your wits?"

"And your respect," he said.

Her expression changed. When she spoke, her voice was very soft. "Always."

Cole smiled.

"But we're not talking about Cole Ryder, USMC," she quickly said, her voice back to business.

Dear God. "No?" he asked, playing along. Hell, what choice did he have? "So, who are we talking about?"

"Your story's hero, Henry Dobbins, US Representative from—"

"His last name is Sloane."

"I like Dobbins better. It sounds weaker."

Uh-huh, Cole thought, then glanced around the wall of darkness behind them and the light from the compound in front of them. "Despite what you've explained, we can't just stay on the very edge of this vegetation. Surely, those drooling fiends will see us here. We have to move deeper inside this perimeter."

"Secondary jungle," she said.

"Right."

"Wrong," she argued, then continued speaking above him. "Not the name, the plan. If we don't stay in this general vicinity, all the bad stuff I said would happen will, in addition to the fact that we'll lose the ocean breeze. It's the only thing keeping insects away, unless you want to build a fire."

"Wouldn't the drooling fiends *and* the insects see that?"

"Exactly," she said, then bounced on her heels as if she were getting excited. "Of course, later in our journey, when there's no possibility of our being seen, we can build a fire at night and cover it with coconut husks to create a smudge that repels mosquitoes. Or we could drip coconut oil into the fire, which creates smoke that works just as well, after we extract the oil, of course. And if we do get bitten, coconut meat is great to reduce the itching. And once we're out of harm's way, we'll be able to catch fish, and collect water, and make beds, and—"

"Oh my God, stop," Cole said. "You're sugarcoating this way too much for me."

Ariel leveled her gaze on him.

"You're really amazing, you know that?" he asked.

Her face betrayed her surprise, while her voice was suddenly hesitant. "Because I know all of this?"

Cole pulled the script from under his arm and leaned against the trunk of a tree. "Because you're a beautiful woman and you know all of this."

Ariel smiled at that compliment, then glanced from him to

the tree trunk and back. "I know that if you lean against that tree too long, you might have a real problem with ticks."

Sweet Jesus, is there no place safe in this forest? Pushing away from the tree, Cole looked over his shoulder to see if anything was hanging on him. Just to make certain there wasn't, he slapped his back with the script.

"You're losing it," Ariel said.

He looked at her. "I'm remaining as calm as I—"

Her laughter interrupted. "I meant your story." She picked up the pages that had fallen away from the rest and handed them to him. "Didn't we talk about trees and ticks this afternoon?"

If they had, Cole was glad he had forgotten. "Like I said, lots to remember. So what now? We're going to sleep standing?"

"Well, we can't lean against trees or fallen logs . . . you'll get ticks that way, too, not to mention the scorpion problem. So until I can find *patza* to use as a repellent, it's really not a good idea."

Okay, he thought. "Maybe I should have planned this for the arctic instead of a tropical—"

"It won't be that bad."

Well, hell, given the soft tenor of her voice it was already getting better. Glancing around, and squinting to see better through the darkness, Cole finally spotted a rock formation near a group of trees. Looking from it back to the compound, Cole knew what he had to do. "Come on."

Ariel glanced down to his fingers surrounding hers, then to where he had been looking, but saw nothing special. "Come on where?"

"Our bedroom."

Before she could comment on that Cole led her to the large rocks. Releasing her hand, he sank to the ground, spread his legs, then patted the insides of his thighs. "Come on, don't make me beg."

As if she ever would. As if she had. The moment the man

had put his mouth on hers, she had lost all rational thought. Even before he expected—or wanted—more, she had willingly delivered it.

"*You* beg?" she asked, her voice incredulous.

Cole's gaze remained on her as he said, "For you I would."

Ariel's eyes widened slightly. "I would never make you beg."

"I know, you're too fine a woman for that. You're too honest. That's why I'd be willing to. You're definitely worth it."

Ariel sank to her knees. Somehow, her legs just wouldn't hold her any longer.

"Come on," Cole said, coaxing her until Ariel was seated between his muscular thighs, her back against his broad chest.

As it moved with his steady breathing, as he drew his legs even closer to her, Ariel's heart continued to race.

You're too fine a woman for that, he had said. *You're definitely worth it.*

Yes, she was. It's what her Uncle Thaddeus had taught her, what she had grown up to believe. To expect the best, because she was the best. But to hear another man say it—to hear this man say it with such candor—was really something.

As Ariel's heart smiled, her gaze roamed the surrounding area. From here, she could still see the compound. Despite that, it would take a great deal of doing for anyone—bad guys, protective uncles, or even Isa—to see them. What's more, there was still an ocean breeze to protect them from insects.

"So," Cole murmured, "how'd I do?"

Ariel ran her forefinger up his left calf, feeling those hard, strong muscles beneath his cotton slacks. "How'd you do what?"

Cole continued to softly moan, then cleared his throat before speaking. "Finding us—that is, Mina and Henry—a safe place to sleep."

"You did good." She ran her forefinger over his huaraches to his long toes.

They briefly splayed. He cleared his throat once more. "Ah, hon, that feels really good. So good that if you want us to—"

"I do," she said, meaning it with all of her heart as she pulled back her hand, "but we can't tonight." Though it killed her, Ariel wanted to anticipate the pleasure that was to come and savor this closeness as Cole's body anchored, comforted, and protected her.

It was a feeling that had been too long denied. It was one of belonging to another human being that she never really had as a child until she started living with her Uncle Thaddeus.

Recalling that, she sighed.

Cole leaned over until he could see the side of her face. "No need to wait if it's going to make you so sad."

Ariel turned her face to his and gently pressed her lips to his mouth. As she pulled back—as Cole was still catching his breath—she murmured, "I'm not sad, I'm enjoying this. Indulge me, please."

He opened his eyes. "You, always. But not the stupid script or the dumb characters."

"It's not stupid," she said. "And they're not dumb. Well, maybe Henry is, at first, until Mina—are you laughing at me?"

Cole tried to sober, but his chest kept pumping against her back with his suppressed laughter. "Sorry."

Lifting her hand, Ariel caressed the side of his face. "You know, we never have him saying that to her in this story, no matter how many times he screws up."

"My mistake." Cole turned his face into her hand and kissed her palm. "I'll pencil it in in the morning."

She smiled to his hot breath tickling her skin. "If we don't follow the script, we might not be here in the morning."

"Oh, come on, it's not that bad." Cole gently wrapped his

arms around her. "When did you become such a worry wart?"

Ariel glanced down at his strong embrace. How nice it looked. So nice, she placed her hands on his forearms at the edge of his folded-back sleeves, then slowly drew her fingers over his deeply tanned skin, those short, dark hairs, as she rested the back of her head against his shoulder. "I was pretty carefree until I was ten and came to live with Uncle Thaddeus."

"He was that hard on you?"

Ariel smiled. "I meant carefree about bugs and animals. Until I met him, I didn't realize most of that stuff existed."

Cole didn't comment.

Ariel didn't mind. She enjoyed the sounds of the night, the feel of his broad chest rising and falling with his easy breathing.

"Met?" he finally asked. "His last name is the same as yours. I thought you were related by blood."

"We are. But he is the black sheep of the Leigh family—at least until I took up that banner." She shrugged. "I didn't actually know he existed, nor did I meet him until I was ten."

Cole brought his legs still closer, until the insides of his thighs hugged her. "What changed when you were ten?"

With that question, Ariel stopped stroking his arms.

Cole was briefly silent, then asked, "Did your parents die then?"

Die? "No, of course not," she said with true surprise. "Actually, they're still alive now."

"Oh, good to hear it . . . but they were seriously ill when you were ten?"

Ariel shook her head. "Both of them have always been as healthy as me . . . and you." She wiggled her butt into his persistent arousal.

Cole's chest quivered with his quiet laughter.

Ariel smiled at how wonderful that felt, and then she

sighed once more. "You really don't know who my folks are, do you?"

"Should I?"

"Don't you ever watch TV?"

"Not when I'm on the edge of a non-rain forest with a beautiful worrywart."

She smiled.

"Are they sitcom stars?" he asked, then continued over her lusty laughter, "Okay, okay—are they in one of those soap operas?"

"Are you kidding?" Ariel laughed until she felt silly and weak.

Cole mumbled, "Maybe I should watch more TV."

"You're fine." She giggled, then forced herself to sober. "I'm honestly glad you've never heard of my folks."

He didn't comment on that. Instead, he adjusted his body, bringing her even deeper within his protective embrace.

So nice, Ariel thought.

"I don't mean to be nosy," he said, "but are they on one of those TV ministries?"

Her giggles had returned. Before they got too bad, she finally fessed up. "They're the anchors of the *Future Report*. And I'm not talking UFOs here."

"Yeah, I know."

That surprised her. "Then you have seen the show?"

"Actually, I heard of it when their viewers went on a rampage—that is," he quickly corrected himself, "when they opposed most of the stuff coming out of the entertainment industry, even the cartoons."

"My parents and their viewers don't like to be entertained," she said.

"No kidding."

"They're very conservative."

"Yeah, I know."

"I don't think you do. The *Future Report* is really grim,

but before my parents got that they were on the *Decency Debate* and before that *Turning Trends*. Talk about bleak. Of course, way, way, way before that they were both on a local station in San Antonio. My dad did this goofy consumer report that had him trying out these inventions that always cost nineteen-ninety-nine and never worked, and my mom was the weather girl with a ten-gallon hat and a pretty snappy wit. Of course, way back then they were in love."

Again, Cole didn't comment, with this silence looking to last the rest of the night.

Figures, Ariel thought. Mention the *L* word to a guy and they suddenly go mute, unable to form complete senten—

"They're divorced?" he finally asked.

Ariel was surprised by the question. She shook her head. "In my opinion, and it's only my opinion, they should be. But there's the audience to consider and their life philosophy, you know?" She briefly paused. "Don't get me wrong, they're good people, but divorce is so messy and public, it's simply easier for them to lead separate lives. In private, they have their affairs. In public, they're the perfect couple. They have this image of what people should be like, and that is very civilized. They really do care what others think."

"And that's why they don't approve of a maverick like Thaddeus?"

"Or me."

Once more, he was briefly silent. "They really believe you're uncivilized because you're a survival expert?"

"Actually, it's because I care more what I think about me than what others do."

Amazing, Cole thought, trying to recall another woman from his past that owned the integrity Ariel did; only there were none. This lady was definitely unique and so damned stunning every part of Cole craved her.

Not only that, he actually enjoyed talking with her. So,

when was the last time that had happened, when he had a beautiful female within his arms on a nice night like this?

With other women, Cole had always wanted to quickly complete the sale. With Ariel, he found himself wanting to get to know her because she was utterly fascinating.

So what was wrong with her parents? Were they really that clueless as to the amazing daughter they had? Were they so caught up in their own stupid lives they didn't realize how much they had hurt her? Cole heard the lingering sadness in her voice, and it made him damned mad. "How'd you get to be so wise? Did you learn all of this from your uncle?"

"Oh, no. I taught it to him."

Cole laughed. "And how long did that take?"

"Years and years. Like I said, I started living with him when I was ten."

His laughter quickly wound down. "Did the courts take you away from your parents?"

"God, no. After I met Uncle Thaddeus, they just kind of forgot about me."

"Forgot about you?"

"It's not as bad as it sounds, really," she quickly explained. "They had their hands full with their work and, well, those extra-curricular activities. They hired nannies to take care of me, but none of them worked out. There was even talk of sending me off to a boarding school, but my father thought a summer vacation with Uncle Thaddeus might be better since it'd show me how great my *real* life was. But the summer vacation turned out to be permanent."

Cole was stunned. He tried to imagine Ariel as a little girl, unwanted by her parents, and meeting Thaddeus for the first time. My God, how scary that must have been for her, not to mention him, given her spirit.

How sad it must have been, too. How in the world could any parent do that to a child? What in the hell was the matter with them? "Permanent, because they forgot about you?" he finally asked.

"You have to understand, for them it was a particularly trying time."

"I'll bet. Anger over a partner's extra-marital affairs usually makes a marriage trying."

"No," she quickly said, "you still don't understand." Leaning forward, she looked over her shoulder at him. "There was never any anger, at least none that I saw. Like I said, they're very civilized."

Cole tried to imagine that or how to comment. At last, he shrugged. "Then my hat's off to both of them."

Ariel's eyes widened slightly, while her stomach fell. *Then my hat's off to both of them?* She had expected better of him; she had thought he'd be as dismayed by her parents' outrageous behavior as she was. "Then you agree with their choices?"

"Hell no, that's not what I'm saying. I'm amazed by their self-control. If it were my wife that was fooling around on me, and my child who was no longer living with me, no damn way would I be civilized."

Ariel caught herself before she smiled, and certainly before she threw her arms around him for saying what he had.

He was absolutely right, of course; she had suspected that from the start. He wouldn't be a civilized man, at least not when it came to his family or his woman. His honor ran too deep. What belonged to him would remain with him.

What a lovely way to live, Ariel thought as she imagined being his woman, waking up in their bed, held prisoner by his arms and one leg draped over hers, because he needed her even in sleep.

When their work demanded that they momentarily part, he would phone her daily; she would train him to do that.

She would reward him when he returned.

They would build a life, a family. She would give him a daughter to protect. That child would be wanted, adored.

He would give his time to her. He would give his life for her.

"No," Ariel finally murmured, "I don't believe you would be civilized."

Before Cole could comment on that or the yearning in her gaze, Ariel turned and snuggled back into his arms.

Bringing her closer, Cole pressed his face to her lush hair, inhaling deeply of its clean, fresh scent.

"So, is that something the Marines taught you?" she asked.

Lifting his face, Cole looked over Ariel's shoulder to his arms holding her close. "That depends. Are you talking about me sniffing your hair or sitting like this?"

Her body trembled with quiet laughter. "I'm talking about you being so uncivilized."

Cole continued to gently stroke her arms with his thumbs as he cradled her against him. "Learned it from my dad."

She inhaled deeply, contentedly, then sighed it out. "You guys are close?"

"Yup."

"He loves your mom?"

"He better."

"Seriously," she said.

Cole used his most earnest voice. "Very much."

"Tell me about them, please."

To Cole's way of thinking there wasn't much to tell. In comparison to her folks, his parents were pretty damned dull. They had gotten married after college, produced four sons, and still liked and respected each other even after all these years. That was the sum total of it, and that's what he told her.

"You know how lucky you are to have experienced such a home, don't you?" Ariel asked.

He had before, but really did now. "Yes, ma'am."

She gently laughed, and it touched his soul.

I warn you, young man, Thaddeus had said, *you are not to romance her, or seduce her, or lead her on, or touch her in any way while she is with you.*

No, sir, Cole thought as Ariel remained in his embrace. He would not seduce her, nor would he lead her on. This woman deserved his respect; she deserved all the good life could give. No way would he ever hurt her.

But there was a part of Thaddeus's warning Cole simply could not live up to. No way could he stop touching her, because that touch would always be honest and protective. For this woman, he could offer nothing less.

Glancing down at her, he murmured, "How you doing?"

She sighed contentedly, then kind of groaned.

"Am I holding you too tight?" he asked.

"You're fine." She pulled his arms back to the way they had been before he loosened his embrace.

Cole smiled. "Then why the groan?"

"Do you really want to hear this?"

Probably not, if she had to ask first. "Sure. Shoot."

"One of us should keep watch tonight—it's in the script," she quickly added, then grabbed it off the forest floor.

Now he groaned. "God, I hate that—hey!" he complained when she smacked the top of his head with it. "That hurt."

"Did not. And don't say it's stupid, please. It's your future."

Yeah, yeah, yeah.

"It is," she said.

"I know," he said.

"So, we really should follow it."

"We could always change it."

"We could, but it wouldn't make sense. The bad guys will eventually find out that Mina and Henry are missing. They'll come looking for them—meaning us—so, you go ahead and sleep, and I'll keep watch so I can tell the actress who plays Mina what it feels like to stay up all night."

Right. "I hate to burst your bubble, hon, but Hollywood actresses stay up really late all the time."

"Not on the edge of a rain forest. Not with the threat of injury or death hanging over them."

This was true. A bad photo in the *National Enquirer* was the worst they usually faced. Still . . . "I don't know. This might not be such a good idea."

"Look, Cole, I've been in far worse situations than this, and I—"

"You think this is bad?"

"No, of course not. That's not what I meant. I'm just trying to say that I am capable of keeping watch. I've done it before."

Not with him, she hadn't. "That's not what I'm worried about. How much do you weigh?"

Ariel's silence said she considered the question odd or politically incorrect. "Why?"

"I don't want to be crushed by your weight after I fall—*ow!*" he complained as she elbowed him in the side. "Now, that did hurt!"

Her voice held a smile. "It was supposed to . . . good night, Cole. Go to sleep."

As if he could with her warm, soft body in his arms.

Inhaling deeply, warning himself to maintain control, Cole carefully swept her hair to the side. Lowering his head, he gently pressed his lips to the back of her neck.

She trembled.

Cole lifted his mouth to her ear and whispered, "We're doing this my way. I'll watch you sleep."

"Okay—wait—what?"

"I'll keep watch while you sleep," he amended. "And that's final."

Chapter Eight

Nothing was final, and to Ariel that was the problem. Even so, she made no argument; she simply didn't have the nerve or the strength.

Nor was she about to slumber. This evening was far too precious.

As the night settled around them, as their silence grew, Ariel listened hard and heard faint laughter from the staff as they made their way to the beach and their boats so they could return to their own islands.

A short time later, she heard the faint sputter of a boat that resisted being started, and then the motor's hum of success. As that sound faded, others replaced it. Leaves were brushed by the wind. A coconut fell, hitting the tree from which it came before thudding to the ground. Quick, light footfalls soon followed as an animal hurried to that treat.

Ariel listened to it all, enjoying nature's music, concentrating on it so that she wouldn't have to face the fact that her first night with Cole was essentially over.

As much as that saddened her, Cole was certainly at peace with his world.

I'll keep watch while you sleep, he had said.

Not unless he did it with his eyes closed.

About fifteen minutes into their silence, Cole's breathing and embrace began to relax.

Five minutes later, he was a goner, and so fully asleep that when Ariel leaned forward and looked over her shoulder at him, he didn't stir at all.

His head hung to the side, his lips were slightly parted, and his expression reminded her of a little boy exhausted from play.

She wondered if he was putting her on, then figured he wasn't, because his breathing remained uniform and slow when she lightly drew her fingertips over his cheek and then gently touched other parts of him.

Of course, the real test was to come.

Ariel snuggled back into him. In that moment, his cock went immediately stiff between the seam of her buttocks before going dead again.

The man was really asleep.

Amazing.

How in the world did he ever get through the Marines, much less Force Recon, with that cavalier attitude? Of course, he had probably taken that service very seriously. Ariel recalled the scar just below his shoulder, only one of countless potential injuries that might have proved fatal. Given that reality, it wasn't surprising that poisonous snakes, scorpions, and the other dangers one might find in a rain forest seemed relatively benign to him, which was why he was blowing this off.

If any other man had done that, no matter what he had survived, Ariel figured she would have been pretty damned pissed and on her way back home. With Cole, well, she was already making excuses and had decided to forgive him.

Girl, you are such a fool, she warned herself, even as her heart responded that that was all right; it needed this chance.

Settling back into his embrace, Ariel told herself that tonight she would be his woman even if he didn't know it. Tonight, she would keep watch and protect him.

She thought about that for a long time and was still thinking about it as she finally drifted off to a peaceful, dreamless sleep.

*   *   *

Cole didn't realize he had even conked out until he woke with a start.

What's that?

Eyes still closed, Cole lifted his head and listened hard, then winced to an animal's ear-splitting shriek.

God, God, God, will you just shut—wait a sec, where am I?

He was afraid to look given that shriek. And then he refused to look when he remembered. He was on the edge of a secondary jungle that had to be gotten through so that he could get to the real rain forest that promised to be just as cruddy or worse than the first one.

Damn. "Oh, God," he moaned as that animal screeched up a storm. "Not again."

What in the hell was the matter with it? Why was it coming closer?

Cole heard those shrieks getting louder, while branches were shaking wildly as if the damn thing were swinging from one to the other like a simian version of Tarzan.

Boobala? he suddenly wondered, then immediately thought of Thaddeus.

Opening one eye, Cole glanced around the muted darkness. It was obviously first light, and now that he noticed it his legs were numb, the volcanic rock he had leaned against all night had carved a dent into the small of his back, while Ariel's weight was still welded to his chest.

Cole figured if he hadn't been as taken with her as he was—which had him fully fucking aroused—he'd be in some serious pain.

As it was, all the discomfort he felt was quickly forgotten as he glanced down.

Ariel's face was turned to the left, eyes closed, long lashes resting above the curve of her smooth cheeks. As she continued to sleep, a neon blue butterfly remained perched on her right knee, its wings slowly opening and closing.

Cole's lips parted in honest surprise and complete awe.

Never had he seen anything quite as beautiful. Ariel looked so perfectly at home here, as if she had been born for this.

She also seemed very young. Her fingers were curled into loose fists that were pressed to her heart as if she were keeping it from harm.

Cole recalled what she had said last night about her goofy parents and imagined her again as a little girl who wanted to be noticed and protected.

Feeling protective now, Cole gently increased his embrace and quickly regretted it as that butterfly fluttered away, while Ariel was suddenly awake.

Lifting her head, she turned and looked at him through sleepy eyes.

Cole's heartbeat quickened to the picture she presented—complete innocence wrapped in female sexuality. *Damn.* He wanted to kiss her so badly he was barely able to control himself. "Morning."

Ariel blinked the sleep out of her eyes, then looked over her shoulder at the quickly dawning day. In the tropics, the sun shot up just as fast as it appeared to fall down. Muttering something beneath her breath, she turned back to him. "It is, isn't it?"

Before Cole could respond, Ariel had already grabbed the script and was on her feet, offering him her free hand.

He arched one brow.

She smiled. "Don't tell me your legs and back don't hurt."

Okay, so he wouldn't tell her that since his legs and back were currently numb. Not that he was going to admit to that either.

Gritting his teeth, Cole pushed to a standing position and was forced to lock his knees to keep from falling over. Keeping that pain out of his voice, he said, "I'm fine."

"I'm amazed."

He paused to swallow. "Why?"

"Well, you are in your thirties and—"

"You'll be there in three years, so be nice."

Ariel arched one slender brow. "Sure you want that?"

Cole smiled. "Well, I don't know." He wanted to move closer, actually right into her, but the pins and needles in his legs wouldn't allow it. Keeping *that* pain out of his voice, he asked, "What else do you have to offer?"

Now she smiled. "Escape."

Uh-huh. "From what?"

She lifted the battered script in her hand. "The bad guys. Time to go into the rain forest so we can't be found by them, after which we'll have to see to getting water, food, building a shelter, making a fire, tending to—"

"Right now, I'd settle for a shower and shave."

Ariel gave him a poor-baby look, then reached out and cradled the side of his face in her free hand. Drawing her thumb across his bristly cheek, she murmured, "That comes later."

"I don't think I can wait three days for—"

"You don't have to," she interrupted, then gently stroked his cheek once more before bringing back her hand. "You can easily keep clean without the modern conveniences, even without water. Yes, you can," she said to his expression, then pointed to his wrinkled shirt and slacks. "Take what you're wearing, for example. That can be cleaned by shaking it out, then letting it set in the sun for a couple of hours."

"Well, if my nudity doesn't bother you, then—"

"I'm giving you an example, not license."

"Why am I not surprised?"

"Really," she said, getting serious, "it won't be that bad. You can keep your clothing clean the way I just said, until we reach a creek or a waterfall, and you can substitute a twig for a toothbrush. All you have to do is chew the end until the fibers separate, then use wood ashes—from a fire—as toothpaste, or a bit of sand from the beach, and *griseb* leaves can easily be used as a substitute for deodorant."

Cole pressed his fingers to his throbbing temple, until he felt something odd there. Pulling it off, he dropped the damp leaf to the forest floor.

"It won't be that bad," Ariel repeated in a voice that was all patience. "Everything you need is right here."

Cole looked at her. A thread of sunlight spilled across her hair, intensifying the red and gold. He recalled how she had looked when asleep with that butterfly on her knee.

Everything you need is right here.

He slowly nodded. "I couldn't agree more."

He's doing it again, Ariel thought, and she had absolutely no protection from his expression or his words. Despite the obvious pain he was feeling, despite the obvious hardships he would face, the man still desired her.

God, but that felt good and made her want him all the more. Only not here, not now. They had his movie to think of, his future to assure. Taking his hand, Ariel said, "Come on, time to escape."

"No." He held back.

Ariel looked over her shoulder at him. "Cole, we simply can't stay here, especially not to make love. The compound's not that far away, and if we want to really be alone, we'll have to go into the rain forest—or rather, through it—until we reach the savanna and—"

"Yeah, I know, I know—but I can't."

She stared at him.

"I can't feel my legs yet," he finally admitted. "If I move, I might fall over."

Oh . . . *oh.* "You poor thing."

He rolled his eyes, then made his voice hard. "Just give me a minute, okay?" Pulling his hand from hers, he gritted his teeth, then walked like Frankenstein towards a coconut palm. "I'll just lean against this trunk until—"

"No," she quickly warned, "you can't. Have you forgotten about the ticks?"

Cole groaned to a stop, then lowered his head and breathed hard. "Tell you what, it's either the tree and ticks or I fall on the ground."

"You don't have to do either. Lean against me." Ariel was

at his side in a moment. After putting his arm around her shoulder, she wrapped her arm around his waist. "Better?"

Cole looked at her. "You really need an answer to that?"

She smiled, then smacked his flat belly with the script.

"Damn," he complained, then frowned to where she had smacked him. "Why are you hitting me on the only spot that still has feeling?"

"It's not the only spot, believe me."

Cole looked farther, then grinned at his erection tenting the soft fabric of his shorts and slacks.

Men. Ariel pulled her gaze from that lovely display and glanced to the right, then to the left.

"Looking for bad guys," Cole asked, "or an out?"

"Neither. I'm looking for *patza.*"

He was momentarily silent. "Boobala's boyfriend?"

Ariel laughed. "No. It's a plant that repels ticks, remember?"

"Sure."

Liar, she thought, but didn't mind. His teasing, his closeness, his continuing desire for her, and his utter masculinity made up for what she now knew was his lack of attention during her survival lectures.

At last, Ariel saw what she needed within all the other vegetation, then looked over her shoulder at him. "Can you stand by yourself yet?"

"Since I was ten months old."

"Aren't you amazing?"

He quietly regarded her. "You really think so?"

Oh, yes. She knew so. "Absolutely."

Cole's expression changed. There was pride in his eyes, coupled with a whole lot of unmet need.

Before things got too out of hand, Ariel eased away to attend to business. "Don't move," she ordered.

Cole sighed. "Who says I can?"

She gave him a soft smile, then slapped the script against his belly. "Please hold this." Before he could comment, Ariel moved through the other vegetation to the *patza* plant. As she studied its leaves, she shouted, "You okay?"

Cole answered in a shout. "Ask me that when I'm thirty-four!"

Ariel started to nod, but stopped, then looked over her shoulder at him.

Cole lifted his gaze from her butt to her eyes. "What?"

She wasn't certain how to answer. *Thirty-four*, he had said. As if she'd still be in his life when that birthday rolled around, perhaps as much as a year from now.

Don't be a fool, she quickly warned herself. *Don't read anything into this. He probably doesn't even realize what he said.*

Ariel studied his face just to be sure. Her shoulders sagged to that clueless expression.

"*What?*" he asked again.

"Nothing," she said, then returned to the task at hand.

When she had several of the plant's large, heart-shaped leaves, Ariel returned to him. "Take off your shirt."

Cole stared at the leaves, then lifted his gaze to hers. "I don't care what the script says; I'm not wearing that."

She smiled. "Of course you're not. That would be stupid."

He looked relieved.

"I'm going to rub this on you."

Just like that his relief vanished, and his brows arched. "Why?"

"As a tick repellent." God, he really wasn't paying attention. "Remember what I said about—"

"Sure." He was obviously lying, and his voice sounded really skeptical, but he finally placed the script on a rock and removed his shirt.

As he looked for a place to lay it, Ariel allowed her gaze to drift down his broad, muscular chest, those short, lusciously dark hairs. She moistened her lips. God, he was gorgeous, and probably watching her.

With her tongue still stroking her lips, she looked up.

Cole lifted his brows as if to say *well, well, well.*

Ariel pulled in her tongue. "Don't move."

"Who says I can?"

Uh-huh. There was one part of him that was having absolutely no problem.

Suppressing a smile, and the urge to stare at the outline of his stiffened shaft, Ariel moved directly in front of him and gently drew one of those leaves across his chest.

His pecs danced, while his taut belly trembled to his sharp intake of breath.

She murmured, "And here I thought you couldn't move."

Cole cleared his throat, but his voice was still husky as hell. "It's the plant. It's a miracle."

Ariel laughed. "This is for ticks!"

"Whatever. Don't stop."

She wasn't about to. With great deliberation and exceeding care, Ariel drew that plant across his shoulders, then moved lower.

Cole's knees briefly sagged. When she started using both hands, he nearly moaned. *God, God, God.* While her right hand stroked those dark hairs on his chest, her other hand repeatedly rubbed that leaf near his right rib cage as if she had forgotten it.

Not that Cole minded. He was far too engaged in watching the morning breeze stir her long hair. During this, her forefinger finally neared that scar below his shoulder. She gently circled it, as if she feared it might still hurt.

Sweet Jesus. It took every bit of Cole's will not to haul her into his arms and enjoy her right here, right now, and for the rest of this—

Her soft voice interrupted his thoughts. "How did this happen?"

Taking a deep, steadying breath, Cole looked down at his scar. "I was riding my bike one day to school and—"

"Liar," she said, but her voice remained soft.

Cole's gaze lifted to her incredible eyes. So clear and cool, while her tawny skin spoke of softness and heat. "You don't believe I ever rode a—"

"Did you get that during one of your Marine operations?"

He finally nodded.

Ariel looked so completely worried that Cole was sorry he had told her the truth.

Lowering her gaze to the scar, she gently stroked that uneven skin with her fingertip. "It must have caused you a lot of pain."

"Not at all. Really," he said as she looked up at him. "At least, not at first. I didn't even know I had been hit until one of my buddies pointed it out to me."

She rested her palm on it.

Cole felt that heat clear to his scalp.

"Were you afraid?" she asked, then quickly added, "Have you been afraid very often during your operations?"

"All the time. To be honest, fear's what keeps you alive."

Ariel regarded him with an expression that was troubled and sad.

"It wasn't that awful," Cole said.

"Yes, it was. But you don't have to be afraid anymore." Lowering her head, she gently kissed his scar.

Her lips were so warm and moist, her tongue so unbelievably hot as she licked that uneven skin, that Cole was quickly dizzy. Never had he been so moved by a woman or as aroused. And if he didn't do something about it soon, well, God, he just didn't know what might happen. "Ariel, *please.*"

She paused, as if suddenly realizing what she was doing. Pulling in her tongue, she straightened and quickly rubbed those leaves all over his chest and arms.

Before Cole could even think of protesting, she said, "Turn around."

He didn't budge. "Why?"

"I need to rub this on your back."

"When you're finished, do I get to do you?"

"I'm not going to be leaning against any trees or—"

"You're not going to be licking my chest again, either," he said, "if you don't intend to go through with everything else that we both want."

Heat rose to Ariel's throat and cheeks. Never in her life had she acted with a man as she was acting with Cole. Hot one minute, cool the next. It just wasn't like her to play games. And she wasn't. She was protecting her heart—not that he knew that.

Inhaling deeply, she looked up at him and made her voice as sincere as she could. "I won't lick your chest again, all right?"

He frowned as if that was not the answer he wanted or expected. "No, it's not all right."

Ariel released the leaves. As they fluttered to the forest floor, she said, "We should get going."

"Where?" he asked. "To do what exactly?"

Ignoring his tone, Ariel remained calm as she took his script off the rock, then lifted it in her hand. "Into the rain forest to enact and research your story."

"Script or screenplay," he corrected, "not story. Aren't you paying attention?"

She was now. "Whatever, okay? We need to get on with this."

He moved closer. "My thoughts exactly. So when are we getting on with what we both want? Exactly when? And don't give me that later nonsense," he said, speaking above her.

"Nonsense?" she asked.

"Ariel, don't play games with me."

Her heart caught. She softened her voice. "I'm not. I wouldn't."

Cole continued to regard her.

Ariel sighed. "I want to make love with you. You know I want to."

"So what's stopping you?"

She glanced at their surroundings, then looked back to him as if to say *this*. Hadn't she already told him that any number of times?

Didn't matter. He was still frowning.

"You're going to make us wait until this research is over?" he asked. "You're going to make us wait three whole days and nights before—"

"Two," she corrected. "We've already been through our first—"

"And I told you I'd stay longer if we needed that."

He had, but even longer would eventually come to an end. Suppressing a sigh, Ariel said the only thing she could. "We need to wait until the time is right. That time's not now. We have work to do, Cole. It's not just your reputation on the line with this movie; it's mine, too."

"Agreed," he said. "But that still doesn't answer when the time will be right for us. You and me."

"When we find the appropriate location." She rested her free hand on his chest. "One that's safe. Protected."

Cole glanced down at her fingers curled within his chest hair. "Protected from what?"

Ariel wasn't about to say. He'd find out soon enough. "Please just trust me on this. The moment we have shelter, water, food, a fire—"

"Good God, we have to go through all of—"

She spoke above him. "Do you want to be interrupted? Do you want to be *stopped* while we're making love?"

Cole finally paused, then shook his head.

"Okay, then," she said, pulling back her hand. "When we have what we need, then—"

"We'll have that tonight," he promised.

The conviction in his voice, his commanding tone, made Ariel's skin tingle. "Then we better get started," she said, and softened her voice even more. "Can you move yet?"

Cole gave her a look, then finished pulling on his shirt. "Given how you were licking me, I might need another moment or two before I'm completely ambulatory."

She smiled. "You have one second. Then I suggest you follow me into the secondary jungle, then to the rain forest where we need to go to escape the bad guys." Before Cole could comment or protest, she lifted the script. "It says so right here."

"Screw the damned story," he said.

"Script or screenplay," Ariel corrected.

"Whatever," he quipped, parroting her, then quickly added, "Before we go, I really do need a few minutes alone."

Ariel nodded quickly. Of course he did. *What is the matter with you?* she chided herself. She had to stop thinking like an expert in survival tactics and start thinking like a woman. "Me, too. Be careful, okay?"

"Don't you worry. Nothing's keeping me from tonight."

Ariel nodded.

As Cole stomped through the vegetation to the left, she moved to the right. When she was hidden within a small clearing bordered by coconut palms, banana plants, ferns, and a riot of other vegetation, she glanced over her shoulder to see that Cole was nowhere in sight.

That could be a bad thing or a good thing.

For the moment, Ariel settled for the latter as she laid the script on the forest floor. As quickly as she could, she pulled off her top and pants, then vigorously shook them in the fresh morning air, at last hanging them over a low branch that was drenched in sun. While those rays freshened her duds still further, she used the ample dew from several large banana leaves as a makeshift sponge bath that was surprisingly effective and refreshing. Next, she picked flower after flower, then rubbed their sweet fragrance over herself despite the fact that it would probably attract insects.

Of course, right now she would risk that in the hopes of attracting Cole.

Glancing over her shoulder, Ariel still didn't see him.

Don't you worry, he had said. *Nothing's keeping me from tonight.*

Ariel believed him. She figured not even real insurgents with atomic bombs would keep him from her side once the sun was down.

Tingling with excitement, she dressed quickly, ran her fingers through her hair until it was tame enough to drape over her shoulders, grabbed the script, then hurried back to where she had left him.

Given Cole's loud swearing and the sound of rustling leaves, he wasn't finding the accommodations as adequate as she had. And here he was an ex-Marine.

Of course, he was now used to the good life in Hollywood, where he'd be returning in just a few days.

Don't go there, she warned herself and did not. She was going to enjoy the time they had, just as soon as they got through the bulk of this research.

Thinking of that, she roamed this area, looking for stuff they would need. By the time Ariel returned, so had Cole.

His hair was finger combed as hers was, several drops of dew still lingered on his bristly cheeks, and a banana leaf was peeking out from beneath his shirt.

"You look nice," she said.

Cole looked to where she was and seemed surprised that she had been staring at that banana leaf, not his groin. Muttering an oath, he pulled the leaf out, then looked at the two bamboo sticks she was holding, one of which she was trying to give him.

"Go on," she said, "this one's yours."

"And here I expected flowers."

"That'll be next time."

He arched one brow, then sniffed. "Is that you?"

Maybe. "Does it smell nice?"

"Very."

"Then it's me," she said.

He smiled, then groaned when she insisted he take the bamboo. "Please don't tell me we're going to rub these two sticks together to make a fire?"

She smiled. "We're not. We're going to use these to push branches aside. Don't touch anything."

He stopped swinging the stick like a sword and looked at her.

"Don't touch anything in the forest," she amended. "Otherwise you could get bitten by an insect or an animal. That would really screw up our plans for—"

"I won't touch anything but you," he promised, then smiled. "Do you bite?"

Her nostrils briefly flared. "If I'm provoked."

"Well, hell, I can't wait."

And she could? "Then you better pay attention."

Cole lifted his gaze from her breasts to her eyes. "Yes, ma'am."

Hmmm. "When you're following me in the forest," she said, "don't look at me."

His gaze swept her again. "Is that your rule or the forest's rule?"

"It's a survival tactic," she said as she struggled not to smile. "You need to pick out a point in the distance—a tree, a group of leaves, something—so long as it's stationary. That will help you maintain a field bearing that keeps your direction true. And I know, I know," she said before he could, "guys never ask for directions, so you don't have to say it."

"I wasn't planning to . . . Have the other guys you've taught said that?"

Every last one of them. Not that Ariel could recall the face or voice of any of them now. Cole, on the other hand, actually looked a bit jealous, as if he didn't enjoy picturing her out here with anyone else.

"Some did," she said.

His expression darkened a bit more. "And what did you tell them?"

Ariel hardly recalled, and told him that.

His mood lightened considerably. "Now about our direction—which way do we go?"

"South."

He nodded agreeably, then glanced around.

"Are you planning to use shadows to determine our direction?" she asked.

"Yup."

"Think we have time for the shadow-tip method?"

Cole looked at her.

"Using your watch would be faster," she said. "All you have to do is—"

"Hold it horizontally," he interrupted, "and point the hour hand at the sun. After that, I halve the angle between my hour hand and the number twelve to get my north-south line."

Ariel's eyes continued to widen. Shoving the script under her left arm, she clapped vigorously. "Very good. You were listening."

"Yes, ma'am."

Ariel smiled. God, she loved it when he used his Marine voice. "Okay," she said, "which way is south?"

Using his watch and the sun, Cole quickly figured it out and inclined his head in that direction.

"Yes!" she said, bouncing on her heels, then quickly stopped. "Of course, using your watch will present a problem once we're actually within the vegetation. Do you know why?"

He shrugged. "One of the monkeys will want it because it's shiny?"

She laughed. "No, of course not!" She sobered once more. "We won't have a clear view of the sun because of the canopy. The watch method, and surely the shadow-tip method, will be useless in there. So, what do we—"

Even before she had finished, Cole was rattling off statistics about moss, growth patterns, trees, what to expect in the Northern Hemisphere and then the Southern Hemisphere so that nature could be used as a guide to determine direction, and by God he was simply flooring her.

"So," he finally concluded, "that's what we look for." He paused briefly. "Are you about to faint?"

"Keep that up and I might."

He grinned. "You ain't seen nothing yet, hon."

Ariel believed him. She ordered herself to calm down before she lost all control and threw herself at him. "I think we're ready to go."

"Whatever it takes to get to tonight," he said, then swung his arm to the side. "Lead the way."

She gave him a sweet smile as she passed, then stopped, backed up, and planted one right on his mouth.

Cole's nostrils were still flared as he opened his eyes. "What was that for?"

"Luck."

"Do I need it?"

She smiled. "Not with me." Her gaze drifted to the forest. "But in there?"

"I'll be fine."

Ariel believed him. But she wanted to be sure. Sobering quickly, she said, "Remember to keep your direction true by picking out a landmark like I said before. And not the trees or vegetation directly in front of you—you need to look farther out—find breaks in the foliage. Once you reach that first landmark, choose another in the distance, and another, and another until we reach an area where we can stop for water, food, shelter—"

"Each other," he interjected.

Oh, yes. She smiled. "Are you ready, Cole?"

"Do you even have to ask?"

Ariel's face flushed with desire. Turning, she went deeper into the vegetation.

Cole followed. Hell, after her vigorous applause and the tender kiss she just gave him, he wasn't about to let her out of his sight or reach.

Besides, this wasn't all that bad. The air was sweetly scented, and the plant life was simply amazing. There were massive trees that were probably hundreds of years old and very young ones that were struggling to survive; there were countless ferns and plants of a type Cole had never seen before; there were several variations of palms; and then there was that sole damp leaf stuck to Ariel's butt.

You need to pick out a point in the distance, she had said, *a tree, a group of leaves, something—so long as it's stationary. That will give you a field bearing that keeps your direction true.*

Okay, so he was a bad boy and not following her directives. Who could blame him with those sweet little cheeks bouncing up and down in front of him, while that leaf was suddenly holding on for dear life as Ariel abruptly stopped.

When Cole lifted his gaze, she was already looking over her shoulder at him.

"You are paying attention, right?" she asked.

"Like I've never done before in my entire life."

Her glee from before was gone. She looked really skeptical now, but nodded slowly, then turned and headed deeper into the vegetation.

And Cole followed, his gaze again riveted to that leaf on her outstanding butt.

Trouble was, Ariel suddenly seemed determined to shed herself of it and him. Her pace had really picked up, she was weaving this way and that, and just as Cole predicted that leaf fell to the forest floor.

Bad girl, he thought, but didn't actually mind since she'd have to do far more than that to lose him. In the deepening green of this forest, her hair was as obvious as a lingering sunset. Inhaling deeply to its beauty, Cole caught the scent of fresh earth, flowers, and ripening fruit as he imagined her wearing nothing but that glorious hair—and those twinkling stars dangling from her navel—as she faced him tonight. He could almost see her rosy nipples, all hard and aroused, peeking through those thick, shiny waves. He thought of her other hair then and wondered once more if it was auburn.

A man could hope.

A man could dream, and by God, Cole did just that as he imagined Ariel lying in his arms, fully nude, fully vulnerable. Her legs would be parted, those hidden lips plump and slick inviting him to taste her sweetness, to linger.

He would. No way would he rush their pleasure. He would

stroke her heated, satiny flesh, licking every bit of it before unfolding his length over hers. And then he would enter her fully, deeply, filling her in an act that was as primitive and as breathtaking as these surroundings.

Wildly colored birds continued to cry out overhead, and monkeys soon followed. Those shrieks grew excited, then frantic as the swishing leaves now rustled wildly to the right, and the left, and even from behind.

With that, Cole's erotic daydream evaporated. Glancing over his left shoulder, he saw nothing but a wall of green. Looking over his right shoulder, the very same scene greeted him. When he checked to see what might be lurking from behind, he was actually surprised that it looked the same as everything else.

This was really something, and definitely the kind of weird sensation he needed in his film.

Not that he was panicked. Oh, no. Feeling as if he had been swallowed up by this forest was just momentary. He'd get his bearings as soon as he went back to that erotic dream of himself and Ariel.

Determined to do just that, Cole brought his gaze back to the front and was greeted by yet another wall of green. Nothing but a solid fucking wall of green.

Holy shit.

He stopped dead and looked again to the left. Swallowing hard, he looked to the right. Warning himself to remain calm, Cole listened hard and heard nothing but his own heart beating out of control.

Where in the fuck is she? He had taken his gaze off her for only a second, and now she was nowhere to be—

"You really should pay attention," she suddenly said from behind.

Cole quickly turned around.

Despite the bamboo stick in one hand and the script in the other, Ariel's arms were crossed under her breasts and she was arching one slender brow as she regarded his panic.

Slowing his breathing, Cole forced his voice to be casual,

even bored, despite the fact that his heart was thudding out of control. "I *was* paying attention."

She leveled her gaze on him. "You were completely lost because you were paying attention to my butt."

"That I was," he admitted, "and with the same interest, I might add, that you used when you stared at my butt last night while we were in my room."

Her brow lowered. She sighed. "I don't want you to get hurt out here."

"I'm a big boy, Ariel."

She wasn't about to argue with that, so she used reason. "I'm trying to teach you something here. For your screenplay. So it'll be better than good; it'll be great. You deserve that. I want to give you that. Please indulge me."

"I'll behave," he promised, then quickly muttered, "at least until tonight."

Ariel warned herself not to comment on that. If she did, they'd never get through this and reach tonight. Whether she liked it or not—and he surely didn't—she had to teach him this junk so that he'd still be in one piece for tonight, at which time she would make love with him until he was so damned breathless, she'd have to give him CPR, which would lead to even more lovemaking.

Thinking of that, Ariel uncrossed her arms and moved past him into the vegetation, even as she remained intensely aware of the sounds coming from behind.

Now, as before, Cole was stomping on vegetation and breaking twigs, branches, and what-not as he followed.

At least she hadn't lost him. She felt buoyed by that until minutes later when a noisy macaw drowned out the noise Cole was making.

Slowing her pace, Ariel finally came to a stop and glanced over her shoulder to see that he was still just a few yards behind her, apparently behaving himself.

"What?" he asked.

Given his mussed hair, his beginning beard, his rumpled

clothes, and the way he was using the bamboo for support as if it were a cane, Ariel couldn't help but tease. "You're actually paying attention."

He arched one brow. "It wouldn't be right if I left you out here all alone, now, would it?"

She smiled. "How sweet of you, but I can take care of myself, and you, and everyone else."

"So you keep saying and saying and saying."

Her smile paused at that unexpected response. One a kick-ass Marine Force Recon dude might use. "That's because I can."

"Uh-huh."

She frowned. "You sound as if you doubt that. You couldn't really doubt that."

"Let's just say I'm not leaving you out of my sight."

"Don't worry, I won't let you get lost, again."

He looked quickly offended. "I wasn't lost, okay?"

"If you say so."

"Maybe I should lead the way."

She laughed.

He did not.

Ariel sobered. "Look, I know this island far better than you and—"

"If you're afraid you can't keep up with me," he said, "it's all right to admit it."

Huh? "Keep up with *you?* I was just about to ask you to hurry it up a bit so *I* wouldn't have to slow down."

"You don't think I can keep up with you?"

"You haven't proven to me, as yet, that you can. But what does it matter? If I were to really hit my stride, you'd never be able to catch me."

"Wanna bet?"

Ariel heard the challenge in his voice and saw the look in his eyes. Gone was the polite officer and gentleman; gone was the man who had acquiesced to a lot of her ideas and plans. In his place was an ex-Marine who wasn't taking that crap anymore.

She saw it in his gaze. It was heated, male, focused, and like nothing Ariel had ever faced before.

Her skin tingled, and her heart raced. She knew any other woman would have started flirting or teasing, or might have even apologized, but she wasn't any other woman.

Arching one slender brow, Ariel turned and ran to see if he could keep up, if he could catch her.

It wouldn't be easy, but it wasn't impossible. The vegetation ahead was sparser, providing brief gaps between the trees. As she swatted the low-lying branches with the bamboo stick in one hand and the script in her other, she wove to the right, the left, then back again until she had proven her point, since he obviously hadn't caught her.

Could be he was lost again and she'd have to save him.

Ariel really didn't mind. Once she found him, she'd finally apologize.

Pausing at last, she bent at the waist, sucked air, then looked over her shoulder to see that she hadn't gone all that far, and that Cole hadn't moved.

Ariel straightened, then stared as he suddenly bolted toward her.

Oh, my God. During that first second she couldn't move; during the next she really tried. Never in her life had Ariel run as fast as she did now, and she knew it wasn't going to do her one bit of good.

Cole was larger, faster, and freaking determined.

She heard him moving through the vegetation like males had since the dawn of time as they pursued females. She heard him closing the gap between them; she heard the pounding of her own heart and her ragged breaths.

I give, I give, I give, her mind cried as she waited for him to grab her, hoping that he'd kiss her, but oddly enough that didn't happen.

At last, her pace slowed, then stopped. She couldn't go another step. Breathing hard, Ariel looked over her shoulder and paused.

Her gaze darted to the right, the left. She stepped forward and squinted as she searched the vegetation, but it was empty of Cole.

Oh, my God, she thought. She'd lost him again, maybe for good this time.

What in the world were you thinking? she chided herself as she looked and looked and looked. *How could you have been so foolish?*

Where is he?

She again looked to the left, to the right, in front of herself, and behind. Bouncing on her heels, Ariel held back panic, then turned once more and gasped.

Cole's hands were planted on his lean hips, and he wasn't breathing all that hard. "Looks like I caught you. So what do I get?"

She wanted to punch him for worrying her. She wanted to scream at him for worrying her.

Dropping the bamboo and the script, Ariel finally moved into him and said, "What do you want?"

Cole's lips turned up in a smile. Slipping his arm around her waist, he hauled her close. "You, right where you are now. Don't you dare move."

Ariel swallowed. He was fully erect and pressing his hips into hers so she damn well knew it. He was arrogant in his success and every bit a male. Desire so quickly flooded through her, Ariel wasn't all that certain she could remain standing. Slipping her arms over his shoulders, she asked, "Are you threatening me?"

"I'm explaining the rules of engagement."

Now, that sounded nice. As Ariel pressed her body even closer to his, as she drove her fingers into his thick, silky hair, she made her own demand. "Make it fast, I'm tired of waiting."

Cole's voice was husky and low. "Yes, ma'am."

With that, his mouth was on hers, his kiss savage, demanding, unrestrained.

As he took what he wanted, he demanded still more. With

one hand cupping her buttocks he pulled her into his thickened rod, while his other hand slipped under her top and bra to cup her right breast.

Ariel moaned, but it was lost as Cole deepened the kiss, not allowing her any sound or escape.

He worked her until she yielded fully; he demanded until she was completely his.

In that moment, his kiss turned tender, and she folded herself into him, making everything else go away.

As they kissed softly, then hard, then softly once more, Cole was barely aware of this world that surrounded them.

In a part of his mind that hardly mattered he heard the always-noisy macaws, chattering monkeys, and finally the wind whispering past the tops of the trees.

It was nothing to compare with Ariel's soft moans, which he again silenced with his tongue.

At last, though, there was another sound, a persistent sound that was vaguely familiar, but which he couldn't quite place.

It was as if something were slapping the air.

And then he had it. It was the *whap-whap-whap* of copter blades.

Pulling his mouth from Ariel's, Cole glanced up to a break in the trees, then looked right back down as she finally stepped away from him and waved to the copter that was now flying overhead.

"Who is that?" he shouted above the noise.

She shouted back, "Uncle Thaddeus."

Cole looked at her.

She lowered her gaze to his and shouted, "Like I said before, we need a place to make love that's safe *and* protected, because my uncle worries about me, you know?"

Chapter Nine

If Cole hadn't known that about her uncle before, he sure as hell knew it now. Man, the old guy wasn't kidding when he said he didn't want her seduced, romanced, led on, aroused, or touched in any way.

Ariel, on the other hand, appeared to be taking that worry in stride as she continued to smile and wave at the copter, as if she wanted to be absolutely certain Thaddeus saw them.

Whether the old guy witnessed any of their action was up for debate as the copter finally flew away.

At just that moment Cole's cell phone rang—from the inside of Ariel's pocket.

Her expression got kind of sheepish. "You really shouldn't sleep so soundly in a forest, you know that, right?"

"I do now." He stepped closer. "Besides taking my phone, what else did you do to me while I was asleep?"

Those honeyed cheeks really pinked up, but she lifted her forefinger as if to say *just a sec* or *screw you, I'm not telling*.

Bringing the phone to her ear, Ariel listened for a moment, then spoke above the waning noise of the copter. "Yes, Uncle Thaddeus, we're fine." Looking at Cole, she arched both brows.

He pressed his thumb and forefinger to the inside corners of his eyes.

Ariel listened for another moment, then said, "No, Uncle

Thaddeus, Cole hasn't crossed any line. Actually, when he woke up this morning, he couldn't even walk for the first few minutes."

Cole dropped his hand and glared at her.

Ariel blew him a kiss, then shook her head as she listened to Thaddeus. "No—that's not what happened. I swear, I did not harm him in any way. He's been a perfect gentleman. What?" She listened again.

Cole had to wonder what the old guy was saying, given that a deep blush was now staining her chest, throat, and cheeks.

"No," she insisted, then paused to clear her throat. "I was just helping him stand up. I told you he couldn't walk at first, and his legs still aren't working as well as they should. He's not used to sleeping out in the open anymore. He hasn't been a Marine in a really long time. He's gotten as soft and as out of shape as the useless politician he's using as a hero in the story. That guy's going to be injured early on, so Cole was kind of enacting all of that with his bum legs and—"

She paused as Cole loudly cleared his throat.

Flicking her gaze to him, Ariel nodded to whatever her uncle was saying, then finally shrugged. "Sure. Okay." Taking the phone from her ear, she offered it to Cole. "He wants to speak to you."

Cole shook his head as he mouthed *no, no, NO.*

Ariel pressed the phone to her chest so Thaddeus couldn't overhear. "He wants to know why your arms were around me as the copter flew overhead. You heard what I told him; now he wants to hear it from you. So here." She shoved the phone at him.

Jesus, Cole thought. The last time he had to explain his romantic activities to an older man was after his junior prom when he and his date necked up a storm on the front porch of her parent's house. Sighing deeply, Cole finally brought the phone to his ear. "Yes, sir."

"What took you so long?" Thaddeus hollered above the noise of the copter. "What are you doing?"

"Talking to you, sir."

"I know that. And you know that. So, don't pretend you don't know what I'm talking about, young man. Now, what were you doing that took you so long to get on this phone?"

Cole lied quickly and effortlessly. "I had a cramp in my leg, sir." His gaze slid to Ariel. She was smiling at his still-hardened cock. "I had to wait until the pain went away, which hasn't really happened yet."

Her cheeks colored. She looked at him.

"You sound as if you're in terrible shape," Thaddeus shouted.

The old guy had no idea. "I'll be fine, sir."

"Well, that remains to be seen."

"Yes—"

"Let's cut to the chase," Thaddeus interrupted in a shout. "Are you falling in love with my niece yet?"

Cole's heart so quickly paused to the question he felt the blood drain from his face.

Ariel stepped toward him and mouthed *what?*

He slowly shook his head. "I'm sorry," he said to Thaddeus, "but there's so much noise I can barely hear what you're—"

"Nonsense," the old guy interrupted, "I can clearly hear you, and I expect an answer."

Cole's heart started thudding.

Ariel mouthed *WHAT?*

His gaze fell to her lips caressing that word. He thought of those lips only a few minutes before when they had been caressing his tongue. He recalled her slender fingers curled into loose fists as they protected her heart, and her worry when she saw his scar, then her promise that he didn't have to be afraid anymore. He remembered her laughter as they argued over his story and her not-so-patient sighs when he was being less than attentive to her survival plans.

Are you falling in love with my niece yet?

Turning his back to her, Cole lowered his voice so she

couldn't overhear. "With all due respect, sir, that is something I would discuss with her, not you."

Whether Thaddeus liked that answer or not, Cole had no idea. Suddenly, there was only copter noise on the other end of this call. Cole was about to end it when Thaddeus suddenly shouted, "Are you still there, young man?"

Cole debated whether to make static sounds, as if they were being cut off, but figured Thaddeus would just keep shouting until the line was clear. "Yes, sir."

"Then please put my niece back on."

Cole wanted to ask why, but didn't dare. "Yes, sir." Turning, he handed her the phone. "For you."

Ariel was reluctant to take the call. What in the world had her uncle said to Cole to make his hand shake so badly, and to get him to look at her as he was doing right now.

It was as if Cole were seeing her for the very first time and discovering something he had missed before. Something that made him look kind of awed, confused, and really scared.

Taking the phone, Ariel turned her back to him and said, "Yes?"

"I like that young man," Thaddeus shouted. "You treat him well, understand?"

Before Ariel could say that she would, Thaddeus added, "I won't be bothering you two again, there's no need. Isa and I are going to that casino you suggested. Say hello, Isa."

She yelled, *"Can you hear me?"*

God. Ariel pulled the phone away from her ear, then brought it right back. "Yes. Hi."

"You have fun! We sure are!"

As Isa giggled, Thaddeus came back on the line. "If I lose the villa at the blackjack table, it's all your fault for suggesting this. I want you to know that. Bye." With that, he ended the call.

"Ah . . . okay," Ariel said to dead air, then closed the phone and looked over her shoulder at Cole.

He was still regarding her.

I like that young man, her uncle had said, *you treat him well, understand?*

Actually, Ariel didn't understand any of this. What had Cole said to her uncle to make the older man suddenly like him, and to offer a promise not to bother them again? Slipping the phone into her pocket, Ariel paused, then pulled it back out and offered it to Cole.

His gaze remained on her as he took it. "Thanks."

"Sure—you okay?"

He nodded cautiously. "Why?"

"Your hand's really shaking."

He seemed surprised when he looked at it, then shoved it and the phone into his pocket.

Ariel cleared her throat to break the tension. "I guess we should get back to enacting out the story, huh?"

He nodded.

Ariel waited for him to tease her about it, or make a comment about tonight, the pleasure that was coming, but Cole did not. Instead, he continued to quietly regard her.

"You sure you're all right?"

He looked uncertain, but still nodded.

Ariel wanted to press for more, but figured she'd better not. Picking up the script and the bamboo sticks, she handed one to Cole.

"Thanks."

"Sure . . . guess we should get started."

Once more, he nodded.

During the next forty-five minutes they moved in silence through the vegetation with Ariel in the lead and Cole bringing up the rear.

More than once she glanced over her shoulder at him. Each time her expression asked *you okay?*

Each time Cole's response was to avoid an answer, because he honestly didn't know.

Physically he knew he should be tired, hungry, and thirsty,

given this trek and the increasing temperature, only he wasn't feeling any of that.

Mentally, though, he was fucking exhausted because his thoughts kept going round and round before endlessly returning to Thaddeus's words.

Are you falling in love with my niece yet?

Never in all of his days had Cole been asked such a question by a woman's relative. Never in all of his days did he reflect on the answer as much as he continued to do now.

Hell, he had just met her. They barely knew each other, and yet Cole was absolutely certain he could pick Ariel's laughter out of a crowd of a hundred other women—no, a thousand. He would recognize her scent and walk and coloring in an instant. She was embedded in his memories as if they had shared a lifetime together, not just a few days.

Already, she was taking care of him as a wife might, right down to keeping him on his feet when his legs went numb and rubbing leaf juice on him to keep the bugs at bay. If she was that good at it when he was only thirty-three, she'd be a real whiz after several decades of practice.

Cole expected to be disturbed by that prospect, but was only disturbed because he wasn't.

You're losing your fucking mind.

Not that it mattered, because Ariel would probably tend to that, too.

Already, she worried over him.

You don't have to be afraid anymore, she had said.

Tell that to his trembling hands and shaky knees, because something was definitely happening here. Try as he might, Cole couldn't recall what the world had been like before he met Ariel. Nor could he recall another female having such a quick impact on him, not even the one who took his virginity and started him on the road to being a man.

That girl had really been something. Her dad was a Marine, which had gotten Cole interested in the military life. Her dad was also super strict, but that girl had been absent without leave during all of those fatherly lectures.

She wore the modest clothes he liked, of course, but absolutely no underwear, which would have given the poor man a stroke if he had known. She did her homework, got straight A's, sang in the choir, and was more uninhibited than a porn star once she was away from his watchful gaze.

That girl pursued sex with Cole as if he were her personal challenge.

At first, she kind of scared him.

After he got over that, they did it everywhere that two kids without driver's licenses and good sense possibly could.

In the rosy aftermath, Cole actually thought he was in love, too young to realize it was gratitude and lingering lust he was feeling.

Now?

As he continued to follow Ariel through the vegetation, he thought about the marriages of the people he knew in LA and those he left behind when he separated from the Marines.

Whether those couples were screaming at each other on a military base or in a mega-mansion, all that yelling was basically the same, as were the breakups.

So far, Cole and all of his brothers had avoided that, since none of them had as yet walked down the aisle.

Until now, he hadn't really wondered why. Could be their parents' marriage was simply too much to live up to or to hope for.

Not that it was particularly exciting, even by a deadly dull midwestern standard.

His folks had met in Kansas during college when his mom was a nursing student and his dad a finance major. When the nursing school needed able-bodied students to pretend to be patients for one of the classes, his dad had signed up. He and Cole's mom had laughed themselves silly while she took his vitals, and never once did they look back.

Cole recalled his mom once telling her friend that she loved his dad because the man cared as much about her happiness as he did his own.

At the time, Cole hadn't understood a word of it. Now, though, he recalled Ariel's words.

Don't say it's stupid, please, she had asked when he had been dissing the script. *It's your future.*

This was true, but he had been all too casual in his response.

I'm trying to teach you something here, she had argued. *For your screenplay. So it'll be better than good; it'll be great. You deserve that. I want to give you that. Please indulge me.*

How could he refuse? She cared about it more than he did, because she honestly cared about him. Maybe she even loved him.

That stopped Cole dead, while his heart beat hard. Was it actually possible that she was falling in love with him . . . or was she just being nice?

"Cole?" Ariel suddenly called out, interrupting his thoughts.

He looked up to see she was nowhere in sight. *Damn, where'd she go?* Cole glanced over his shoulder to see if she was behind him now, like before, only she wasn't. Turning back, he saw she was yards away and coming toward him.

"Cole?" she said again.

"What?"

She stopped as if that question offended her. "What are you doing?"

Well, actually, he was recalling something about her he had forgotten. That look she gave him—a mother's look—when she thought he was being a naughty little boy or was acting totally clueless.

Maybe he should chase her through the forest again to show her exactly what he could do and precisely what he did know. Then again, maybe he should just play dumb. "Doing?" he asked in his most clueless voice.

Ariel frowned. "Why are you stopping? We only have a very short distance left."

"To what?"

Her frown deepened. "To where we're going, of course."

"Going?"

Her expression said he was either nuts or just being difficult, and then every muscle in her face quickly fell. "Please don't tell me you ate something while we've been walking."

She was back to being worried about him, obviously believing that he had gorged on something poisonous or hallucinogenic; unless she was simply concerned about their enactment of the script. "Why? Isn't it in the screen—"

"Did you?"

She so quickly ran toward him, Cole retreated a step before her stick impaled him. "No," he finally answered, then added, "You dropped the script back—"

"You're sure?"

"Yeah. I saw it fall into that pile of leaves back—"

"Are you sure you didn't eat anything?" She pressed her free hand against his chest as she stared at the corners of his mouth, looking for evidence.

"I think I'd remember if I had eaten some—what are you doing?"

"Feeling your forehead."

Well, hell, he knew that. "For what?"

"To see if you're hot."

Of course he was hot. He was in a tropical jungle for God's sake, and she was so close he could just about feel each worried breath she took.

"You're feeling all right?" she asked.

Cole's gaze lowered to her hand cupping his face, while the scant breeze brought her sweet fragrance to him. "Better than one might expect."

She nodded absently as she continued to study his eyes, possibly looking for some rare tropical illness that she had expertly avoided.

Cole wanted to sigh but didn't dare. Could be she'd misinterpret that for heart failure. "Do you worry this much about everyone you take through the forest?"

"No one else has gotten lost as much as you."

"I did *not* get lost."

Her brows lifted slightly. "Okay."

"No, it's not. Do you do this for all your clients?"

Ariel lowered her hand and retreated a step. "I wouldn't let anyone just die out here."

That was hardly the answer Cole had been looking for. He debated whether to pursue it, but figured he should quit while ahead. "That's good to know."

She nodded absently, then glanced over her shoulder to where she had dropped the script. "Are you really, really thirsty?"

No, he was moderately thirsty. Did she now think he had rabies? "If I say yes, are you going to make me stick out my tongue?"

She turned back to him. "Well, that would depend on where you want to put your tongue once it's out."

Cole was about to grin, but did not. Did she flirt with all of her clients this way? After all, she hadn't really answered him the last time he asked.

"I'll bet some water will perk you right up," she said.

Only if it's blasting from a shower head in a five-star hotel. "There's a creek up ahead?"

"Not exactly."

Uh-huh. "What exactly?"

Her lovely eyes lit up in excitement. Taking his free hand, Ariel led him through the vegetation. "I'll show you."

Given her glee, Cole wasn't about to hold back. Whatever they were hurrying toward had to be better than what they had just come through.

Maybe Thaddeus had built a second villa on this part of the island. Maybe Ariel was going to let them fudge on the rest of the script. Maybe he and she would spend the rest of today and tonight in a real bed and wake up to real food and real water being served by a really devoted staff.

A man could hope. A man could dream. At least until Ariel came to an abrupt halt.

"The script," she said, suddenly remembering it. "You stay here while I go back to get it. It'll only take a sec."

It took three and a half minutes.

As she came down the path waving it over her head, Cole shouted, "Thank God, I thought you were lost!"

Her laughter was lusty and didn't stop until she reached him.

"Here," she said, handing him those soggy and increasingly muddy pages.

Cole held the thing away from himself. "Do we really need this anymore? Don't you already know it by heart?"

"Only the parts I fixed. I did fax a copy to Gwen before we left the villa. I could call her when I forget—"

"That's okay. We'll keep this." He continued to hold it at arm's length.

"Just wave it in the air," Ariel advised, "once the mud dries it'll fall right off."

"Something to look forward to."

"Not like what's ahead. Come on."

As Cole followed her through the last of the vegetation, he waved the script to dry it out and twice dropped the damned thing.

He picked it up again and returned to her, at which point she suddenly stopped and inclined her head to the left. "Look."

Cole fingered sweat out of his eyes, then swung his gaze in that direction.

Ariel continued to bounce on her heels. "Nice, huh?"

For a wide expanse of grassy land that was lumpy from all those volcanic rocks and dotted with stunted trees roasting in the sun, yeah, it was really nice. "Uh-huh."

"And see," she said, then pointed, "over there are palms."

Cole took her at her word, since his attention had already been captured by something white glistening in the sun. *Are those bones?*

"It has exactly what we need," Ariel said, then dropped her stick. "Come on."

The only part of Cole that moved was his gaze as he lifted it to the sky, all that empty space that Thaddeus's helicopter could fly over. "We're not camping here, are we?" he asked, then quickly added the obvious, "It is kind of exposed."

"It's as safe as any other place now."

Now? Cole thought, then looked at her. "Why is that?"

She seemed reluctant to answer. At last, she said, "The bad guys in your story wouldn't think to come this far as yet. After all, if you're playing Henry, then you'd be a useless politician, and despite Mina's expertise, which is mine, the insurgents don't think much of females. I think we're safe here."

Only from each other, Cole thought, given that she was already putting distance between them as she actually jogged across the lumpy ground. He shouted, "Where are you going?"

Ariel stopped and turned to face him, presenting a picture that brought Cole to his knees, at least figuratively.

That amazing hair flamed red and gold in the unrestricted sun; loose tendrils danced around her face with the gentle breeze that pushed her thin top against those pebbled nipples.

"To those palms." She pointed.

Cole finally dragged his gaze from her breasts to those trees that in no way compared to the beauty of her soft, heated flesh and that simply breathtaking hair.

"You are thirsty, aren't you?" she asked.

Until she posed that question, Cole had actually been aroused. Now he was back to being thirsty and hungry and frustrated and fucking lonely.

As far as he was concerned, this was just too damned much reality. Hell, even during his Force Recon days he'd had emergency gear to fall back on. Never had he been forced to survive with nothing but his bare hands. He finally slogged across the lumpy ground toward her. "There's some kind of body of water around here?"

Ariel continued studying the ground in her immediate vicinity. After a moment, she moved to the right and hunkered down to pick up a stone. "Look at this." She lifted it for him to see.

Cole widened his eyes in appreciation, even though he hadn't a clue why she was so excited. The damn thing looked like a lot of the other rocks here—flat with sharp edges. Given its color it might have been coal or flint.

Good God, he suddenly thought, were they going to use that to make fire?

Running his tongue around his fuzzy mouth, he asked once more, "There's some kind of body of water around here?"

Ariel pushed to her feet, then brushed debris from the rock. "Creek's over there." She inclined her head to the left. "Waterfall's over there." She inclined her head in yet another direction. "Either of them will take another hour or so to get to. Even though my gal Mina wouldn't break a sweat during that kind of trek, your guy Henry wouldn't last ten minutes, which is why we're here. Thank goodness, too, given the problem you had earlier with your legs."

Cole lowered his head and breathed hard. "Ah, hon, I'm not really as unfit as Henry, all right?"

"I'm glad you're aware of that. You're not delirious yet. Good."

Cole lifted his head.

She smiled. "But you are thirsty, right?"

"In a minute or two I'll actually be frothing at the mouth. But," he interrupted her, "no matter how thirsty I am, you'd better not be telling me that you're going to hike an hour or so to a waterfall, fill up whatever it is you'll fill up with water, then haul that back here to me because you think I'm incapable of walk—are you laughing at me?"

"Sorry," she said, then continued.

Cole would have turned and left, if he could have recalled how to get back to the damned villa.

Ariel finally noticed his pissy mood and sobered. "Not only would my doing that be counterproductive, it's not necessary." Turning, she jogged to those palms she was so taken with, then lifted her head and studied something at the top.

Cole's gaze drifted down that glorious hair, the ends of which were pointing to her sweet little ass.

"Cole."

Suppressing a sigh, he looked up and was surprised by her smile. "Yeah?"

"Come here . . . please."

That word and her soft expression drew Cole to her faster than the lumpy ground allowed.

"Careful!" she said.

Cole straightened his twisted leg and pretended it didn't hurt as he continued to move toward her.

Ariel smiled, then looked up at that tree again.

Cole studied the faint vein throbbing at the base of her throat, at least until she moved from this tree to the next.

He wished to God she'd just stay still. Once his twisted knee stopped aching, Cole joined her at that tree, looked up, and didn't even see a damned coconut, which left only one other thing to quench their thirst. "Before you suggest we lick dew off those leaves, there are ones much closer to the ground on any number of plants. Better still," he quickly added, "shouldn't we just wait for the daily rainstorm to collect water?"

"During the dry season?" She continued to regard the top of that tree. "You do know that daily rainstorms are a tourist's myth, right?"

Cole wondered if she had told him that back at the villa. "Yeah . . . I just wasn't sure you knew that."

Ariel lifted her brows as she continued to stare at the tree. "I do now. Of course, at this time of year all we have to do is look at the sky to know rain isn't expected until the end of the week."

Cole raised his face to the cloudless sky that offered no clues about anything.

"It's a real shame, you know?"

She had lost him. "What's a real shame?"

"That we missed our chance to lick dew off the leaves this morning because you were taking so much time trying to walk."

Cole lowered his head and looked at her. "Now this is my fault?"

"Well, sure." She turned her face to his. "Next time you create a hero, make sure he doesn't piss off the bad guys in the middle of nowhere." She continued over his laughter. "Next time have him stay at a luxury resort with round-the-clock room service."

"Believe me, next time it's a five-star hotel or nothing."

"Too late for that now, but this one's good." She stroked the thickened vine snaking up the trunk of that palm.

Cole suddenly noticed it and in that moment recalled a forgotten fact from his military training. How tropical vines could actually be a source of fresh water.

Which Ariel obviously knew.

In one fluid movement she smacked the edge of that rock against the topmost part of the vine, using just enough force so that it was nicked rather than severed.

"Nailed it," she said, complimenting herself, then looked over her shoulder at him. "Put your hand there." She pointed to a part of the vine that was approximately two feet above the ground.

Cole didn't move. "Just out of curiosity, how's your depth perception?"

"Let's just say I'll have no problem finding the most important parts of you—that is, if we ever get water."

With no more delay Cole hunkered down, put his hand where she wanted, then flinched as she slammed the side of the rock against the tree—no more than an inch below his hand—cleanly severing that vine.

"Nailed it," she said again, then tapped her fingers against his shoulder.

Cole took another ragged breath and looked up.

"Just lift the vine to your mouth," she said, "and let the water drip inside."

"You first."

Ariel sighed. "Cole, I swear it's not poisoned."

"I know that. But you're as thirsty as I am, so you go first. When you've had your fill, then—and only then—will it be my turn."

He was being too kind, Ariel thought. The man was obviously thirsty, not to mention pretty bummed about all this, but God love him he was still horny.

Not wanting to lose that interest by arguing, Ariel drank first.

As she did, Cole grabbed the rock and went to another tree.

Ariel's first thought was to tell him to wait for her help. Her next was to keep quiet and hope for the best.

It took him more than a few tries, but at last he battered that poor vine into submission and held it out to her as if it were a bouquet of roses.

Ariel smiled, then shook her head. "It's your turn now . . . please."

He didn't have to be told twice. Once he was finished, Cole wiped his mouth off with the back of his hand. "You know, I don't believe water's ever tasted so good."

"Not even when you were in the desert on one of your Marine operations?"

"I didn't have to work at it like this."

Ariel slowly nodded. "Deserving something makes all the difference in appreciating it." How else was love supposed to blossom and last unless both parties were worthy? How else could a marriage be secure unless the participants proved their devotion each and every day by caring for each other and worrying about each other?

Not that they were out here to research that, Ariel reminded herself. Just as soon as Cole had far more information than he had ever wanted for this movie, he'd be history . . . they'd be history, with that history starting in just two days.

"Everything all right?" Cole suddenly asked.

Of course it wasn't. With each passing moment Ariel's feelings for this man just grew deeper and more complicated. Good sense told her to stop this right now, tell him she couldn't go further into this research, lie about why, then have a copter pick him up and take him away forever.

Trouble was, her heart wouldn't allow that.

"Sure," she finally said, then cleared the catch in her voice. "Now to food."

Cole sighed, then glanced up. "Surely there are coconuts up there somewhere."

"Surely, but there are insects down here."

He closed his eyes.

"No need to faint," Ariel said, then raised both brows as he looked at her. God, but she loved teasing him. How she would miss that. Not that she would allow herself to think about that now. Clearing her throat once more, she said, "Insects are very high in protein, way more than beef. Your average steak is only twenty percent protein, while some insects have up to eighty per—"

"Tempting as that may sound, I don't think my guy Henry's that macho or desperate as yet." Cole looked past her. "Aren't those bananas over there?"

"Well, sure, if you want to do this the easy way."

Cole laughed. "I was crippled for nearly ten minutes when I first woke up, I've got leaf juice all over my chest and arms so I don't attract ticks, I've still got bits of bark in my mouth from sucking water out of vines, and you think I've been taking the easy way out?"

"Guess not—but," she interrupted, "we haven't even reached a location where we can build our beds or a fire, or make traps so we can catch fish, or collect fruit to supplement our diet, or locate a dependable source of water, or clean our clothes or make—"

"Uh, Ariel," Cole interrupted, "must you keep sugarcoating this for me?"

"People have been doing this since the dawn of time, Cole. Boy Scouts have been doing this since the dawn of time."

He wasn't about to argue with that logic; he was just too damned tired. Already this was turning out to be worse than his Force Recon days. Then, he hadn't had to build every fucking thing from scratch. Then, he hadn't had a luscious female distracting him while he built it. And if that weren't bad enough, there was always the possibility of Thaddeus showing up in his copter to ask if Cole was falling in love with her yet.

What man wouldn't?

Not that Cole wanted to explore that anymore than he already had, at least not now. He needed some R&R—she needed some R&R.

When will the time be right for us? You and me? he had asked this morning.

When we find the appropriate location, she had said. *One that's safe. Protected. The moment we have shelter, water, food, a fire . . .*

He turned to her. "Which way did you say the waterfall was?"

She told him.

Cole nodded. "Come on, we'll shop for food along the way to that dependable source of water, the shelter we'll select nearby, the fire I'll build, and the bed I'll construct, which we most definitely will use before this day is over and all through the night."

Chapter Ten

He started them off at a steady pace, which turned quickly brisk once they left the uneven ground of the savanna. Not once did he speak, nor did he stop to study the vegetation or smell the proverbial roses.

The soldier in him had a target in mind with the prize being her body beneath his, open and yielding, hot and welcoming.

It wasn't love, of course, but Ariel reveled in his desire of her, his promise of *all through the night.*

She would make certain he kept that pledge and that his strong embrace imprisoned her from dusk to dawn. That he used her in a way no man had ever done before, greedily and tenderly, until all doubt of what the future might, or might not, bring was forgotten, at least until he left.

She didn't want to think of that now.

Today, this very moment, she was his woman, and so Ariel followed rather than led, content in Cole's new role as their guide. A role he seemed well prepared for as he used various survival techniques and his overwhelming need to keep them on course.

Good, good boy.

At last, though, Ariel knew he was testing the limits of his endurance, just as all men did, so she started to hold back.

Cole didn't appear to notice until they had gone another

eighth of a mile and he was yards and yards ahead of her. At last, he stopped, glanced over his shoulder and shouted, "Am I going too fast for you?"

Now, there was a question. They had met less than seventy-two hours before, she had already been blessed with seeing him nude, they had spent their first night in the wild sleeping in each other's arms, they had kissed like kids that found the experience completely new and exciting, he had secured her promise that they would make love tonight—or in his words, *all through the night*—and now he was hell-bent on getting to that waterfall so both their desires could be met.

"I was about to ask you the same," said Ariel as she joined him. "I'll slow down even more if you need to rest."

Cole's expression said she was nuts. "Do I look like I need to rest?"

He looked like a male in his prime. Despite the previous pace, he hadn't even broken a sweat, he wasn't breathing all that hard now, his eyes were clear, his beginning beard and tousled hair were oh-so-rugged, and his body—*mmmm, his body*—a shiver of delight tore through Ariel as she recalled its male power and beauty. "Actually, you look aroused."

He grinned.

"But you also sound hungry. Hold these, please."

He took the bamboo stick and script from her. Reaching over, Ariel gently tapped his flat belly as it continued to loudly growl. "You should eat."

Cole looked down as that tapping turned to gentle strokes. "I fully intend to. Later."

Mmmm. She would make certain he also kept that promise. "That's good to hear, but I'm talking about food. And now, not later," she insisted, then quickly added to his protests, "You need to keep up your strength so you can keep up with me."

That got him to stop arguing, at least for a millisecond. "No insects. I refuse."

"Well, if you want to do this the easy way."

He laughed until she held up an orange. He dropped both sticks and the screenplay as she tossed it to him.

"Good going," she said when he caught it, "but you dropped the script."

He arched one dark brow. "Where'd you get this?"

Ariel looked up from that poor battered script and pointed behind herself. "Those bushes we passed back there, before you broke into a run." Ignoring his expression, she pulled a large banana out of her back pocket, lifted his shirt, then stuck that fruit into the waistband of his slacks above the fly. "Go on, eat."

Cole looked from the banana to her. "You first. Believe me, I won't mind."

Later, she thought. "I'm way ahead of you," she said. Keeping her gaze on him, Ariel reached over and pulled a ripe mango from a low-lying branch.

Cole glanced at that and all the other fruit surrounding them in an area that had once been cultivated. His brows lifted in surprise. "I'm usually better at this than I have been. More attentive, that is." He looked at her—all of her. "I'm not making excuses, mind you—but I have been somewhat distracted."

Ariel watched his gaze ride over her breasts, then lower to her navel where those dangling diamond stars were still hidden beneath her clothing. After swallowing the mouthful of mango, she said, "If you say so."

Cole's fingers paused on the orange he was peeling.

Ariel looked at him from beneath her lashes and spoke in a very soft voice. "But don't you worry. I forgive you."

Cole arched one brow as he ripped that orange naked and quickly devoured it.

Tossing the finished mango aside, Ariel pulled another banana out of her back pocket.

Amazing, Cole thought. While he had been leading her headlong in the direction of the waterfall so he could see to all of their needs, she had been grocery shopping. This lady was just full of surprises.

And they just didn't stop.

Cole stopped peeling his banana as she started to peel hers. With that fruit snuggled into the palm of one hand, her long, slender fingers stroked its length before circling the top.

His brows lifted slightly; he continued to watch.

With great care, Ariel finally lowered a section of the peel, baring part of the fruit. Inhaling deeply, as if that had taken quite a bit out of her, she finally continued.

Cole's brows lifted once more.

At last, she lowered the last of the peel. Lifting her gaze to his, she drew her tongue over her lips, then brought the banana to her mouth and leisurely licked its length.

My God, my God, my God. Cole's stiffened cock pushed so hard against his thin clothing, the thing was damned near pointing at her. As his breathing picked up, her tongue continued snaking to the top of the fruit. There she paused and parted her lips still farther to slip that elongated treat as far as she could into her mouth.

In all of his days, and they weren't celibate by any means, Cole had never seen anything like this. She even made eating wanton. "Are you trying to kill me?"

Ariel lazily chewed the fruit. Once she had swallowed, that sweet little tongue was right back out casually licking her lips. At last she said, "No need to whine. If you want part of this, all you have to do is ask." Running her finger up the remaining fruit, she then brought that finger to Cole's mouth.

His lids fluttered wildly as Ariel drew her finger over his bottom lip until Cole felt that tingling clear to the roots of his teeth. "Oh, shit," he said, "that's enough."

She seemed surprised. "Really—*whoa.*"

"Too late for that." Already he had slung her over his shoulder, securing her with one arm as he slid his free hand to her ass. "We've wasted too much time already."

Ariel pulled up his shirt, then pressed her palms against the small of his back. "If you say so."

God, she was driving him crazy. "Hold on," he warned, "I'm not slowing down for anything this time."

"Wait!" she shouted as he took that first step.

"*No*—why?"

"The script. Yes, we do need it," she argued, then continued to speak above him, "just slide me a little farther down your back and I can reach it from—"

"Hold on." Gritting his teeth, Cole hunkered down until Ariel was able to reach the damn thing.

"Got it. Go on. What are you waiting—ow!" she complained as he playfully smacked her butt. "That hurt."

Tell that to his knees. Tensing every muscle in his body, Cole finally grunted to a standing position and breathed hard.

Ariel, on the other hand, playfully bounced her legs against him. "You all right?"

Cole held back a growl and took that first critical step, then another. When he was absolutely certain he wouldn't fall over or drop her, he finally relaxed. "You are so going to pay for this when I get you to that waterfall."

"I doubt it since you're going east now, instead of due south, which is where the water—" Ariel abruptly paused as Cole changed course. "Good boy."

He slid his hand between the seam of her buttocks and smiled to her sharp intake of breath. "I haven't been a boy for a very long time."

"Now you tell me." With her free hand, she continued stroking his back.

It felt so good Cole nearly forgot all the pain he was in, pain that was keeping him on track. *Focus,* he ordered himself or they'd never get to that damned water—

His thoughts abruptly paused as Ariel slipped her free hand beneath the waistband of his slacks and shorts and stroked his bare ass.

"Hold on, hold on, hold on!" he shouted as he staggered to a stop, bent over, and unceremoniously put Ariel on her feet.

The script dropped from her hand as she stumbled back a few steps, before going right back to him. "What's the matter? Did you step on something? Did something bite you? Is your heart okay?" She pressed her palm against his chest. "How old are you really? If you're past forty, men your age can have heart—"

"Quiet," Cole growled.

Ariel giggled, then moved into him and lifted her face to his. "Really," she asked, "are you okay?"

"Hell no, I'm not okay. Not when you're fondling my ass like that."

Her eyes widened slightly. She slipped her hands around his waist to his butt and squeezed both cheeks. "You mean like—"

She didn't get the last words out—she didn't even come close. Cole was on her as he had never been on a woman before, and by God Ariel gave it right back. Wrapping one leg around his, she suckled his tongue until it went as deeply as it could into her mouth, even as she pressed her hands against his ass to bring his rigid cock that much closer.

Damn, she was something.

And Cole thanked her for that by grinding his hips against hers and continuing the kiss until neither of them could do it anymore.

With their foreheads pressed together, they both heaved air.

At last, Ariel swallowed, then panted out her words, "You okay?"

"Never been better." Cole wheezed in more air, then finally added, "Unless you hear a copter."

Ariel rolled her forehead over his. "Don't you worry." She paused to swallow. "Uncle Thaddeus won't be disturbing us."

Now there was a surprise. "Did you call him on my cell to tell him that?"

"Didn't have to."

"Then how do you know he won't—"

"I just do." She ran her forefinger down his torso to his navel to his fly which she gently stroked. "But if you keep attacking me, we're never going to get to that waterfall."

Cole continued to breathe hard as she stroked his thickened rod through the thin fabric of his slacks and shorts. "Sorry."

"That's okay," she murmured, "I forgive you."

Uh-huh. At last, he placed his hand over hers to stop all that stroking, then took several calming breaths. "What you need to do is quit fondling me until we get there, understand?"

Ariel pressed her lips to his throat, cheek, and finally his ear where she whispered, "Yes, sir."

Cole's eyes rolled into the back of his head as she wiggled her tongue into his ear. "Oh, hell, I give," he sighed, "do whatever you want with me."

Oddly enough, that caused her to stop. "To the waterfall it is," she said, then gently kissed his cheek, retrieved the sticks and script, then led them due south.

Never in his life had Cole wanted to get to a place as badly as he did that damned waterfall. Suddenly, this trek seemed endless with everything looking the same, as if they were walking in circles. When Cole looked up into the trees, monkeys looked right back down, just as they had only a few minutes before. Their expressions seemed amused, as if they knew something he only suspected. When he and Ariel passed a macaw that seemed to be no different from the last that was also shrieking nonstop, Cole finally asked, "You're sure we're going the right way or at least in a straight line?"

Ariel smiled. "Well, I don't know. Once or twice we did use your watch for direction. Is it set for daylight or standard time?"

He scowled.

Her laughter was lusty. "Sorry."

"You will be."

"I doubt it. Here we are."

Cole's pace slowed, then stopped as he looked up. His jaw actually sagged at the series of volcanic rocks in the distance. They were black, jagged, fucking foreboding, and looked for all the world like a tropical version of hell.

And that didn't begin to address what surrounded them, a forest so damned dense he and Ariel would need more than a machete—possibly a bulldozer—to get through it.

He looked at her.

She lifted her brows. "The rocks and having to climb them to get to the waterfall *are* in my notes." She lifted the script to remind him where those notes were.

Hell, he thought. He really should have read what she had penciled in.

"Now, you did say you wanted something more exciting in this movie than onions, right?"

He arched one brow in answer.

Ariel easily continued despite that. "You did say filmmaking needs something different, something exciting, something unique. Something the audience would enjoy." She paused to catch her breath. "You didn't like the onions, so I'm giving you this . . . different, exciting, unique." She gestured to those volcanic rocks.

Cole didn't bother to look at them again; they were burned into his memory. "I was talking about dealing with the insect problem."

Her eyes widened slightly. "Oh."

His gaze drifted to her lips as they simply hugged that word.

"You do know how to climb, don't you?" she asked.

Of course he knew how to climb. Of course, it had been a while since he had done so with gear, and even longer since he had done so without. "You're kidding, right?" he asked, not willing to admit that he was a bit rusty.

Ariel gave him a luminous smile that showed all her dimples. "Guess I was. Our dependable source of water is just past those rocks. Come on."

Her tone and expression challenged, but for the moment Cole could only watch as she slipped the script into the waistband of her pants, then bolted across the small savanna leading to those rocks and started to climb them with the same ease a mountain goat would use—or Mina, her native girl that the government had turned into a Marine.

Planting his hands on his lean hips, Cole lowered his head and breathed hard. Never in all of his days had he been forced to work this hard for a woman . . . one he just had to impress, which wasn't going to be easy since she was proving to be better at this than he had ever been. Hell, she was even better at plotting screenplays than he was, and that was definitely hurting his male pride, not to mention his—

"Cole!" she called out, breaking into his thoughts. "Aren't you coming?"

She would ask that. Glancing up, he took a deep breath, then bolted across the clearing as she had.

Not that it mattered. She was well up those rocks and scrambling to the top as he finally reached the bottom.

"Take your time!" she called out. "Catch your breath!"

Right. Still breathing hard, Cole tackled those rocks as if they had personally offended him. He was so focused, he didn't allow himself to stop until he had gotten halfway.

At last he rested, then looked down to see he hadn't gone as far as he first thought. Looking up, he met Ariel's gaze. She wore her usual worried expression, even though she was straddling the topmost point and casually swinging her legs as she fanned herself with the script.

"Are you all right?" she called out.

"*Fine,*" he growled.

She nodded cautiously, then looked really worried as she called out, "I could get a vine to help pull you up!"

Cole tightened his jaw.

"Oh-kay." She lifted both hands in surrender, then continued to casually fan herself with his script, as if she'd been teasing all along. "Do it the hard way."

His gaze narrowed.

She smiled. "Would you feel more comfortable if I wasn't watching you?"

He continued to glare at her.

"Oh-kay," she called out, then pointed over her shoulder. "I'll be over there."

As she disappeared from view, Cole breathed hard, then continued to haul himself up the damned rocks, while cursing himself for getting into this mess.

Why in the hell hadn't he read her notes? Why had he been so cavalier about this? Not only was it causing him no end of frustration, but Ariel wasn't about to let him off the hook for not taking her skills seriously. Again and again and again she showed him the error of his ways.

She could have been a drill sergeant, while he probably seemed no more than a horny bastard wanting only to get into her pants.

Pausing again, Cole really swore. What he wanted from her was so far beyond mere sex. Never in his life had Cole respected a woman more. Ariel Leigh could do anything. And, by God, once he was on the other side of these fucking rocks he was going to let her know how much he admired her skill, strength, know-how, and talent. It wasn't just sex with him and hadn't been since that first night at supper; he liked her as a person. He admired her honesty and lack of guile. She touched him in a way no other woman had. And if he ever got up these stinking rocks, he was going to tell her that!

Panting like a dog that was about to die, Cole finally struggled to the top and heard the faint rush of water past the pounding of blood in his ears.

The blessed waterfall. *So what?* Closing his eyes, he continued to breathe hard, even though he just knew Ariel was watching him.

Somehow it no longer mattered if she saw his shortcomings. From this moment forward he was going to be as honest with her as she was always being with him.

Swallowing hard, Cole at last opened his eyes, expecting to see her concern. To his surprise, she wasn't on the rocks anymore.

He looked from the base of the rocks to the left and felt his heart pause.

The waterfall was far smaller than he expected, a slender rush of water that spilled into a dark blue pool surrounded by dazzling red, orange, and yellow tropical flowers that grew right up to the forest that hugged this area.

Palms swayed in the gentle breeze; lush foliage, drenched in moisture, sparkled beneath the light of the sun; and within all of that beauty was Ariel.

My God, Cole thought, pushing to his knees as he stared at her.

She was nude, except for those diamond stars dangling from her navel. They twinkled wildly in the light, creating a rainbow of color across her taut, tanned flesh. As water tumbled and misted around her, she remained beneath a gentle trickle, her face lifted to expose her lovely throat, her lips parted as she drank her fill, her eyes closed, her arms raised as she smoothed down her dampened hair.

A few of those tresses had escaped with one curling beneath her left breast.

Her nipples were a deep pink and arched toward the sky.

It was more than a man could bear. It was more than any man should be allowed. Need so quickly hungered through Cole it stole his breath and thickened his cock as his gaze rode her firm breasts, those delicate nipples, her navel, and that precious jewelry that shone more brightly than the beads of water skimming over her silky belly until they became trapped in those delicate curls between her legs.

That hair was a dark auburn as he had dreamt . . . as he had hoped.

Wow, he thought once more. Never in his life had Cole seen anything more humbling or arousing. This was how a woman should look—natural and pure with none of the embellishments Hollywood and the beauty industry promoted. No makeup on earth, no plastic surgeon's skill or enhancement, could match this beauty.

For the first time in Cole's life his heart knelt to a woman. The frustration he had felt, the exhaustion he had endured, was quickly forgotten as he hurried down this side of the rocks and finally reached the edge of the pool.

As if sensing his presence, Ariel's head slowly lowered, and her lids fluttered open. There was need in her eyes, a female welcome that was vulnerable, but impatient, as Cole pulled off his clothing, tossing it and his watch to the side. Naked he faced her, his thickened cock demanding notice.

Ariel's gaze caressed its hard length. She smiled.

Cole grinned, then dove into the deepest part of the pool, knifing through it toward her. Reaching the bank, he emerged, leaving a trail of water across the smooth stones as he moved closer, then pulled her into his arms.

At last, Ariel thought, lifting her face to his. Beads of water clung to his long lashes and bristly cheeks. A male appetite like none she had ever seen darkened his eyes and drew her still closer.

She pressed her thighs, belly, and chest to his, offering all of herself, but even that seemed inadequate. She parted her legs, then lifted her head as he kissed the length of her throat. His lips were still cooled from the water, though his tongue was hot. Ariel held back for as long as she could, and then a sigh so soft only she knew it existed escaped her lips.

In that same moment, Cole cupped her right breast in his palm, lifting it as he lowered his mouth. His lips circled the taut nipple; his roughened cheeks scraped her tender skin, while his fingers expertly worked her supple flesh.

He didn't hold back and offered her no escape. Laving her nipple with his tongue, he next drew it into his mouth and suckled hard as he moved his hands down her, resting one across her buttocks and the other on those curls between her legs. There, he explored, finally parting those lips to slip two fingers inside her opening, while his thumb rested on her clitoris.

Ariel's back arched to that possession, which drove his fingers still deeper. As her flesh tightened around him, he separated his fingers, stretching her, owning her before he drew his thumb over her sensitive nub.

The sensation was so intense Ariel was caught off guard.

It was precisely what Cole had wanted. As he lifted his head from her breast, he pressed his hand against her buttocks to keep her still, while he stroked her clit.

Ariel's breaths came in quick, shallow pants, but Cole didn't concede. His strokes were lazy and deliberate until she sagged into him, resting her head on his shoulder to await the pleasure.

He wasn't about to let that happen just yet.

Ariel squeezed her eyes tight; her fingers balled into fists as Cole continued to slowly draw his thumb over her clit, teasing that erect nub until Ariel simply couldn't stand it any longer. The insides of her thighs ached; her breathing continued to pick up.

As it did, Cole moved his thumb from her clit, denying her completion even as his strength kept her close.

She whimpered.

Cole paid no heed. Again, he separated those fingers that were trapped within her to stretch that flesh, to prepare it for his thick, hot cock. During this, he ran his thumb to the right of her swollen clit, to the left, always coming close, but never quite touching it.

"You're driving me crazy!" she finally cried.

His answer was to press his mouth to her neck, while his thumb all too slowly circled that nub, making her wait and want.

Ariel moaned; it was all the power he had left her. She was his to use and enjoy.

The man in him, she knew, expected nothing less; the soldier in him demanded full control, at least in this.

Ariel gave it and was rewarded with the promise of completion, but only a promise as his touch continued to tempt and tease.

Soon, she was drawn into this moment that muted all else. The water hushed from above and behind; the birds grew still; the wind only whispered.

Through it all Cole continued until Ariel was lulled by the sweet torture, then taken so deep she could barely catch her breath as he unexpectedly brought her to completion, insisting that she hide nothing, that she show him the pleasure he had given her.

She had no other choice.

Shivering uncontrollably, Ariel pressed her length into Cole, whimpering, then crying out as he continued to stroke and tease.

At last, she begged him to give her a moment, only a moment.

He did not. He worked her until she was limp and exhausted, but even then he wouldn't remove his fingers. Instead, Cole eased them still farther into her tight, wet opening.

Ariel softly moaned.

Cole smiled, but in no way did that mean he was going to allow her even a second of peace. She had put him through his paces, she had just dragged him through hell, and now she would pay.

Lifting his hand from her ass, he brought it to her right breast, fondling that achingly soft globe even as he ran his thumb over her slick nether lips.

She trembled with each new stroke.

When she was consumed with this latest pleasure, Cole finally removed his fingers from her.

Ariel's head remained lowered; her breathing hitched.

As the last shiver tore through her, Cole knew it was time for more.

Resting his hands on the flare of her hips, he was about to sink to his knees so that he could bury his face in her delicate curls, so that he could lick her clit until he drove her to the edge once more, but Ariel suddenly stepped back.

Cole lifted his head.

She continued to shake hers.

He was stunned into a brief silence. "What are you doing?"

She swallowed, then panted out her words. "Catching my breath."

He grinned. "To hell with that, get back here."

She didn't budge.

Cole's smile quickly faded. He wasn't certain what to think, so he did the only thing he could; he spoke from the heart. "I want to taste you, Ariel, all of you . . . You do want that, right?"

"Of course I do, and you will, but not yet."

"Why?"

She pointed to an area behind him. "Sit down—please."

Cole glanced over his shoulder to the mound of smooth rocks on the edge of the pool. Again, he wasn't certain what to think. "If I do sit down, what do you plan to do?"

"Oh, you'll see."

Suddenly, there was enough seduction in her voice to make a grown man weak, and to fill Cole's mind with images of her straddling him so that he could finally enter her.

He met her gaze. "Yes, ma'am."

She smiled.

Padding to those rocks, Cole turned and sat, then gestured her to him.

Ariel's gaze remained on his tight balls and stiffened cock as she moved closer, but not close enough.

She stopped just short of his reach so that Cole couldn't pull her onto his lap.

He told himself to be patient, but still blurted, "What's wrong?"

She continued to quietly regard his thickened rod and testicles, and even that scar just below his shoulder, before meeting his gaze. "Absolutely nothing." Her expression and voice softened even more. "You're perfect just as you are."

Cole's eyes widened to the compliment.

Ariel took that moment to finally go to him. She sank to her knees between his legs.

Cole looked down, then inhaled sharply as she lifted his stiffened cock, caressing it in the palm of one hand, while she cradled his balls in the other.

Never had a woman touched him with such reverence. Never had a woman delighted in his maleness as much as Ariel seemed to.

"My God," he whispered, then moaned—a low moan from deep within, a male sound of pure delight as Ariel finally lowered her head and licked his length.

He tasted more wonderful than she had imagined, and Ariel was not about to rush this pleasure.

As she carefully fondled his hot, tight sac, she pressed her face to that dark thatch of hair above the base of his shaft. To her delight, his male scent remained despite that brief swim.

She inhaled deeply of his musk, filling herself with it before flicking her tongue over this hair dampening it still further.

Cole wiggled. Out of the corner of her eye, Ariel saw his toes splay.

Already she was driving him crazy. *Poor baby.* She hadn't even begun.

Drawing her thumb over his cock's blunt head, Ariel slowly licked the base of his shaft.

"Oh, yes," he whispered.

Ariel sighed, then brought her thumb from the top of the head to the back. As she lightly stroked that uneven skin she drew her tongue up his full length.

Cole quickly tensed.

She knew he was struggling for control. Control she was not about to give.

Without pause, Ariel finally—and fully—took him into her

mouth, suckling him still deeper, sweeping her tongue over his thickness and heat.

Cole finally cried out, "Ariel, *no!* I can't hold off!"

Her heart smiled. She didn't want him to hold off. She wanted to give him this pleasure that she had never given another man. Before Cole, she hadn't wanted to.

He was different. Ariel loved him without pause, already and perhaps foolishly, but there it was, making her want to explore and worship each part of him.

She did, filling herself with his scent, fondling his balls, suckling his cock until his protests turned to gasps of delight as she brought him to completion.

A moment later, she finally released his rod, but only because she wanted to watch his chest heave with his strained breathing, while his jaw clenched to the unbearable pleasure that made him briefly weak.

Ariel smiled at what she had done. Before he could recover, she lowered her head, then licked his balls.

"Ahh!" he cried.

Mmmm, she thought, running her tongue over that wrinkled skin.

Cole finally placed his hands on either side of her head. "Stop!" he ordered.

She wasn't about to and certainly did not, until he lifted her head.

Cole continued breathing hard as his gaze lowered to her tongue.

Ariel brought it back into her mouth. "What?"

He laughed, and then he groaned, and then he sighed.

In that moment he looked so very weary that a wave of tenderness washed over Ariel. Straightening, she cradled his face in her palms, then ran her thumbs over his bristly cheeks as she gently touched her lips to his. "You okay?"

He swallowed. "What do you think?"

"Well, I don't know. A man your age might not survive

such—ow!" she complained as he playfully smacked her butt. "That hurt."

"Did not. Admit it."

She gently kissed his lips instead, then his poor scar before easing back.

Cole inhaled deeply once more.

As he opened his eyes, Ariel saw a yearning in his gaze that hadn't been there before.

She wanted to believe it was more than just gratitude. She hoped it might be the beginning of love, but warned herself not to dwell on that.

She had him for this moment in time, and a few more moments to come, and that might be the sum total of it. Although that ached to her very core, Ariel knew it was more than she had ever dreamt possible, and certainly more than most women got in a lifetime.

"Thank you," he said.

She smiled. "Thank *you.*"

Cole grinned. "Not yet. But you will." He reached out to pull her onto his lap.

Ariel easily pushed to her feet, then backed away.

Cole not only looked surprised, but hurt. "You don't want me inside of you?"

"You *were* inside of me."

He arched one dark brow, then looked hurt again. "I'm talking about our making love."

Poor baby. "We will," she promised in her softest voice, then got real, "only we can't now."

He seemed to be digesting that, before he frowned. "Just give me a few seconds and I'll—"

"I know you will," she said, "but I can't give you those few seconds."

"Why not?" His gaze rode her flesh. When he spoke again, his voice sounded distracted. "I'm nude, you're nude, except for those stars dangling from your navel—by the way," he quickly said, then lifted his gaze to hers, "don't *ever* take those off, understand?" Before Ariel could comment, Cole continued as his gaze lowered to her navel, then lifted to her breasts, "We're here, we're obviously ready and aroused, so what's the problem?"

"The sun."

He briefly paused, looked up, then squinted at the sun that was directly overhead. "You're worried about sunburn?" He lowered his head and looked at her bronzed nudity which was the same as his—there were absolutely no tan lines. "Can't we just move into the—are you laughing at me?"

Ariel couldn't help it. "You don't understand," she said. "The sun is at just the right point for us to build a fire—which we'll need tonight," she quickly added, speaking above him, "*if* you want to make love to me without being bothered or stopped by insects, animals, or—"

"Okay, okay, okay."

Pushing to his feet, Cole slung his arm around Ariel's naked shoulders and pulled her close. "Let's see about building that fire."

Chapter Eleven

Ariel blithely followed Cole's lead until she saw that he was heading for a small clearing. Although it was perfect as a campsite, there was one problem.

At last she held back.

He glanced over his shoulder at her. "You like that spot to the left better?"

"I'd like to get dressed," she said.

Cole gave her a mischievous smile. "You're not going to start being difficult, are you?"

"I haven't stopped."

He looked thoughtful. "I think that's what I like about you." He got serious. "But getting dressed is out of the question. I want you just the way you are."

Ariel gave him her sweetest smile. "Yes, sir."

Cole grinned, then led them even farther away from their clothing.

"Of course," she finally added, "don't blame me if tonight's off because I got bitten by something, or scratched by something, or injured by something because I'm walking around in my birthday—"

"Right," Cole interrupted, then led her back to their clothes. "Let's get dressed."

"Actually, we should wash our clothes out while we have the chance."

He frowned. "What about the sun? What about it being in the perfect spot for us to build a fire?"

She patiently explained. "It will only take us a minute or two to wash our clothes. The sun's not going to drop out of the sky in that period of time. Of course, if you want to take only a minute or two to make love, then—"

"Right." He sighed. "Let's wash out our clothes; then we'll get dressed."

"Whatever you say," she murmured, then lifted her brows to his expression.

It hardly got better as they brought their respective clothing to the edge of the pool.

"Okay, what now?" Cole asked.

"That's on page seventy-five of the script. You did read my notes, didn't you?"

He looked busted. "You didn't actually add the characters washing their clothes, did you?"

"Of course not. That's not something that would interest an audience."

Cole muttered something beneath his breath, then sank to his knees next to her.

Ariel leaned toward him and murmured, "I wrote that they're washing each other, using nothing but their tongues."

His shoulders shook with his laughter. "Good to know. So, what now? We beat our clothes with a rock?"

Only if they wanted to wear rags. "Using soap would be much better."

Cole glanced at the ground as if some might be growing there.

"We have to make it," Ariel said.

"How long would that take?"

"Well, that depends. If we use animal fat, which is our best choice—but not readily available, since I'm totally opposed to harming a live animal—we'd have to find one that died of natural causes first, and then we'd have to—"

"What's the second best choice?"

"Well, that would be sand. Of course, we'd have to go back to the beach to get—"

"Third best."

"That would be wood ashes from a fire, which we'd have to build first to—"

"How about plain old water?"

She smiled. "That'll work."

Cole shook his head as he plunged his clothing into the water, swirled them around once, then pulled the soggy bundle out. "Done."

"Ah, there's something on one of the legs of your—"

"*Jesus.*" Cole quickly and repeatedly snapped his pants until the long-legged black thing flew off.

"Want me to wash them for you?" Ariel asked.

He continued to breathe hard as he shook his head. "It'll go faster if we do each other's. Give me your bra and panties."

That's the spirit Ariel liked to hear, but insisted on washing her own stuff. Three minutes later their duds were clean and still dripping water as they got dressed.

Cole made a face to the damp fabric sucking his skin. "I think I liked dry and dirty better."

"They'll be dry by the time you build the fire. Come on, we're losing the sun."

He nodded, then stopped. "Wait a sec."

"Why?"

He frowned. "It didn't occur to me till now, but what's the sun being at just the right point have to do with our building a fire?"

Ariel had wondered when he'd get around to thinking about that. "Everything, if we're going to be using your watch."

Cole looked down at it, then back at her. "You're going to use this crystal to start a fire?"

"No. You are. Unless," she quickly added, "you want to rub two sticks together."

"I'd rather rub us together."

"That makes pleasure, not fire."

"Maybe in everybody else's world, but in ours—"

"We won't get to yours until you pay attention to mine."

"*Yours?*" he asked.

"Ours," she corrected.

Cole smiled. "Okay, what kind of fire do you want—a tepee, lean-to, pyramid, or a cross-ditch?"

"I think a tepee would be—" Ariel abruptly paused, then looked at him. "You know about the different types of fires?" She edged closer. "You've already done all of this during your Marine operations? You already know all of this?"

At least some of it, he thought, and thanks to his big mouth she knew it, too. So, he talked fast. "It's been quite a while since I was taught those skills, and I never once needed to build a fire during an operation."

Ariel nodded slowly, but still looked disappointed, as if she had wanted to go on and on impressing, overwhelming, and simply outdoing him with her expertise. "I guess you know what we need to use then, huh?"

Cole decided to lie. Hell, at this point he would have done anything to see her as happy as she had been just a moment before. He liked her that much . . . he loved her that much. There, he finally admitted it to himself, and the sky didn't cave in, and even the fucking sun didn't drop into the ocean.

This was a woman like no other, and by God, Cole didn't mind falling in love with her. It felt oddly comfortable and so completely overwhelming he was suddenly dizzy.

She stepped closer. "Hey, you okay?"

"Just thinking too hard," he said.

"No need. That's why I'm here."

God, she was something. No wonder he was falling in love with her. As Cole thought about that, he didn't get as dizzy as the first time. "I'm glad you are." He met her gaze.

Her brows lifted slightly. "You sure you're okay?"

"Never been better. Now, about the fire."

She continued to look at him expectantly, as though she was waiting for him to pass out.

He cleared his throat and got his bearings. "I can't recall all the particulars about making one," he said. "Now, if you want me to disarm a bomb, jump from a helicopter, throw a—"

"Maybe for your next story," she said, then smiled. "Okay, here's what you need."

Cole nodded to show her he was finally listening as she explained the ins and outs of fire. There seemed to be no end to her knowledge of tinder, kindling, and fuel.

As she went on and on about each, she got increasingly excited.

He, on the other hand, found himself falling more deeply in love. God, it was weird, but Cole simply couldn't help himself.

Ariel finally noticed. "Everything all right?"

He nodded.

"You heard everything I said?"

"Sure did."

She looked skeptical. "What makes the best tin—"

"Dried husk fiber from coconuts."

She smiled. "You were listening."

And falling in love.

"Oh-kay," she said, "go find me that stuff—if you think you can."

She was challenging him again, but Cole decided to forgive her. He also warned himself to make some mistakes when he was choosing the *stuff* so her glee continued uninterrupted.

As it turned out, he wasn't the whiz he thought. He just seemed to naturally pick out the wrong material. At last, though, he dropped the appropriate fixin's at her feet.

"Wonderful," she said. "But this area isn't protected from the wind."

Of course it isn't, he thought, *that would be too easy.* "I'm on it." Like a born-again Boy Scout he roamed the area until he found the perfect spot, then hauled all the fixins to it.

Ariel applauded until Cole hauled her into his arms, kissed her like crazy, and only stopped when both of them were having trouble standing.

Breathing hard, he said, "Save the applause till later for the important stuff."

"Yes, sir."

Concentrating on the task at hand, Cole sank to his knees and arranged a mound of tinder, then surrounded it on three sides by kindling that formed a cone or tepee. Taking a flat rock, he placed more tinder on it. "Stand back," he warned, "I'm about to make magic."

"You'll have to take off your watch first."

"I knew that," he said, then removed it.

Ariel immediately wiggled her fingers. "Give it to me."

"Why? I thought I was going to do this."

"You're going to start the fire." She glanced at his hands. "But you're not going to be able to pry out the crystal with those short nails."

He glanced at her hands. "Yours are as short as mine."

"I wasn't going to use my nails."

He frowned. "You're not going to pry it out with your teeth, are you?"

Now she frowned. "Of course not. I'm adaptable, not un-civilized."

"I didn't mean any—"

"Cole, the sun isn't always going to be as strong as it is right—thanks," she said as he handed her the watch.

He remained kneeling in front of his unlit tepee, obviously useless to her plans, as Ariel glanced around. At last she regarded a rock that was a twin to the one with the extra tinder. Going to it, she hunkered down, then lifted his watch above her shoulder.

Cole shouted, "Whoa—wait!"

Ariel flinched, then so quickly lost her balance she fell

from a squat to her butt. Looking over her shoulder at him, she frowned. "Wait? Why?"

Cole pushed to his feet and went to her. "You're going to break it to get the crystal out?"

"I'm going to smack it to get the crystal out. Hopefully, it won't break. Either way, it's do this or go without a fire."

"There's no third choice?"

Ariel arched one brow. "It's just a watch, Cole."

"Maybe to you, but it's one I happen to really like."

Her expression changed from barely patient to somewhat embarrassed to surprisingly sad. "I didn't know this meant so much to you. Here." She extended the watch. "Go on. Take it. I didn't know someone special gave it to you. I wouldn't want to hurt her gift to you, especially if it's so—"

"What are you talking about? There is no her, and there is no gift. I bought that myself, because I like it, so why do we have to ruin it?"

Ariel nodded slowly, then tossed him the watch. "Sorry," she said when he missed catching it. "Please get that crystal out for us, you and me, without ruining it. You have fifteen minutes."

"I have fifteen minutes to do *this*, but not to make love to you before I build us a fire?"

She looked concerned. "Is that all the time you'll need when we—"

"You are *so* going to pay for this."

"Something to look forward to." She sobered. "Now you have fourteen minutes and forty-five seconds to—"

"Yeah, yeah, yeah." Cole sank to the ground. "Block out some time, baby, because you and I are gonna have lots of it once I get this out."

"Uh-huh. Now you have fourteen minutes. No more."

"I don't need more." He bent his head to the task.

Three minutes later, he tossed the still-intact watch back to her. "Vaporize the damned thing for all I care."

She smiled. "No need to go that far." Pushing to her knees,

Ariel lifted her arm and smacked the side of the watch against the edge of the rock. Just like that, the crystal popped out and rolled onto a soft cushion of grass.

"You're amazing," he said.

She smiled. "You ain't seen nuthin' yet." Once the crystal was in her palm, Ariel offered it to him and murmured, "Light my fire."

Cole laughed and took the damned thing. "Faster than you'll believe possible."

"No need to rush. Pace yourself."

"Like hell. Break out the marshmallows, baby, 'cause I'm on a roll."

"In that case, I'll just watch." Sinking back to the grass, Ariel pulled up her knees and wrapped her arms around her legs.

Cole gave her a smile, then moved the lens over the extra tinder, angling it to concentrate the rays of the sun.

"Here we go," he said.

"I can't wait," she said.

Ten minutes later she was still waiting, while Cole mentally swore. *Burn, damn you, burn!*

The tinder continued to play dead.

Fuck. What in the hell was he doing wrong now? He recalled being shown this and doing this during his survival training, only he hadn't recalled that it had taken most of the afternoon to work. At last he looked at Ariel. "Bear with me, okay?"

Her eyes widened slightly. "I'm not going anywhere, Cole."

The surprise in her voice, her obvious patience with him, made Cole want her all the more. It also made him want to do this so damned well that he'd make her smile. "Thanks."

"Thank *you*—look."

He turned his head to where she pointed and stared at the thin wisp of smoke rising from the tinder. "Oh, my God, look at that!"

"Magic," she said.

The lady wasn't kidding. Cole stared at that smoldering tinder as if it were the Holy Grail. With great care, and more than a bit of fear, he carefully blew on it until the smoke turned to flame. At last he slid that baby blaze on top of the fireclay, then sagged to his back on the ground, draping his left arm over his eyes.

A moment passed before Ariel murmured, "Did you faint?"

He laughed. "This is fucking hard, you know that?"

"Uh-huh."

"But at least we're done."

Ariel cleared her throat. "You should really feed the fire some small bits of kindling now, so it doesn't go—"

"I'm on it," he interrupted, then grunted to a sitting position and fed the damned thing.

A half hour later it snapped, crackled, and popped as it burned up a storm. At last, Cole relaxed. "Call me crazy, but I don't think it's going to go out anytime soon."

"Because you did it so well," Ariel said.

Cole slid his gaze to her. "You ain't seen nuthin' yet."

"Oh, but I have," she corrected, "though I want to see more."

"Oh, yeah?" He wiggled his brows.

She smiled, then got deadly serious. "Now it's time to catch some fish."

His smile paused.

"You're not hungry?" she asked.

He leveled his gaze on her.

Okay, so she was testing his limits, and not just in wilderness survival. Even so, they couldn't just come out here and play Adam and Eve for a few days, then hope their survival and the research for his story would take care of itself. Even if this didn't involve their lives and her reputation, it involved his.

Even if Ariel hadn't loved him, she still would have wanted

his movie to be the greatest ever. She wanted people to rave about it. And even when she saw it alone, because their time together had ended, she wanted to know that she had played a small part in seeing his dream come true.

Of course, given the way Cole was currently glaring at her, he had forgotten all about his movie.

Lucky that you have me, she thought, then pushed to her feet.

Cole looked up at her. "What are you doing?"

Ariel walked around him. "If you won't catch me a fish, then I'll just have to catch one for myself, which is probably what would happen with Mina and Henry. After all, he is a useless politician who—"

"What he is is *my* character!" Cole called out. "And his name is *Roarke,* and I don't give a damn if he catches fish in this screenplay or not!"

Ariel stopped. His words cut so deeply that for a moment she felt as if she couldn't breathe. At last, she looked over her shoulder at him and spoke in a voice that was surprisingly even. "I give a damn."

Cole's expression changed. He pushed to his feet. "I didn't mean—"

"Sure you did. You haven't liked any of my suggestions, even though Gwen approved them all, so stay where you are. I'll just catch a fish by my—"

"To hell with that." He went to her. "If you want a damned fish, I'll catch you a damned fish."

"Don't do me any favors."

"I'm not. I'm giving you what you want."

"I don't want it, Cole! I want you to want it!"

"Well I—oh, hell," he said, interrupting himself. Lowering his head, he breathed hard. "Ariel, I want you, pure and simple." He lifted his head to look at her. "Believe me, I am not about to apologize for that. But," he added, speaking above her, "I also want your expertise. Since that's what I'm apparently going to be getting first, I will catch you that damned fish."

She regarded him for a long moment, then finally moved into him, resting her hand on his chest. "You really do want my expertise?"

Cole glanced up from her fingers stroking him. "Are you kidding? I wouldn't have gotten this far today without it."

She smiled. "You actually like my ideas for your story?"

"No—not at first," he quickly amended, "but they grew on me."

"They *grew* on—"

"Okay, okay," he interrupted. "Most of them make a lot of sense, so I'm going to use them—but only because they make a lot of sense."

She pulled back her hand. "Most? Not all?"

His shoulders slumped.

Ariel gave him a dimpled smile. "Thanks." She pushed to her toes and kissed his bristly cheek.

Cole briefly closed his eyes and hoped to God they never argued again. Seeing her pissed just killed him. "Where are these damned fish?"

She gently eased back. "Well, that depends. What kind do you prefer?"

Opening his eyes, Cole leaned down to her until their lips nearly touched. "The kind in a restaurant found on a plate."

She murmured, "If you want to do it the easy way."

"Please, God."

She laughed, then pulled back. "If you're not particular about the kind of fish you catch, then I'd say we need to go to the deep area of the pool over there." She pointed. "Or an area with overhanging brush, or any place we see that has submerged rocks or logs since fish usually gather in places like that."

"Sounds good, let's go." He took her hand, then glanced over his shoulder when she held back. "What now?"

"Aren't you forgetting something?"

Cole looked down at her body, then down at his. "Oh. Just a sec." He went to get his watch and the crystal. Returning to her, he asked, "Think you can pop the top back on?"

"Not if we're fighting a fire, I can't."

His expression changed; he looked over his shoulder to it. "I should bank that before we leave, right?"

"Just like it says on page seventy-eight of the script."

Cole looked to where she had left it—on the ground soaking up more moisture and mud beneath the rock that kept it from blowing away in the wind. "You're actually sticking to that, aren't you?" He looked at her. "We're really not going to make love until we reach page ninety-eight, are we?"

"It's not like we haven't done *anything*, Cole."

As his gaze turned inward to their waterfall adventure, his mouth turned up in a smile. "But we're really not going to make love until we reach page—"

"Deserving something makes all the difference in appreciating it," she said, then continued when he met her gaze. "We have a lot to do."

Cole made a face, then mumbled, "Let me bank the fire—unless you want to do it."

She shook her head. "I have full confidence in you."

That got him to smile. Ariel returned it, then kept her fingers crossed as he went to the fire. Within minutes he had kicked just enough dirt on it to protect the coals so they'd be ready to use later.

Pleased with himself, Cole swaggered back to Ariel and again took her hand. "Let's go get those fish."

"Sure—but," she quickly added, again holding back, "shouldn't you decide first what you plan to use to get the fish?"

Probably. "Is it in the script?"

"We discussed it back at the compound."

Cole nodded agreeably. What else could he do since he didn't recall discussing fish? Maybe it was time to tell her what he did remember from his SERE training—that food was nothing more than a crutch—that willpower would, and should, rule the day.

Trouble was, her willpower seemed to be much stronger than his. Holding back a sigh, Cole regarded their surroundings. "There's wood all around us. Lots and lots of branches. Surely we could use one of those as a spear."

"We could," she agreed.

"Great. Let's go."

Ariel didn't budge. "Have you ever speared a fish?"

"Have you?"

She nodded.

Figures. Despite her continuing one-upmanship, Cole was not about to cave. "It seems the easiest route, and," he quickly added, "the most interesting to use in the film."

"If you say so."

If you say so? Damn. He really hated it when she so easily agreed with him, because it meant only one thing. The proverbial other shoe was about to drop. She was going to give him a million reasons to Sunday why this plan wouldn't work, but no way was he going to concede his point. Not on this. "Actually, I do." He released her hand. "In fact, this is something the male lead can match the female lead in, given that he will have at least some superior strength, because he will be taller and heavier than she is."

"If you say so."

He laughed, then quickly sobered. "Oh, hon, that's not my idea to have her smaller and weaker. The suits will insist upon it, believe me."

She frowned. "Suits?"

"The powers that be in Hollywood. Studio heads, the money people. None of them are going to accept a female lead with hairier knuckles than my guy."

"Then they're in big trouble. Useless politicians wouldn't have hairy knuckles; they'd all get waxes during their manicures."

Cole's shoulders shook with his suppressed laughter. "He is going to be spearing fish, got it?"

"Yes, sir."

"Okay, then." Cole glanced over his shoulder at the pool, then right back to her. "So, what do he and Mina do?"

"When?"

Cole arched one brow. "Don't play coy with me."

Ariel's gaze drifted to his fly and what was behind it—his satisfied cock that she had so expertly pleasured. "Oh, sorry." She met his gaze. "I won't from now on."

He sighed.

That seemed to do the trick, because suddenly her voice was contrite. "Forgive me. I'll behave."

"Only for now," he said, "later you can do whatever the hell you want."

She smiled, then quickly sobered as she got down to business. "Okay, to spear fish, first you need a spear—you do know that, right?"

Jesus. "Well, I don't know. Was it in your notes?"

"Of course not. I don't advise this for your story—but," she quickly added, "since your heart is set on this, I'm willing to go along."

Cole briefly wondered if he should remind her that this was still his screenplay, at least so far as the contracts he signed were concerned.

"Anyway," she said, "the first thing you need to do is to cut a sapling to use as your spear. It should be long and straight."

Cole nodded, even as he wondered how he was going to cut wood without the benefit of a knife.

"Okay then," Ariel said, her gaze carefully monitoring his reactions. "Once you have the spear in hand, you'll then need to sharpen the end of it into a point—or attach a knife to the end of it. Of course," she quickly added, "you don't have a knife, but that's okay, a piece of sharpened metal will also do. Of course you don't have a piece of sharpened metal, but that's—" she abruptly paused, then asked, "Is something wrong?"

Cole lifted his head and opened his eyes. "Nope. Just listening hard."

Ariel nodded slowly. "Good . . . where was I?"

"Telling me about all the stuff I don't have. This is just a thought," he said, "but why don't we concentrate on what I might have?"

"If you say so."

Cole gritted his teeth and spoke through them. "I do."

"Okay, then. Since you don't have a knife or a piece of sharpened metal, a jagged piece of bone would do."

Now she was talking. "That's a good idea."

Ariel smiled. "Thanks." Her eyes sparkled, just as they always did when she started to get enthused. "Now all you have to do is find an animal that's died of natural causes, since we wouldn't want to harm anything in the forest, and then all you'd have to do is check to make certain it didn't die of something that could possibly infect and kill you, and after that you'd only have to separate the meat from the bone. Since you don't have a knife, you'd have to use your bare hands, unless you wanted to use the sharp end of a rock. But then, you'd have to be careful not to pound too hard or you'd be crushing the bones, which would defeat your purpose." She paused to take a deep breath, then looked at him expectantly.

Cole warned himself to be patient. "How about we look for bones that are just lying around?"

"You could do that. Of course," she quickly added, "you'd have to be on the scene pretty close to when the animal died. Once it's down, it does become food for the other animals, and in a few hours, or less, usually there's nothing left."

Cole lowered his head again. "I'm not trying to be difficult here, but he's *got* to spear these freaking fish. It'll look good on film to have him throwing the damn spear and nailing one of them."

"Okay—but it wouldn't be accurate."

Cole ran his hand down his face, then lifted it. "Why not?"

"You never throw a spear at fish; you could lose the spear

that way. Then where would he be? Making another spear, that's what."

God. This was Boy Scout hell. "Okay, so he doesn't throw the spear. What does he do? Smack them in the head with it to knock them senseless?"

Ariel frowned. "Of course not. He'd wade into the pool where the fish are the most plentiful. He'd have to give them a chance to get used to his presence. Once they were, he'd wait for the right moment, then simply push the spear down to impale one of them."

Cole nodded as he pictured that from a director's point of view. There could be an overhead wide shot of his poor guy in the middle of a huge body of water with nothing but a spear in his hand. He'd be naked to the waist, and his back would already be sunburned—possibly even clawed from some animal attack. As the camera zoomed in on those fish swimming past his legs, the shot would cut to his face. His cheeks would be hollowed out from hunger. Sweat would be dripping into his eyes. His gaze would be focused, murderous as he watched those damned fish casually swimming by without a care in the world, while he knew they were the only thing standing between him and starvation. He'd know that he had only one shot at this; if he failed, all the other fish would zip away. He'd have to be patient despite his hunger; he'd have to wait for the right moment—at last it would come, and he would shout his success.

Cole nodded as he pictured all of that. It could definitely work. "And once he had impaled one of them, he'd be able to hold it up in a moment of victory."

"Only in your story."

"What do you mean only in my story?"

"In real life, the moment he tried to lift the fish, it'd slip off the end of the spear. The only way he could avoid that would be to hold it down with the spear, then bend over and grab it with his free hand. Of course, all of this is contingent upon whether there's lots of fish swimming around and he's aware of light refraction and how it distorts objects in the water."

Cole rubbed his throbbing temple. "Okay, let's say for the sake of argument the character in my screenplay doesn't know how to spear fish, because up until now he's been totally useless. Are you telling me that his only other option is to make a freaking fishing pole *and* hooks *and* lures?"

"It's not as difficult as it sounds."

Cole looked at her.

Ariel cautiously explained, "You can easily use broken seashells or thorns or tortoise shells or pieces of coconut shells or even bones for hooks."

"If you can find them."

"Well, sure."

Cole rolled his eyes.

"Not interesting enough for your story?" she asked.

"Not easy enough," he corrected.

Ariel frowned. "Hank wouldn't look for those things so he could fish for Mina?"

"No, he—Hank?" Cole asked.

Ariel gave him a wicked look as she turned into him and gently stroked his chest. "I think he deserves a name change if he did for Mina what you did for me at the waterfall, don't you agree?"

Oh, she was really something. Teasing one minute and yielding the next. Cole leaned close and murmured, "Absolutely. But is that all he's going to get?"

Ariel looked at him from beneath her lashes. "He wants more?" Before Cole could answer, she casually said, "All right." Stepping back, she quickly removed her top.

Cole stared at her tightened nipples pressing against that incredibly dainty bra. Now this was a surprise he didn't mind. He started to unbutton his shirt.

"Oh," Ariel suddenly said, "would you rather I use yours?"

Cole looked up from his buttons. "Use my what?"

"Your shirt to catch the fish."

Okay, now she'd lost him. "You've taken off your top to fish? You're going to use your top as a lure?"

"Net," she corrected as she glanced around the clearing, then went to the edge of the vegetation and selected a branch. Testing it for suppleness, she returned to Cole.

He watched as she knotted the neck of her top, then bent the branch until it formed a circle, securing it with one of the sleeves. With that accomplished, she slipped the rest of the top over that circle until she had made her net.

Cole's eyes continued to widen. "I'm not complaining, mind you, I always like it when you're even partially un-dressed, but you actually think *that*"—he pointed to the net—"is going to catch any fish?"

"It's either this or we poison them."

He laughed, until he noticed that she was dead serious. "Really?"

"Uh-huh. All we have to do is use a plant that produces rotenone. It's really something. It'll kill or, at the very least, stun a large number of fish so you can catch them—actually," she interrupted herself, "you don't even have to do that since the fish rise helplessly to the surface. And I know what you're thinking. If it kills them, will it kill you? Absolutely not. Rotenone has no effect on warm-blooded creatures. Of course," she quickly added, "there aren't any rotenone-producing plants on this island, but there are other poisonous plants that you could add to your story." She started to bounce on her heels, again. "Could be Mina and Hank whip up a witch's brew of those plants and somehow get the bad guys to drink it and—"

Cole finally interrupted. "You're pulling my leg, right?"

Ariel worked her mouth around as if she were trying very hard not to smile. Going to him, she murmured, "Let's just say I will . . . later."

Before Cole could comment, she stepped back and said, "But first, let's catch those fish."

Chapter Twelve

It took some doing, and more than a few breathless kisses, before Ariel was able to coax Cole toward the pool.

Before they reached it, she turned around and walked backward as she talked. "Once we're at the edge keep your voice lowered. We don't want to scare away the fish."

He nodded absently as his gaze remained on her nipples pushing against the delicate cups of her bra.

"Cole, did you hear me?"

"Loud and clear." He grabbed her arm, stopping her. "You get that from Victoria's Secret?"

Ariel looked down at the dainty silk and lace bra that was the same shade of green as her eyes. It, like those dangling diamond stars, had been a knee-jerk response to her awful encounter with that corporate pilot. "Actually, it's from *Field and Stream.*"

Cole laughed.

"Shhhh," Ariel said, then inclined her head toward the pool. "The fish, remember?"

"Not when I've got a Victoria's Secret vision right in front of me. Come on, fess up," he said, "that's definitely a Vicki's Delight."

Ariel arched one brow. "How would you know? You frequent their stores very often?"

"Never once been inside, but," he quickly added as his gaze lifted to hers, "I have looked at their display windows."

Uh-huh. Ariel guessed he had probably dated some of the babes in their catalogues. Babes that didn't fish or climb rocks or build fires. Babes that were so damned female they had to go into therapy over a few split ends.

Ariel knew she shouldn't ask, but just had to. "Did you like what you saw in those windows?"

Cole quietly regarded her, then murmured, "I like what I see here."

She smiled, until his gaze grew quickly heated. "Uh-uh," she warned, pulling her arm from him, "we have to catch some fish."

The heat in his eyes remained.

"Cole."

"I haven't said a thing, Ariel. I haven't *done* a thing."

"Well, that's not entirely true. Back at the waterfall you—"

"That was days ago, maybe even weeks. I haven't done anything since then. You keep stopping me."

"Not because I want to. If it were up to me, I'd have a pizza delivered."

"Good idea. We could work it into the screenplay that the government turned Mina's long-lost brother into the delivery guy."

Ariel laughed, then quickly stopped, remembering the fish. "Will you be serious?" she asked in a lowered voice, then quickly continued, "I'm simply trying to keep us on track. And, believe me, I appreciate the fact that you've been more than cooperative, but then you are an officer and a gentleman."

"*Was* an officer and a—"

"You still are and you know it."

He frowned. "Lucky for you I am, because if I weren't—"

She interrupted, "I'd still trust you, because you're a good man."

That doused his passion faster than a cold shower. Oddly enough though, he didn't look pissed or frustrated. He seemed genuinely touched by her words. "You really think so?"

"Absolutely."

He smiled. "So that's what you told your uncle to make sure he wouldn't bother us later when we actually and finally do make love?"

"Nope."

He seemed surprised.

Ariel finally confessed. "Uncle Thaddeus said I should treat you well because he likes you."

Cole's brows shot up. "No shit—I mean, no kidding?"

"Hard to believe, I know, but there you have it." She shrugged. "After that he said he wouldn't be bothering us anymore."

"You believe him?"

"Oh, yeah. When we last talked he was headed for the casinos to lose the villa at a blackjack table, which he said would be all my fault. But, at least, Isa seemed pleased."

"She was with him, huh?"

"I don't think she'll ever be without him from that moment forward. It's not something she could bear."

Cole's expression changed. When he spoke his voice sounded distracted. "She really loves him?"

More than you will ever know, Ariel thought, thinking of herself and him. "Yes, she adores him."

Cole's expression changed again, as if he finally realized they weren't talking about Thaddeus and Isa anymore.

Ariel suppressed a sigh. Before things got too heavy or Cole passed out, she decided to return to the task at hand. "Once we get to the edge of the pool just watch what I do, okay?"

"Whatever you want."

Good God, she thought. It wasn't only what she wanted. She wanted him to want it, too! Not that Ariel was about to get into that now. They had fish to catch.

Damn. Moving to the edge of the water, she turned to Cole and put her finger to her lips, gesturing him to silence.

He seemed distracted as ever as he finally nodded.

Suppressing yet another sigh, Ariel crept along the water's edge until she reached the most advantageous part of the pool—a shallow spot where the fish were visible—then lowered the makeshift net into the water. Her movements were exceedingly gentle so as not to scare the game.

So far, so good. The little buggers had briefly flitted away, but when they sensed no real danger, they began to return.

During this, Ariel tried to remain focused, but could not.

In her peripheral vision she saw Cole edging closer. Looking over her shoulder at him, Ariel shook her head.

He stopped, then swung his arms out as he mouthed, *What are you doing?*

Waiting, she mouthed right back.

His expression said he could see that. He continued to edge closer.

Again, she shook her head.

He ignored that admonition, stopping only when they were side by side. Lowering his mouth to her ear, he whispered, "What are you waiting for?"

Ariel's lids fluttered to his breath tickling her ear. My God, but that felt good. Not that she should dwell on that now, or the weird expression he had worn when she sort of told him she loved him.

Sighing deeply, she finally moved her head until she could whisper in his ear. "I'm waiting for the fish to get accustomed to the trap."

Cole moved his mouth back to her ear and whispered, "Oh," then gently pressed his lips to her cheek.

Ariel nearly dropped the trap.

"Careful," he whispered.

She lowered her head and breathed hard.

He whispered, "Want me to take over?"

Well, of course she did. At least in some matters, like pursuing her and committing to her and promising to always be with her. Not that that was likely to happen. At last, she shook her head, got her bearings, and focused on these damned fish as she had never focused before.

Cole seemed to sense her changed mood, because he didn't move or whisper.

He waited as she did, then inhaled sharply as she finally—and easily—scooped two fish out of the water, tossing them on the bank.

Cole's head snapped to where they had landed, their frantic thrashing as they tried to get back into the water. "Damn," he said in a normal voice.

Despite that unacceptable volume, Ariel couldn't help but smile. He really loved the way she caught fish . . . now if only he could love everything else about her.

Will you just knock it off, she warned herself, then moved around him.

He turned. "What are—"

"Shhhhhh."

Okay, okay! he mouthed, then followed her and whispered, "What are you doing?"

"Catching more fish," she said in a low voice, "two won't be enough for us." She went to another area she liked and dipped her net.

Cole quickly joined her and whispered, "Let me do it."

Ariel looked up. For once, the man wasn't faking it. His gaze was actually on the makeshift net, not her nipples or butt. Despite that, or maybe because of it, she couldn't help but tease. "You sure you're ready for this?"

Cole slid his gaze to her, then smiled as she handed him the net. He continued to whisper, "How many do you want?"

"You decide, just so long as you don't empty the pool."

He arched one brow. "I swear I'll leave at least one or two to repopulate."

"Two would probably be best."

"You think?"

"Go fish." She pointed to the pool.

Cole nodded absently as he was already focused on catching those fish. Just as she had, he kept his movements to a minimum and didn't once talk, cough, or make any unnecessary noise.

Not even a groan when ten minutes passed and he came up empty.

At last, he lifted the makeshift net and glared at it.

Ariel leaned over and whispered in his ear. "Something wrong?"

He turned his head to her and whispered, "Besides the fact that we still haven't made love?"

She gave him an innocent look, then kept her voice low, "We need to eat first."

"Yeah, I know. It's called foreplay. After that, then we'll make love."

"We need to eat fish," she corrected in a whisper.

"Yeah, I know." He held up the net. "There must be a hole in this thing that the fish are swimming through, because it's not working."

"Must be," she said.

"Or maybe I need a little more practice?" he whispered.

"If you say so."

He rolled his eyes, then moved to another shallow part of the pool as if her presence, in addition to flaws in the net, was causing the fish to slip through it.

After he carefully studied every part of the net and found no obvious hole, Cole again placed it in the pool, waited a few seconds, then jerked it upward, dousing himself with water.

Ariel lowered her head as her shoulders trembled with suppressed laughter.

"This isn't funny," he said in his normal voice.

"Shhhh!" she said, then continued to tremble as she tried not to laugh.

"To hell with this," he said, then tossed the net on the bank and entered the water.

Ariel's laughter quickly paused. She frowned. "What are you doing?"

"Catching these damn fish."

Her brows lifted as Cole hunkered down, then slipped his arms into the water to catch those fish bare-handed.

"Use the net," Ariel said, "it will work if you only give it a—"

"*Shhhh.*"

Ariel lifted her hands in surrender and waited to see what wouldn't happen.

Two minutes passed, then four more. Even so, Cole kept his head down and his gaze on the water as he turned in a very slow circle, presumably following the movements of the fish.

At last, Ariel sank down to the bank, getting comfortable. Could be this would take the rest of the day since he was doing everything wrong. He was supposed to be reaching under the bank, not where he presently was. He was supposed to be letting his arms move with the water's flow, not swishing them back and forth as if he were washing clothes. He was supposed to be unobtrusive to the fish, not frightening—

Ariel's thoughts abruptly paused as Cole gasped.

"What?" she shouted.

"Gotcha!" he shouted, then flung two fish into the air.

Ariel's head lifted, and her brows rose as she watched those buggers sailing through the air in a wide arc, before plopping onto the bank.

Cole pushed to a standing position, let out a wild *whoop*, then started to boogie.

"Cole!" Ariel suddenly shouted.

His hips gyrated for a moment more before he met her gaze. "What?"

She pointed. "Your fish."

He turned to look. "What about my—oh, no you don't!" he growled as one of those fish wiggled from the bank back into the pool.

Splashing through the water, Cole slapped it with both palms as he tried to grab that fish.

As Ariel watched from the side, man and fish struggled for several minutes before Cole tossed the unlucky creature back onto the bank, then quickly tore out of the water, lifted a rock and brained it.

Breathing hard, he finally turned to Ariel.

Her gaze dropped to his wet clothing that hugged his muscular body, not to mention that male treasure behind his fly.

"Well?" Cole said.

Ariel met his gaze, smiled broadly, and applauded. "Oh, damn," she suddenly said, then stopped. "I forgot, I'm supposed to be saving my applause for the important—"

"This is important. This is huge."

Her gaze drifted back to his lovely, yet hidden, cock. "Sure is."

He laughed, then whined. "Come on. I did good."

"That you did." She applauded wildly.

He made an elaborate bow from the waist. While still in that position, he lifted his head and gaze to her. "Hungry?"

You have no idea, Ariel thought. "Oh, yes," she murmured.

Cole grinned, then started to straighten, but abruptly stopped.

"What's wrong?" she asked. "Are you in pain?"

He shook his head. "There's something . . ." He didn't finish as he lifted his shirt, pulled his slacks and shorts away from his body, then looked down. Given the face he made, he didn't like what he saw.

"What's down there?" she asked.

His gaze lifted to her.

"Other than the usual wonderful stuff?" she finally added.

He arched one brow, then made another face as he pushed his hand into his shorts only to pull out a soggy piece of vegetation.

"Ooooh, that looks nasty," Ariel said, "did it bite you?"

He looked at her. "You want to be cute or do you want to eat?"

"Well, given your snotty attitude, I don't know."

"Let me put it this way," he said. "You want to be cute or do you want to eat in every sense of the word?"

She slowly smiled. "Now there's a plan despite your snotty attitude."

To her surprise, Cole didn't grin. "You want me, but you don't want my fish, too?"

Her gaze flicked to the one he had clobbered with that rock. Even the birds probably wouldn't want it now. She looked back at him and lied. "Of course I want your fish."

At last he smiled. "That first, me later. Come on, baby," he said, then held out his hand. "Tonight, supper's on me."

Although Ariel was glad that Cole was finally getting into this survival stuff, allowing him to prepare their meal all by himself could prove problematic.

Of course, he seemed blissfully unaware of that, at least at first.

Like most men of his caliber, he could disarm a bomb, jump out of a helicopter, and fire missiles to blow up the bad guys, but gathering food and tending a fire seemed to stump him at every turn.

"Were you *ever* a Boy Scout?" Ariel finally asked.

She was again fully dressed, and they were both sitting around the fire that he had yet to reignite.

Cole finally looked up. His face was reddened from blowing and blowing and blowing to get the fresh tinder to flame. "Even better than that. I graduated from the Naval Academy."

Of course. But had he ever been a Boy Scout, since the only skills he seemed to be lacking were those taught to that group. "I knew that."

He seemed surprised. "You read my bio?"

"Uncle Thaddeus told me."

"Ah, when he begged you to help me because you don't like Hollywood types."

"He actually told you that?"

"He told me a lot of things," Cole muttered, "none of which I intend to get into now. There's work to do, remember?"

Ariel arched one brow. He was doing to her what she was always doing to him—avoiding the subject. "Actually, I do," she said, then leaned down and gently blew on the tinder that was closest to her.

Just like that, the fire was reignited.

"What do you know," Ariel said, then leveled her gaze on him. "Now we have time to talk about what you and my uncle talked about."

Cole continued to frown at the fire before lifting his gaze to her. "No, we don't. There's too much to do."

Before Ariel could counter that, Cole was on his feet, collecting kindling to feed the fire. After he tended to that, he jumped back to his feet and disappeared into the surrounding forest.

Ariel tapped her fingers against the ground, warning herself not to ask what in the world he was doing.

Two minutes later, she was on her feet, pacing the area as she told herself not to worry.

Three minutes after that, she shouted, "Cole!"

He so quickly ran out of the forest some of the stuff in his arms fell to the ground. "What? What's wrong?"

She lifted her shoulders in a small shrug. "Nothing. I was just wondering what you were doing."

"Like hell," he said as he went to her. "You thought I was lost."

"I worry about you," she said.

His expression changed, and his frown softened. "Yeah, I know, but I had to get this." He dropped the load in his arms at her feet.

Ariel looked down, then grinned. "You remembered!"

"Damn right." He finished brushing debris off his sleeves, then pointed. "There's enough coconut husks there to repel every insect on Planet Earth."

"No kidding." She looked up as he drew her into his arms, then rested his forehead against hers.

"Nothing is going to interrupt us tonight," he said, his voice very soft. "Nothing."

She smiled. "Well, at least not insects."

"Nothing," he corrected, then gave her a lusty kiss and a playful pat on the butt, before releasing her. "Okay, now to the fish. You want them fried, barbequed, broiled, or baked?"

"Cleaned would be nice."

His upper lip curled as he considered what that chore involved. "Guess we can't just cook them clear through, guts and all, huh?"

"We could, but I don't advise it."

That lip starting curling again. "Cleaning and gutting a fish without a knife is going to be messy."

Ariel cupped the side of his face in her hand. "I know, but remember, Boy Scouts have been doing it since the dawn of time."

"They have not!" He laughed.

"Okay," she conceded, "they've been doing it since the nineteen forties, about the time you were born—no—don't!" she squealed.

"You've been asking for it, baby, and now you're gonna pay." He continued to tickle her.

He was driving her nuts. Ariel tried to run, but it did no good. Cole was far faster and certainly stronger. He had her on the ground in a moment, where he unfolded his body, fully trapping hers so that he could tickle her uninterrupted.

"No!" she shrieked.

"Be nice," he said.

"I—I—I—stop!"

He finally did when she started to hiccup.

"You okay?" he asked.

Ariel opened one eye and glared at him, at least until she hiccupped again.

"Want me to scare those out of you?"

She hiccupped again, then quickly said, "I think the forest fire will do that."

Cole's expression changed. He looked over to the fire he had again forgotten. "Damn." Jumping to his feet, he returned to it.

Ariel gulped air, then held it until her hiccups had passed.

"You okay?" he finally called out.

Was he kidding? She was lying limp on the ground, still breathless and weak from that tickling, plus the ache in her heart, because she was really going to miss moments like this when he was gone.

"Ariel, are you—"

"I'm fine," she lied.

"Good," he called out, then added, "you need help getting up?"

That was the least of her worries. Ariel knew she was going to need help getting over him. Of course, that wasn't going to happen for the rest of today and all of tomorrow. So now was not the time to think about it. "Nope."

With as much ease as she could muster—and so that she could continue to impress him—Ariel jumped to her feet and jogged in place.

Cole didn't notice. His head remained bent to the fish he was trying to clean with nothing but his bare hands, wits, and a lot of swearing that he probably learned in the Marines.

Ariel finally joined him and rested her hand on his shoulder. He looked up.

"Thanks," she said.

He seemed surprised. "For what?"

Tickling her, kissing her, putting up with her crap, and wanting to make love with her. "Just thanks." Bending down, she gently kissed his lips, then sank to the ground and crossed her legs. "How you doing?"

"Well, the kiss was great, but this?" He looked down at the soggy mess in his hands.

Ariel figured it was far too late to suggest using a sharp-edged rock, rather than his closely clipped nails, to gut those things. "Looks good," she lied.

His expression brightened. He worked even faster as he finished mutilating their food. "Let me rinse these babies out in the pool. Be right back."

"You better be," Ariel whispered as she watched him stride away.

When he reached the edge of the water and looked over his shoulder to see if she was watching, Ariel smiled.

She had no choice. She knew she would always watch him in protection and in love.

Cole grinned as if he was pleased. Of course, he hadn't heard her thoughts.

As he hunkered down, Ariel watched the thin fabric of his slacks straining against his muscular thighs. Her gaze drifted over his broad back as he dunked those mangled fish into the water to wash them clean.

As he worked, she wondered what kind of woman he could truly love . . . one he would be willing to offer his heart and his name.

Accepting a man's heart had always seemed easy to Ariel, if the right guy came along. It was accepting his name that gave her the most pause. It was an old-fashioned concept that Ariel had never really endorsed, not even with her college guy, but then she hadn't really been in love with him.

If Cole had been hers, if there was even the remotest possibility that he could be hers, Ariel knew she would willingly take his name and give it to their children.

Already she had decided one daughter wouldn't be enough; they should also have a son. And, if Cole agreed, even more children than that.

For the first time in her life, Ariel actually yearned to be a mother, a notion that until now had seemed remote at best, and altogether unwise given her own childhood.

What if she didn't live up to her children's expectations as her own parents had not lived up to hers? What if she made the same mistakes they had?

Oh, God no, she quickly thought. If Cole were hers, no matter how bad things became—even if he cheated on her repeatedly and without pause—no way could Ariel do the same to him.

No way did she think he would cheat. He was an officer and a gentleman. He was a man of integrity and honor.

He was a man who would not wed unless he was very certain that he adored the woman who became his wife.

Which begged the question—what did any of this matter when their time together was nothing more than a job?

The day after tomorrow Cole would have all that he needed for his movie, along with a sunburned face, a variety of cuts, scrapes, and bruises, and a fading memory of the good—but limited—time they had.

Ariel sighed.

"Hey, I'm going as fast as I can."

She looked up, surprised to see that he had returned.

He seemed surprised that she hadn't continued watching him. "Something wrong?" he asked.

Ariel picked a bit of fish meat up off the ground.

"Damn," Cole said, "these suckers keep falling apart." Now he sighed. "Guess putting them on a spit for a little barbeque is out of the question."

"Not at all. A Boy Scout would know that."

"Look, I joined the Girl Scouts—are you laughing at me?"

It was either that or cry. God, how Ariel loved being with him. "Sorry," she finally said, then cleared the laughter and sorrow from her voice. "Those can still go on a spit. All you have to do is pull some of those fibers from the coconut husks, then wash them, then braid them into long ropes, then wrap that around—"

He finally interrupted, "Guess putting them on a spit for a little barbeque is out of the question."

She smiled. "Guess so."

"Right. Here."

Ariel leaned away as he tried to hand her those soggy fish. "Whoa, I'm not eating them raw."

"I haven't asked you to. But if you don't hold these while I get something to fry them in, I'll have to lay them on the ground. If you haven't yet noticed, it's kind of dirty."

"The fire will take care of that."

His upper lip curled.

"Or," Ariel finally added, "you could try putting them on a clean banana leaf."

"Now, why didn't I think of that? I'll just hold them in my mouth while I go looking for—"

"Just a sec." Pushing to her feet, Ariel got what he needed and returned with it. "Just lay those babies on this."

Once Cole scraped them off his palms onto that clean leaf, he glanced around.

Ariel sensed a question was coming, so she simply waited.

To her surprise, Cole went to the script that was still under the rock.

She glanced down at the fish and figured within a half hour, at most, the smell of these things would draw all sorts of nasty dinner guests.

Not that Cole seemed to notice or care. His head was bent to the battered script as he slowly thumbed through it.

Ariel frowned. "What are you doing?"

"Reading." He briefly looked up before returning his gaze to the script. "What page did you say the sex scene was—"

She interrupted, "If you take any longer getting these fish cooked, there won't be a sex scene."

He nodded as if he couldn't care less, then continued thumbing through the script until he found what he was looking for.

Ariel lowered her head and breathed hard until she was

overwhelmed by the raw odor of the fish. *God.* She held their food at arm's length.

"Here it is," he suddenly said, then read aloud as he went to her. "In this part, the useless politician and Mina, the girl hero, will be making supper. Mina will be doing most of the work." Cole paused, then looked up. "Liar."

Ariel couldn't help but laugh. "You're reading about supper, not sex?"

"I'll get to that." He looked back down, then read aloud once more. "Although the useless politician will suggest putting the fish on a spit, which won't work at—" Cole abruptly paused, then arched one brow.

Ariel cleared her throat. "If I had suspected you were going to read that, I wouldn't have written it."

Cole didn't comment. He glanced back down, found his place, then continued reading aloud. "Won't work at all. But Mina is patient with the man." Cole paused to roll his eyes, then continued reading. "She then easily *and expertly* suggests the only possible and best solution, which is boiling the fish." He made a face. "Yuck."

"It was the best solution," Ariel said.

He looked up. He actually looked hopeful. "Was?"

"Uh-huh, before you removed most of the skin."

"Damn, I'm sorry," he said.

She laughed. "No, you're not. But boiling fish while it's still clothed does retain all the fat and oil, which gives you the most nutrients."

His expression said he could care less.

"Nutrients, of course, give you energy," she said, "which you'll need when we finally reach page ninety—"

He finally interrupted, "To hell with nutrients, *you* give me energy."

Aw, he was so damned sweet, and suddenly glancing around again.

Ariel waited while he visually searched the area, after which he looked back to the script, read several pages, then finally lifted his head to her. "Okay, I give, what do I use for a frying pan?"

"Well, that depends."

He muttered, "On what?"

"How long you intend to go looking for it." She lifted the fish. "Smell."

He backed away instead. "We better hurry."

"Uh-huh."

"So, what do I—"

Ariel interrupted and talked fast. "Get a large flat rock and place it next to the fire. Once it gets hot, I'll let these things ooze from the leaf onto—"

He interrupted, "Ooze?"

"Drop," she corrected, "and let them fry. Now, if you don't mind getting that rock."

"I'm on it." Cole looked right, left, then turned to see what was behind him before finding what he liked. He pointed. "That one over there looks good."

"Too big."

He paused, then swung his finger a bit to the right. "How about—"

"Too porous."

He gave her a frown. "How can you tell that's too porous from way over here?"

"It's near the pool. The rocks there have tiny little holes in them, because they're porous."

"Yeah. So?"

"Porous usually means they have moisture in them, and that usually means that once they're heated they'll explode. Of course," she added to his expression, "we could use exploding rocks as weapons against the bad guys when they catch up with—"

He interrupted, "If those bastards catch up with you and me tonight, then *they* can damn well build our bed."

Ariel laughed. "Tell you what, while you're seeing to our supper, I'll build our bed."

"No. I want to do it all."

He meant it; she saw that in his eyes, and that touched Ariel more than if he had said she was gorgeous and hot and all that other stuff guys said that didn't mean a thing.

Being committed to this as much as she was meant everything.

She softened her voice and spoke from the heart. "I want that, too, *in bed,* which we'll get to that much faster if you let me help you with—"

"Right." He took the banana leaf and gently placed it on the ground, then sighed when a bit of the fish slipped off of it.

"That's going to be really good," she said.

He briefly laughed, then spoke in a hard voice. "Get to work."

"Yes, sir—but if you have any questions just—"

"I know, I know, look in the script."

Actually, she had been about to suggest that he ask her, but the script would have to do. Already Cole had forgotten her as he looked at one rock after another, finally choosing one that was perfect.

Ariel smiled.

He didn't notice that either as he went to the pool, then used the dampened edge of his shirt to clean off the rock before bringing it back to the fire.

As he continued to worry over the food, muttering profanities when it refused to cooperate, Ariel figured she should start working on their sleeping arrangements.

Once she had selected a spot that was dry and close enough to the fire for protection, she began to wonder what it would be like to pick out a condo with him, or a house, then to fill it with children, laughter, and love.

It would certainly be more civilized, not to mention more enduring, than this.

Not that this wasn't lovely and more than Ariel had ever hoped for.

There was just enough wind to cool the balmy air, while

the sounds of the water gently tumbling into the pool so quickly lulled. Behind that, she heard monkeys playing and birds calling out to their mates.

Enjoy this while you can, she warned herself and allowed herself a long moment of reflection before getting back to work.

Not that it was all that hard. She quickly decided that they needed a modified swamp bed—king-sized, of course, because Cole was so tall.

Ariel smiled at that and the thought of what lay ahead as she gathered the branches she needed, then positioned them until they formed a rectangle on the ground. She next laid smaller branches lengthwise across them, then kept repeating the process until the bed was about a foot high.

Returning to the forest, she came back with numerous banana leaves and gauzy coconut fibers. Alternating the leaves and the fibers, she soon had their mattress.

As Ariel tested it out, finding it comfy enough even for a Hollywood type, she finally looked over to Cole.

He was sucking his thumb.

Her brows lifted. Either he was frustrated as hell or he had just burnt his thumb on that smoldering rock. *Poor baby,* she thought. He was such a mess. His hair was still spiked from that brief swim, his once-clean clothes were again streaked with dirt, and there were now wood ashes smudged on his left cheek and ear.

He looked really terrible and so completely wonderful that Ariel's eyes stung with quick tears.

Never had a man worked so hard to impress her with a meal. Never had she known anyone so very lousy at it.

She held back a giggle, then quickly averted her gaze as Cole lifted his.

"Everything all right?" he asked.

"Uh-huh. Just putting the finishing touches on the bed."

"Hey," he said as if he just now noticed it. "Nice."

"Thanks." She looked at him.

"Uh-uh," he said, "don't watch me. I want to surprise you."

Ariel figured he would do that without even trying, but still nodded. "Sure. I'll go wash up."

"Just your hands," he said. "Don't do anything naked until I'm with you, okay?"

She laughed. "Absolutely. Be back in a sec."

"Ah, better make it several, okay?"

"Sure." Ariel made certain not to look at the fire, the smoldering rock, or those mutilated fish as she headed for the waterfall, then bypassed it to go to the edge of the forest.

Once there, she looked to see how far she had come, then pushed to her toes which gave her just a glimpse of the top of Cole's head.

He was far enough away so that he couldn't overhear anything.

At last, Ariel pulled out his cell phone that she had again taken without him noticing. How in the world did he survive in an area like LA that surely had its share of pickpockets?

Of course, while he was here he was safe. She would make damned certain of that.

Lowering her gaze to the phone, Ariel selected Gwen's number from the address book.

Fifteen rings later, the woman snarled, "What in the hell do you want?"

"Bad time to talk?" Ariel asked.

"That depends. *Who is this?* I'm a cop by the way," she quickly added, "and your number has already gone from this phone to the computer system at the station, which goes straight to Washington and the Feds. Within seconds they not only have the location where you're calling from, but a satellite system is currently taking pictures of you. So smile, you're on CIA Camera."

"Can they really do that?" Ariel asked. "If they can," she quickly added, "I'll put it in Cole's story. That's cool."

There was a brief pause filled with cell phone static, before Gwen said, "Arianna?"

"Ariel," she corrected, not for the first time. In fact, each time she spoke to the woman, Gwen got her name wrong.

"Right," Gwen said now. "What time is it there, hon?"

Ariel told her.

"Hey, that's not too far off from what it is here." Gwen's voice dropped several degrees. "But guess who just got into bed after working twenty hours straight?"

"I shouldn't have called, but I had a few minutes to kill."

"Really?" Her voice got downright frosty. "Glad you thought of me to kill them with. So what's Cole doing while you're calling me?"

"Getting our supper, in a manner of speaking."

Gwen suddenly laughed. "You have him hunting down animals with a spear?"

"No, of course not." Ariel frowned. What was it with these people and their love affair with spears? "He's cooking fish on a rock."

Gwen laughed so hard it was several minutes before she could speak. "Oh, my God, I can't stand it! Does your cell have a camera? If it does, please send me a picture of that."

"It doesn't," Ariel said in her own frosty tone, "so I won't."

Gwen was momentarily silent. "No need to get all protective of him, hon. Cole can take care of himself."

"Not out here, he can't."

Gwen was laughing again.

Ariel sighed, then decided to ask the question that had been nagging her ever since Cole brought up the subject. "You know, since he's having trouble with this research, I was wondering—"

"He hasn't hurt himself, has he?" Gwen suddenly interrupted, her tone deadly serious. "I mean, we don't want insurance problems, you know."

"No, he hasn't hurt himself . . . at least, not yet."

"Keep in mind," Gwen said, "you gotta keep him safe. If he gets hurt and we have to wait for him to recover, that will add millions to the production." Her voice got frosty again. "We can't have that."

Ariel shook her head. "I won't let him get hurt."

"Thank God."

"But he may need to stay a few more days to complete this—"

"No, absolutely not," Gwen cut in. "We have work to do. Day after tomorrow he's gotta be done with you."

Ariel's heart sank. As Gwen continued to speak, it was Cole's voice that she heard.

I'll stay longer if I have to.

At the time he had meant it, but Gwen had spoken the brutal truth.

Day after tomorrow he's gotta be done with you.

Ariel's eyes filled with tears.

"Hey, you still there?" Gwen suddenly asked.

"Yeah."

"Then please see to it that this is done on time. Already he's stayed too long. This was only supposed to be for one day. I mean, does the script really need this much realism?"

"Yes, it does," Ariel finally snapped. "And he's not leaving until the day after tomorrow, *got it?*"

"Easy, hon. I'm only telling you our schedule. We got commitments, you know? Already one of the money people is bitching about delays, you know."

She did now.

"Look at it this way," Gwen said in a much softer tone, "once we iron out the new script, he'll be back on your island to shoot this damn thing. You can see him again then."

Surrounded by other people, Ariel thought, without a moment to give to her.

Could be he wouldn't even notice her anymore.

"Yes, I can," she finally said.

"Good, now just go back to his fish and his rock." She started laughing again. "That is so damned fun—"

"Ariel!" Cole suddenly called out.

"Gotta go," she quickly said to Gwen, then shut the cell phone and dropped it into her pocket. "Yeah!" she shouted to him.

"Where the hell are you?"

She was on the edge of despair—not that Ariel could shout that to him.

Day after tomorrow he's gotta be done with you, Gwen had said.

Dammit! Ariel thought, covering her face with her hands. Already she was hurting and he hadn't even left.

"Ariel?" Cole shouted again.

She dropped her hands. "I'm coming, all right?"

He was briefly silent, then shouting, "Ah, not yet. Give me a few more minutes, okay? I just wanted to make sure you were all right!"

Not ever again, she thought.

"You are, aren't you?" he shouted.

New tears stung her eyes. "Sure!" She tightened her hands into fists. "I can take care of myself! I'm an expert at that!"

"Look, I'll hurry it up!" he shouted, as if his dillydallying were the problem. "Just give me five more minutes!"

Five more minutes, she thought, when what she wanted and needed was a lifetime. "Sure."

"What?"

"I said *sure!*"

Uh-huh, Cole thought, not about to argue with that tone of voice. Something had happened after she had strolled away from him, and he hadn't a clue what it might be.

Maybe she was just hungry. Maybe she was pissed because he was taking so damned long.

Quicker than his expertise and blistered fingertips allowed, Cole gathered the rest of the stuff for their meal and set it up.

He was about to shout for her to *come and get it* when he figured it'd be better if he picked her up for their date. That's what an officer and a gentleman would do.

After Cole attended the fire so that it wouldn't do anything it wasn't supposed to in the short time he'd be gone, then washed his hands in the pool, he went in search of her.

Minutes later, he saw that she was seated on a moderately large rock with her head down and her elbows resting on her knees.

Cole wasn't certain if she was thinking or praying. He cleared his voice.

Her head snapped up.

His brows rose. My God, it looked as if she'd been crying. "Hey," he quickly said, then went to her. "What happened? What's wrong?"

Ariel shook her head and used the backs of her hands to dry her eyes. "I just stubbed my toe, that's all."

Cole was already on his knees. "Let me see it."

"No. It's okay."

"Not if it made you cry. Come on, I want to see it, and we better make it quick since I left the fire burning back—"

"Okay, okay," she said, then pulled off her moccasin and lifted her foot. "See, it's fine."

Actually, it looked far better than his felt. Still, he leaned down and kissed it, then wiggled his tongue between her big and longest toes.

She laughed.

"That's my girl." Cole shoved her moccasin back on, grabbed her hand, and pulled her to her feet. "Come on, the fire's getting hot, and all the food's getting cold."

She jogged with him. "*All* the food?"

He briefly met her gaze. "I have a surprise for you."

She looked close to tears again.

"It's good, really," he promised, then hurried her back to the fire and their meal. Moving his arm in a wide sweeping gesture, he said, "Your table, ma'am."

Ariel's eyes filled with more tears as she looked at the fish that had third-degree burns, the mulberry fruit he really shouldn't have chosen as a dessert, those unripe mangos, and those red-dish flowers that appeared to be from the canna lily plant.

Fear quickly replaced her sorrow. "Have you eaten any of that yet?"

"No . . . why?" He glanced down at their food. "Did I pick something poisonous?"

"Not exactly, but those red flowers—"

"Aren't part of our meal," he said, then added, "they're for decoration. They're for you."

Her eyes welled up again.

Cole quickly misunderstood. "Hey, if they're poisonous, tell me. I'll get rid of—"

He abruptly stopped as Ariel threw her arms around him. "Don't," she murmured, "they're beautiful. Everything's beautiful."

"Really?" he asked.

Ariel pressed her face against his neck. "Oh, yeah, though you shouldn't eat too many of those black berries. They'll give you a stomachache."

"I'll pace myself."

"Only with that."

He laughed, then eased away. "Go on, sit down and dig in."

Ariel sank to the ground and accepted the banana leaf he gave her to use as a plate.

Just as he was about to join her, he abruptly stopped.

"What's wrong?" she asked. "Is it your back?"

"No." He straightened. "We need some napkins. Be right back."

Ariel nodded, until she saw that he was headed for the manchineel tree. "Whoa, hold it!" she shouted.

Cole stopped dead, then looked over his shoulder at her. "Why? What's wrong?"

"Those leaves cause dermatitis. Better stick with banana leaves."

He brought back his hands and wiped them on the back of his slacks, even though he hadn't touched anything.

When he returned, minutes later, it was with enough banana leaves for a party of ten.

Ariel smiled. "You're really something, you know that?"

His brows lifted as he sank to the ground. "Something good, I hope."

"The very best," she said, "and I don't want you doing another thing, you hear me?"

He glanced at the fire and the food. "Afraid I'll screw this up more than I already have?"

"Nonsense. You've done a wonderful job. And because you did, now it's my turn to serve you."

Cole looked at his blistered fingers, then showed them to her. "And not a minute too soon."

Ariel laughed, then cupped his right hand in hers and brought it to her mouth. With great care she ran her tongue over his battered fingertips, then pressed her lips to his palm.

The gesture was so tender, so filled with affection, that Cole tried to recall another woman treating him like this, but could not.

There had been lots of females that had wanted sex with him, and plenty that wanted marriage, but he had never felt truly important to them.

Ariel made him feel as if he were the center of her world when he knew the truth. This woman was his equal in every way, and in more than a few matters she was superior to him.

Even so, at this moment she seemed content to serve.

After ministering to his hands, she found a part of his fish that wasn't burnt and brought it to his lips.

"No," he said, "that's for you."

"I'll take half."

At last, he agreed, but still she insisted on feeding it to him. Once she had slipped that morsel into his mouth, once he had chewed and swallowed, Ariel leaned forward, then licked the remaining juice from his lips.

"More?" she murmured.

His lips were still tingling, while his nostrils flared with each new breath. At last, Cole forced his eyes to open. "Okay."

Ariel smiled, then fed him a few of those berries, using her fingertips and tongue to clean that juice from the corners of his mouth.

She left his side briefly, then returned with some bananas and oranges. She took great pains to give him only the very best portions.

As she labored over this, the sun began to set, turning the tops of the trees the same reddish gold as her hair, while the breeze stirred those thick, glossy waves.

In that moment, he caught her scent. It was as fresh as the pool and as heated as her gaze.

Her eyes sparkled in the waning light, while her expression softened as she fed him the very last of the orange.

This time, Cole took her hand and licked the remaining juice from her fingers.

When he lifted his head, Ariel's gaze was already on him.

Without pause, she moved into his arms, settling there. For a long moment they simply gazed at each other because it seemed enough.

And then it did not.

Cole lowered his mouth to hers, kissing her gently, tenderly, to thank her for all she had done.

In this moment, and so many others, she had made him feel worthy; she had made him feel like a man.

And now, she opened her mouth to his, inviting him inside.

Cole didn't pause. Soon, his kiss turned as needy and savage as hers. There was no mistaking her actions; she wanted him in a way no other woman had.

As he finally ended the kiss, as he finally opened his eyes, Ariel met his gaze and whispered, "Make love with me, please."

Chapter Thirteen

Please, she had said, as if there were any doubt he truly wanted her. This, when he had thought of little else since beginning their trek.

She was really something.

She was about to become his.

Lifting his hand to her cheek, Cole carefully drew his fingers across her velvety skin.

Ariel's lids fluttered closed; her delicate nostrils briefly flared as his fingertips continued to trace her features.

At last, he said, "Let me take care of a few things first."

Those lids fluttered open, while her slender brows drew together. "What things?"

"The fire for one." He touched the tip of his nose against hers, then smiled as she went briefly cross-eyed. "I've learned my lesson; I'm not leaving it to its own devices anymore."

"You won't be." Her gaze slid to the side. "Our bed's right over there."

Cole liked the sound of that. Even so, he shook his head. "We're not going to use the bed just yet. I have other plans."

Her brows lifted; her voice hushed. "Okay."

Cole grinned at her naked enthusiasm, that arousing honesty that was more potent than all the Victoria's Secret lingerie in the world.

After Ariel had moved from his embrace, he took care of

the fire, building a fortress of non-exploding rocks around it so those flames had nowhere to escape.

Rubbing his palms against the sides of his slacks, Cole pushed to his feet and whistled.

Ariel looked over her shoulder at him. "What?"

What else? She was naked to the waist.

"I thought I told you not to do anything naked until I was with you."

She gave him a wicked smile. "You are with me, and I'm not naked."

"Tell that to your nipples."

She looked down at them, then turned to him. "You tell them."

If he could find words. Cole's mouth was already too dry to speak. Dear God, but she was luscious. Draped in the brief light of the fiery sunset and those flickering flames, Ariel's nipples were a deep strawberry shade surrounded by perfectly seamless flesh that was dewy with health and youth.

Drawn to that beauty, like any sane man, Cole sank to his knees before her, then cupped her breasts in his palms.

Ariel moved into his touch. She rested her fingertips against his bristly cheek.

Cole felt quickly embarrassed. "I don't usually look this bad."

"You're beautiful," she whispered, "now hush."

He did far more than that as he lowered his head to her left breast to run his tongue over that nipple. Once it was taut and her breathing had picked up, he moved to the other. At last, he rested his face between her breasts, pressing that achingly soft flesh even closer so that it aroused and comforted.

Ariel's heart beat as wildly as his own, but neither of them rushed. It seemed important—no, vital—to experience each moment, to lock it away just in case it never happened quite like this again.

Cole couldn't imagine another moment being as perfect, and they had yet to begin.

At last, he lifted his face to her.

Ariel's smile was soft and welcoming.

My God, I love you, he thought, *I really do.*

It was a truth Cole had known before, but it seemed real now and so sacred all he could do was gaze at her.

Never in his life had he been content to do only this with a woman when the promise of sex awaited.

Now he simply could not rush.

Slipping his arms around the flare of her hips, Cole brought her so close he felt each breath she took. "Comfortable?"

"Very."

He smiled. "So, what happened to your bra?"

Her belly quivered with her soft laughter. "You really like it, don't you?"

His gaze lifted as she played with his messy hair. "Not as much as I like your skin, but I am curious why you started without me."

"I didn't get undressed for you."

Okay, that wasn't the answer he had been looking for. "If not me, then who?"

"What," she corrected, then inclined her head to the left.

Cole wasn't all that inclined to look. *What* could mean lots of nonhuman things, like monkeys or snakes or something else he wasn't particularly fond of. Nor did it address why she would strip to the waist for those creatures.

At last he turned his head to the left.

"Up," she said.

He started to push to his feet.

"No." She laughed. "I meant, look up."

Cole sank back to his knees and did as she directed. Only then did he notice that she had tied her bra to one of the upper branches of a bamboo tree.

"Afraid one of the girl monkeys is going to take it?" he asked.

"Not it," she corrected again, "the food you worked so hard to provide."

Cole looked at her, then back to the bra. Now that he noticed, those cups did appear filled. "You're protecting our food with your bra?"

"And that tree. The branch is far too small to support the weight of most animals and high enough from the ground so they can't jump up and snatch our stash."

"In your bra."

"It was either that or use your shorts."

Cole looked back at her. "All you had to do was ask."

"Okay." She leaned down and murmured, "Make love with me, please."

There it was again, that word that no other woman had used when wanting sex with him.

Of course, those acts had been about lust, not a need that continued to astonish. "I'd be honored."

Ariel smiled, then inhaled deeply and easily as he pressed his lips to her torso before pushing to his feet.

Once there, Cole quickly unbuttoned his shirt and pulled it off. "No, don't take those off," he said as Ariel started to undo the tie at the waist of her pants.

She looked up. "You're sure about that?"

"Very. Put this on." He held out his shirt so she could slip into it.

"Aren't we doing this backward?" she asked. "I mean, shouldn't we—or at least I—be getting undressed?"

"You will. Now, don't give me any trouble."

"I've been nothing but cooperative, admit it."

"Uh-huh."

Ariel smiled as she slipped into his shirt.

Resting his hands on her biceps, Cole leaned down and whispered in her ear. "That looks good on you."

She glanced down at his shirt that was so big on her the tails fell nearly to her knees. Turning her face to his, she said, "Please don't tell me you want to wear my stuff now."

"Can't. It's up in the tree."

She laughed.

"I don't want you getting bitten by anything—but me, of course—because you're foolishly walking around in your birth-day suit."

Ariel's gaze lowered to his naked chest. "What about you?"

"I'm a guy. Insects just won't fuck with me."

She laughed again. "Oh, *please.*"

"You doubt that?" Before she could answer, Cole hauled her close and kissed her hard and deep.

When he was finished, she sagged against his chest. "No, sir."

He smiled to her hitching breaths tickling his skin. "No, sir, what?"

"I don't doubt you're a guy." She paused to swallow. "But the insect thing? Oh, *please.*"

"You are so asking for it."

"Ah, but will I get it?"

"Just you wait."

"Again?"

Easing back, he captured her hand in his own. "Quiet, got it? And follow me."

"Anywhere," she said without pause.

God, she was something.

But hardly as pliant as she led a man to believe. Once Cole headed for that part of the pool farthest from the falls, Ariel was firmly taking the lead, which caused her to drag him along.

At least, until Cole held back, not wanting to rush, not wanting this to end.

Once it did, he'd have to make some very big decisions. He'd have to admit his love and await her verdict. He'd have to decide the next step, if there was a next step.

No way was he ready for that tonight, so he simply could not rush.

Ariel finally noticed. Coming to a stop, she looked over her shoulder at him. It was now fully dark, but the moon cast soft shadows on her face and sparkled in her eyes. "Here?" she asked.

"There," he said, inclining his head toward the pool. "Follow me."

"Anywhere," she said once more and obediently slowed her pace so that it matched his.

Hand in hand they walked in silence toward that sleek body of water. At their end, the pool was tranquil and dark, except for one spot that reflected the heavy moon. At the falls, the misting water sparkled like those countless stars dusting the sky.

The scene was more beautiful than Cole would have ever imagined, and would be one he used in his film thanks to Ariel and all of her amazing ideas.

At last he stopped and turned to her. "Get naked," he ordered.

"You're sure?" Her voice was as wicked as her expression. "You're absolutely—"

"You are so asking for it."

"Ah, but will I get it?" she asked, stripping faster than the law allowed or a man could bear.

As she straightened, Cole's gaze settled on the diamond stars that dangled beneath her navel and pointed straight to those delicate curls. It was only then that he noticed she was talking. "I'm sorry, what?"

"Never mind."

Ah, but he did. As she stepped away from the clothing, that small movement gently rippled her taut muscles. Moonlight skimmed over her narrow shoulders, touching the tips of her nipples and those amazing stars.

"Am I going too fast for you?" she asked.

He arched one brow.

If anything, that made her more mischievous. "If you're afraid you can't keep up with me, it's all right to admit it."

So they were back to that dance that had already been played out in the forest with him easily winning. Because of that, Cole felt game again and decided to play along. "You don't think I can keep up with you?"

Her gaze lowered to the cargo pants and huaraches he still wore, while she was buck naked. She met his gaze. "I'm just wondering if you'll be able to catch me."

"Catch—"

Cole didn't finish; Ariel didn't give him the chance as she quickly turned, then effortlessly dove into the pool.

By the time she had surfaced, he wore only one huarache.

Smoothing back her hair as she treaded water, Ariel called out, "That's it, take your time! Pace your—"

This time she didn't finish, as Cole kicked off that sandal and dove in after her.

Ariel laughed, then went right back under, swimming as close as she could to the bottom while her gaze searched the surface. At last, she saw Cole's beautiful body silhouetted against the moonlight that shone overhead.

Moving quickly, she swam to the surface, coming upon him from behind.

Cole knew. In the very moment Ariel reached him, he quickly turned and lunged for her.

Squealing and laughing, she fell backward into the water and headed for the bottom, swimming harder than she ever had before.

Didn't matter. The man was fast as hell and determined, too.

But Ariel had one advantage—a smaller body that was far more supple than his. As Cole reached her, as he placed his hand on her butt, Ariel rolled over in the water, then swam in the opposite direction, and as far away as possible.

Finally breaking through to the surface, she gulped air, then dove right back in when the moon revealed his approach. By God, if the man wanted her, then he'd just have to catch her. If tonight was going to be the sum total of their relationship, then Ariel wanted to make certain he remembered it.

She wanted him to crave it as he had nothing else in his life.

And so she swam, and swam, and swam until she was momentarily exhausted and near the falls.

Breaking through to the surface, Ariel gulped air and treaded water as her gaze skimmed the pool that revealed nothing. After fingering water out of her eyes, she continued to search the surface, starting at the farthermost point, then edging closer to herself.

Still nothing.

She didn't understand, but wasn't yet panicked.

Cole was an excellent swimmer. He couldn't have gotten into trouble within this small pool. He couldn't have drowned.

Frowning, Ariel looked down on either side of her own body to see if Cole was using a reed so that he could breathe under—

"Looking for me?" he suddenly asked from behind.

Ariel flinched, then glanced over her shoulder to see that he had been sitting on the bank all along, just to the side of the waterfall and directly behind her.

She arched her body to go back under the water, but Cole was too fast.

With more ease than Ariel believed possible he caught her, holding her with one arm as he swam them both to the bank on the right. His embrace continued to imprison as the water grew shallow—only waist deep—while a series of rocks offered a place to recline. Once his back was to those rocks, Cole turned her to face him.

Beads of water clung to his eyelashes and beard. His eyes were hooded, his voice hard. "You're not getting away from me again."

Ariel's lips parted in surprise as he slipped his hands beneath her buttocks, then pulled her up until she was straddling his lean hips. As her knees and shins pressed against the rocks, he leaned against them for support, then lowered his hand to his stiffened cock.

Ariel breathed hard; she lifted her face to the sky, then let out a pleased moan as he unceremoniously buried his flesh in hers. He was a large man and knew it as he worked her body until she had no choice but to accept all of his.

Once they were flesh to flesh, their curls touching, Cole said, "Look at me." His voice was raw with unashamed need.

Lowering her head, Ariel opened her eyes.

His expression was pure male . . . demanding, hungry, expecting to be satisfied.

Ariel caressed the back of his neck; she tightened her muscles around his stiff cock.

Cole's lids fluttered. "More," he said.

She worked her muscles, forcing them to stroke his flesh.

"Ariel," he whispered, then accused, "you made me wait so damn long."

"I won't anymore."

"You put me through hell."

"I brought you to this."

"You'll bring me a fucking lot more."

"I will," she promised, then closed her eyes as his mouth captured hers.

Without pause Cole plunged his tongue inside so that she was filled here and below, without any chance of escape.

Ariel wanted no separation; she craved the peace that only his body could bring.

Cole kissed her deeply, greedily, as he moved his hips until his thickened rod slid partially out of her, only to thrust back inside.

When Ariel moaned in response, he silenced her with his tongue.

He allowed her no rest after that; his body used hers as her body used his.

Ariel could not hold back. She had wanted him from the moment they met and now returned his kiss with unrestrained need. Her hunger matched his; her hands couldn't touch him enough.

At last, and together, they reached a climax that tore a growl of delight from deep within Cole. Despite her own cries, Ariel felt the strength of his against her breasts and belly.

As she continued to breathe hard, Cole slipped his right

forearm beneath her buttocks, then wrapped his other arm around her waist as he buried his face against her neck.

His breath was hot and weary, but his embrace remained firm. "More," he said.

Ariel couldn't help but smile. She kissed his damp hair and bristly cheek, then lowered her mouth to his ear. "In time."

"Now," he insisted.

Her smile returned. The man wanted more; then she would give him more. As she worked her still-throbbing muscles around his weary shaft, Ariel slipped her right hand beneath her thigh to reach his sac.

The second she cradled it in her palm, Cole gasped, "Oh, hell—*stop!*"

"Now?"

With great effort, he lifted his head and frowned. And then he was shivering again as she fondled his balls. "Dammit, Ariel, *no.*"

Despite that protest she did precisely what she wanted and surely what he needed until Cole was clinging to her as wave after wave of pleasure tore through him.

As he struggled for breath, Ariel ran her tongue over the curve of his ear.

He panted out his words. "You don't take orders very well, do you?"

"Never have." She paused to kiss his temple. "I'm a bad, bad girl."

"You will be. I haven't even started with you yet."

Ariel briefly closed her eyes as she savored those words. And then she looked at him and got wicked. "Prove it."

It was a challenge that calmed Cole's strained breathing and renewed his energy faster than Ariel would have thought possible.

Her brows rose as he turned them around, then moved his hips until her body released his.

She frowned at that, then looked down as he plopped her on the bank. "Was I getting too heavy for—"

"Quiet," he ordered, then without warning, pushed her back onto the grass. Before she could recover, his hands were between her thighs, spreading them widely. He next lifted her legs until her heels were on the edge of the bank which fully exposed her body to him.

"Don't you dare move," he said.

"I won't," she promised, then did, lifting her arms above her head to fully expose her breasts.

Cole said nothing at all; he seemed unable to find words.

During the following moments Ariel watched as he gazed at the most intimate parts of her.

Never had she been this exposed to any man; never had she realized how deliciously female it felt.

The insides of her thighs continued to tense as desire pooled between her legs, thickening those lips even more, making them slick, preparing them for what was to come.

At last, Cole touched her.

Ariel's breath caught. Her back arched as he slid his fingers down the insides of her thighs to her opening.

For a moment he paused, and then he showed his intent as he filled her once more with his fingers, then rested his other hand on her flat belly. As he ran those fingers over the dangling stars, his thumb stroked her delicate curls.

His touch was surprisingly gentle and quickly lulled. Ariel's breathing grew lazy; her lids fluttered closed as he stroked and filled, delivering a sweet pleasure.

But that was hardly his true intent; he had only begun.

Separating those fingers within her to stretch and to arouse, Cole next pressed his other hand against her belly to keep her movements to a minimum.

Seconds later she was imprisoned within this embrace, and only then did Cole lower his head between her legs.

Ariel inhaled sharply; a shiver tore through her as he slowly licked her plump, slick lips, his hot tongue tracing the contours of flesh before flicking against her erect nub.

Ariel's back arched at the sensation, but Cole wasn't about

to allow any movement; not until he was finished, not until he was fully satisfied.

As he gently increased the pressure on her belly, he slipped his fingers even deeper. During this his tongue slowly worked her nub until she cried out, wanting completion, needing it.

Cole's response was to withdraw his tongue and suckle the inside of her left thigh.

Ariel's chest heaved with her strained breathing; her mind cursed him for not allowing a climax! She tried to lift her body to make it happen, but he held her down.

He made her wait.

Ariel thrashed her head from side to side, but that caused him to move farther from her core. Breathing hard, she finally obeyed and fully yielded to him.

A moment passed and then another as she remained open, vulnerable, waiting.

At last he returned to her opening, flicking his tongue over her clit.

When he suckled that hardened nub, Ariel bit her lower lip to quiet her moans. As his fingers stretched and worked her, her hands tightened into fists. As he teased her with his mouth and tongue, she opened her legs still farther, giving him full access and control.

The male in Cole took it without pause. The ex-Marine demanded still more.

The following moments blurred for Ariel as he alternately stroked her clit with his tongue and thumb, even as he slipped his fingers out of her, only to work them back inside.

Within seconds her world was his hands, his mouth, and that small part of her that begged for release.

Each time her body tensed, wanting it, he would withdraw the pleasure, teaching her patience and obedience to his will, at least in this.

Ariel loved him, so she yielded. She adored him, so she endured, and was amply rewarded as he at last brought her to the edge, allowing her to soar.

As the world spun, Ariel pressed her fists to her temples and lifted her chin to the sky. As completion shuddered through her, she shouted her release, then moaned and whimpered.

It hardly mattered as Cole was not yet finished with her.

He gave her absolutely no rest as he straightened, then removed his fingers so that his cock could quickly enter her with one hard thrust.

Ariel's back arched to his filling her again, taking her again, plunging over and over until she quickly reached the next climax.

This time, Cole held back.

As she lay breathless and weak, his head remained down, his chest pumping hard as he struggled for control.

Ariel was not about to give it. Despite her fatigue she forced her muscles to tighten around his thickened cock once more.

Cole's nostrils flared; he lifted his head.

Ariel held his gaze as she tightened, then relaxed; tightened, then relaxed those muscles.

He lifted his face to the sky. The muscles in his neck and shoulders were bunched as he continued to resist.

Ariel brought her legs closer, using his torso as an anchor as she rocked her hips.

His jaw tightened, and then a low growl suddenly escaped the back of his throat as she worked her muscles again.

Tightening his grip on her knees, Cole's hips thrust forward as he plunged deeply within her only to ease out, then plunge again and again and again.

Her body rocked with the force of his passion. His shuddered once it was spent.

The sounds of their lovemaking lingered, joining the other night music before Cole bent forward at the waist, resting his head between her breasts.

Ariel worked her fingers through his damp hair.

Cole inhaled deeply, then sighed it out. "Comfortable?"

Ariel regarded the starry sky, the misting waterfall, and his impressive nudity as he remained joined with her beneath the shimmering moon. *Comfortable?* he had asked. She was enchanted. "Oh, yeah."

His shoulders shook with his weary laughter. "Me, too."

She smiled. "So, is this what you did while you were on camping trips with the Girl Scouts?"

His laughter deepened. He slid his hands from her waist to the swell of her breasts. "Hardly. What about you?"

She gently bounced her legs against his torso. "What about me?"

"Did you do the Scout thing—did you even go to school?"

Ariel stopped bouncing her legs and playing with his hair. For a moment, she was tempted to smack him upside the head. "Not only did I attend school, I even graduated from college."

"Hold on, that's not what I meant." He tried to lift his head, but that much effort appeared beyond him at the moment. His weary sigh warmed her chest, while his deep voice rumbled against it. "I meant, did you go to a regular school or did your uncle have tutors come to this island?"

Ariel started to play with his hair again. "Uncle Thaddeus insisted I go to a regular school. He didn't want me to be spoiled rotten."

Cole offered a small nod. "So what went wrong with his plan?"

This time Ariel gave in to her first reaction and very gently smacked him on the side of the head.

Cole moaned as if he'd been shot.

"I barely touched you," she said, "even though you deserved far worse, admit it."

Cole finally lifted his head and glanced down at their joined bodies before meeting her gaze. "Barely touched me?"

She smiled.

He pulled back his hands and straightened. "You went to school all by yourself at ten?"

Now, there was an unexpected question. "Yeah. Didn't you?"

"I didn't have to go from this island to another to go to—"

"Neither did I." She wrapped her legs around his hips, keeping him inside her just in case he had other ideas. "Uncle Thaddeus bought a ranch in Texas so I could attend a regular school. We only spent my summer vacations here, and," she quickly added, "in Africa, South America, Europe, and wherever else his work took him."

"And here I was feeling sorry for you."

"You're kidding—why?"

He mumbled something.

"What?"

"Because of your parents," he finally blurted, then sounded cautious again. "You know, your lack of family."

"Uncle Thaddeus *is* my family."

Cole wasn't about to argue with that, not after what she had just told him. "He's a good man."

"The very best—or, at least, one of the very best."

Cole slowly nodded, sensing she might be including him in that statement. Not that that gave him the courage to tell her how he felt. Good times and good sex were one thing; love and the commitment it entailed was another thing entirely.

Although he had braved some pretty bad crap in his military operations, the thought of not being totally wanted by this woman scared him shitless. He still wasn't ready to face rejection tonight. He wasn't certain he'd ever be able to face *Uncle* Thaddeus.

The man had predicted Cole would lose his heart; trouble was, he hadn't said what might happen after that.

Uncle Thaddeus said I should treat you well because he likes you, Ariel had said.

Could be that was the truth or a whopper of a lie—the very first in her otherwise honest life—just so she could make him feel better. Who knew?

What if the old guy disapproved of any relationship between them? Hell, Ariel was so attached to the man—he had done so very much for her—Cole wouldn't have been a bit surprised if she let that guide her decision.

Jesus, what a mess he had gotten himself into.

"Am I holding you too tight?" she asked.

Cole met her gaze. "What? No. Why?"

"You were breathing kind of hard . . . actually, you still are."

He looked down at his chest which was really pumping away. "I was just thinking."

"Oh." She tightened her muscles around his cock again. "About what?"

Cole couldn't help but smile. Damn, she was something. And dammit, he didn't want to ruin this moment with worry about the future. *Deal with it tomorrow,* he ordered himself. Tonight was theirs to enjoy.

Running his hands up her body, he whispered, "My screenplay."

Ariel's smile briefly faded, then returned. "Like hell."

"No, really." He casually fondled her breasts, then next focused on those adorable diamond stars, tapping them first with his right forefinger, then his left. "I was thinking of opening the film with a shot of these."

She was briefly silent. "In *my* navel?"

"Of course not. In Hank's."

She laughed. "Liar."

"You don't think a useless politician would wear body jewelry like this?"

"Women's underwear, maybe; body jewelry, I doubt it."

"There's a distinction?"

"When was the last time you stapled your shorts to your skin just to keep them on?"

Cole got the picture and immediately stopped tapping those diamonds. "It really hurt to have your navel pierced, huh?"

"Well, it wasn't like having a baby—show me the man that could live through *that.*"

Uh-huh. He started tapping again. "Guess that's why you and all the other gals out there are in charge."

"You're finally conceding that?"

He flicked his gaze to her and held back a smile. "Looks like we're well past page ninety-eight of the script by now, huh?"

"And well to the middle of the very next page. Ninety-nine, right?"

Ah, she was definitely something. "Could be. But I'm fresh out of ideas, so what now?"

Ariel's answer was to push to a sitting position and wreathe her arms around his neck. "I'm glad you asked."

Chapter Fourteen

He liked her enthusiasm and was more than willing to hand over the reins to whatever she had planned for the coming minutes and hours. After all, her ideas for the script hadn't been half bad, while that chase she just put him through had been pretty damned amazing.

Cole could hardly imagine what might happen next as she slipped from his embrace and into the water.

"Follow me," she said.

"Anywhere," he said.

Ariel's eyes sparkled, and then she turned and swam toward the opposite bank.

This time, unlike the last, her pace was easy, as if she wanted the anticipation to build, or thought he might need a few more minutes to regain his strength for what was to come.

Whatever her purpose, Cole used these quiet moments to imagine how their bodies looked from overhead. Their tanned flesh, now paled by the moonlight, contrasted sharply against the dark pool. How frail their nudity must have appeared, how completely unfit for a life out in the wild.

How wrong that perception was.

Cole had witnessed Ariel's strength; he marveled at her abilities and was again stunned by her beauty as she effortlessly pulled herself out of the water, then stood, feet fully apart, arms by her sides as she waited for him on the bank.

Ribbons of water trailed down her sleek nudity, reflecting the moonlight in a hundred places.

Never in all of his days had Cole witnessed anything as amazing.

Treading water, he called out, "Don't move!"

"I won't," she said, then did, knowing instinctively what he wanted.

As he watched, she lifted her hands to her hair, then pulled it off her shoulders.

The movement arched her back, angling her nipples until they pointed to the sky. Beads of water briefly clung to the areolas, twinkling in the light before gliding over the swell of her breasts to her taut belly.

Cole watched those muscles move with her breathing, which was completely relaxed despite her nudity and his gaze.

If anything, being watched made her wanton.

She was now lifting her chin to the sky, even as she lowered both hands to her breasts, casually fondling them as her thumbs flicked over the nipples.

Cole stared; his mind whispered *more*.

Ariel instinctively obeyed as she released her right breast, sliding that hand down to her amazing body jewelry. She stroked those sparkling stars with the same reverence she might have shown his cock, then slipped her hand still farther, working it through the delicate curls until she reached her clit.

There, she lingered, moving her forefinger in a slow circle that stole Cole's breath as she brought herself to climax, allowing him to see now what he could not when he had been pleasuring her.

His gaze lifted from those muscles tensing in her thighs to her taut belly to her breasts that quivered with each shuddering breath.

It was a show like no other and brought him to her faster than any plea.

As Cole emerged from the water, Ariel lowered her face to look at him. Her eyes were briefly unfocused with pleasure, then sparkling with mischief. "Follow me."

Still? Cole was about to protest that he wanted her here, now, again, but decided against it . . . at least for the time being. "Anywhere," he finally said.

She smiled, then turned her back to him and bent at the waist to pick up her clothing.

Cole's gaze instantly fell to her ass, those plush cheeks and what he could see of her short auburn curls. Her body was just begging to be mounted, and his cock responded in kind.

At just that moment, she looked over her shoulder. Her gaze noted his stiffened rod before lifting to his eyes. "You should get your clothes."

Cole didn't move. "Why?"

"You'll need them if you're going to follow me."

"What's wrong with staying here?"

"You can see better back at the fire."

Cole heard her words, but it was a very long moment before they registered. At last, he forced himself to regain control, which wasn't easy, given that she remained in that same position. Teasing. Tempting. Thrilling.

"Back to the fire it is," he said, then went to get his clothing.

"Don't get dressed," she said.

Cole looked over his shoulder at her. She had straightened and now faced him with her feet apart and her arms to the sides, hiding absolutely nothing.

"I wasn't planning to," he said.

She smiled. "You can wear your huaraches if you want."

"And you can wear your moccasins and those stars, but nothing else."

"I wasn't planning to wear anything else."

Good girl, he thought, his gaze holding hers as he slipped his feet into his sandals, while she did the same with her moccasins.

He extended his hand.

"Thanks." She draped her clothes over his outstretched arm.

Cole looked down to that, then right back up. He had wanted her fingers, not her damned clothes.

"Follow me," she said.

"This better be good."

Ariel had already turned her back to him; now she looked over her shoulder once more. "Have I disappointed you yet?"

"The night's still young."

"Worried about being able to keep—"

"I *am* up."

She grinned. "Yeah, I know. So if you want some relief, you better follow me."

Fucking anywhere, he thought, then stared at her sweet little cheeks bouncing up and down as she led him away from the pool to their fire.

Or rather his fire. Cole quickly prayed that the damned thing hadn't gone out. Dear God, if he had known she'd be behaving like this tonight, he would have started another fire to keep as a spare just in case the first one went—

"You still behind me?" she asked, cutting into his thoughts.

Cole made his voice as casual as hers. "Where else would I be?"

"Well, I don't know." She abruptly stopped, then turned completely around to face him. As her gaze settled on his frustrated cock, her voice grew thoughtful. "Wouldn't want the insects stealing you away, because you're undressed."

"Don't you worry; they wouldn't dare fuck with me."

"That's right." Her voice was now fully distracted as her gaze remained on his rod. "You're a man."

She said that word with such awe, such reverence, Cole was momentarily stunned.

Ariel, on the other hand, had already turned and continued toward their fire.

Please be burning, Cole prayed as he continued to follow. *Please give me enough light so I can see every fucking thing. Please don't make me go through hell to get you restart—*

"Oh, damn," Ariel suddenly said, breaking into his thoughts as they got back to camp. "Look."

Was she kidding? No way did he want to look at a dead fire that would take divine intervention to burst back into flame. "Do we really need it?" he asked.

"Well, no. Not if you're willing to sleep on the ground."

Cole frowned, not understanding, then finally looked to where she was. The bananas leaves had been taken off their bed and scattered about the ground.

"Damn monkeys," Cole said, noting the muddy paw print on one of those leaves, "but look at the fire." Moving toward it, he smiled at those still-buoyant flames.

Ariel joined him. "Wow."

Okay, now she was making fun. Cole glanced over his shoulder to see that her gaze was on his continued arousal, not his fire. *Good girl.* "You don't sound impressed," he teased. "Isn't it good enough for you?"

She moistened her lips before answering. "It'll do." She finally glanced up. "Where do you want me?"

Ah, she was letting him choose. Cole glanced around the area that the fire illuminated.

"There," she said and left his side.

So much for letting him choose.

As he turned, Ariel continued to a series of large, low rocks that glowed a deep rust in the light of the fire.

Pausing only long enough to look over her shoulder at him, she then sank to her knees and bent at the waist, resting her forearms against the first rock. As she lowered her head and spread her legs widely apart, she arched her back.

Cole dropped their clothing on the ground. His gaze

drifted over her buttocks that she continued to raise to give him full access.

"Take your time," she said at last. "Pace yourself."

To hell with that. Cole was behind her in a moment, his hands covering her smooth cheeks. "More," he demanded, and she obeyed, arching her back even farther.

God, God, God, he thought. "Don't you dare move," he said.

This time she did not. This time she was his to use as he pleased.

It was more than Cole had ever hoped for, more than any woman had ever offered. This position was as feral as their surroundings.

In the forest around them animals moved through the brush making small, furtive sounds. Above, wind rustled leaves as it swept past.

Here, Ariel moaned loudly, lewdly, as Cole slipped one hand beneath her, pressing it to her belly, while his other hand explored her curls and opening.

"More," he said.

Again, she obeyed, lifting her buttocks as far as she could so that he had easy access to pleasure.

In that moment Cole entered her, knowing that was precisely what she wanted. She wasn't coy and hardly needed to be coaxed. This was an amazing woman who wasn't afraid of a man's body or his desires.

Cole delivered his passion, thrusting into her as males had done with females since the dawn of time. There was no hesitation in his actions, no apology in what he took from her or delivered. His grip tightened on her hips as his thrusts increased. His balls tapped against her flesh as his cock drove deep, then partially retreated, only to drive deep once more.

He brought them to a climax that was more powerful than all of the others; he remained inside as he wrapped both arms around her waist and lowered his head to her smooth back.

After a few moments, Ariel swallowed, then panted her words. "Thank you."

Cole finished kissing her back. He murmured, "I'm not finished."

"That's why I'm thanking you."

He laughed, then gulped more air and finally found the strength to take her yet again.

Once that lovemaking was over, he finally pulled out and sprawled faceup on the ground.

Ariel was still breathing hard when she finally staggered to her feet. "Don't get up on my account."

Cole laughed until that proved too hard. "Okay. Thanks."

"You bet." Yawning, Ariel shuffled to her clothes and finally pulled them on despite her fatigue. As she passed Cole she dropped his clothes on his head.

He didn't even bother to move them until she was putting husks on the fire as an insect smudge.

"Don't hurt my fire," he ordered.

Ariel leveled her gaze on him.

He gave her a sweet smile, then gestured her close. "Come here."

"Can't." She yawned once more. "Gotta fix the bed."

"To hell with that," he said, then yawned. "Just lay on top of me." He patted his flat belly.

As tempting as that looked, Ariel shook her head. "The last time I slept against you, you couldn't walk for days so—"

"Minutes," he corrected, then pushed to his elbow after two tries. "Just give me a sec and I'll help you."

Uh-huh. Already he had slipped back to the ground and was yawning loudly. Shortly after that, he was asleep.

Scratching her butt, Ariel returned to the edge of the forest and gathered clean banana leaves to rebuild the mattress.

Once it was finished, she padded to Cole and hunkered down near his head.

His face was turned to the side, his lips parted with his

quiet breathing. Ariel reached out to smooth his messy hair, but then thought better of it, not wanting to disturb him.

There wouldn't be another chance to see him like this. Tomorrow they would start back for the villa. The following morning he would be leaving.

Her eyes stung with quick tears, even as her smile widened. Oh, God, but she was screwed up. She was completely happy and more miserable than she had ever thought possible.

If only they didn't have to go back just yet.

Day after tomorrow he's gotta be done with you, Gwen had said.

As much as Ariel hated to admit it, she knew that Gwen was right. The world didn't stop for weary hearts or hopeless love.

Swallowing hard, Ariel brushed the tears from her eyes and ordered herself to enjoy what she had, to make the most of every minute.

She smoothed back Cole's hair and pressed her lips to his bristly cheek, then gasped as he unexpectedly grabbed her around the waist, bringing her to the ground.

As he rolled on top of her with absolutely no trouble at all, he narrowed his gaze, trying to focus. Once he had, his brows lifted. "Oh, it's you."

She frowned. "You were expecting?"

Cole touched the tip of his nose to hers. "I was dreaming of Boobala."

Ariel laughed. "BooBoo!"

"God, I've got them all over my body." He lifted his head and yawned, then rolled them over until she was on top. "Go on, kiss all of them to make them better so I can fall asleep."

Uh-huh. He was well on the way there now, and all by himself. "Come on," she said, rolling off of him, "we have to go to bed."

Grumbling, he finally shifted to a sitting position, then grumbled some more when she suggested he get dressed. At last, though, Ariel was able to lead him to their bed, which he pretty much filled all by himself.

"Nice," he said.

It was that and so much more as he opened his arms and she slipped inside.

Within seconds he had fallen back to sleep. Within minutes, Ariel followed, sinking into an exhausted slumber that made no room for dreams.

It wasn't until hours later that Ariel became aware of Cole's absence. She no longer felt the heavy weight of his arm across her waist, or the heated scent of his body as he pressed close.

Why did he leave? More importantly, where was he?

Rubbing sleep out of her eyes, Ariel lifted her head and looked from the forest to the horizon. It was nearing first light. It was the beginning of their last day, and already he was gone.

Her gaze lowered, then went to the right as she heard the fire suddenly pop.

Cole was sitting next to it. Near his right side was a mound of wood to feed those precious flames; in his hands was the script, which he was reading.

Ariel watched him for a long moment before he felt her gaze.

"Mornin'," he said.

She wondered what he had been reading, since he seemed kind of bummed. "Hi. How's your boo-boos?"

"They'll live. Now me?" He shrugged.

"You're in pain?"

He seemed uncertain how to answer that, then looked back to the script. "Lots to cover today."

Our last day, she thought.

Cole looked at her again. "Mind if we get started?"

Ariel did. She wanted to stay here forever, or at least until he told her he loved her and made love to her. "Not at all."

Cole finally nodded.

After that, he seemed driven by a need to learn absolutely everything there was about survival on this island. He asked question after question about stuff she had put in the script, and stuff she had left out.

It was as if their lovemaking had finally cleared his mind for what they should have been doing all along.

Once they had taken a brief swim, then eaten the food Ariel had stashed in her bra, they washed their clothes and returned to the fire.

Cole looked more reluctant to put it out than to leave her forever.

Suppressing a sigh, Ariel gave him some space as she waited near a coconut palm. Several minutes passed as Cole's head remained bent to that fire as if he loved it. And then he looked really pissed as he put it out, finally stomping on it to make certain it was dead.

Ariel would have teased him with applause, but her heart just wasn't in it.

Cole, on the other hand, seemed to have gotten his second wind as he approached. "We'll need water for the trip back."

Not if they took the shortcut she knew about. Not that she was about to tell him that. "Yes, we will."

"In the script you wrote that there were several ways to carry water, none of which you detailed."

Well, no. Ariel hadn't thought he'd ever be this interested. So, she lied, "I thought I'd leave that up to you."

Cole nodded, then looked past her to the forest. "I'll bet the stomach of an animal could—"

"Not on this island."

He nodded once more. "Then that leaves a hollowed-out piece of wood or a coconut that's been drained." He met her gaze. "I'll go with the coconuts, you find a piece of wood that you feel will work. We'll test each on our way back to the—" He abruptly paused, then looked in the direction from which they had first entered this area.

Ariel knew what he was thinking, but didn't comment.

Cole finally looked back at her. "We'll have to climb those rocks again to get to the other side."

Only if they didn't use the shortcut.

"There's got to be another way," he quickly said, then glanced around, "a shortcut."

Ariel still didn't comment, but did frown as Cole left her side and really got his bearings as he regarded the area surrounding them.

At last he turned and pointed. "We can use that route." He looked at her. "Right?"

Unfortunately. Still, Ariel kept that disappointment out of her voice. "We *could* go that way, but—"

"We'll have to go that way," he interrupted, "if we're hauling water."

Ariel debated whether she should tell him about the creek just ahead and decided she wouldn't. If he wanted to make containers, fine. If he wanted to haul water, fine. At least it would delay the moment they returned to the—

"Well, let's get to it," he said, breaking into her thoughts.

Her shoulders sagged. "Fine."

"Oh, it'll be better than that," he said. "Bet I can really show you a thing or two this time."

Ariel finally met his gaze. "Excuse me?"

He repeated what he had just said.

She quickly frowned. "You're kidding, right?"

"You don't think I can?"

She didn't freaking care if he could! She didn't care about anything except seeing him stay, which wasn't about to happen! "If *you* think you can, then I suggest you *prove it.*"

Cole didn't comment. He had only been trying to impress her, to show her that these survival skills were as important to him as they were to her. He sure as hell hadn't been trying to piss her off.

Ever since she had awakened her mood had gone from quiet to foul. Cole might have asked if she was nearing that time of the month, but figured she'd slug him if he did. He might have asked if she was as sorry as he that this was the last day of their adventure, but he simply wasn't that brave a man.

Could be she was in a pissy mood because she was sorry about last night. Could be he had been reading things into her desire for him, making it far more than it was.

To address that now and have her tell him that she kinda-sorta liked sleeping with him, but hey, it was nothing more than that would make the return journey more awful than Cole could bear.

The most prudent thing to do was what he had decided this morning when she was asleep. Enjoy today with her, no matter her shitty mood, prove that he respected her field as much as he loved her, then spill his guts once they had a chance to clean up and rest back at the villa.

For now he kept his distance, leaving her to find a piece of wood to use as a container—or a weapon—while he struggled with his first and, hopefully, last coconut.

Patience, Cole ordered himself before he found the perfect rock to put a hole into his coconut so he could then drain the liquid and replace it with water from the falls. Holding that rock between his feet, pointed side up, he next ran his hand over the three depressions at the top of the fruit. When he had found the softest, he lifted the coconut in both hands, then froze as Ariel shouted, "Ohmygod, *stop!* You'll hurt yourself!"

Jesus. She had nearly given him a stroke; but, at least, she still seemed to care. He looked at her. "I wasn't going to slam it down on the rock, so just relax."

She was back to being pissed. "If you weren't going to slam it down on that rock, then what—"

"Watch and learn." Before she could bitch about that, Cole positioned the softest part of the coconut on the pointed end of the rock, then grabbed another rock and whacked the fruit, which caused the rock between his feet to fall over and the coconut to roll out of his hands.

"So long as you're all right," Ariel said and resumed looking for her own container.

Shit. After a number of tries Cole decided to just smash in the top, then hold what remained like a drinking cup during the trek back.

He had just hurled the coconut against a rock for the fifth time—without putting so much as a dent in it—when Ariel strolled by.

He turned. "Okay, what do you suggest?"

"Draining it first," she said as she continued strolling. "Otherwise you'll get coconut milk on everything."

Like that would actually matter if the character in his story was dying of thirst? "Care to show me how?" he snapped, then felt quickly bad. "Please, will you just show me how?"

Ariel stopped and turned to him. "You don't have to plead with me, Cole. I'd be happy to."

That was a surprise, given how sad she looked. Good Lord, her emotions were all over the place, and he didn't know what to do. "Thanks."

Her eyes filled with tears.

"Really," he added, just in case she wasn't convinced. He even debated taking her into his arms to comfort her, but didn't get the chance. Already she was heading for his coconut.

"Here's what you do," she said.

Cole cautiously nodded, then watched as she expertly, and easily, used that same pointed rock to put a hole in the top of the nut. After she brushed it off, she lifted it to him. "Thirsty?"

More like humbled. "You first."

To his surprise, she straightened and handed it to him. "I'm not thirsty, Cole, but thanks."

Before he could respond, she resumed her search for a piece of wood to use as a container.

Once she had that in hand, Cole followed her to the falls so that they could wash out and fill their respective receptacles. As usual, she finished first and waited quietly for him.

When Cole finally turned around, she was looking at the series of rocks where they had made love last night. Her gaze was turned inward, her expression unreadable.

As he approached, she looked past him to the direction they would take. "We better get going," she said.

Minutes later they were on their way with Ariel letting Cole take the lead. That way she could look at him uninterrupted and without him noticing if she started to cry.

Her gaze moved from those blades of grass stuck to the back of his head to the berry stains on his butt, which he had gotten this morning as he unknowingly sat on their stash.

She smiled in tenderness, then sighed in sorrow.

These little things would be the hardest to forget, along with his laughter, his teasing, the way he so quickly fell asleep, his raw male need when he made love, and his amazing strength.

He was a powerful man, and yet she so wanted to protect him. He had gained true competency in this survival stuff, and yet she couldn't resist helping.

But that's what love did . . . it gave all that was possible, even when it wasn't needed, and then it provided still more.

"You still behind me?" he suddenly asked.

Always. If not with her presence, then with her heart. "Where else would I be?"

"Running for cover."

Cover? "Why?"

"It seems there's a creek up ahead." Cole finally stopped and turned to her. "One you failed to mention."

She quickly lied, "It's in my notes."

His easy laughter crinkled the corners of his eyes. "Like hell. Before you got up this morning I read every single note you made." He unexpectedly sobered. "You did a good job."

Her eyes filled with tears.

Cole looked quickly worried, just as he had earlier when she nearly cried. "Really," he said, "you did a good—are you laughing at me?"

Ariel dropped her container, then waved her hands in front of herself as she tried to stop. God, she was so screwed up. Sad one moment, happy the next. "I'm just dazzled by your compliment."

"Okay then," he said, then looked back to the creek. "Guess we—or rather Hank and Mina—won't be needing this either." He tossed his coconut to the side.

A monkey quickly shrieked.

Ariel watched as the animal hightailed it out of there. "When the bad guys catch up with Hank, maybe he should use that as a weapon."

"I have a better idea—or rather you had a better idea," Cole said. "You mentioned a bola on page 120 of the script." He held up his arm, then moved it in a circular motion as if he were swinging that multicorded weapon that had stones attached at the ends. "Let's make one and test it out—it'll look good on film."

"Yeah, when your actor uses that film to sue you because he gave himself a lobotomy."

Cole stopped swinging his arm and rocking his hips. "You don't want to do this?"

She answered without pause. "Of course I do."

"Then what's the problem?"

Ariel wasn't certain how to answer that, and then she was. All of her life she had been brutally honest, not wanting to go the way of her parents, so she decided to just be herself now. "It'll take some doing to make it and for you to learn how to use it without hurting yourself. You need to get back. Your time's almost up."

"I'll make time," he said, then before Ariel could argue the point, he added, "come on. I want this for my film."

* * *

To Cole's relief the bola did it. Suddenly, Ariel's luminous smile was back.

He considered that her change in mood might be because their day wouldn't end as quickly, but continued to warn himself not to read too much into anything. Could be she was just happy he was finally appreciating her survival skills. Could be these last few days, no matter how wonderful, hadn't completely changed what Thaddeus had first said about her.

I had to use all my powers of persuasion to even get Ariel to agree to do this, the old guy had said, *given that she abhors Hollywood types.*

She wasn't too keen on useless politicians either, but that's why Cole adored her. Her strength and integrity were stunning, while her endless commands were worthy of a drill sergeant.

"Pound harder," she said.

They were currently beating the spiked leaves of the agave plant with rocks so that the fibers could be removed and braided for the cords of the bola.

Cole briefly wondered if he'd have the strength to spill his guts after all of this.

"Not slower," Ariel said. "Hard—" She didn't finish as Cole really pounded the damned thing.

"That's it!" she said. "Just keep it up!"

He arched one brow.

Ariel laughed.

Cole stopped pounding.

So did she. "What?"

Tell her you love her, he ordered himself. *To hell with the rest of this crap, just tell her you love her.*

Ariel glanced down at his hands. "Did you hurt yourself? Are you in pain?"

He would be if she didn't love him in return. God help him, but Cole still wasn't ready to face that, or the possibility that she actually did love him out here, but once they got back to the villa she would decide otherwise because of Thaddeus's disapproval.

Oddly enough, that gave Cole an idea. It might be best to do this the old-fashioned way, since Thaddeus was obviously an old-fashioned type of guy, and ask him for Ariel's hand before asking her.

"Cole?"

He decided to play dumb. "What?"

She gave him that *bad boy* look again. "Why'd you stop pounding?"

"Haven't," he said as he resumed, all while making his plans.

As Ariel put Cole through the paces of constructing that bola, then its appropriate use, she noticed how his attention kept drifting only to snap back, which seemed to give him an enormous amount of renewed energy.

At last, she asked, "Are you thinking about your story?"

Cole looked at her, then down to the bola that hung useless in his hand when he should have been practicing with it. "Yeah." He stepped back, swung that bola like nobody's business, and finally threw it at the target they had set up.

Ariel's eyes widened as he hit the thing dead on. "So, what were you thinking?"

"When?"

She ordered herself to be patient. "When you were thinking about your story?"

He went to get the bola, then carefully studied it before returning. "When do we signal for help?"

"Help?"

"Yeah. In the script. Old Hank and Mina have to signal for help eventually, right?"

"Sure . . . everything has to eventually come to an end."

Cole looked up from the bola. He seemed as surprised as she that she had actually said that. Glancing past her to the forest, he asked, "So what do you suggest they do?"

Stay with each other. Love each other. Build a life together. Not that Ariel had the nerve to say any of that. "It's your story."

Cole didn't comment. He continued looking at the forest, then glanced at the bola in his hand. "Guess they can't use those diamonds in your navel to attract any airplanes, huh?"

She smiled at his joke, then sighed. "Guess not."

He nodded. "Guess we really should be heading back."

Her heart quickly ached. "What about the rest of the research?"

Cole's head remained down as he watched the bola swinging back and forth. "We can talk about it on the way."

They didn't talk at all for the first twenty minutes, though Ariel struggled to find something to say.

By the time they were an hour into their journey, Cole's quiet mood finally seemed to lift. Ariel wanted to attribute it to her sparkling conversation. Of course, it could have been the tropical almonds, wild grapes, and apples she picked that perked him right up rather than the details she had been providing about island weaponry.

As Cole finished the last of the almonds, Ariel said, "Bet you miss real food like you've never missed it before."

He wiped his hands on the back of his berry-stained slacks and shook his head. "This has been nice."

The words were out of her mouth before Ariel could stop them. "Because it's not forever."

Cole gave her an odd look, then turned to the left and checked his watch against the sun. "If we take that way"—he paused to point—"we should reach the villa in no time at all."

Again, her heart ached. "Uh-huh."

"Is that all right with you?" he asked.

Ariel lied with a nod.

It was hard to keep up with him after that. The man simply would not slow down, and there was no way Ariel could stop him. Sooner than she would have liked they reached the edge of the secondary jungle.

The villa was just ahead.

"Home sweet home," Cole said, then grabbed her.

Ariel's eyes widened to his bear hug, then closed to his kiss.

When she was, at last, limp and breathless Cole finally released her. "Looks like we made it."

She swallowed. "You had any doubt?"

"Not with you at my side, baby." He playfully swatted her butt.

Ariel looked from it to him, or rather for him as he strode across the lawn. When she finally caught up just outside the villa's entrance, he glanced over his shoulder. "There you are."

"Where else would I be?"

"Well, I don't know." He opened the door for her. "After a long soak in the tub, I would hope you'd be joining me for supper."

Ariel's brows lifted in surprise. She ran to catch up with him again as he quickly moved through the villa to the halls leading to their bedrooms. "Hey, wait!" she finally said.

At last, he did.

"You want us to have supper?" she asked.

"You're not hungry?" He wiggled his brows.

Ariel grinned. "Are you kid—"

She abruptly paused as his cell phone rang.

Cole mumbled, "Bet it's your uncle."

Ariel wiggled her fingers for the phone. "Give it to me, I'll handle him."

"Nope. That's my job." Cole opened the phone and brought it to his ear. "Just a sec." He pressed it against his chest and turned to her. "Take your soak. I'll meet you in an hour. Wait," he quickly said before she even had a chance to move. "Where do you want to eat, the piazza or outside where we first met?"

She smiled. "Where we first met—if that's okay with you."

He smiled. "Perfect. I'll let the staff know." He quickly frowned. "Well, what are you waiting for—go!"

Oh, she did, but hardly as fast as he wanted. Giving him a

wicked smile, Ariel turned and casually strolled down the hall.

It wasn't until Cole went in the opposite direction to the kitchen, and was finally focused on his call, that Ariel hurried to her room.

Chapter Fifteen

Once inside, she leaned against the door and reminded herself that she had an hour. As a rule, it took Ariel less than thirty minutes to get ready for the day.

Of course, now she was getting ready for Cole and their last night together.

Oh God, oh God, oh God, she thought, knowing she just had to make tonight special so that it didn't end. She hadn't a clue how that might be possible, but she had to try.

"So what do other women do?" she asked aloud and came up empty.

Damn. Pacing her room, she finally had a thought. What if she kept him waiting; not for a long time, of course, but just for a little bit? Would that be so wrong? Would that be too much like her parents' less-than-honest approach to romance?

Of course, if she made Cole wait that would increase his anticipation and appreciation, right?

Damn right. Ariel had hardly forgotten what happened at the pool when she forced him to chase her; first for fun, but later to prove that he truly wanted her before they made love.

And she wouldn't be more than twenty minutes late for their supper, on the dot. "Please let this be right," she said aloud as she filled the tub.

After her soak, Ariel wondered if any of the female staff had makeup she could borrow, then decided against asking.

Cole had seen her at her worst and hadn't been scared off, so she drenched herself in perfume and left it at that.

Until she worried about what to wear. There was always the outfit that bared her navel. Then again, something less revealing might make him want to see more later, after supper, in his bedroom, right?

Ariel lowered her head and breathed hard. How in the world did other women go through this crap each and every day of their lives?

How could she not if it meant getting Cole?

Biting her lower lip, Ariel troubled over whether to wear her beige top and shorts or the green top and silky slacks.

At last, she flipped a coin and pulled on the green duds, then looked at the clock on her nightstand. Even with all of her indecision, she was still five minutes early. *Damn.*

She bounced in place for a few seconds, then decided she would be early. That's just the way she was, unsophisticated and uninhibited and completely in love. Crossing her room to the door, Ariel grabbed the handle, but didn't turn it.

Make him wait, her mind ordered. *Make him want.*

For the next twenty minutes Ariel paced the bedroom. At last, she was fashionably late and wondering why Cole hadn't stormed down the hall and pounded on her door so that she'd get a move on.

Damn it, she thought. He couldn't have finally passed out from exhaustion.

She entered his room without even bothering to knock. After what they shared, there wasn't a whole lot the man could hide from her, especially the fact that he wasn't in his room and hadn't been in his room.

Ariel checked his overnight bag and found his clothes undisturbed. When she went into the bathroom, she immediately saw that the tub was dry.

Where is he?

Leaving his room, Ariel ran down the hall and nearly knocked over Isa.

"Whoa, sorry," Ariel said.

"Little Ariel!" Isa cried, then frowned. "You must be more careful." She smiled. "You came back!"

Ariel nodded, then stated the obvious. "So did you."

"Your uncle won big at the tables and wanted to get out before anyone broke his legs."

Ariel nodded distractedly as she looked over the woman's head. "Have you seen Cole?"

"He is outside with his people."

Ariel looked back to Isa. "What? Who? What people?"

"People who flew in and people he is outside with. That's all I know. Don't ask me no more."

Ariel frowned. "Did he tell you that he and I were going to have supper together? Did he ask you to set it up outside?"

"Not in the kitchen as that is where I stay. Your uncle and me had one big fight on the way back—only not that big," she quickly added, "a little one for lovers, so I stay in the kitchen until he comes to me to apologize. As I wait, Mr. Cole goes outside to say hi to his friends, not to me. But who am I? Only the cook."

"Sorry," Ariel said, not understanding any of this. "Is he by the tables outside?"

"They are on the beach. Boys. Girls. All of them."

Boys? Girls? "There're children outside?" Ariel asked. Cole had child—

"Girls your age. Boys his age, maybe younger."

Girls my age? Who were these people? Why were they here? How had they even found out he was here?

Unless he told them.

"Come to the kitchen with me," Isa ordered, "you can see them from—"

"Thanks, but no, I'll just go outside."

"And I will still wait for your stubborn uncle," Isa said, then headed for the kitchen.

Once the older woman was out of sight, Ariel ordered herself to get moving. After all, it was obvious Cole wasn't coming to get her.

Pushing aside that disappointment, Ariel told herself that there had to be a very good reason these *girls* and *boys* were here. One Cole would explain just as soon as he got rid of them so that he and she could enjoy their supper alone, just as he had promised.

The moment Ariel went outside she heard loud male laughter being carried on the wind. Her heart raced as she listened for Cole in that crowd, even as her mind whispered that she had foolishly made him wait and he hadn't even noticed; he hadn't even come for her.

There was another burst of laughter. This time she clearly heard a female voice among the others.

Girls your age, Isa had said.

It doesn't mean anything, Ariel told herself as she finally rounded the corner of the compound that led to the beach.

Below, on sand as white as powdered sugar, a volleyball net had been set up. Four young men stripped to their cargo shorts were laughing as they played the game.

To the right of them, within the shade of palms, a long table had been set up with food and beer. Lingering near it was a short, thin woman with dark brown hair cut Cleopatra-style, exceptionally pale skin, glasses, and a cell phone to her ear.

The woman paced as well as she could on the sand as that same female laughter rang out. It was tinkling, youthful.

Ariel glanced in that direction. Just past a group of palms, she saw what appeared to be the bottom of Cole's berry-stained pants fluttering in the breeze.

Moving down the slope that led to the beach, Ariel finally stopped as she saw him standing next to a tall, older man who was dressed like a tourist and a young blond woman who wore a thong bikini that showed off her exceptional figure.

Ariel's stomach fell as that girl casually leaned into Cole, touching the small of his back and then his butt as she laughed.

Cole indulged that laughter and the girl's touch as he took a sip of his beer, apparently enjoying himself when Ariel knew she had been troubling over what to wear and when to arrive for their supper.

"Hey!" the dark-haired woman suddenly called out.

Ariel's gaze darted from Cole to that woman, who was now gesturing her closer.

Ariel didn't want to go closer, but had no choice since she didn't want to appear the fool—or more of a fool. This, when she had never before cared what anyone thought. But that was before Cole. At last, she moved down the slope toward the woman, hoping that he would finally notice and come to greet her.

"Oh, you bad, *bad* boy," the girl suddenly said, then laughed again as she gave him a hug.

Ariel stopped. For a moment she could barely breathe, her heart ached that much.

"Hey," the dark-haired woman said again, but in a much lowered tone as she came toward Ariel. Quickly grabbing her arm, she turned Ariel around and led them down the beach away from Cole and the others.

"Here's the deal," the woman said in a voice Ariel could barely hear. "Meachum was bitching about the delay. It's the same old story everyone's heard before; you let someone back a project and suddenly they're God." She swore loudly, then continued, "He obviously had to be appeased, and we wanted to convince Niki, too, not to mention bringing some of the crew here for establishing shots—they're the ones over there playing volleyball—so there you have it."

Ariel stopped and pulled away. "There I have what? What are you talking about?" She looked over her shoulder as that young woman laughed again and touched Cole's butt again. "Who are you?"

"Gwen Rudd. Who else would I be?"

Ariel looked down as Gwen's arm again slipped through hers so the woman could resume leading them even farther away from Cole.

"You kept him too long," she accused. "Meachum nearly bit my head off this morning, and so I said, 'Well, hey, why not see where this baby's going to be filmed?' The SOB wouldn't budge, until I threw in Niki."

"Niki?"

"Yeah, the perfect bod and face that's talking to Meachum and Cole."

Ariel looked over her shoulder to them, noticing again what she had before—Niki's dainty height, perfect body, and breathtaking features. She was the epitome of a female, and Ariel hated herself for envying her.

"So anyway," Gwen continued, "you need to really play up how keeping Cole here and how all of your ideas for the script are really going to help the film. Tell Meachum you helped Schwartzenegger prepare for his role in *Predator* and—"

Ariel cut in. "I had nothing to do with that." She frowned. "I was still a kid when that came out."

"So?" Gwen looked as if she were nuts. "Just say it, he won't do the math. Everybody in Hollywood looks about your age thanks to the miracle of plastic surgery." She paused to chuckle, then talked fast. "The idea is to convince Meachum that this is a go, while also being very nice to him, since it is his stinking money after all. When he talks about his tire industry, or condom plant, or whatever the hell it is that's made him rich, drool a little; you know, pretend like you're actually interested."

"He's paying for Cole's film?"

"Now you have it. He's our sugar daddy, okay?"

"Niki's his daughter?" That's why Cole was letting her touch and hug him?

"Daughter?" Gwen asked, then laughed so hard her face turned red. "Wow, you're a riot, Adrienne."

Ariel frowned at the woman getting her name wrong

again, then nearly lost her footing on the sand as Gwen turned them both around to head back to the others.

"By the way," Gwen said, leaning into Ariel as her voice remained lowered, "be extra nice to Niki. She's a real diva, you know? One successful reality show and these kids think they're on the same level as Julia Roberts and Nicole Kidman."

"She's an actress?" Ariel asked.

Gwen laughed once more. "Well, she thinks so; now, the critics? Of course," she quickly added in a much sobered tone, "don't bring up that direct-to-video release she starred in. She gets snottier than usual if anyone mentions it."

Ariel didn't comment as the wind continued to bring them Niki's buoyant laughter.

"Okay, get ready for this," Gwen said as they passed the table with Dos Equis, seafood, fruit, and other island fare that was being tended to by a man Ariel had just now noticed and had never seen before in her life.

"By the way," Gwen quickly added, "Meachum likes to be called Doc. Don't ask me why, I don't want to know. Niki is *Ms.* Noel, at least for as long as she's in this film. Please remember that, Adrienne."

Ariel finally came to a stop. "It's *Ariel,* not Adrienne, not Arianna—*Ariel.* Would you like me to write it for you in the sand?"

"Easy, hon," Gwen quickly said, "I'm trying my best, all right? Now just be—"

She didn't finish as Ariel pulled away from her and turned.

At just that moment, Cole looked to the left and immediately paused. *Ariel?* My God, she looked glorious. Her hair was fiery in the late afternoon sun, and her tawny skin simply glowed, while her eyes—oh, shit, her eyes were filled with confusion and what appeared to be hurt.

That, of course, didn't stop Gwen, who continued to say something to Ariel in a very low voice.

Niki, on the other hand, was now talking loudly as she tried to get Cole's attention.

Suppressing his irritation, he spoke in his nicest voice. "Just a sec, okay?"

She ran her forefinger down his arm. "Don't be long." She swung her gaze to Meachum. "Right, Doc?"

"Whatever you say, hon. You listen to her, Ryder. We want to keep the little lady happy."

The *little lady* again squeezed Cole's butt.

This was worse than schmoozing a female general. As he edged away from her he saw that Ariel was about to leave.

"Ariel," he said.

"Who?" Niki asked Doc.

He lifted his shoulders. "Beats me."

With the dismissive tone of their voices, Ariel stopped turning away.

In that moment, it was as if a veil had been drawn over her eyes. Gone was the hurt that he had not joined her at the table for their supper. Gone was the confusion that he had forgotten about her.

He had not. Cole had repeatedly tried to get away from these people, but first Gwen stopped him, then Niki had, and Meachum kept asking the dumbest fucking questions Cole had ever heard in his life, and he would tell Ariel all of that as soon as they were alone . . . if they were ever alone.

"Please," Cole said, extending his hand, "come here and let me introduce you to the others."

Her gaze dipped to his hand, then returned to his eyes. She seemed so quickly vulnerable and unsure, Cole didn't know what to say.

Unfortunately, Niki took up the slack.

"Why?" the girl asked, then spoke to Meachum. "Is that supposed to be someone important?"

Ariel looked at her.

Cole held back an oath and talked fast. "That's what I'm about to tell—"

Ariel cut in. "Please don't bother."

"It's no bother," he said. "I want to."

She seemed uncertain how to take that, but at least she didn't leave.

"Niki, Doc," Cole quickly said, glancing at them, "this is Ariel Leigh, the premiere survival expert in her field and an exceptional young woman." He looked at her, and his tone intensified. "I wouldn't have made it through the last few days if it hadn't been for—"

Niki's laughter drowned him out.

Cole frowned.

Her laughter quickly wound down; she appeared honestly surprised that he was so pissed.

"What?" she asked.

Cole was not about to answer that in mixed company.

At last, Niki frowned, then spoke to Meachum. "Does Cole look like he *made it* to you?" Her gaze swept his grubby appearance. "Now, be honest," she purred, "did Ms. Expert here wrestle you to the—"

Cole interrupted, "*Ariel* showed me how to make this a better film." He spoke to her. "Isn't that right?"

Ariel's gaze remained on Niki for a long moment, before moving to him.

Cole finally cleared his throat to break the silence. "Why don't you tell them about the ideas you had for the script?"

"Good idea," Gwen said.

Ariel said nothing.

Cole turned to the others. "It was Ariel's idea to include a female lead."

Niki was obviously unimpressed as she continued to regard Ariel with bored amusement.

Cole moved to the right, blocking her view. "Ariel suggested plot developments I had never even considered, then took us through each sequence to make certain that everything would work on film."

"She helped Arnold get through *Predator,*" Gwen quickly added.

"Good film," Meachum said, then spoke to Ariel. "You

stay in touch with Arnold? Can you get him for this project?"

Cole answered for her. "I believe he's busy being the governor of California."

Meachum quickly countered. "Not if the price is right."

"Isn't he a little old for the lead?" Niki asked. "And I don't like his accent."

"Neither do we," Gwen said. "Besides, we're looking to get better box office than Arnold. He's old news."

"So, these ideas of yours," Meachum said to Ariel, "tell me about them."

She kept her gaze on Cole.

"Ariel's far too modest," he quickly said, since she wouldn't say one damn thing. "So allow me." With that, Cole boasted about every single thing she had done or talked him through, from building a bed out of branches and banana leaves, to making that bola, to starting a fire with the crystal of his watch, to catching fish with her shirt.

Meachum looked honestly impressed, while Niki eyed the food and booze on the table to the side.

Thank God, Cole thought. At least it wasn't Ariel in her line of sight. Turning to her, Cole smiled. "Is there nothing you can't do?"

Ariel's gaze moved from his mouth to his eyes. Never had she loved a man more; never would she love another in the same way that she loved him.

And yet, she had no way to answer that question or the pride she heard in his voice.

What was it that Gwen just said? That they had to impress these people? Was that why Cole was boasting about her, so that he could convince them that his movie was worth the money and effort?

Ariel had known that from the start. Because of that and her feelings for Cole she had given her all. She didn't care about impressing anyone but him. These other people didn't matter. They would never matter. As much as she loved Cole, as awkward as she had felt only a moment before, she was still the same person deep inside.

Is there nothing you can't do? he had asked.

She couldn't live a life where truth was twisted to fit the occasion and where the opinion of others mattered more than the reality of those you loved. She couldn't live in a world where beautiful women threw themselves at a man she adored. She couldn't live with the thought that one day he might leave her because someone else came along, someone who was impossible to compete against.

Niki was what every man foolishly wanted, when Ariel knew she never would be. She was unsophisticated and uninhibited, especially with a man she so loved.

A man who had not once revealed his feelings.

Just as she had not revealed hers. For once, Ariel was glad she had been less than honest.

Is there nothing you can't do?

At last, she answered, "I can't stay."

Cole started to nod, until he realized what she had said. "What?"

Ariel looked from him to the others and said again, "I can't stay."

"Wait a sec," he said, even though she hadn't moved. "You're leaving?"

"I agreed to help you for three days," she said, her tone cordial, as if she were speaking to a client. "That time's up. Now I have other work to do."

"You're helping another screenwriter?" Meachum asked.

Ariel shook her head.

Cole quickly asked, "Where's your other job?"

It was a moment before Ariel met his gaze. "I can't say. It's classified."

"You work with the government?" Meachum asked.

"At times," she said to him, then addressed Cole. "My job with you is done. Now I have this other job to do."

Cole was stunned. That's all he was to her—a fucking *job?*

No way. He didn't believe it, and he wasn't about to believe her. She was understandably pissed because these people had put a crimp in their plans, but she had no right to casually dismiss what they had shared just because she was pissed. "You're actually *leaving?*"

Ariel's cheeks flushed to his tone, but her voice remained calm, distant. "I can't stay."

"You mean you won't."

Her neck and chest flushed as she glanced at the others. "None of you need me." She turned back to Cole and used that same calm, distant voice. "None of—"

"Well, I might," Niki suddenly interrupted, then gestured to the table. "See that booze? I don't like booze. I need water to keep hydrated. Now be a good expert and find me a Perrier to drink. I'm thirsty."

Ariel flicked her gaze at the girl, then returned it to Cole. "Didn't you hear her? She's thirsty. So you better show her how to get that drink."

He tightened his jaw.

Niki frowned. "What's there to show? Isn't there bottled stuff in refrigerators out here?"

"There's lots of stuff out here," Gwen quickly said, then looked helplessly around until her gaze settled on the crew still playing their noisy game of volleyball. "Hey, I've got an idea. Why don't we join those guys? We can work off some of this excess energy."

Cole didn't comment as his gaze remained on Ariel.

"I think we really should play," Gwen said, then whistled for the ball. Once she had it, she threw it at Cole, hitting him in the shoulder.

He ignored that as he kept his gaze on Ariel.

"Come on," Gwen pleaded, "let's play."

"No," he said.

"Go on," Ariel said. *"Play."*

His expression darkened. "So you can just blithely take off?"

Blithely? Ariel thought. She had given him everything she could since the moment they met, and now he wanted her to stay to appease the movie's backer and this nitwit actress? This, when her heart was breaking?

No damned way. Not that Ariel was about to tell him that in front of an audience. If it killed her, she would not behave like a jealous fool; she would not give *Ms.* Noel the satisfaction. She would be dignified about this whole sorry mess, and then keep her damn vow never to get involved with a Hollywood type again. "I'm doing what I have to. Besides, you really don't need me to stay."

"What are you talking about? I've been begging you to—"

"You don't have to beg me, Cole. You *know* that."

He quietly regarded her, then said, "Whatever you say, sweetheart."

"I'm not your sweetheart."

His expression changed. He looked as if she had slapped him.

Ariel's heart quickly ached, but she couldn't take it back. These were his people, not hers. This was his world, not hers . . . it would never be hers.

"Let me tell you something," he said.

"Good Lord," Niki whined, "can I please have some water to drink?"

Ariel looked at the girl. "There's water all over this island. All you have to do is find it. Would you like for me to draw you a map?"

"No need," Cole quickly said, "I can do it for her."

Ariel turned to him. "Only because I taught you how."

Again, he quietly regarded her. When he spoke, his voice was measured. "You're kidding, right? I already knew the stuff you showed me out there and far more, all right?"

It wasn't. She looked quickly surprised.

In that moment Cole realized what he had said and instantly regretted it, but it was too late.

"You lied to me?" she asked.

Only on some things. And only because he had wanted to be with her, didn't she know that?

Given her expression, she did not, so Cole quickly back-pedaled. "No, I didn't lie. It's just that I knew some of the—"

"You lied to me?" she asked again.

"No!" he insisted, "I—"

"Hey," Gwen interjected, "why don't we play a game of—"

"Yes, why don't we?" Ariel interrupted as her gaze remained on him. "Unless you're going to also lie about knowing how to play—"

"I know how to play the damned game," he said, "and I did not lie to—"

His words stopped as Ariel picked up the ball and in one fluid movement slammed it so hard that it sailed well over his head.

Cole closed his eyes.

"Guess you don't know how to play," Ariel said. "Guess you were lying this time, too."

Cole opened his eyes, wanting to shout that he fucking loved her and would she please just give him a chance to say that?

Given her expression, Cole knew she wouldn't hear him, and she surely wouldn't believe him. "Don't go," he finally asked.

Her gaze momentarily softened, then closed to him again. "I have to," she said. "I can't—"

"So you've said again and again and again," Niki muttered.

Ariel looked at the girl, then back to him. "Was *she* your idea for the girl hero?"

Cole sighed, "I—"

Ariel interrupted, "Hey, it's your story. If you think she'll make a good Mina, what business is it of mine? If you think she even remotely looks like Mina should look, then who am I to—"

"Whoa, wait a minute," Niki interrupted, "who the hell is

Mina?" She spoke to Gwen. "I was promised the role of Shannon."

Ariel frowned. "What part is that?"

"The lead, what else?" Niki said.

Ariel looked at her.

Gwen talked fast. "We thought Mina was a bit unattractive as a name, and since Niki likes the name Shannon, we decided—"

Ariel interrupted, "You're going to have an island girl named Shannon?" She spoke to Cole. "Even though you know how important it is that this be accurate, you actually agreed to that stupid name?"

"It's not stupid," Niki quickly said, "and of course he agreed. I'm the star. So back off, got it? You're just tech support."

"Wait just a minute," Cole said.

"No, she's right," Ariel said, then so quickly approached Niki the girl was required to take a step back.

"I may only be tech support," Ariel said, "but let me tell you something, you're going to need a lot of it out there." She pointed past this nitwit to the rain forest. "Not to mention luck."

Niki retreated another step. Ariel followed.

She finally looked past Ariel to Cole. "What's she talking about?"

Before he could answer, Ariel said, "The elements, nature, what else?"

Niki's slender brows drew together. "What elements?"

"Well, let's see, when we're out of the dry season there are those daily downpours that constitute a part of the elements. If you people don't get on this story and fast, you're going to be making this movie right in the middle of the rainy season."

Niki looked to Gwen for confirmation of this, but Gwen was already staring at the ocean as her lips moved in what seemed to be a quiet oath.

"As to nature," Ariel continued, "let's start with the bats. Bet you didn't know we have lots of them out here, did you? Bet you didn't know they're just going to love all that blond hair."

Niki looked at her.

Ariel continued, "Bet you didn't know that you're going to have to drink water from a vine, and knock fish senseless with rocks after you catch them with your bare hands, and take off your bra to hold fruit, not the audience's attention, and rub leaves over your body as insect repellent, and climb a small mountain to get to a waterfall, and make certain the rocks you use to fry your food don't explode, and—"

"What is she talking about?" Niki finally interrupted. "I'm not doing that. My contract says I have a stand-in for all of the physical stuff."

"Maybe so," Ariel said, "but they'll still have to dirty you up a bit so you look like you've done *some* work and so that everyone can then pretend that you can actually act."

Gwen kneaded her forehead, while Meachum and the crew quietly watched as Niki suddenly turned on Cole.

"Why didn't you hire a *real* writer to write this damn thing?" She next shouted at Gwen, "Why do we have to settle for *him* as the screenwriter? He's GI Joe, not a freaking wri—"

"Don't even go there," Ariel warned, her voice quickly hard. "Cole's a good writer. He's good at everything he does. He's *perfect*. You apologize or you can damned well get off this island and swim back to Hollywood."

Niki tightened her jaw and spoke through clenched teeth. "I will not be in this goddamn thing if *she's* going to be—"

Ariel again interrupted, "Don't you worry, I am not going to be here. I am leav—"

"Ariel!" Cole interrupted. "Will you just wait?"

She could not. She never should have come in the first place; she knew that now. As she turned to him this last time, Ariel warned herself to be cool, to act as if she didn't care.

Tears quickly stung her eyes as she regarded his messy hair, beard, and rumpled clothing. He looked so wonderful, a part of her died. God, how she would miss him. That sorrow was in her voice as she said, "Good luck, Cole."

Before he could speak, Ariel turned and quickly headed for the villa.

Cole just as quickly followed, until Gwen caught up and grabbed his arm.

"Hey," she said, pulling him back until he almost fell on the sand, "where do you think you're going?"

He looked over his shoulder at her. "Where do you think?"

She kept her voice low. "You can straighten this out with Adrian, la—"

"Ariel," he corrected. "Her name is Ariel." He shook her off.

She caught up with him again. "Okay, okay, don't bite my head off. And don't go," she insisted, grabbing his arm again, then yanked him to a stop. "We're going to lose Niki if you don't placate her; and if we lose her, we'll lose Meachum. You want that? You want the film to—"

"I don't care about the fucking film," he said. "I care about Ariel."

He shook her off again and finally got to the top of the slope only to see Thaddeus.

Oh, hell, *he* was back? Could this get any worse?

"Hi," Cole said, then tried to bypass the old guy, but Thaddeus was faster than his age would have allowed and was back to sporting that damned cane, which he swung directly in Cole's path.

"Just one minute, young man."

Fuck, Cole thought, then made his voice as nice as the situation allowed. "Sorry, sir, but I just don't have a min—"

"Then you'll make time for one." His hand went to his hat as the wind tried to pull it off. "That is my niece you're attempting to follow, and this is my island."

Cole's hands tightened into fists, but he continued to make his voice nice. "Yes, sir, I understand that, sir, but I really need to speak with Ariel for a few—"

Thaddeus interrupted. "You need to leave her alone until she cools off. She ran by me without so much as a hello or a kiss, which she has never done before. I know my niece. She won't listen to a thing you have to say now. You've disappointed her. You shouldn't have done that."

Cole finally lost his cool. "It's not like I was trying, all right? Gwen called me when I was on my way to set up supper. She and everyone else were already on their way in the copter. I argued with her to turn around, not to land here, but she said the film wouldn't get the green light if she and the others couldn't come, so I finally said all right, thinking I could get rid of them before Ariel came out, which I obviously didn't, so—"

Thaddeus interrupted once more. "Do you plan to disappoint my niece very often?"

Huh? "Of course not! But hell, I'm only human! Sir," he finally added.

Thaddeus ran his gaze up and down Cole's grubby appearance. "At the moment it would appear you're slightly less than human." His eyes twinkled. "It would also appear that Ariel really put you through the wringer."

"I've never enjoyed anything more."

"My, my, you are a glutton for punishment, but then," he said with a wistful look in his eyes, "women are well worth it, are they not?"

Ariel was, and Cole was damn well prepared to tell her that if Thaddeus would just get out of his way. "That they are, sir. If you don't mind, sir, I'd really like to—"

"Of course you would," Thaddeus interrupted without moving that cane one inch, "but I insist on knowing your intentions." Those eyes no longer twinkled.

"I love your niece, sir, just as you predicted."

That gaze did not soften.

"And," Cole quickly added, "I'd like to ask you for Ariel's hand."

"You want to marry her?"

"If she'll have me."

Thaddeus frowned. "You haven't asked her?"

"I was going to, sir, until you got in the way."

His frown deepened. "You waited until *now* to—"

"I'll admit I've been a coward. Each time I tried to tell her I love her, the moment just wasn't—"

"You have yet to even tell her *that?*"

Cole pressed his fingers to his temple. Thaddeus was making this out to be far worse than it sounded. "As I said, the moment was never quite right."

"What moment is? No, you listen to me," Thaddeus interrupted. "When I asked you if you had, as yet, fallen in love with Ariel, I believe your exact words were, 'With all due respect, sir, that is something I would discuss with her, not with you.' Apparently, you chose to forget that as you have obviously delayed putting her into the equation."

"That I have, but have you ever been in love?"

"I am now."

Yeah, Cole thought, and it had only taken him ten years to declare himself to Isa, and most likely because she had finally threatened bodily harm. Not that Cole was about to bring that up. As Thaddeus so aptly stated, Ariel was *his* niece and this was *his* island. He tried to explain. "I wasn't certain if she felt as deeply as I did, and if you'll excuse my bluntness, sir, I sure as hell did not want to be out in the middle of nowhere with a woman I just bared my soul to if she didn't feel the same, especially when I had no way of getting back here."

"I see your problem."

Thank you, Cole thought.

"But the moment you saw the villa again, you should have—"

"Excuse me for interrupting, sir, but I wanted to clean up a bit and romance her at supper. I wanted to make certain she said yes, given that I didn't know if she would say yes. I still don't know if she'll say yes. At this rate, I'll *never* know if she'll—"

"Yes, yes," Thaddeus interrupted. "You young people are always so damned dramatic."

"Mister Thaddeus!" Isa suddenly shouted from across the lawn. "Why are you out here and not in my kitchen?"

The old guy rolled his eyes, but not before that mischievous glint had returned. "I am coming!" he shouted to her, then spoke sotto voce to Cole. "It pays to keep a woman waiting just a bit—not my niece, of course," he added, "but most women."

"I'll remember that, sir."

"No you will not, because you won't be doing that to my niece. Nor will you ever be unfaithful to her, is that understood?"

More than the old guy knew. Cole loved Ariel in a way he never thought possible. And now, he wanted only to tell her that. "Yes, sir, I'll be the perfect—"

Cole's words abruptly paused as he heard an engine, then the increasing *whap-whap-whap* of copter blades.

His head turned to the left as Ariel effortlessly guided that Bell into the sky.

I can't stay, she had said, and was leaving now.

Thaddeus shouted above the noise. "It would appear you've lost your chance to speak to her."

Cole's jaw clenched; he looked at the old guy.

Thaddeus appeared unconcerned with what his delay had caused. "No need to be angry with me, young man. You were the one who failed to tell my niece how you felt. I suggest that you don't let that happen again. If you love her, then—"

"I do, sir!"

"Then I suggest you pursue her as she's never been pursued before. And *if* you're able to catch up with her, I suggest that this time you tell her what's in your heart."

Chapter Sixteen

If you're able to catch up with her, Thaddeus had said. To Cole that seemed an odd choice of words, but then Thaddeus wasn't exactly known for playing it straight, except when he had said, *Before this is over, you will dearly love Ariel.*

Of course, right on the heels of that he had continually said, *You are not to romance her, or seduce her, or lead her on, or touch her in any way while she is with you.*

Uh-huh. Well, Cole had survived that, so he damned well *would* catch up with her, at which time his real worries would only begin. What in the world could he say to convince Ariel of his love and fidelity?

With any other woman a simple *I love you, babe* probably would have done the trick, but not with Ariel. Given what she had experienced firsthand with her parents' marriage, well, Cole knew he sure as hell better not disappoint her in that aspect of their lives.

He, on the other hand, knew she had better not disappoint him when it came to trust. How dare she just assume the worst and leave? How dare she not even give him a chance?

She was definitely going to hear about that the moment he had her in his sights.

To start that ball rolling, Cole grilled Thaddeus every way

he knew how, but the man kept insisting that he had no idea where she might be going.

"She is an adult," Thaddeus said. "She is allowed to go wherever she pleases."

"Agreed, but surely you keep corporate records of the jobs she does."

Thaddeus scratched the back of his head, then slapped his hand on his hat before it blew off. "I'm not a good book-keeper. Never have—"

Cole interrupted, "When you get paid up front for a job, when Ariel gets paid up front for a job, who keeps those records?"

"My man in the States, but," he quickly added as Cole pulled out his cell phone to call the guy, "Ariel has her own man—to do her bookkeeping."

Jesus. Cole ordered himself to be patient. "Any idea what that man's name is?"

"Ariel's very independent; she doesn't tell me everything. Believe me, I have tried to learn more, but—" He abruptly stopped as Isa again hollered for him. "It appears I have to go." He gently patted Cole's shoulder. "Don't look so tragic, young man, you'll find a way."

With no help from you, he thought.

Thaddeus turned to go to Isa, but then paused and spoke over his shoulder. "Remember, young man, deserving some-thing makes all the difference in appreciating it. I am com-ing!" he hollered to Isa.

As the two of them briefly bickered, then walked arm-in-arm back to the villa, Cole had to wonder how much the old guy did know. After all, his last comment was exactly what Ariel had said when they were in the rain forest.

Not that it mattered. With, or without, the old guy's help, Cole was going to find her.

During those first minutes, Cole called every airport close to the island to see if she had landed there.

She had not.

In the time following that, Cole checked airports and heli-pads in wider and wider circles away from the island, but no one had a record of her flight. Doing a little math, he deter-mined her fuel from fully loaded to bone dry and when she'd need more for every conceivable scenario, and where she might have to get it.

Despite that, no one had a record of her refueling the Bell at any commercial or even private port of entry.

It was only then that Cole recalled something he had for-gotten.

Where's your other job? he had asked just before she bolted.

I can't say. It's classified.

You work with the government? Meachum had asked.

At times.

Cole was quickly grateful that he had a military past and had kept in contact with most of his fellow officers.

Gwen, on the other hand, kept bugging him to come back to the beach to, at least, say goodbye to the others.

"Can't," he said

"Won't," she said.

"That's right. Bye."

She remained in the doorway of the office Thaddeus had allowed Cole to use and swore up a blue streak.

When even that didn't get his attention, she finally begged, "Please tell me how long you're going to stay here."

"Until I find Ariel."

"You're serious?"

Cole looked up from the computer search he was doing for military installations.

Gwen's expression said he was fucking nuts.

That he was. Love did that to a man. "If you want to back out of this," he said, "it's not a problem. I'll see you get paid for whatever's in your contract."

"Screw you."

"Aw, hon, you did that when you showed up with the others."

"Okay, okay, I'm sorry!" She finally came into the room, then paced it. "But I'm not backing out. You're a pain in the ass to work with, but compared to the other lunatics I've dealt with over the years, you're pretty damn easy."

"I love you, too. Now please get out of here and get rid of those people and fix the project's schedule yourself—if you intend to stay on."

"You know I do."

"Then go. I'll get in touch with you as soon as I can. Oh, Gwen?" he said as she started to leave.

She looked over her shoulder at him. "What?"

"Thanks."

She gave him the finger, then blew him a kiss.

Cole smiled and got back to the matter at hand.

Two days later, he was still working on it. No matter his service record, no matter how many medals he had been awarded, no matter the contacts he still maintained, the red tape he had to go through would have killed any other man.

Not him. Cole loved Ariel, and by God he was going to fucking tell her that as soon as he finished yelling at her for putting him through this crap.

If I were to really hit my stride, you'd never *be able to catch me,* she had once said.

Just watch me, baby, he thought.

Minutes later, he was on the phone with a buddy that had served with him in Force Recon. "That's not good enough," Cole said to the man's comments. "You'll have to do more than just try."

His buddy was briefly silent, then sounding slightly pissed. "Like what, Ryder? Let's face it, if the records of where she's working don't exist, then—"

"They *always* exist. All you have to do is find—"

This time he interrupted. "How? Short of a *60 Minutes* exposé or a psychic, of course."

"Use what you have to—I don't care. Just get me the damned location. I'll give you an hour."

Two days later, his buddy finally came up empty.

Cole growled, "What do you mean there are no records of who she's working—"

"That's just what I mean," the man interrupted. "She must be doing this for a civilian outfit or something so damned secret even the Pentagon doesn't know about it."

"Since when are they on top of everything?"

"Point taken, and I will keep trying, but I have to tell you, it ain't lookin' good."

It was far worse than that. Even the damned military couldn't find her.

Cole had finally had enough and cornered Thaddeus again. "Where is she? Please, you have to tell me."

"I would if I could, but I don't get involved in Ariel's affairs."

Right, Cole thought, sourly.

"Do you still love my niece?" Thaddeus asked.

Cole responded without pause. "You know I do. You knew I would from Day One. So, where is she?"

"I don't know, Cole."

It was the first time Thaddeus had used his name, and to Cole that was as significant as the look in the man's eyes. He really didn't know. This was no game to him, either.

"Has she ever done this before?" Cole asked.

"She goes off on her own from time to time, but always checks in to let me know that she's all right."

"Has she checked in this time?"

"She's sent an e-mail each day to tell me not to worry, that she's all—"

"And you forgot to tell me that?"

"It doesn't give her location, Cole."

"Not her physical location, no. But you have her e-mail address. Give it to me, I'll write her a note. I'll explain everything. I'll—"

"She's blocked my address."

Cole covered his eyes with his hand.

"You're not giving up, are you?" Thaddeus asked. "You will find her?"

"Damn right, I will."

"And you'll take care of her?"

Cole lowered his hand. "Are you serious? It's more like she'll take care of me since she can do *anything*."

"Then you'll always need her to do that?"

"Till the day I die, sir."

"Good luck then, Cole."

"Thanks, but I won't need it. I *will* find her."

As Thaddeus left the room, Cole turned to the window. *Dammit,* he thought, *where are you?*

Ariel remained at a small window in the compound. It shuddered with the suddenly stiff wind that continued unchecked across this arid landscape. Gritty dirt sounded like hundreds of nails as it was driven against the surface.

Glancing over her shoulder, Ariel noted the hour on the numerous wall clocks that covered every time zone and major location on the planet. She and her students should have been outside by now, but at the last moment she had been asked to delay the lesson for an hour.

Ariel was savvy enough not to ask why, knowing she wouldn't receive an answer.

"Just hang tight," the official had told her. He was a short, squat man with a long jagged scar on his jaw.

Ariel had nodded absently to him, even as she thought of another scar . . . this one just below the shoulder. A scar she had kissed.

How did this happen? she had asked Cole, and he had joked, *I was riding my bike one day to school.*

It must have caused you a lot of pain. Were you afraid? Have you been afraid very often during your operations?

All the time.

You don't have to be afraid anymore.

It had been three and a half weeks since Ariel had last seen him. She wondered who was keeping him safe now.

She wondered, again, if she should have left.

It was a decision that had seemed right at the time, but even as Ariel had been taking off in the copter, she wanted to return. She wanted to tell Cole that she loved him. She needed to be honest about that.

Only how could she do that with so many people around? The time just wasn't right, and once she had reached her destination, indecision gripped her.

What if he didn't feel as strongly as she did? Could be that's why he never offered his heart.

So how then could she have asked him to reveal his feelings when he was stuck on her uncle's island and in her care? How could she have asked that in front of all of his people?

She obviously couldn't.

Of course, she could have returned after those people had left—she might have even cornered Cole in Hollywood and demanded an answer to how he felt.

Trouble was, Ariel didn't want to have to ask. She wanted him to offer. She needed him to want this as much as she did.

At the very least, she expected that he would have written an e-mail that her uncle could have forwarded. Ariel thought of that each night she wrote Thaddeus to let him know she was safe. Come morning, she always hoped for a return message that would tell her something about Cole.

Each morning she received nothing. Always nothing.

"Ms. Leigh?"

She lifted her head, unaware that the official had returned. Glancing at that wall of clocks again, Ariel was surprised that more than an hour had passed.

"The men are outside," he said.

Ariel nodded and grabbed the head gear she would wear later, then exited the building. The wind was down and the morning was not yet hot, but that would most definitely come.

She looked up.

Thirty men, each wearing full camouflage gear, awaited her in three neat lines. Although there were slight differences in height and body frame, no one man was distinguishable from the other; all had their features hidden.

Ariel adjusted her sunglasses, thankful for the reflective lenses that hid the pain in her eyes. She wondered, briefly, if she should have worn these on the beach that last day with Cole. Maybe then, he wouldn't have seen her anger or hurt. Maybe then, the situation wouldn't have gotten so out of—

"Ms. Leigh?" the official said.

Ariel looked at him, surprised she had drifted again. Clearing her throat, she faced the men and told them what to expect today in terms of temperature extremes.

After she allowed that to sink in, she said, "As you'll recall during our earlier meetings, sand and rock in this area can, and does, reach up to sixty degrees Celsius or one hundred forty degrees Fahrenheit, well above the air temperature. To travel within those extremes, rather than seeking shelter in a wadis where there is thicker vegetation and where your camouflage gear will come into play, is a death sentence, is that understood?"

There was a chorus of "Yes, ma'am," with one voice answering last.

Ariel looked up from the headgear she was holding.

For some reason that last voice had sounded like Cole's. Only that was impossible, that was just nuts, so she ordered herself to stay on point.

Clearing her throat once more, Ariel pointed to one of the men in the first row. "You," she said, "name the seven environmental factors that need to be faced in this desert."

"Yes, ma'am!" He rattled them off with ease and spoke in

an accent Ariel couldn't quite place, but then most of these men were from remote corners of the globe.

And none of them, she reminded herself, were Cole.

Stop it, she thought, then got back on point. "You," she said, pointing to another man, this one in the back row, "what area should be most avoided in a desert environment?"

"One that has a high mineral content near ground surface, ma'am."

She pointed to another man. "And why is that?"

He flawlessly rattled off the answer, betraying only a slight accent from the Baltic region.

"Is that correct?" she asked the group as a whole.

Once more, there was a chorus of "Yes, ma'am," with that same lone voice answering after the others.

Ariel's heart started to race. She looked up at the sun. The day had yet to get truly hot, but already she was perspiring badly. Looking back to these men—with every last one of them unknown to her in their gear—she told herself she was imagining things.

"You," she said, pointing to a man she had not called on before, then asked him a question about desert survival.

He answered immediately, flawlessly, and in a voice that hardly stirred her soul.

"You," she said to yet another, then asked him a question, which he answered.

"Do you all agree with that?" she asked.

For the third time all of the other men answered as one, with that same lone voice holding back until last.

It's not possible, she thought. No one, not even her uncle, knew she was here. Besides, if Cole hadn't even thought to send her a damned e-mail, why would he come here?

He wouldn't, she told herself. *You're losing your mind.* Even so, she wanted to be sure.

She approached the men. "There appears to be one among you who isn't as certain of that as the others." She moved down that first line to the right and spoke to the man on the end. "Are you the one who has doubts?"

"No, ma'am."

His voice was firm, but not Cole's.

She asked the next man the same question and received the same answer in a voice that was definitely not Cole's. She went through that first line and then the next, until she was finally at the last line. Only ten men left.

It's not possible, she told herself. *He can't be here.* "You," she said to the first in line. "Do you have doubts?"

"No, ma'am."

In that moment, the world seemed to pause, and then it spun out of control. Lowering her head to stop her dizziness, Ariel told herself this wasn't possible. He hadn't sent her so much as an e-mail, so how could he be here now? How could that voice be his?

It's not, she told herself, then opened her eyes and saw that the man had removed his headgear, which was now in his hands.

Lifting her head, she met Cole's eyes.

Ariel's lips parted as her gaze touched each part of his face.

It was thinner than she recalled, as if he hadn't been eating. There were worry lines on his forehead and laugh lines at the corners of his eyes. His gaze questioned, and Ariel quickly answered as she moved into him, wreathing her arms around his neck.

Cole dropped his gear, then quickly embraced her as he told the other guys to beat it.

For a long moment all Ariel could do was to hold tight as tears rolled down her cheeks. *My God,* she thought, this couldn't be happening, and yet it was. "You're here," she said.

"Of course I am." He tightened his embrace. "Did you actually think you could get away from me?"

"I was hoping I couldn't."

Cole just had to smile. It was the answer he wanted, the

one he had been waiting for. Even so, he wasn't going to let her off the hook that easily. "Ariel, you put me through hell to find you and this place."

She slowly nodded, then shook her head and started to cry again.

Oh, hell. "Don't do that," he said in a much softer voice, then held her even tighter than before.

Ariel pressed her face against his neck. Her voice trembled, "How did you find—"

"A friend of a friend of a friend just so happens to know the guy running this place."

"But this isn't a military operation."

No kidding, Cole thought, wondering who in the hell these guys were. CIA? Soldiers of fortune? International bounty hunters? "If it had been, I would have found you three weeks ago."

New tears slipped down Ariel's face as she gently eased away. She smiled, then started to cry once more as Cole removed her sunglasses so that he could see her eyes. "You've been looking for me that long?"

"I never stopped looking, Ariel, from the moment you left. I would have told you I love you if you had only given me a chance, but you didn't. So here I am wearing two tons of gear, because even now I wasn't all that certain how you'd take my being here when you so abruptly—"

She finally interrupted, "You love me?"

"Hell, yes! Would I be here if I didn't? Would I be dressed like this if I didn't?"

"Well, I don't know," she said, then threw her arms around him again and cried, "I love you, too!"

This time, Cole held back

Oh, God, she thought. "What's wrong?"

"You love me? Then why the hell did you leave me?"

Her heart ached at the pain she heard in his voice, pain she had put there. "I was wrong, and I swear, it will never happen again."

Cole didn't seem all that convinced as he gently removed her arms from around his neck and eased away. "You need to trust me, Ariel."

"I know."

"I believe the words are *I do.*"

"I know."

He sighed.

"I reacted badly," she said, "I admit it. But even after I left I thought you'd at least send me a note to—"

"A note?" he interrupted. "How could I? I didn't know where you were until a few hours ago when I got the man in charge to stall you so I could get here and gear up."

"I meant, you could've e-mailed me. Uncle Thaddeus would have forwarded it to—"

"How could he? You blocked his address."

"He actually told you that?"

"Oh, hell," Cole said, "what a family you got."

"Well, now with you it's pretty good."

He quietly regarded her.

"Very good," she amended.

Cole sighed. "You need to know I'll always be there for you. You can't have doubts about that, Ariel."

"I know."

He arched one brow, at least until she cupped his face in her hands and murmured, "Please believe me that I will trust you from this moment forward. *Please.*"

He frowned. "You don't have to beg, you know that."

"Forgive me, then, for not giving you a chance," she said. "I'm asking, not beg—"

"Come here." Cole pulled her into his arms and looked at her for a long moment; he looked at her as if she were his, then kissed her deeply because she was.

A sudden and wild whoop went out from her students who had obviously lingered, despite Cole's admonition to get lost.

Ariel gently pulled away from him and whispered, "Just a

sec." Glancing over her shoulder, she shouted, "Quiet!" The men all fell silent. "Now go away," she ordered, then looked at Cole and murmured, "because I'm busy."

His gaze was suddenly as playful as his voice. "Busy?" he asked. "Is that what you call this?"

No, she thought. She called this a friendship that was real, a respect every woman craved, an intimacy that could not be denied, and a love that would make an angel smile.

"I call this the beginning of a very, very long engagement," she murmured as she cupped his face in her hands, then brought his head down until their lips nearly touched. "So pay attention, soldier, and take my breath away."

Treat yourself to heavenly romance
by Lori Foster with
"Once in a Blue Moon,"
from our STAR QUALITY anthology,
available now from Brava . . .

Stan's gaze lifted and locked with hers. Sensation crackled between them. His awareness of her as a sexual woman ratcheted up another notch. Even without hearing Jenna's thoughts, what she wanted from him, with him, was obvious to any red-blooded male. Heat blazed in her eyes and flushed her cheeks. A pulse fluttered in her pale throat. Her lips parted . . .

Amazing. A mom of two, a quiet bookworm, a woman who remained circumspect in every aspect of her life—and she lusted after him with wanton creativity.

Not since the skill had first come to him when he was a kid of twelve, twenty-eight years ago, had Stan so appreciated the strange effect a blue moon had on him. It started with the waxing gibbous, then expanded and increased as the moon became full, the ability was so clean, so acute, that it used to scare him.

His parents didn't know. The one time he'd tried to tell them they'd freaked out, thinking he was mental or miserable or having some kind of psychosis. He'd retrenched and never mentioned it to them again.

When he was twenty and away at college, he signed up for a course on parapsychology. One classmate who specialized in the effects of the moon gave him an explanation that made sense. At least in part.

According to his friend, wavelengths of light came from a full moon and that affected his inner pathogens. With further studies, Stan had learned that different colors of lights caused varying emotional reactions in people. It made sense that the light of a full moon, twice in the same month, could cause effects.

In him, it heightened his sixth sense to the level that he could hear other people's tedious inner musings.

Now he could hear, *feel*, Jenna's most private yearnings, and for once he appreciated his gift. Nothing tedious in being wanted sexually. Especially when the level of want bordered on desperate.

She needed a good lay. She needed him.

He wanted to oblige her. Damn, did he want to oblige her.

Casually, Stan moved closer to her until he invaded her space, and her alarm thumped louder with every beat of her heart. He left himself wide open to her, relishing each tingle she felt, absorbing each small shiver of excitement—and letting it excite him in return. He no longer cared that he had a near-lethal erection.

Reaching out, he brushed the side of his thumb along her jaw line, up and over her downy cheek, tickling the dangling earrings that suddenly seemed damn sexy. "Maybe you need the ice tea," he murmured, his attention dipping to her naked mouth. Jenna never wore lipstick, and he liked the look of her soft full lips, glistening from the glide of her tongue. Oh yeah, he liked that a lot. "You feel . . . warm, Jenna."

Her breaths came fast and uneven. "I've been . . . working."

And fantasizing. About him.

Lazily, Stan continued to touch her. "Me, too. Out in the sun all day. It's so damn humid, I know I'm sweaty." His thumb stroked lower, near the corner of her mouth. "But I didn't have time to change."

Her eyelids got heavy, drooping over her green eyes. Shakily, she lifted a hand and closed it over his wrist—but she didn't push him away. "You look . . . fine." *Downright edible.* She cleared her throat. "No reason to change."

Stan's slow smile alarmed her further. "You don't mind my jeans and clumpy boots?" He used both hands now to cup her face, relishing the velvet texture of her skin. "They're such a contrast to you, all soft and pretty and fresh."

Her eyes widened, dark with confusion and curbed excitement, searching his. He leaned forward, wanting her mouth, needing to know her taste—

The bell over the door chimed.

Jenna jerked away so quickly, she left Stan holding air. Face hot, she ducked to the back of the store and into the storage room, closing the door softly behind her.

Well, hell. He'd probably rushed things, Stan realized.

And please turn the page for a very funny
sneak peek at Susanna Carr's
CONFESSIONS OF A "WICKED" WOMAN,
coming in June 2005 from Brava . . .

"I know my rights!" someone yelled in the distance.

Jack swiveled his head in the direction of the holding cells.

"I watch *Court TV*!" The feminine voice didn't sound familiar. The words were clipped as if she had a slight accent.

He turned back to Mackey and saw the man munching ferociously on something. "What's going—?"

Mackey slid the file to him. "Indecent exposure."

Damn. Jack set his mouth into a firm line and reluctantly took the folder that already sported greasy fingerprints. He didn't like the new ordinance Alderman Zimmer pushed through. Probably because he knew it was inspired by the Zimmer girls who tried to dress like their favorite pop stars.

He might not like the ordinance, but until it changed, he had to enforce it. Jack walked to where he heard the woman yelling about some plot point in a popular courtroom drama. He wondered if he could get to the bottom of this and find a solution that would satisfy everyone. He didn't think so.

Pushing the door and walked into the holding cell area, Jack's steps faltered the moment he saw the woman.

The first thing he noticed was her shoulder-length brunette hair. No brush would survive those tangles. Streaks of blond zigzagged in the wild mass, indicating she lived where there was sunshine and lots of it.

Jack's gaze skipped down. Her lean body was almost all arms and legs. The shoes were bold and exaggerated. The heels alone looked lethal.

The pale blue jeans were damp and stretched tight at her knees and thighs. The pants hung lower than any he had ever seen. He was sure more than one red-blooded male stared at them, waiting with bated breath for the waistband to slide. The sequins winked back at him, as if letting him know it was going to be a long wait.

Jack's fingers tingled when he gazed at her bare stomach. She didn't have a rock hard muscle, but her flat abdomen had a touch of curve to cushion the palm of his hand. He wanted to reach out and touch the pale, smooth skin that promised to be warm, soft and silky.

What was he thinking? Bad idea. Jack shook that wayward thought away, but it held firm. His hands felt heavy as he imagined how it would feel to dip his fingers into her navel. Followed by the tip of his tongue.

Jack swallowed roughly, his throat tight. She really needed to cover that belly button up. Like with a diamond.

No, that would be worse. Jack squeezed his eyes shut, but the vision remained, taunting him. Much, much worse.

He forced his eyes open and fixated his attention on her halter. Her tight nipples pushed against the sodden fabric that stretched across her small breasts. It was as if everything she wore was one size too small.

The woman jutted her hip to one side, her fist resting on the other. Her shoulders were angled, ready to deflect any challenge that came her way. She tossed her head back, her angry gaze colliding with his silently assessing eyes.

Jack felt the energy whoosh through him, his blood crackling in the aftermath. His skin felt tight, his body heavy as he met the big brown eyes head on.

The flaked mascara didn't diminish the raw power of her uncompromising gaze. There was no other trace of makeup n her lean, angular cheeks or her wide mouth.

That mouth. His cock stirred with interest.

Those lips promised the most beautiful smile while whispering the dirtiest jokes. That mouth could give perfect, deep-throated head or the most mind-blowing kiss without any effort.

It was every man's fantasy.

Fantasy? No. Jack took an instinctive step back, a flash of anxiety searing through his gut. Not his. He was *not* interested in this woman who was behind bars. At all.

He was the sheriff. Jack purposefully reclaimed the step he lost. He was a man of authority. Integrity. At least, he was trying to be.

Old Man Schneider's words mocked him.

Trouble's coming.

Yeah. She had arrived.

The woman's glittering eyes narrowed and she shifted her stance. "What are you looking at?" she barked out.

He wasn't sure, but he was going to guess his most difficult challenge. Wrapped up in the most tempting package. He wondered if this was how Samson felt right before Delilah whacked off his hair along with his strength.

Jack flinched as the door behind him banged open.

"Quit hollering," he heard Venus Gold order the other woman. "Here's something dry for you to wear. I even remembered the shoes."

The brunette didn't look grateful.

"Oh, hey, Jack." Venus appeared next to him. "Didn't see you there."

"Venus," he said hoarsely and cleared his tight throat. He gave a cursory glance at his former classmate. "Nice rain gear."

She smiled prettily. "Thank you."

"Wait a second!" The other woman said in a huff. "She's wearing something see-through and it's *nice*?"

"In case you haven't noticed," Venus replied, walking to the cell. "My dress covers me from my shoulders to mid-thigh. Just as the law requires. It never indicated that the material had to be . . . what's the word? Opaque."

Jack felt his mouth twitch in a smile. He could always count on Venus Gold to tease the law.

"Don't worry," Venus looked over her shoulder at him. "No nail files in these clothes."

"Imagine my relief," he muttered. Now if only his body wasn't on full alert. Jack unclenched his fingers from the folder he held and opened it.

"Who *are* you?" the brunette asked, her question brimming with attitude.

He kept his attention on the paper in front of him. "I'm Jack Logan. The sheriff." And she was Stephanie Monroe, according to the file. Somehow the name fit. "What's going on here?"

"False arrest, according to Stephanie," Venus answered as she wiggled a shoe between the bars.

"Were you read your rights?"

"What?" Stephanie asked, the shoe clattering onto the ground. "Yeah."

He flipped the paper over and looked at the next form. "Do you know why you were arrested?"

"No."

"No?" He glanced up and saw Stephanie squatting down to grab the shoe from the floor. To his disappointment, the jeans didn't dip at all. "It says here you were cited for indecent exposure."

"In case of rain, there's a good chance my clothes will get wet with a possibility of becoming transparent."

Jack's shaky restraint and wild imagination could have done without that forecast.

"But it would be accidental and not"—she cast a withering glare at Venus—"intentional."

"Try not to get me arrested," Venus suggested as she shoved the last of the clothing between the bars. "Or there'll be no one to bail you out."

Jack snapped the file shut. "Even if your clothes were dry, they wouldn't meet the legal requirements."

Stephanie scoffed. "What kind of place expects a dress code?"

"A nice one."

Jack immediately regretted his quick reply. He was fully aware that his hometown wasn't paradise and was often the first and most vocal to point out the problems. But like most natives, he didn't like it when outsiders complained about Mayfield.

He didn't mean anything about Stephanie, or how she wasn't suitable to visit a nice small town. But Jack knew she took it that way and took it to heart. He saw how she flinched. She pressed her lips tightly together and turned her back sharply. Stephanie kicked off her shoes and focused on her task of spreading her clothes onto the thin cot of her cell.

Venus's lips drew into an O as the tense silence stretched. "You know, I think I'm going to see how Mackey is doing on releasing you. I'll be right back."

Jack watched her scurry for the door. He scrunched his eyes for a second and resolutely turned back to Stephanie. Whatever he had to say disappeared in his throat as Stephanie pulled the string from her halter top and let it fall.